Asterix ®

VOLUME ONE

PAPERCUTZ™

ASTERIX GRAPHIC NOVELS

Paperbacks

ASTERIX

Vol. 1

ASTERIX

Vol. 2

ASTERIX

Vol. 3

ASTERIX

Vol. 4

Coming Soon

ASTERIX

Vol. 5

Coming Soon

ASTERIX

Vol. 6

Hardcovers

ASTERIX

Vol. 1

ASTERIX

Vol. 2

ASTERIX

Vol. 3

ASTERIX

Vol. 4

Coming Soon

ASTERIX

Vol. 5

Coming Soon

ASTERIX

Vol. 6

R. GOSCINNY
ASTERIX
A. UDERZO
THE CHIEFTAIN'S
daughter

Vol. 38

ASTERIX graphic novels are available in paperback for $14.99 each and in hardcover for $22.99 each; ASTERIX Vol. 38 is available in hardcover only for $9.99 each at booksellers everywhere. Order online at papercutz.com. Or call 1-800-886-1223, Monday through Friday, 9 – 5 EST. MC, Visa, and AmEx accepted. To order by mail, please add $5.00 for postage and handling for first book ordered, $1.00 for each additional book and make check payable to NBM Publishing. Send to: Papercutz, 160 Broadway, Suite 700, East Wing, New York, NY 10038.

ASTERIX graphic novels are also available digitally wherever e-books are sold.

PAPERCUTZ.COM

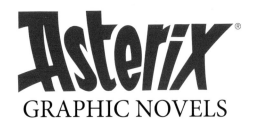

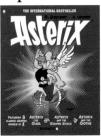

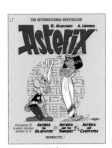

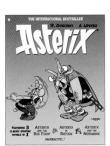

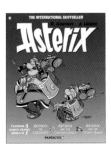

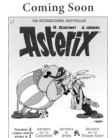

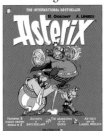

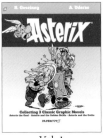

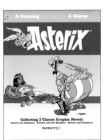

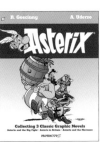

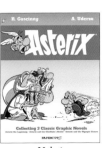

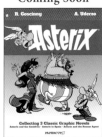

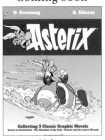

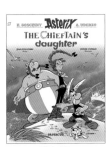

VOLUME ONE

Collecting
ASTERIX THE GAUL
ASTERIX AND THE GOLDEN SICKLE
ASTERIX AND THE GOTHS

Written by RENÉ GOSCINNY
Illustrated by ALBERT UDERZO

NEW YORK

VOLUME ONE

Collecting…
Asterix the Gaul
Asterix and the Golden Sickle
Asterix and the Goths

ASTERIX® - OBELIX ® - IDEFIX ® -DOGMATIX ®

Original titles: *Astérix le Gaulois, La Serpe d'or* and *Astérix et les Goths*
© 1961 GOSCINNY/UDERZO
© 1962 GOSCINNY/UDERZO
© 1963 GOSCINNY/UDERZO
© 1999 Hachette Livre
for this edition and its American translation

Published by: Papercutz
Third Papercutz edition: August 2021

Printed by Ultimate Print, Malaysia

Paperback ISBN: 978-1-5458-0566-4
Hardcover ISBN: 978-1-5458-0565-7

JOE JOHNSON – Translation
JAYJAY JACKSON – Design
BRYAN SENKA – Lettering
JULIE TILLET, LAURA STAUFFER – Special Thanks
JEFF WHITMAN – Managing Editor
JIM SALICRUP
Editor-in-Chief

Papercutz books may be purchased for business or promotional use. For information on bulk purchases please contact Macmillan Corporate and Premium Sales Department at (800) 221-7945 x5442.

Distributed by Macmillan

www.asterix.com   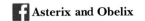 Asterix and Obelix   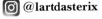 @lartdasterix

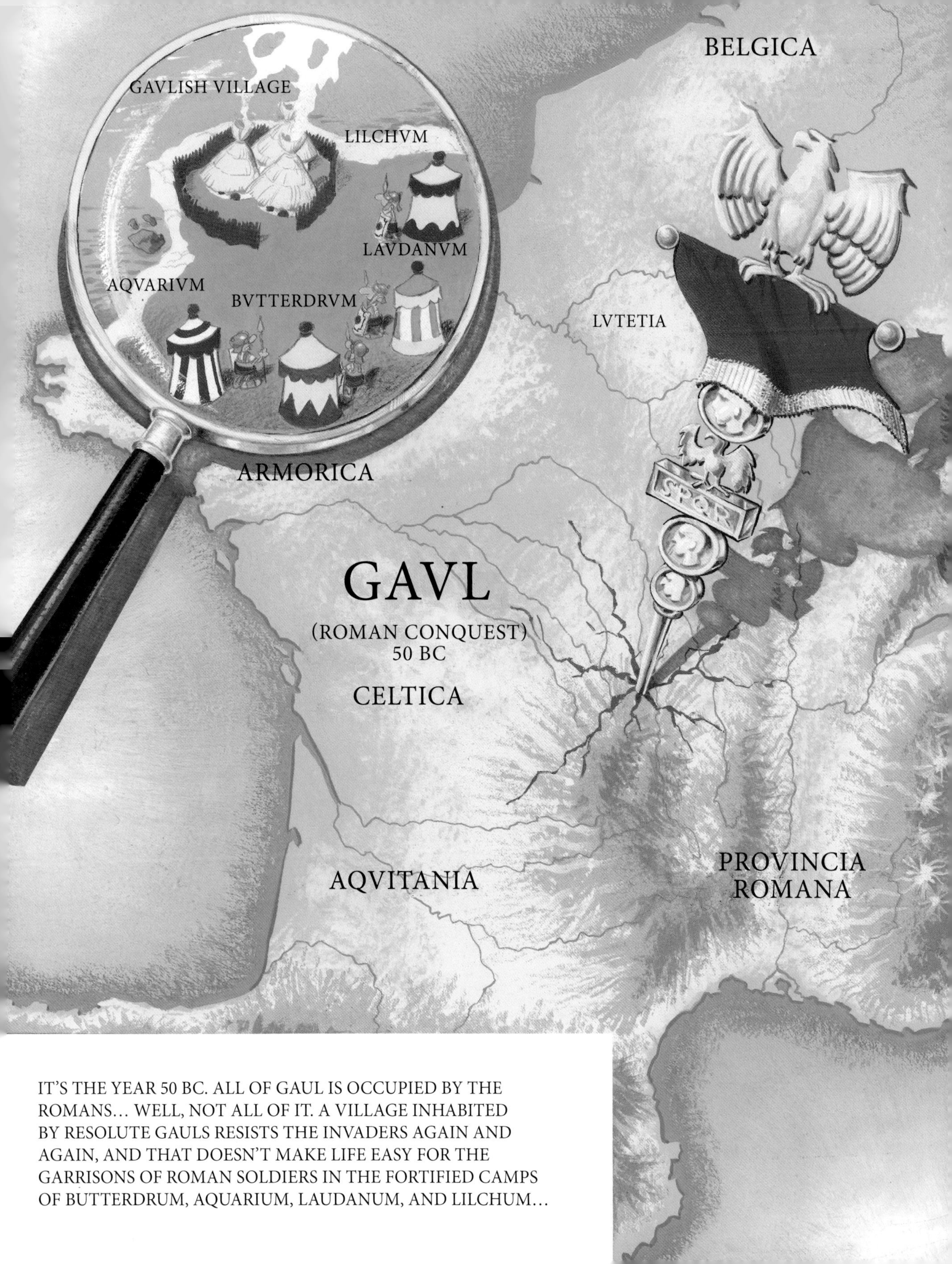
BELGICA
GAVLISH VILLAGE
LILCHVM
LAVDANVM
AQVARIVM
BVTTERDRVM
LVTETIA
ARMORICA
SPQR
GAVL
(ROMAN CONQUEST)
50 BC
CELTICA
AQVITANIA
PROVINCIA
ROMANA

IT'S THE YEAR 50 BC. ALL OF GAUL IS OCCUPIED BY THE ROMANS… WELL, NOT ALL OF IT. A VILLAGE INHABITED BY RESOLUTE GAULS RESISTS THE INVADERS AGAIN AND AGAIN, AND THAT DOESN'T MAKE LIFE EASY FOR THE GARRISONS OF ROMAN SOLDIERS IN THE FORTIFIED CAMPS OF BUTTERDRUM, AQUARIUM, LAUDANUM, AND LILCHUM…

ASTERIX, THE HERO OF THESE ADVENTURES. A SHREWD, LITTLE WARRIOR WITH A KEEN INTELLIGENCE. ALL DANGEROUS MISSIONS ARE ENTRUSTED TO HIM WITHOUT HESITATION. ASTERIX GETS HIS SUPERHUMAN STRENGTH FROM THE DRUID PANORAMIX'S MAGIC POTION…

OBELIX IS ASTERIX'S CLOSE FRIEND. A MENHIR (TALL, UPRIGHT, STONE MONUMENTS) DELIVERY MAN, HE LOVES EATING WILD BOAR AND GETTING INTO BRAWLS. OBELIX IS ALWAYS READY TO DROP EVERYTHING TO GO OFF ON A NEW ADVENTURE WITH ASTERIX. HE'S ACCOMPANIED BY **DOGMATIX**, THE ONLY KNOWN ECO-DOG, WHO HOWLS IN DESPAIR WHENEVER SOMEONE CUTS DOWN A TREE.

PANORAMIX, THE VILLAGE'S VENERABLE DRUID. GATHERS THE MISTLETOE AND PREPARES MAGIC POTIONS. HIS GREATEST SUCCESS IS THE POTION THAT GIVES SUPER-STRENGTH TO THE USER, BUT PANORAMIX HAS OTHER RECIPES UP HIS SLEEVE…

CACOFONIX IS THE BARD. OPINIONS ABOUT HIS TALENTS ARE DIVIDED: HE THINKS HE'S AWESOME, EVERYBODY ELSE THINKS HE'S AWFUL, BUT WHEN HE DOESN'T SING ANYTHING, HE'S A CHEERFUL COMPANION AND WELL-LIKED…

VITALSTATISTIX, FINALLY, IS THE TRIBE'S CHIEF. MAJESTIC, COURAGEOUS, IRRITABLE, THE OLD WARRIOR IS RESPECTED BY HIS MEN AND FEARED BY HIS ENEMIES. VITALSTATISTIX HAS ONLY ONE FEAR: THAT THE SKY WILL FALL ON HIS HEAD BUT, AS HE SAYS TO HIMSELF: "THAT'LL BE THE DAY!"

R. GOSCINNY **Asterix** A. UDERZO

Asterix
THE GAUL

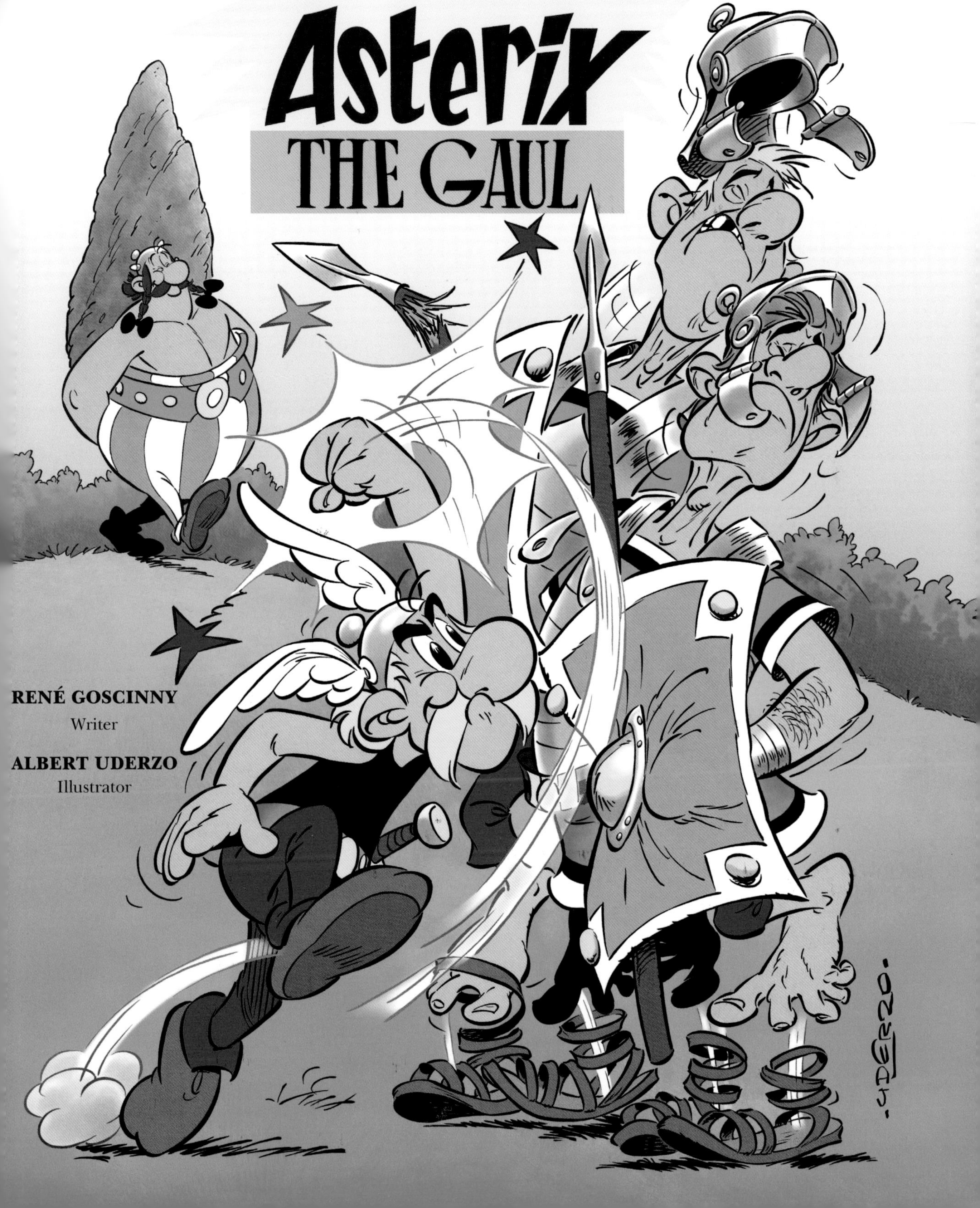

UDERZO.

RENÉ GOSCINNY
Writer

ALBERT UDERZO
Illustrator

ASTERIX THE GAUL

Written by RENÉ GOSCINNY *and illustrated by* ALBERT UDERZO

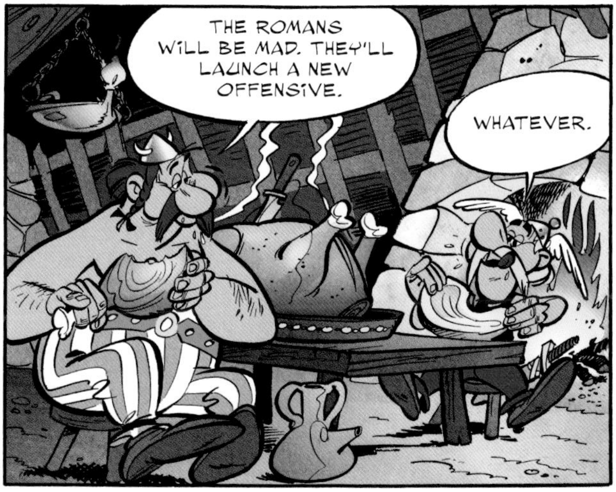
THE ROMANS WILL BE MAD. THEY'LL LAUNCH A NEW OFFENSIVE.
WHATEVER.

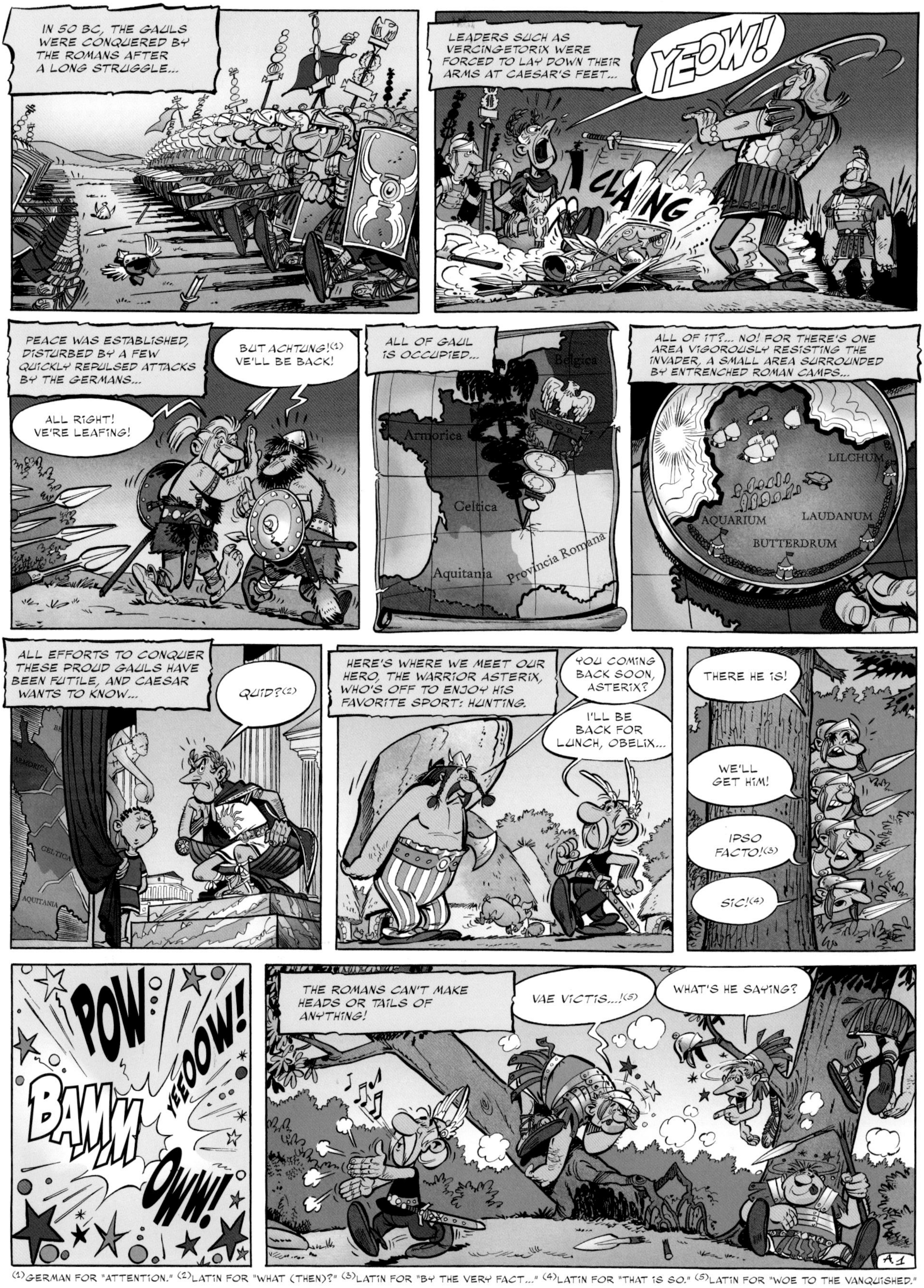
IN 50 BC, THE GAULS WERE CONQUERED BY THE ROMANS AFTER A LONG STRUGGLE...
LEADERS SUCH AS VERCINGETORIX WERE FORCED TO LAY DOWN THEIR ARMS AT CAESAR'S FEET...
YEOW!
CLANG
PEACE WAS ESTABLISHED, DISTURBED BY A FEW QUICKLY REPULSED ATTACKS BY THE GERMANS...
BUT ACHTUNG![1] VE'LL BE BACK!
ALL RIGHT! VE'RE LEAFING!
ALL OF GAUL IS OCCUPIED...
Belgica
Armorica
S.P.Q.R.
Celtica
Aquitania
Provincia Romana
ALL OF IT?... NO! FOR THERE'S ONE AREA VIGOROUSLY RESISTING THE INVADER, A SMALL AREA SURROUNDED BY ENTRENCHED ROMAN CAMPS...
LILCHUM
AQUARIUM
LAUDANUM
BUTTERDRUM
ALL EFFORTS TO CONQUER THESE PROUD GAULS HAVE BEEN FUTILE, AND CAESAR WANTS TO KNOW...
QUID?[2]
ARMORICA
CELTICA
AQUITANIA
HERE'S WHERE WE MEET OUR HERO, THE WARRIOR ASTERIX, WHO'S OFF TO ENJOY HIS FAVORITE SPORT: HUNTING.
YOU COMING BACK SOON, ASTERIX?
I'LL BE BACK FOR LUNCH, OBELIX...
THERE HE IS!
WE'LL GET HIM!
IPSO FACTO![3]
SIC![4]
POW
YEOOW!
BAMM
YEEOOW
OWW!
THE ROMANS CAN'T MAKE HEADS OR TAILS OF ANYTHING!
VAE VICTIS...![5]
WHAT'S HE SAYING?
A.1

[1] GERMAN FOR "ATTENTION." [2] LATIN FOR "WHAT (THEN)?" [3] LATIN FOR "BY THE VERY FACT..." [4] LATIN FOR "THAT IS SO." [5] LATIN FOR "WOE TO THE VANQUISHED."

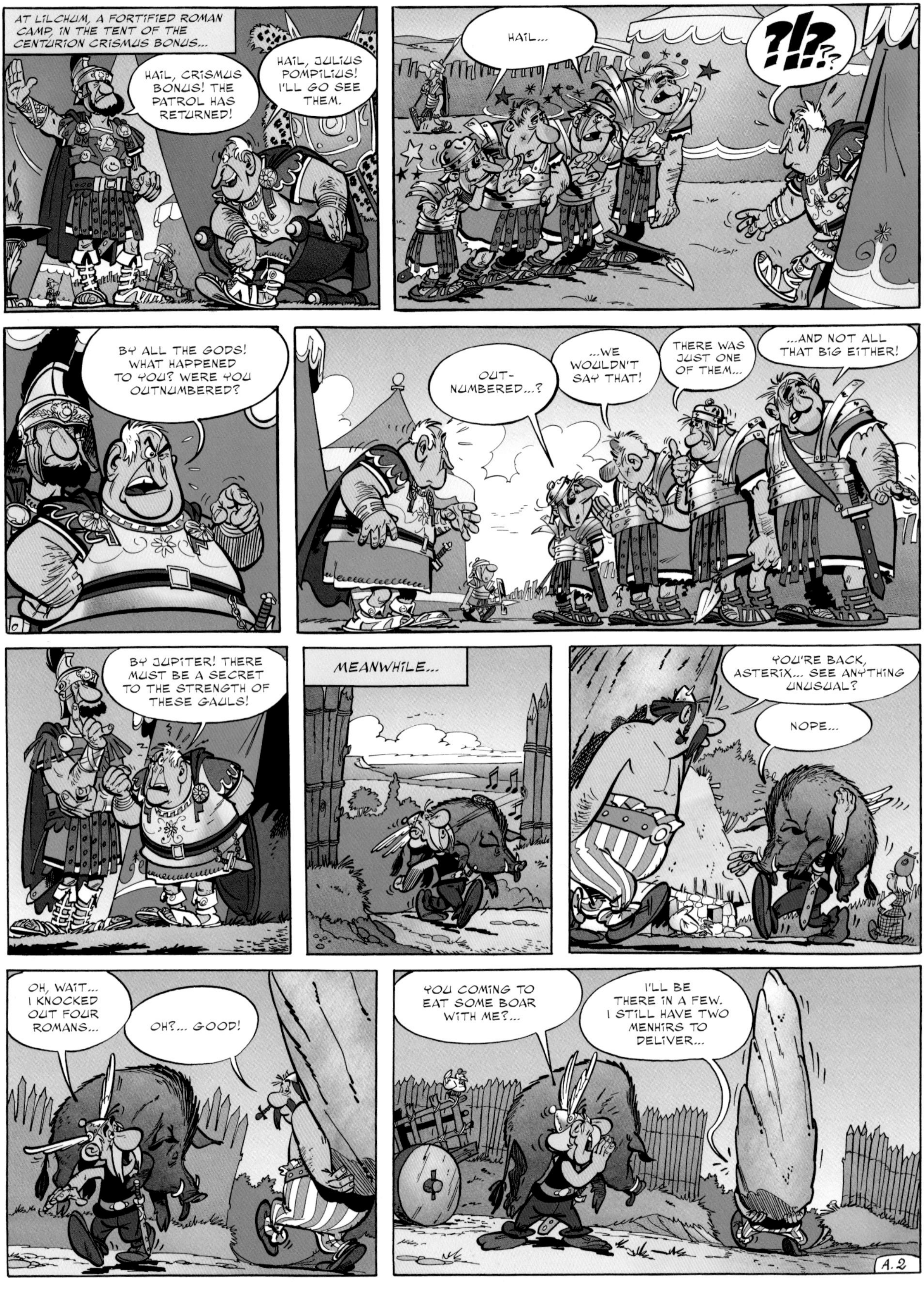
AT LILCHUM, A FORTIFIED ROMAN CAMP, IN THE TENT OF THE CENTURION CRISMUS BONUS...
HAIL, CRISMUS BONUS! THE PATROL HAS RETURNED!
HAIL, JULIUS POMPILIUS! I'LL GO SEE THEM.
HAIL...
?!?
BY ALL THE GODS! WHAT HAPPENED TO YOU? WERE YOU OUTNUMBERED?
OUT-NUMBERED...?
...WE WOULDN'T SAY THAT!
THERE WAS JUST ONE OF THEM...
...AND NOT ALL THAT BIG EITHER!
BY JUPITER! THERE MUST BE A SECRET TO THE STRENGTH OF THESE GAULS!
MEANWHILE...
YOU'RE BACK, ASTERIX... SEE ANYTHING UNUSUAL?
NOPE...
OH, WAIT... I KNOCKED OUT FOUR ROMANS...
OH?... GOOD!
YOU COMING TO EAT SOME BOAR WITH ME?...
I'LL BE THERE IN A FEW. I STILL HAVE TWO MENHIRS TO DELIVER...
A. 2

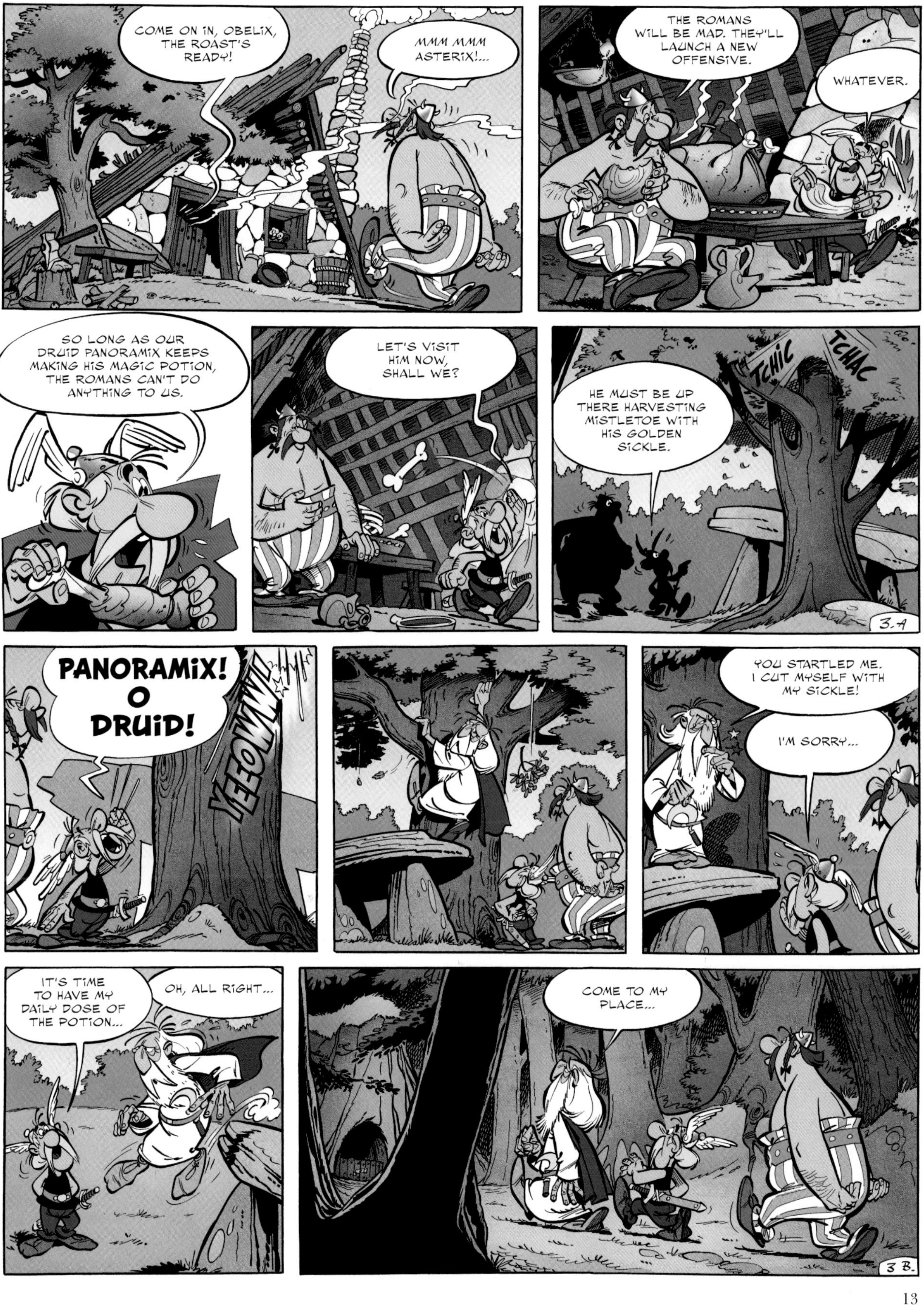
COME ON IN, OBELIX, THE ROAST'S READY!
MMM MMM ASTERIX!...
THE ROMANS WILL BE MAD. THEY'LL LAUNCH A NEW OFFENSIVE.
WHATEVER.
SO LONG AS OUR DRUID PANORAMIX KEEPS MAKING HIS MAGIC POTION, THE ROMANS CAN'T DO ANYTHING TO US.
LET'S VISIT HIM NOW, SHALL WE?
TCHIC
TCHAC
HE MUST BE UP THERE HARVESTING MISTLETOE WITH HIS GOLDEN SICKLE.
3.A
PANORAMIX! O DRUID!
YEOWWL!
YOU STARTLED ME. I CUT MYSELF WITH MY SICKLE!
I'M SORRY...
IT'S TIME TO HAVE MY DAILY DOSE OF THE POTION...
OH, ALL RIGHT...
COME TO MY PLACE...
3 B.

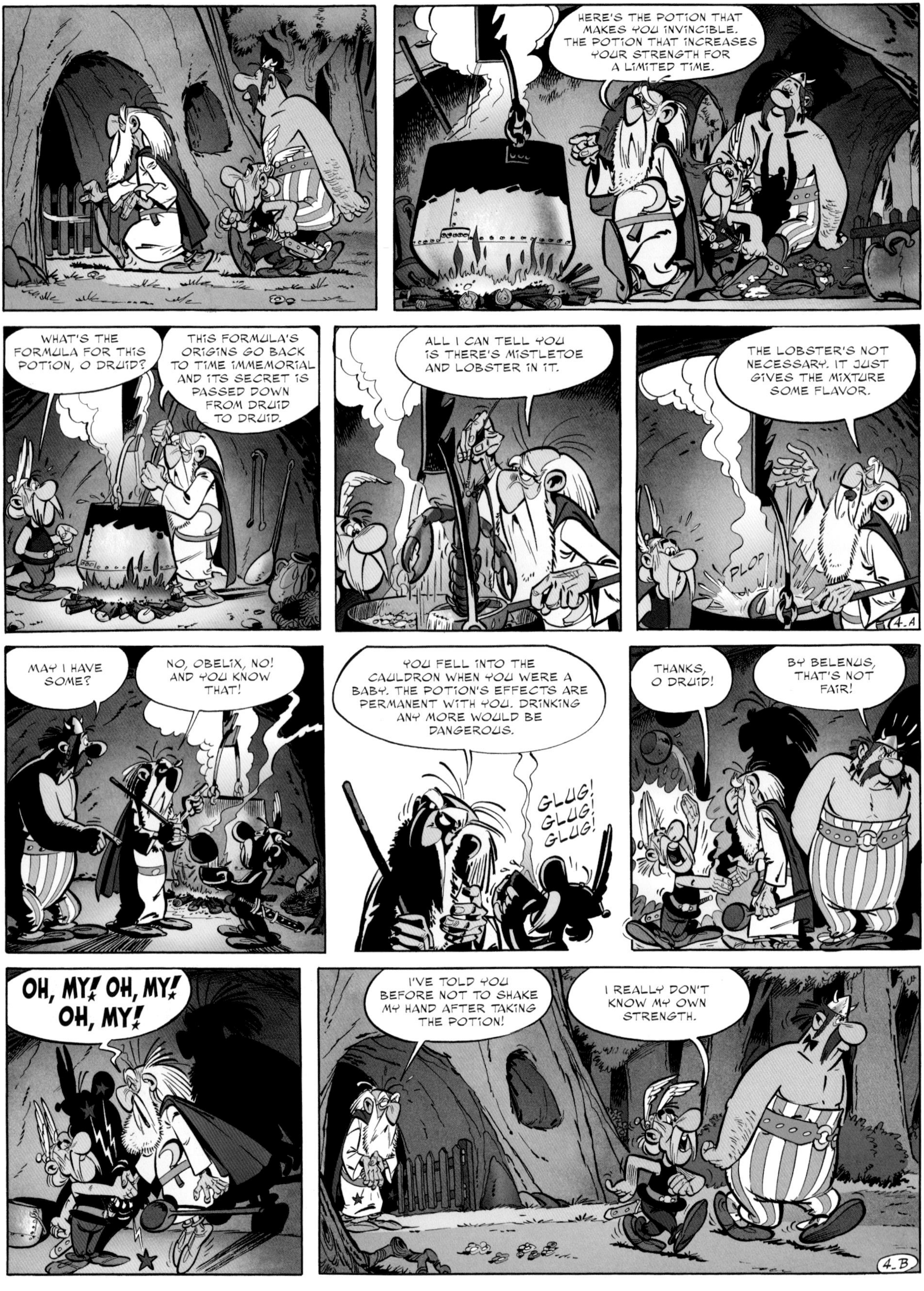
HERE'S THE POTION THAT MAKES YOU INVINCIBLE. THE POTION THAT INCREASES YOUR STRENGTH FOR A LIMITED TIME.
WHAT'S THE FORMULA FOR THIS POTION, O DRUID?
THIS FORMULA'S ORIGINS GO BACK TO TIME IMMEMORIAL AND ITS SECRET IS PASSED DOWN FROM DRUID TO DRUID.
ALL I CAN TELL YOU IS THERE'S MISTLETOE AND LOBSTER IN IT.
THE LOBSTER'S NOT NECESSARY. IT JUST GIVES THE MIXTURE SOME FLAVOR.
PLOP
4-A
MAY I HAVE SOME?
NO, OBELIX, NO! AND YOU KNOW THAT!
YOU FELL INTO THE CAULDRON WHEN YOU WERE A BABY. THE POTION'S EFFECTS ARE PERMANENT WITH YOU. DRINKING ANY MORE WOULD BE DANGEROUS.
GLUG! GLUG! GLUG!
THANKS, O DRUID!
BY BELENUS, THAT'S NOT FAIR!
OH, MY! OH, MY! OH, MY!
I'VE TOLD YOU BEFORE NOT TO SHAKE MY HAND AFTER TAKING THE POTION!
I REALLY DON'T KNOW MY OWN STRENGTH.
4-B

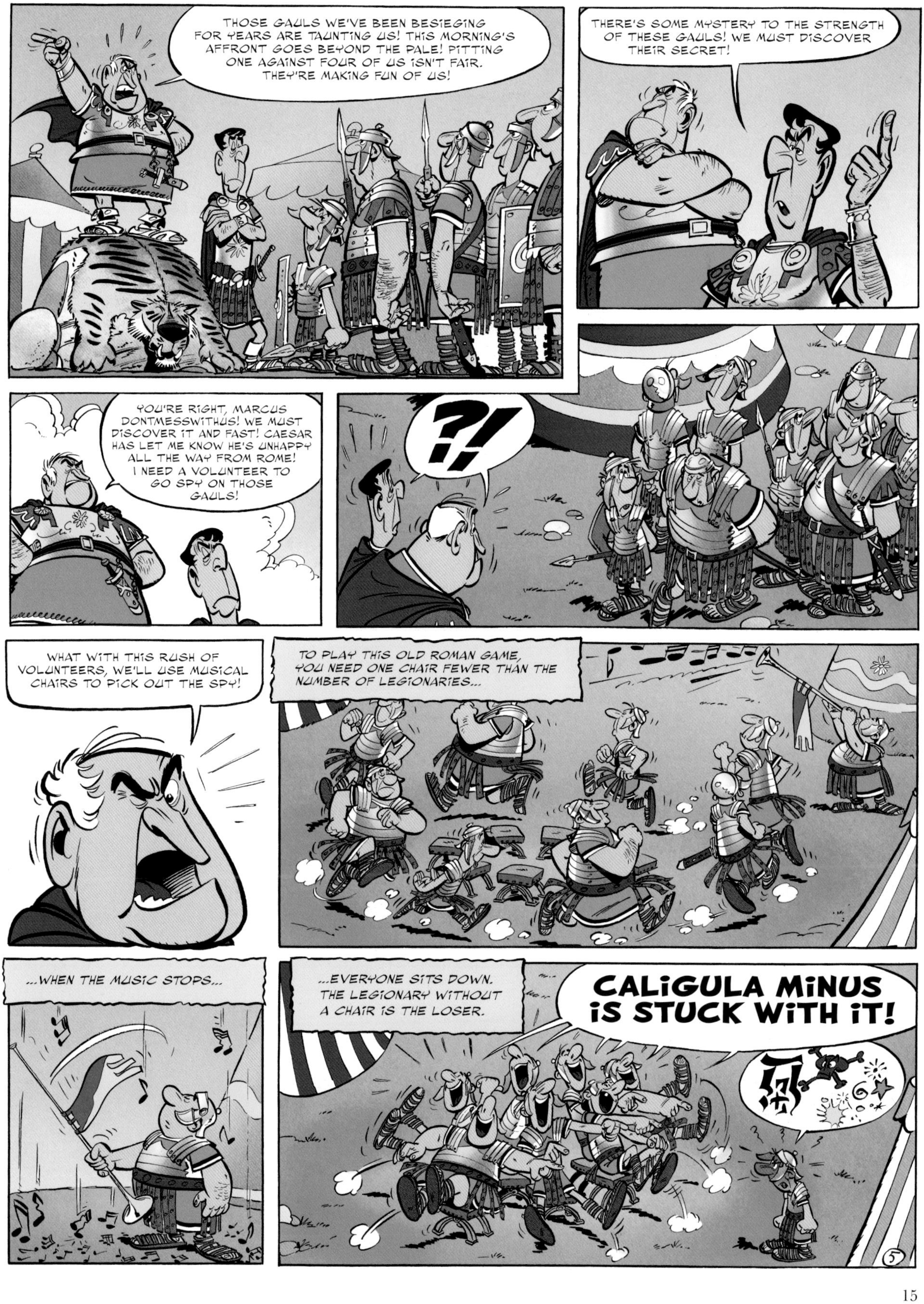
THOSE GAULS WE'VE BEEN BESIEGING FOR YEARS ARE TAUNTING US! THIS MORNING'S AFFRONT GOES BEYOND THE PALE! PITTING ONE AGAINST FOUR OF US ISN'T FAIR. THEY'RE MAKING FUN OF US!
THERE'S SOME MYSTERY TO THE STRENGTH OF THESE GAULS! WE MUST DISCOVER THEIR SECRET!
YOU'RE RIGHT, MARCUS DONTMESSWITHUS! WE MUST DISCOVER IT AND FAST! CAESAR HAS LET ME KNOW HE'S UNHAPPY ALL THE WAY FROM ROME! I NEED A VOLUNTEER TO GO SPY ON THOSE GAULS!
?!
WHAT WITH THIS RUSH OF VOLUNTEERS, WE'LL USE MUSICAL CHAIRS TO PICK OUT THE SPY!
TO PLAY THIS OLD ROMAN GAME, YOU NEED ONE CHAIR FEWER THAN THE NUMBER OF LEGIONARIES...
...WHEN THE MUSIC STOPS...
...EVERYONE SITS DOWN. THE LEGIONARY WITHOUT A CHAIR IS THE LOSER.
CALIGULA MINUS IS STUCK WITH IT!

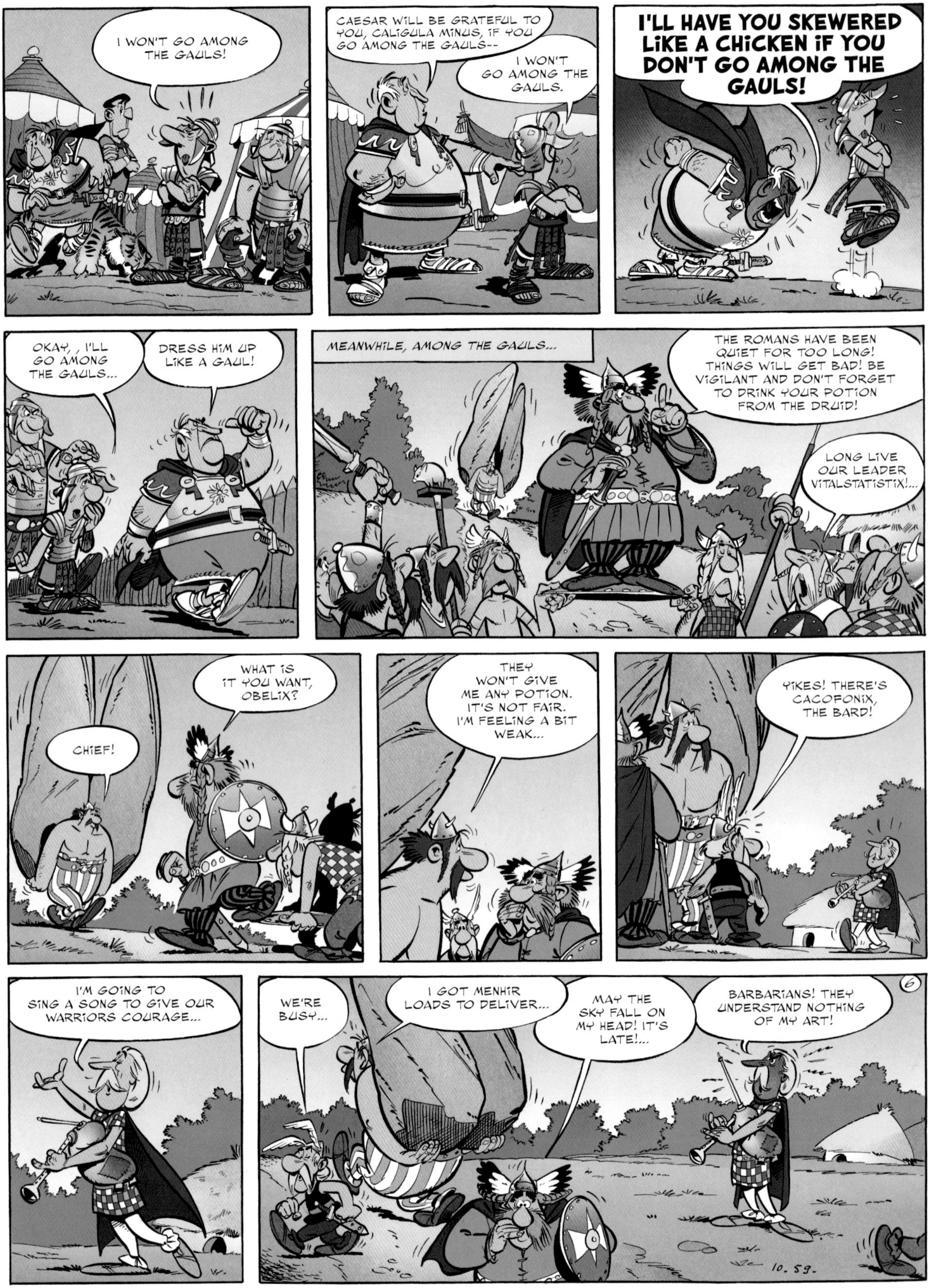
I WON'T GO AMONG THE GAULS!
CAESAR WILL BE GRATEFUL TO YOU, CALIGULA MINUS, IF YOU GO AMONG THE GAULS--
I WON'T GO AMONG THE GAULS.
I'LL HAVE YOU SKEWERED LIKE A CHICKEN IF YOU DON'T GO AMONG THE GAULS!
OKAY, , I'LL GO AMONG THE GAULS...
DRESS HIM UP LIKE A GAUL!
MEANWHILE, AMONG THE GAULS...
THE ROMANS HAVE BEEN QUIET FOR TOO LONG! THINGS WILL GET BAD! BE VIGILANT AND DON'T FORGET TO DRINK YOUR POTION FROM THE DRUID!
LONG LIVE OUR LEADER VITALSTATISTIX!...
CHIEF!
WHAT IS IT YOU WANT, OBELIX?
THEY WON'T GIVE ME ANY POTION. IT'S NOT FAIR. I'M FEELING A BIT WEAK...
YIKES! THERE'S CACOFONIX, THE BARD!
I'M GOING TO SING A SONG TO GIVE OUR WARRIORS COURAGE...
WE'RE BUSY...
I GOT MENHIR LOADS TO DELIVER...
MAY THE SKY FALL ON MY HEAD! IT'S LATE!...
BARBARIANS! THEY UNDERSTAND NOTHING OF MY ART!
6
10.59.

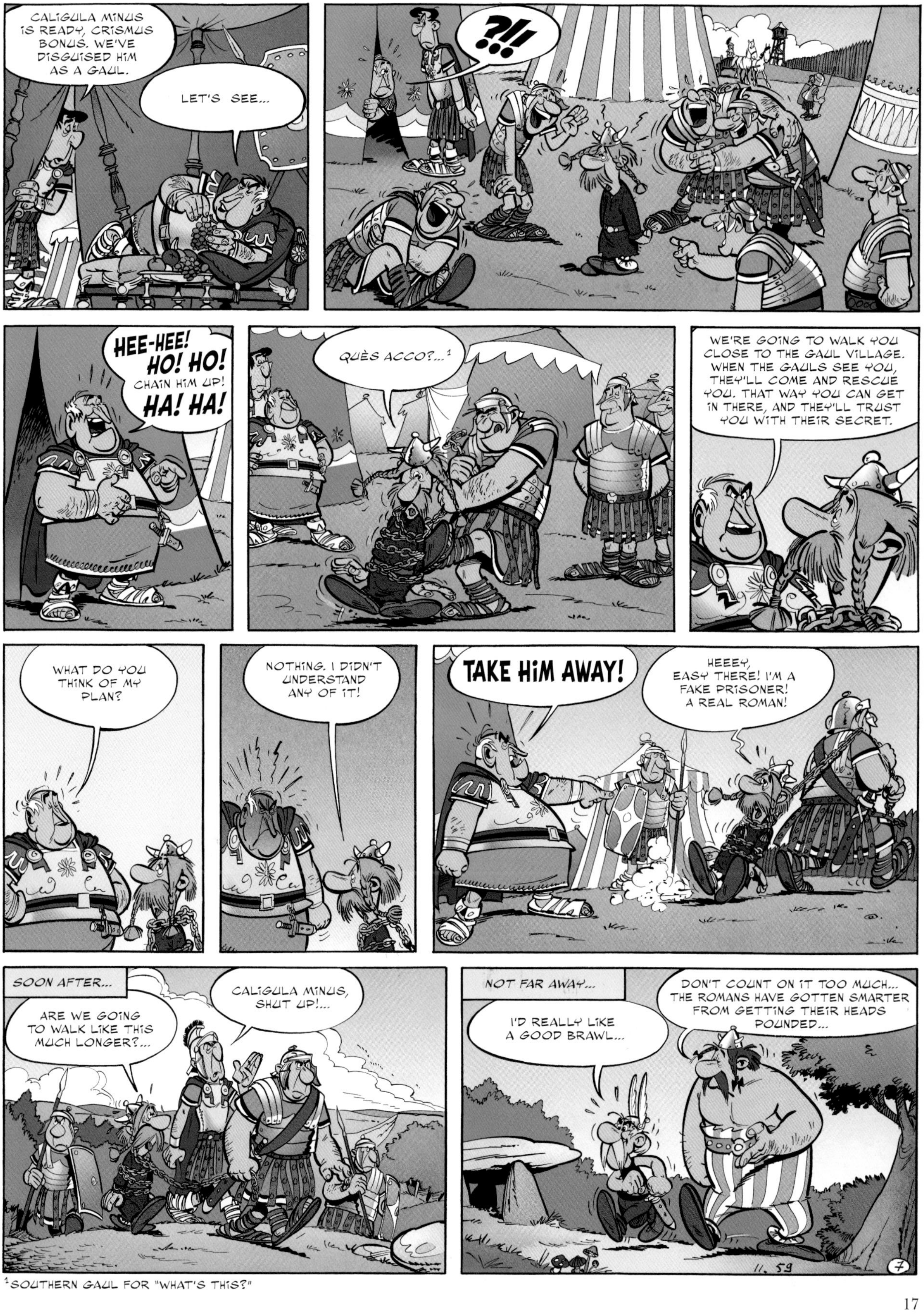

CALIGULA MINUS IS READY, CRISMUS BONUS. WE'VE DISGUISED HIM AS A GAUL.
LET'S SEE...
?!!
HEE-HEE! HO! HO! CHAIN HIM UP! HA! HA!
QUÈS ACCO?...¹
WE'RE GOING TO WALK YOU CLOSE TO THE GAUL VILLAGE. WHEN THE GAULS SEE YOU, THEY'LL COME AND RESCUE YOU. THAT WAY YOU CAN GET IN THERE, AND THEY'LL TRUST YOU WITH THEIR SECRET.
WHAT DO YOU THINK OF MY PLAN?
NOTHING. I DIDN'T UNDERSTAND ANY OF IT!
TAKE HIM AWAY!
HEEEY, EASY THERE! I'M A FAKE PRISONER! A REAL ROMAN!
SOON AFTER...
ARE WE GOING TO WALK LIKE THIS MUCH LONGER?...
CALIGULA MINUS, SHUT UP!...
NOT FAR AWAY...
I'D REALLY LIKE A GOOD BRAWL...
DON'T COUNT ON IT TOO MUCH... THE ROMANS HAVE GOTTEN SMARTER FROM GETTING THEIR HEADS POUNDED...
11.59
7

¹SOUTHERN GAUL FOR "WHAT'S THIS?"

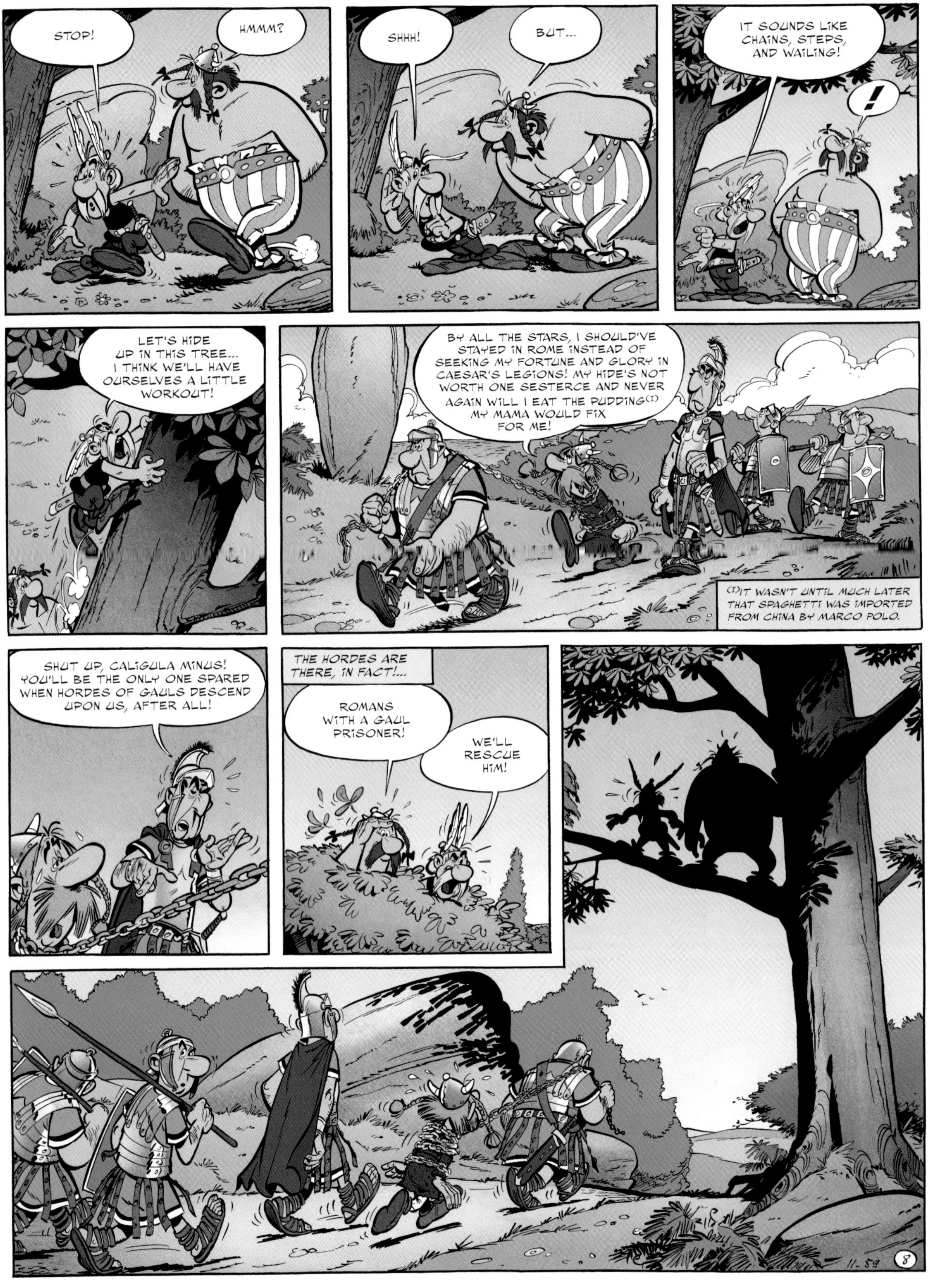
STOP!
HMMM?
SHHH!
BUT...
IT SOUNDS LIKE CHAINS, STEPS, AND WAILING!
!
LET'S HIDE UP IN THIS TREE... I THINK WE'LL HAVE OURSELVES A LITTLE WORKOUT!
BY ALL THE STARS, I SHOULD'VE STAYED IN ROME INSTEAD OF SEEKING MY FORTUNE AND GLORY IN CAESAR'S LEGIONS! MY HIDE'S NOT WORTH ONE SESTERCE AND NEVER AGAIN WILL I EAT THE PUDDING(1) MY MAMA WOULD FIX FOR ME!
(1)IT WASN'T UNTIL MUCH LATER THAT SPAGHETTI WAS IMPORTED FROM CHINA BY MARCO POLO.
SHUT UP, CALIGULA MINUS! YOU'LL BE THE ONLY ONE SPARED WHEN HORDES OF GAULS DESCEND UPON US, AFTER ALL!
THE HORDES ARE THERE, IN FACT!...
ROMANS WITH A GAUL PRISONER!
WE'LL RESCUE HIM!
11-59
8

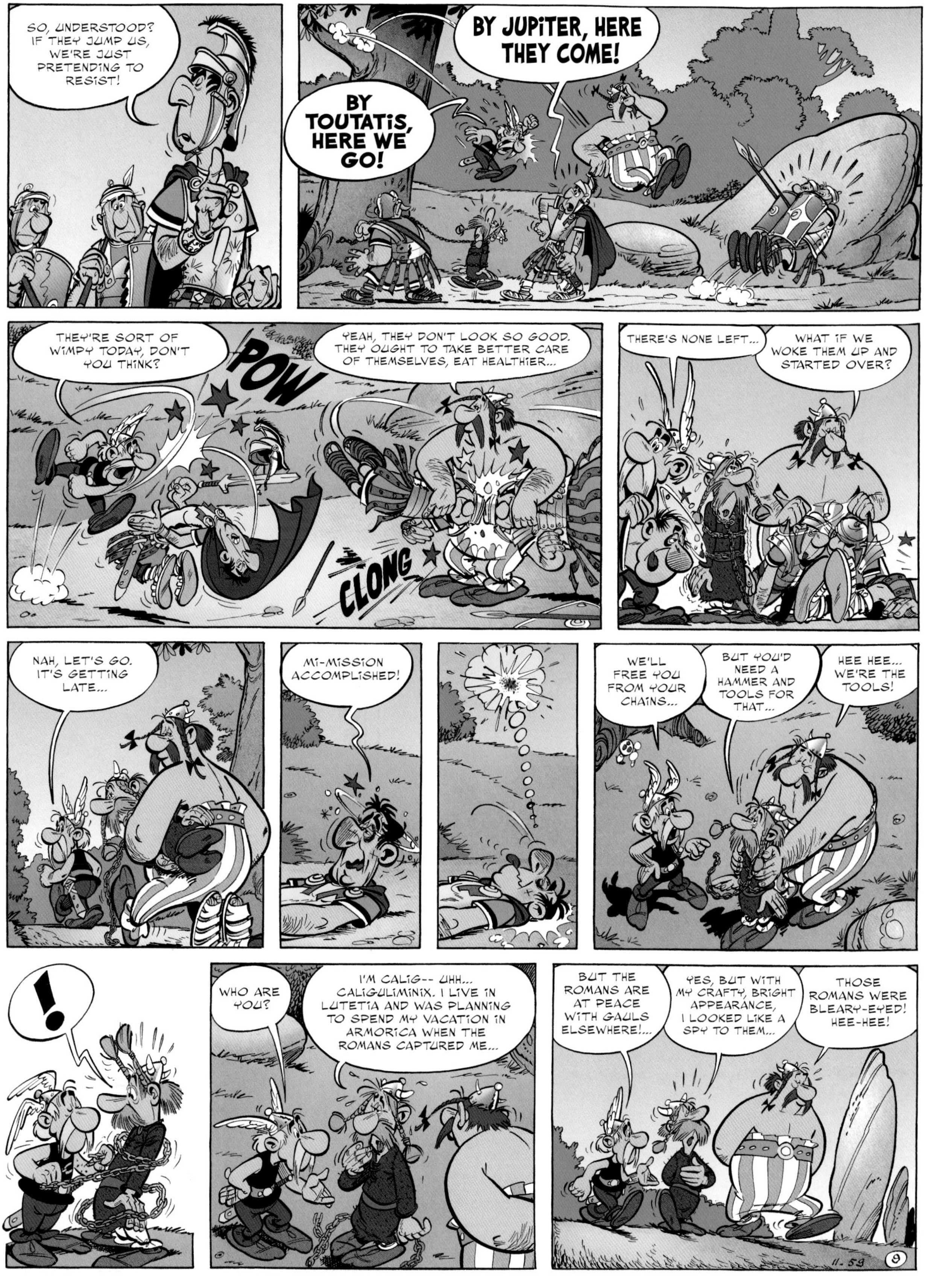
SO, UNDERSTOOD? IF THEY JUMP US, WE'RE JUST PRETENDING TO RESIST!
BY JUPITER, HERE THEY COME!
BY TOUTATIS, HERE WE GO!
THEY'RE SORT OF WIMPY TODAY, DON'T YOU THINK?
POW
YEAH, THEY DON'T LOOK SO GOOD. THEY OUGHT TO TAKE BETTER CARE OF THEMSELVES, EAT HEALTHIER...
CLONG
THERE'S NONE LEFT...
WHAT IF WE WOKE THEM UP AND STARTED OVER?
NAH, LET'S GO. IT'S GETTING LATE...
MI-MISSION ACCOMPLISHED!
WE'LL FREE YOU FROM YOUR CHAINS...
BUT YOU'D NEED A HAMMER AND TOOLS FOR THAT...
HEE HEE... WE'RE THE TOOLS!
!
WHO ARE YOU?
I'M CALIG-- UHH... CALIGULIMINIX. I LIVE IN LUTETIA AND WAS PLANNING TO SPEND MY VACATION IN ARMORICA WHEN THE ROMANS CAPTURED ME...
BUT THE ROMANS ARE AT PEACE WITH GAULS ELSEWHERE!...
YES, BUT WITH MY CRAFTY, BRIGHT APPEARANCE, I LOOKED LIKE A SPY TO THEM...
THOSE ROMANS WERE BLEARY-EYED! HEE-HEE!
11.59
9

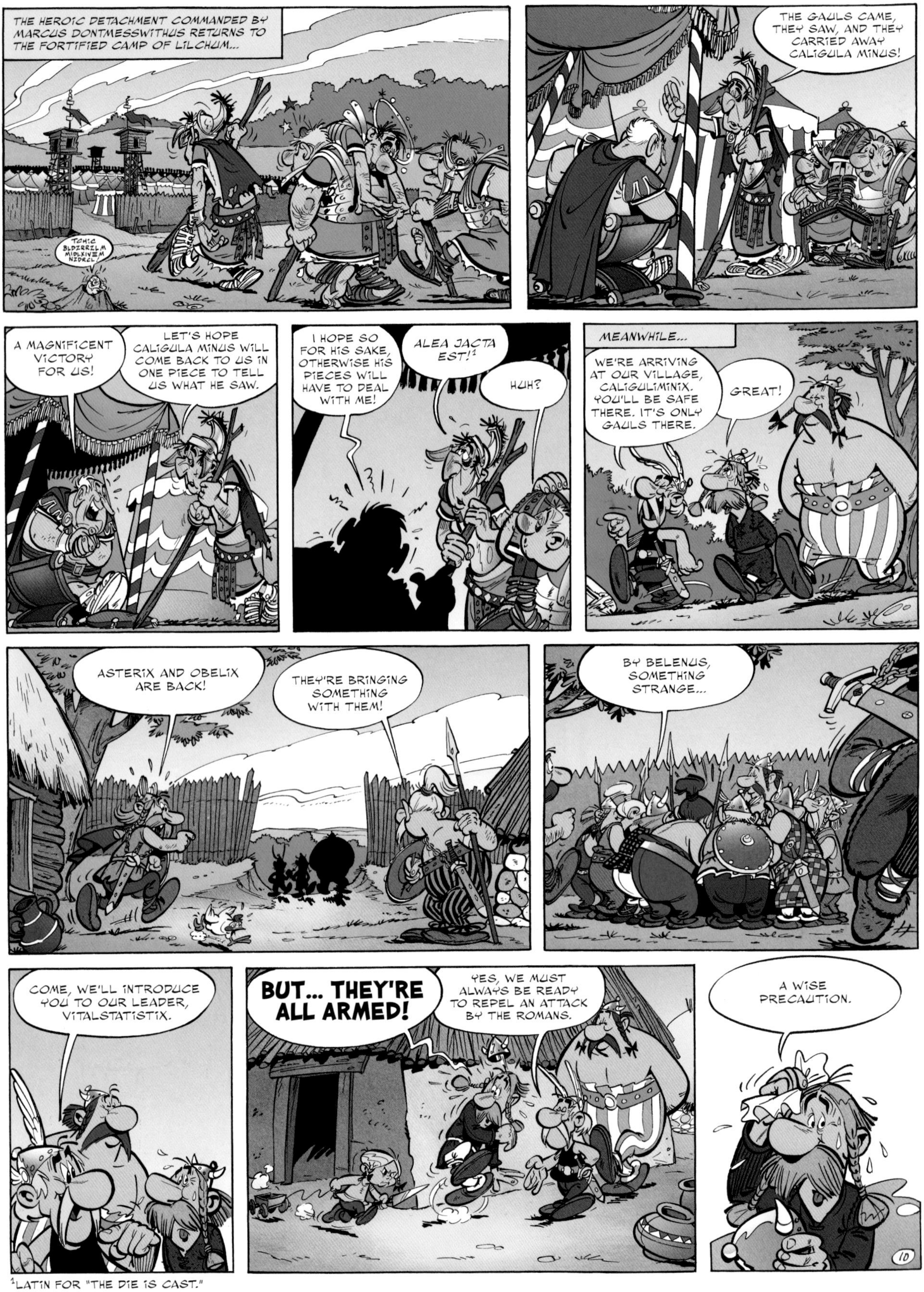
THE HEROIC DETACHMENT COMMANDED BY MARCUS DONTMESSWITHUS RETURNS TO THE FORTIFIED CAMP OF LILCHUM...
THE GAULS CAME, THEY SAW, AND THEY CARRIED AWAY CALIGULA MINUS!
A MAGNIFICENT VICTORY FOR US!
LET'S HOPE CALIGULA MINUS WILL COME BACK TO US IN ONE PIECE TO TELL US WHAT HE SAW.
I HOPE SO FOR HIS SAKE, OTHERWISE HIS PIECES WILL HAVE TO DEAL WITH ME!
ALEA JACTA EST![1]
HUH?
MEANWHILE...
WE'RE ARRIVING AT OUR VILLAGE, CALIGULIMINIX. YOU'LL BE SAFE THERE. IT'S ONLY GAULS THERE.
GREAT!
ASTERIX AND OBELIX ARE BACK!
THEY'RE BRINGING SOMETHING WITH THEM!
BY BELENUS, SOMETHING STRANGE...
COME, WE'LL INTRODUCE YOU TO OUR LEADER, VITALSTATISTIX.
BUT... THEY'RE ALL ARMED!
YES, WE MUST ALWAYS BE READY TO REPEL AN ATTACK BY THE ROMANS.
A WISE PRECAUTION.
10

[1] LATIN FOR "THE DIE IS CAST."

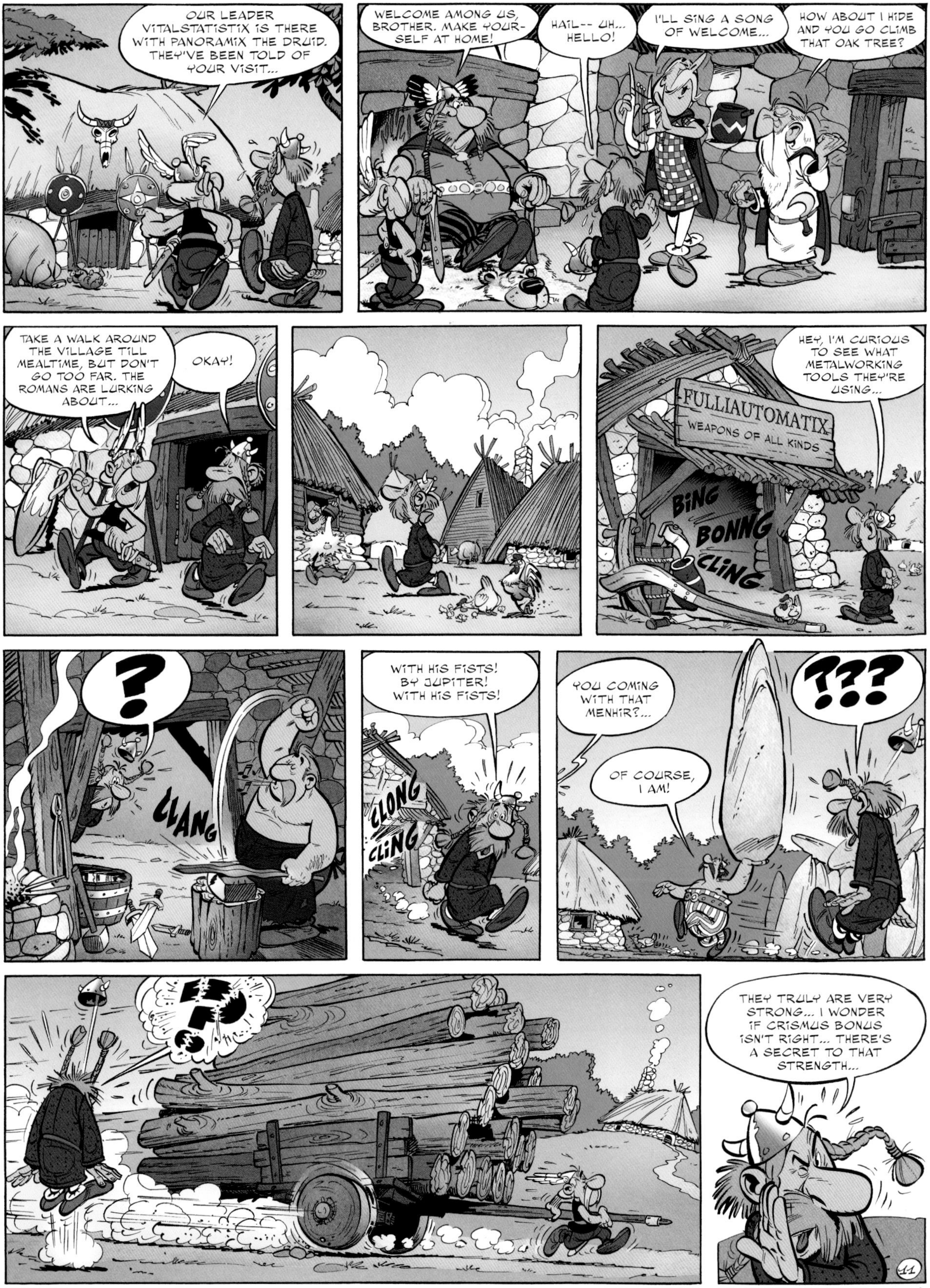

OUR LEADER VITALSTATISTIX IS THERE WITH PANORAMIX THE DRUID. THEY'VE BEEN TOLD OF YOUR VISIT...
WELCOME AMONG US, BROTHER. MAKE YOURSELF AT HOME!
HAIL-- UH... HELLO!
I'LL SING A SONG OF WELCOME...
HOW ABOUT I HIDE AND YOU GO CLIMB THAT OAK TREE?
TAKE A WALK AROUND THE VILLAGE TILL MEALTIME, BUT DON'T GO TOO FAR. THE ROMANS ARE LURKING ABOUT...
OKAY!
HEY, I'M CURIOUS TO SEE WHAT METALWORKING TOOLS THEY'RE USING...
FULLIAUTOMATIX
WEAPONS OF ALL KINDS
BING
BONNG
CLING
?
CLANG
WITH HIS FISTS! BY JUPITER! WITH HIS FISTS!
CLONG
CLING
YOU COMING WITH THAT MENHIR?...
OF COURSE, I AM!
???
THEY TRULY ARE VERY STRONG... I WONDER IF CRISMUS BONUS ISN'T RIGHT... THERE'S A SECRET TO THAT STRENGTH...
11

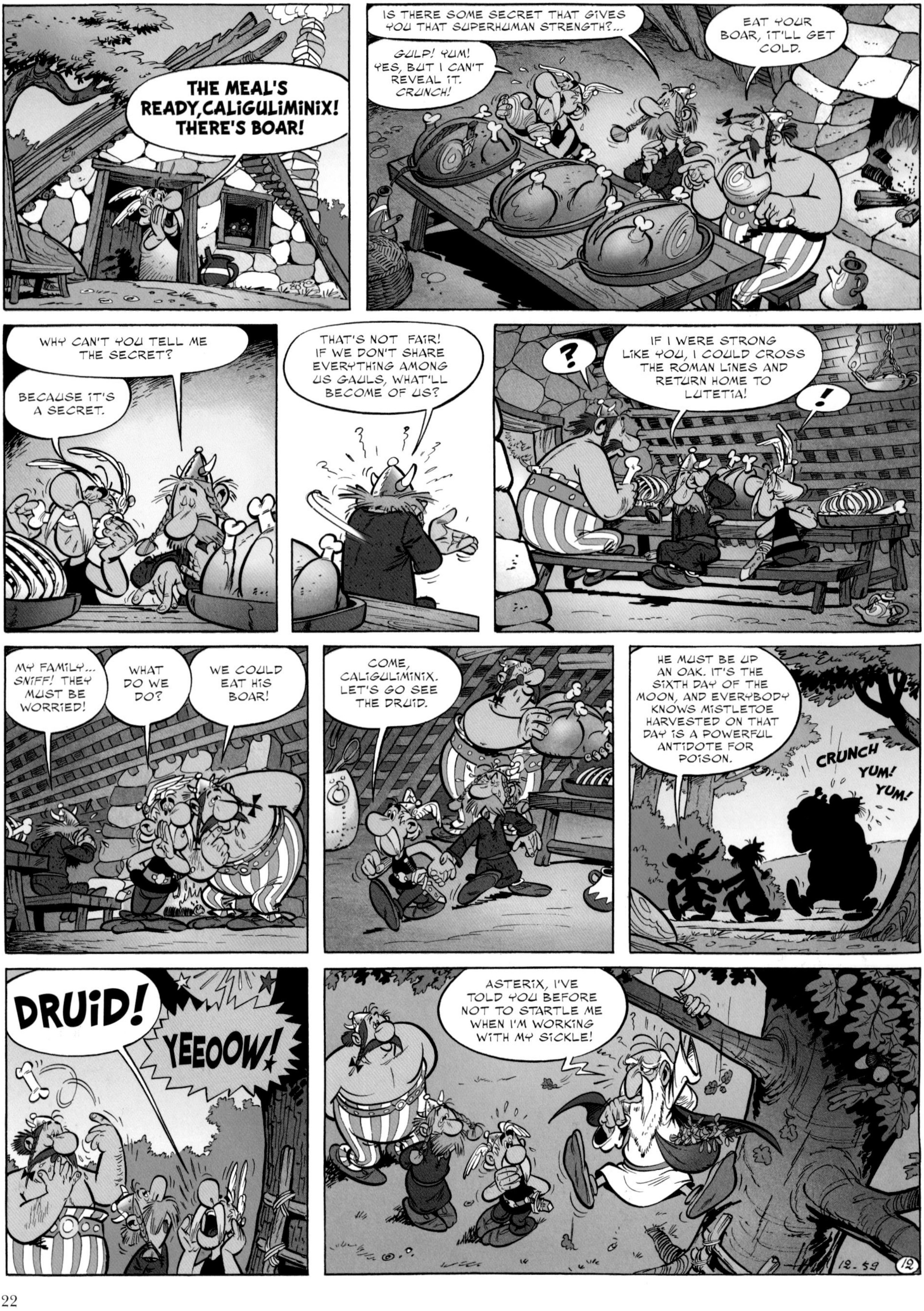

THE MEAL'S READY, CALIGULIMINIX! THERE'S BOAR!
IS THERE SOME SECRET THAT GIVES YOU THAT SUPERHUMAN STRENGTH?...
GULP! YUM! YES, BUT I CAN'T REVEAL IT. CRUNCH!
EAT YOUR BOAR, IT'LL GET COLD.
WHY CAN'T YOU TELL ME THE SECRET?
BECAUSE IT'S A SECRET.
THAT'S NOT FAIR! IF WE DON'T SHARE EVERYTHING AMONG US GAULS, WHAT'LL BECOME OF US?
?
IF I WERE STRONG LIKE YOU, I COULD CROSS THE ROMAN LINES AND RETURN HOME TO LUTETIA!
!
MY FAMILY... SNIFF! THEY MUST BE WORRIED!
WHAT DO WE DO?
WE COULD EAT HIS BOAR!
COME, CALIGULIMINIX. LET'S GO SEE THE DRUID.
HE MUST BE UP AN OAK. IT'S THE SIXTH DAY OF THE MOON, AND EVERYBODY KNOWS MISTLETOE HARVESTED ON THAT DAY IS A POWERFUL ANTIDOTE FOR POISON.
CRUNCH
YUM!
YUM!
DRUID!
YEEOOW!
ASTERIX, I'VE TOLD YOU BEFORE NOT TO STARTLE ME WHEN I'M WORKING WITH MY SICKLE!
12-59
12

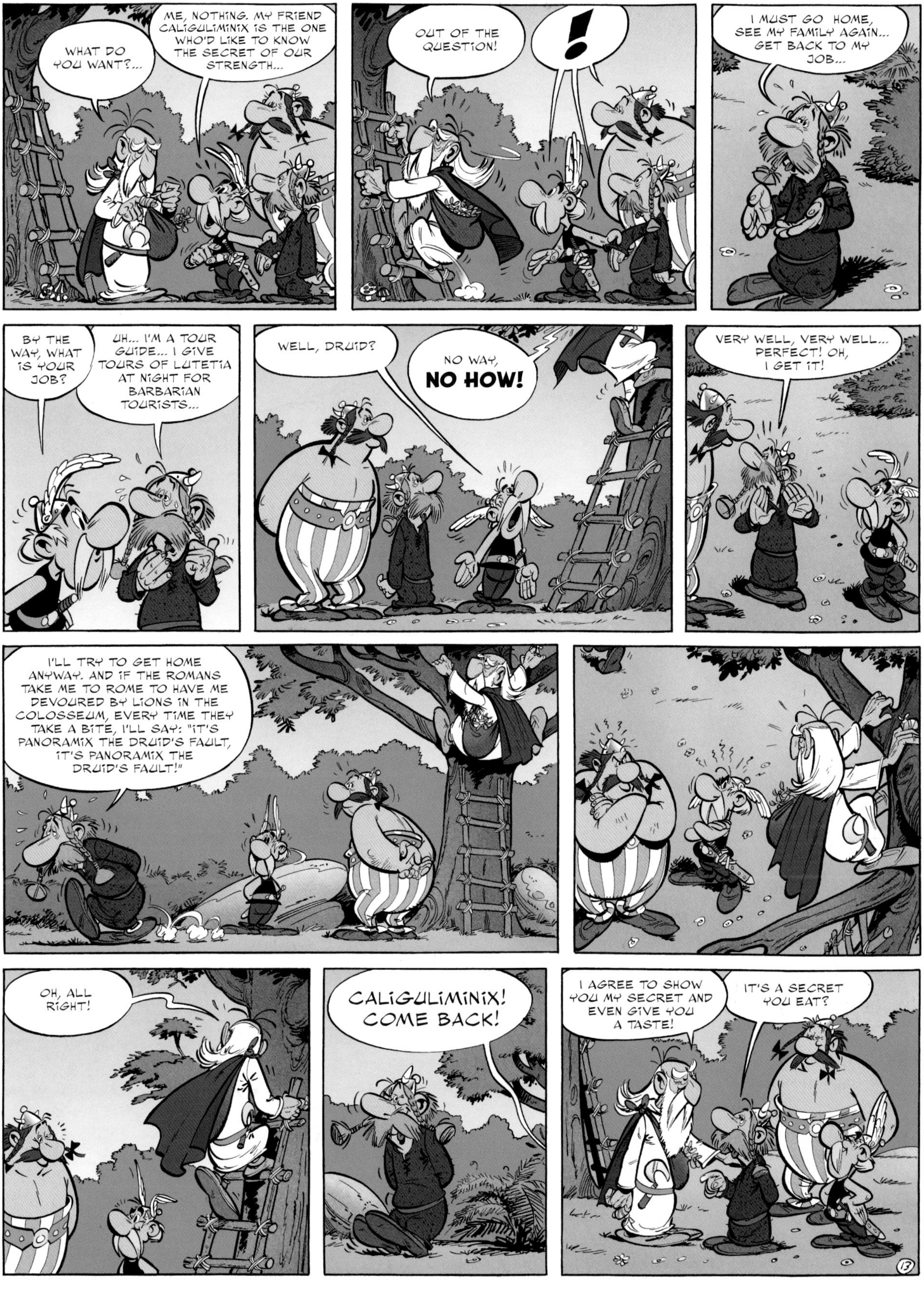
WHAT DO YOU WANT?...
ME, NOTHING. MY FRIEND CALIGULIMINIX IS THE ONE WHO'D LIKE TO KNOW THE SECRET OF OUR STRENGTH...
OUT OF THE QUESTION!
!
I MUST GO HOME, SEE MY FAMILY AGAIN... GET BACK TO MY JOB...
BY THE WAY, WHAT IS YOUR JOB?
UH... I'M A TOUR GUIDE... I GIVE TOURS OF LUTETIA AT NIGHT FOR BARBARIAN TOURISTS...
WELL, DRUID?
NO WAY, NO HOW!
VERY WELL, VERY WELL... PERFECT! OH, I GET IT!
I'LL TRY TO GET HOME ANYWAY. AND IF THE ROMANS TAKE ME TO ROME TO HAVE ME DEVOURED BY LIONS IN THE COLOSSEUM, EVERY TIME THEY TAKE A BITE, I'LL SAY: "IT'S PANORAMIX THE DRUID'S FAULT, IT'S PANORAMIX THE DRUID'S FAULT!"
OH, ALL RIGHT!
CALIGULIMINIX! COME BACK!
I AGREE TO SHOW YOU MY SECRET AND EVEN GIVE YOU A TASTE!
IT'S A SECRET YOU EAT?
13

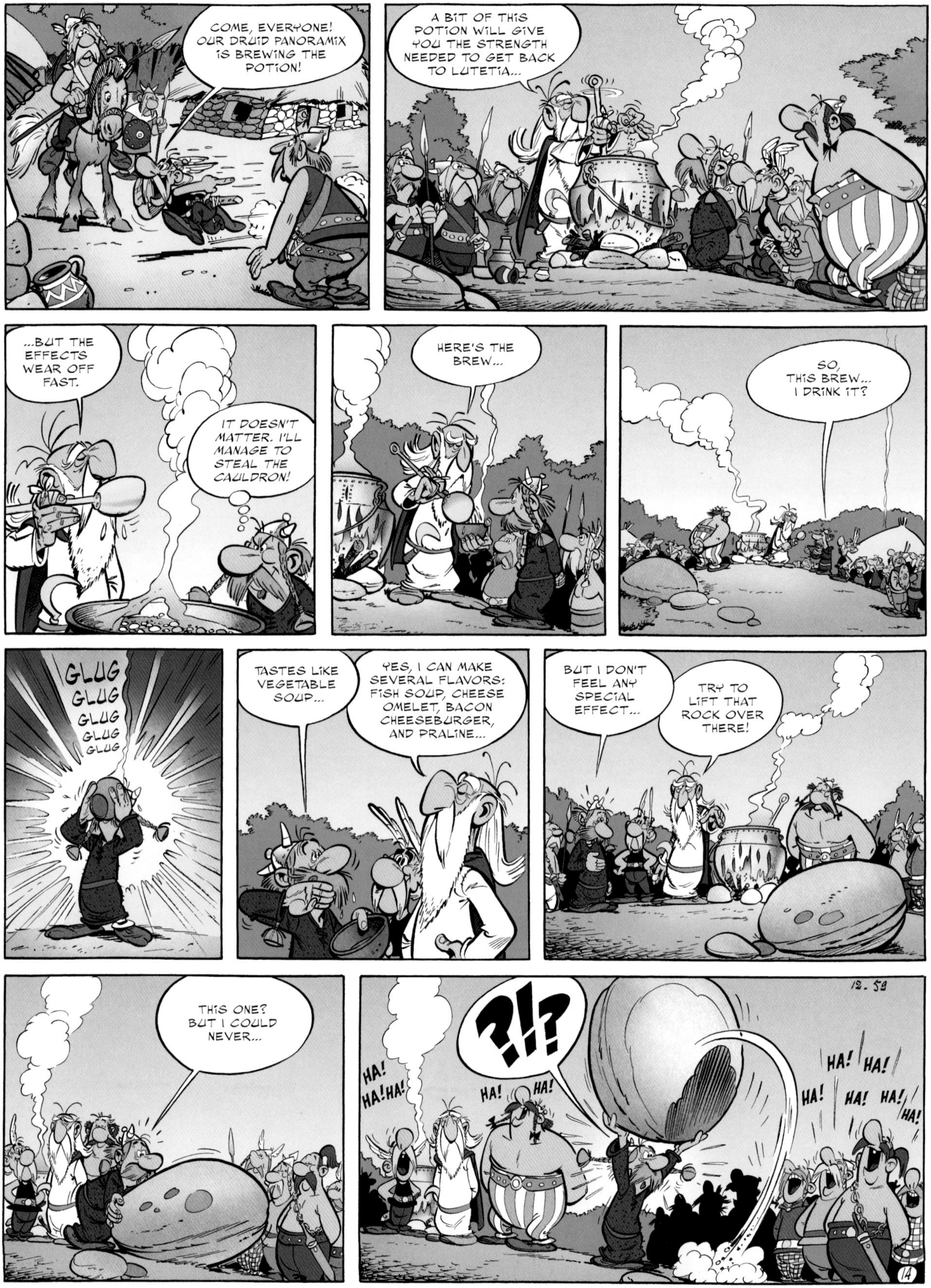
COME, EVERYONE! OUR DRUID PANORAMIX IS BREWING THE POTION!
A BIT OF THIS POTION WILL GIVE YOU THE STRENGTH NEEDED TO GET BACK TO LUTETIA...
...BUT THE EFFECTS WEAR OFF FAST.
IT DOESN'T MATTER. I'LL MANAGE TO STEAL THE CAULDRON!
HERE'S THE BREW...
SO, THIS BREW... I DRINK IT?
GLUG GLUG GLUG GLUG GLUG
TASTES LIKE VEGETABLE SOUP...
YES, I CAN MAKE SEVERAL FLAVORS: FISH SOUP, CHEESE OMELET, BACON CHEESEBURGER, AND PRALINE...
BUT I DON'T FEEL ANY SPECIAL EFFECT...
TRY TO LIFT THAT ROCK OVER THERE!
THIS ONE? BUT I COULD NEVER...
12.59
?!?
HA! HA! HA!
HA! HA!
HA! HA! HA! HA! HA! HA!
14

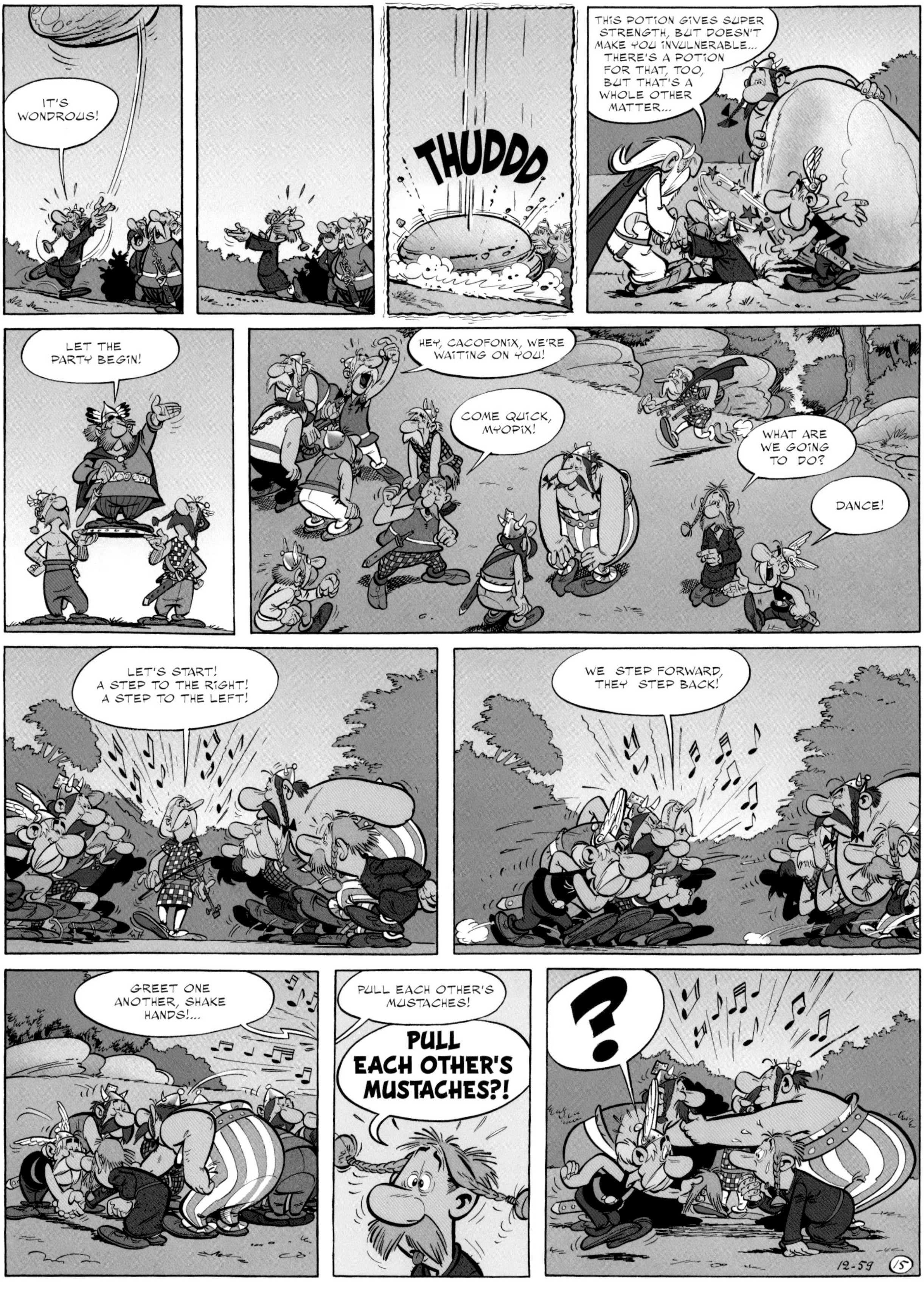

IT'S WONDROUS!
THUDDD
THIS POTION GIVES SUPER STRENGTH, BUT DOESN'T MAKE YOU INVULNERABLE... THERE'S A POTION FOR THAT, TOO, BUT THAT'S A WHOLE OTHER MATTER...
LET THE PARTY BEGIN!
HEY, CACOFONIX, WE'RE WAITING ON YOU!
COME QUICK, MYOPIX!
WHAT ARE WE GOING TO DO?
DANCE!
LET'S START! A STEP TO THE RIGHT! A STEP TO THE LEFT!
WE STEP FORWARD, THEY STEP BACK!
GREET ONE ANOTHER, SHAKE HANDS!...
PULL EACH OTHER'S MUSTACHES!
PULL EACH OTHER'S MUSTACHES?!
?
12-59
15

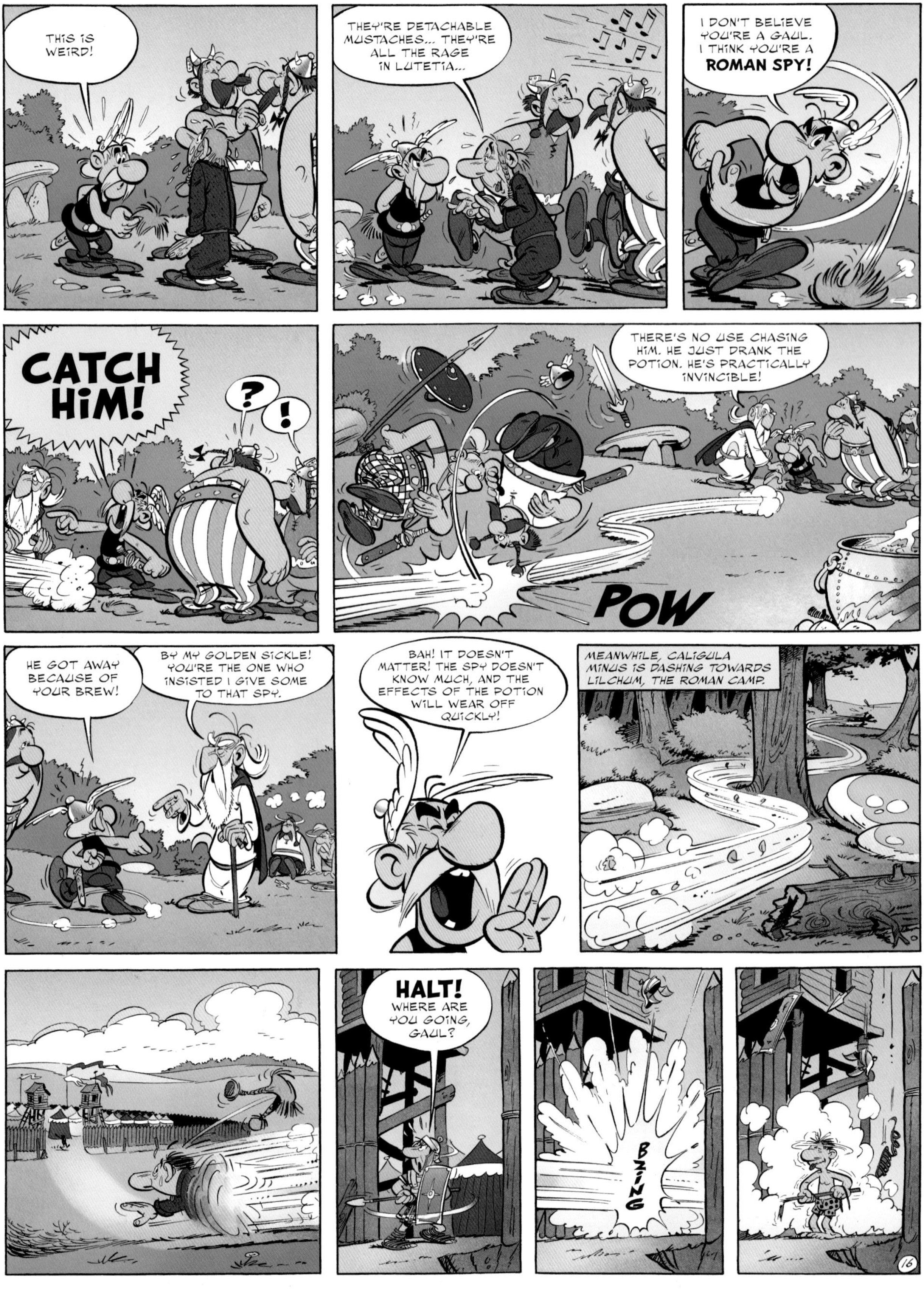

THIS IS WEIRD!
THEY'RE DETACHABLE MUSTACHES... THEY'RE ALL THE RAGE IN LUTETIA...
I DON'T BELIEVE YOU'RE A GAUL. I THINK YOU'RE A ROMAN SPY!
CATCH HIM!
?
!
THERE'S NO USE CHASING HIM. HE JUST DRANK THE POTION. HE'S PRACTICALLY INVINCIBLE!
POW
HE GOT AWAY BECAUSE OF YOUR BREW!
BY MY GOLDEN SICKLE! YOU'RE THE ONE WHO INSISTED I GIVE SOME TO THAT SPY.
BAH! IT DOESN'T MATTER! THE SPY DOESN'T KNOW MUCH, AND THE EFFECTS OF THE POTION WILL WEAR OFF QUICKLY!
MEANWHILE, CALIGULA MINUS IS DASHING TOWARDS LILCHUM, THE ROMAN CAMP.
HALT! WHERE ARE YOU GOING, GAUL?
BZING
16

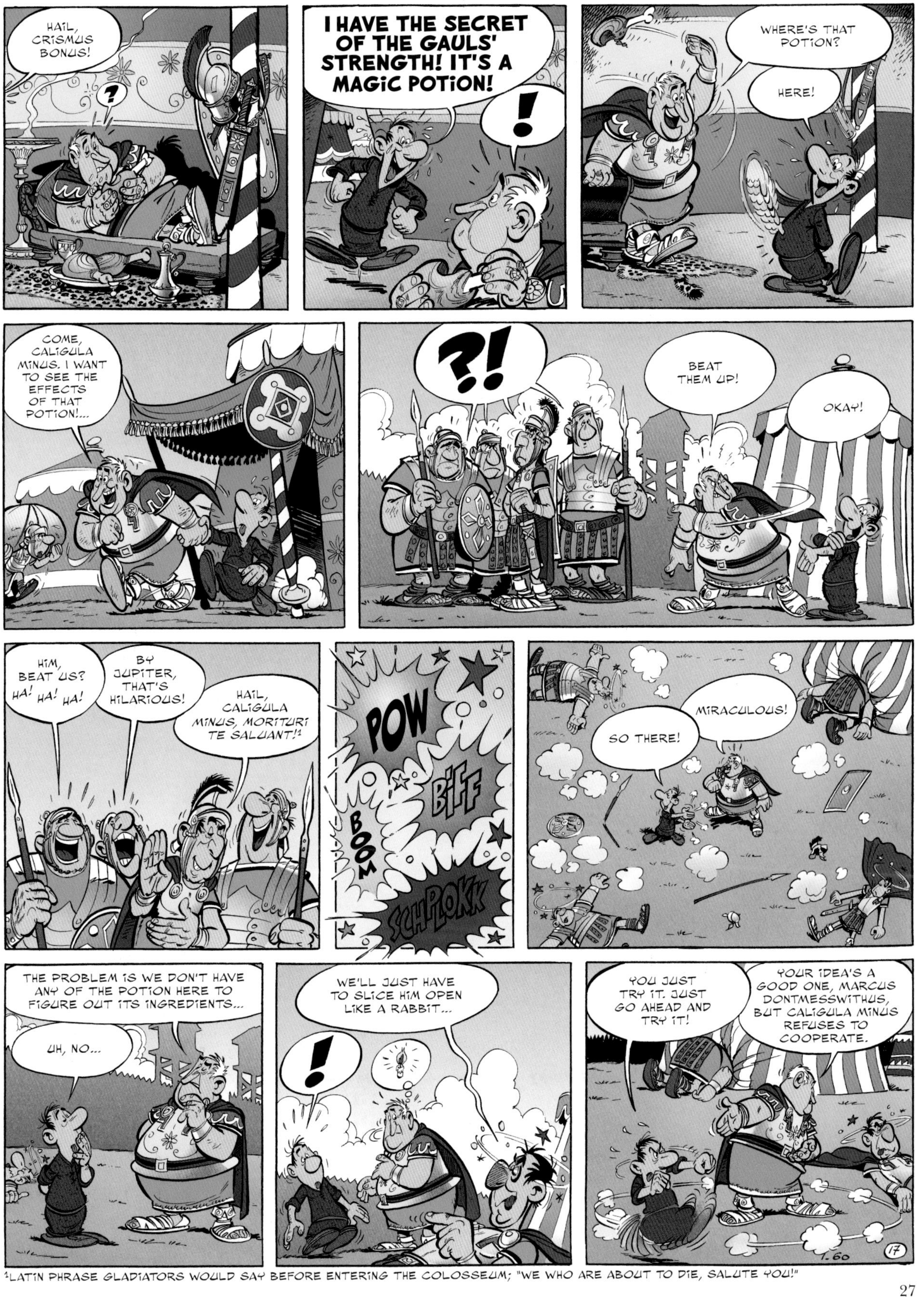
HAIL, CRISMUS BONUS!
?
I HAVE THE SECRET OF THE GAULS' STRENGTH! IT'S A MAGIC POTION!
!
WHERE'S THAT POTION?
HERE!
COME, CALIGULA MINUS. I WANT TO SEE THE EFFECTS OF THAT POTION!...
?!
BEAT THEM UP!
OKAY!
HIM, BEAT US? HA! HA! HA!
BY JUPITER, THAT'S HILARIOUS!
HAIL, CALIGULA MINUS, MORITURI TE SALUANT!1
POW
BIFF
BOOM
SCHPLOKK
MIRACULOUS!
SO THERE!
THE PROBLEM IS WE DON'T HAVE ANY OF THE POTION HERE TO FIGURE OUT ITS INGREDIENTS...
UH, NO...
WE'LL JUST HAVE TO SLICE HIM OPEN LIKE A RABBIT...
!
YOU JUST TRY IT. JUST GO AHEAD AND TRY IT!
YOUR IDEA'S A GOOD ONE, MARCUS DONTMESSWITHUS, BUT CALIGULA MINUS REFUSES TO COOPERATE.
17

[1]LATIN PHRASE GLADIATORS WOULD SAY BEFORE ENTERING THE COLOSSEUM; "WE WHO ARE ABOUT TO DIE, SALUTE YOU!"

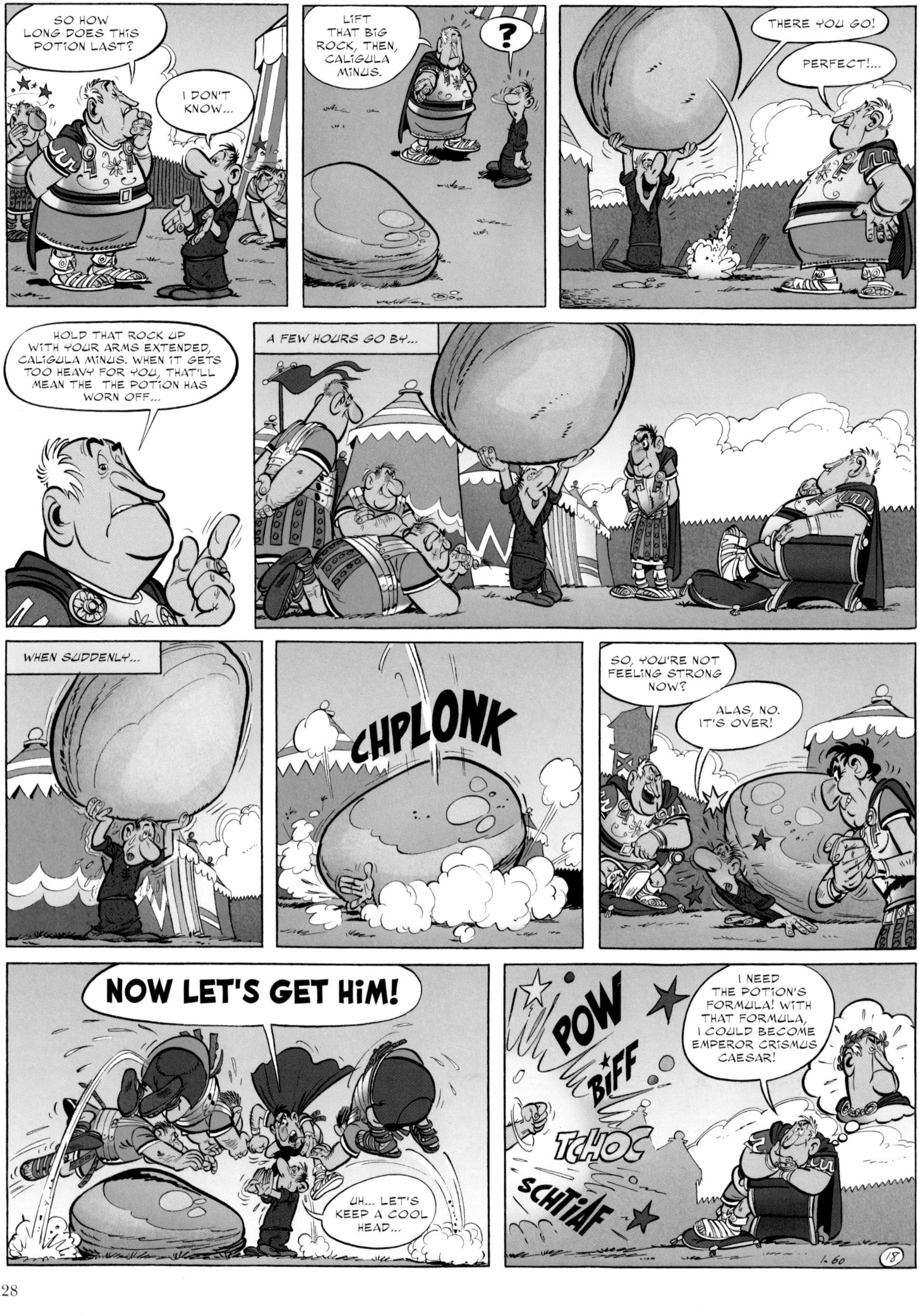
SO HOW LONG DOES THIS POTION LAST?
I DON'T KNOW...
LIFT THAT BIG ROCK, THEN, CALIGULA MINUS.
?
THERE YOU GO!
PERFECT!...
HOLD THAT ROCK UP WITH YOUR ARMS EXTENDED, CALIGULA MINUS. WHEN IT GETS TOO HEAVY FOR YOU, THAT'LL MEAN THE THE POTION HAS WORN OFF...
A FEW HOURS GO BY...
WHEN SUDDENLY...
CHPLONK
SO, YOU'RE NOT FEELING STRONG NOW?
ALAS, NO. IT'S OVER!
NOW LET'S GET HIM!
UH... LET'S KEEP A COOL HEAD...
POW
BIFF
TCHOC
SCHTIAF
I NEED THE POTION'S FORMULA! WITH THAT FORMULA, I COULD BECOME EMPEROR CRISMUS CAESAR!
18

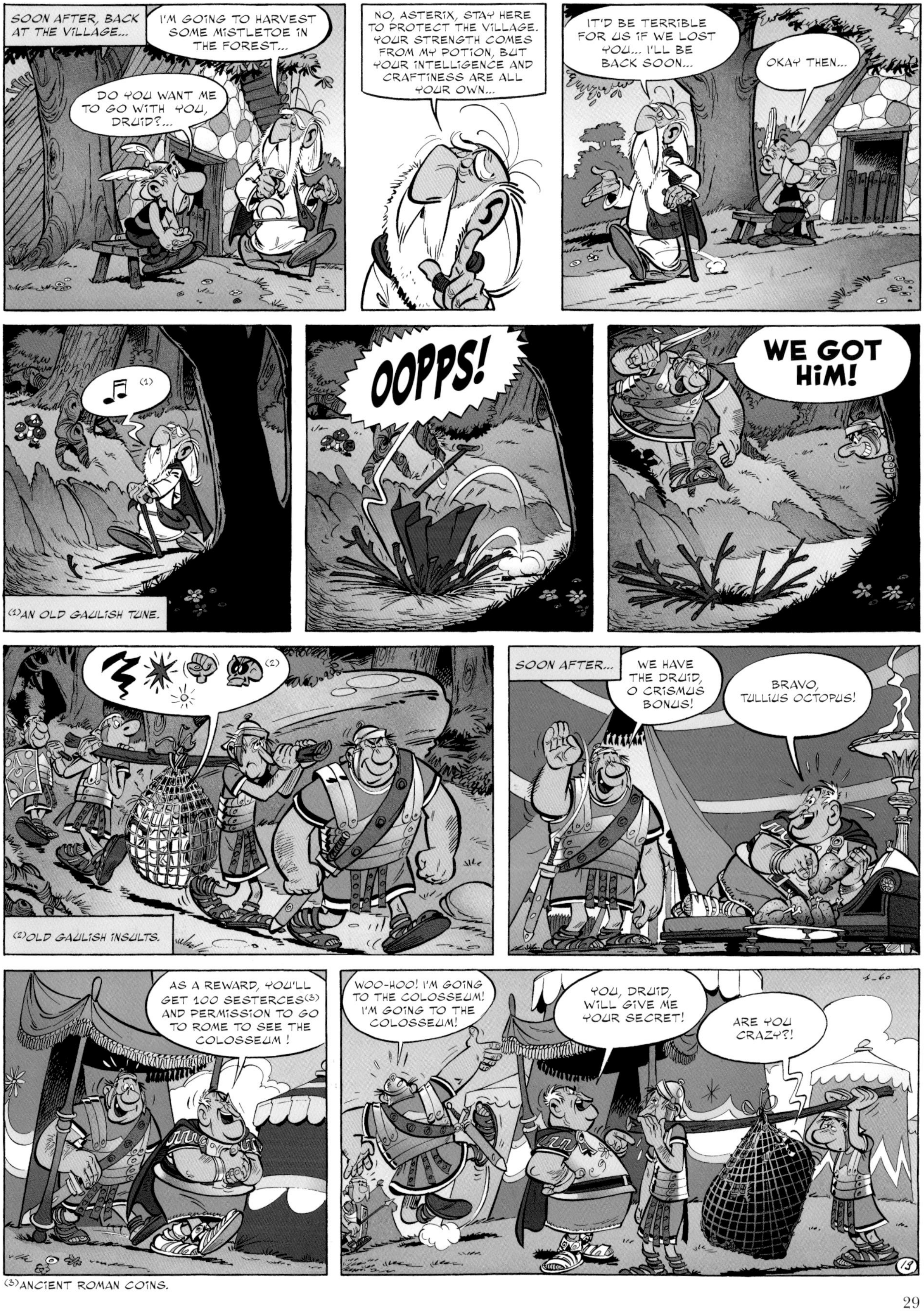
SOON AFTER, BACK AT THE VILLAGE...
I'M GOING TO HARVEST SOME MISTLETOE IN THE FOREST...
DO YOU WANT ME TO GO WITH YOU, DRUID?...
NO, ASTERIX, STAY HERE TO PROTECT THE VILLAGE. YOUR STRENGTH COMES FROM MY POTION, BUT YOUR INTELLIGENCE AND CRAFTINESS ARE ALL YOUR OWN...
IT'D BE TERRIBLE FOR US IF WE LOST YOU... I'LL BE BACK SOON...
OKAY THEN...
♫ (1)
(1) AN OLD GAULISH TUNE.
OOPPS!
WE GOT HIM!
(2)
(2) OLD GAULISH INSULTS.
SOON AFTER...
WE HAVE THE DRUID, O CRISMUS BONUS!
BRAVO, TULLIUS OCTOPUS!
AS A REWARD, YOU'LL GET 100 SESTERCES(3) AND PERMISSION TO GO TO ROME TO SEE THE COLOSSEUM !
WOO-HOO! I'M GOING TO THE COLOSSEUM! I'M GOING TO THE COLOSSEUM!
YOU, DRUID, WILL GIVE ME YOUR SECRET!
ARE YOU CRAZY?!
4-60
13

(3) ANCIENT ROMAN COINS.

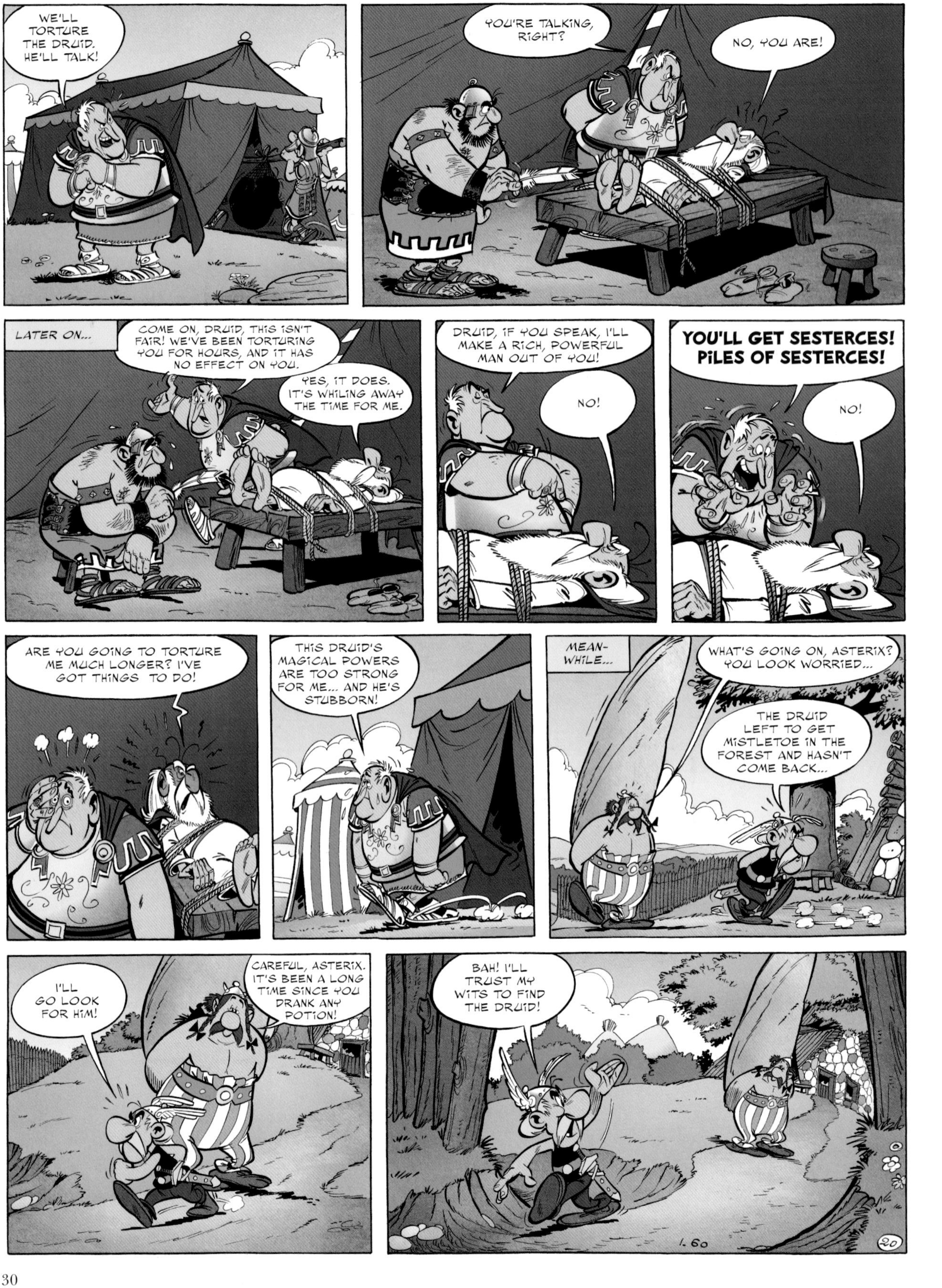
WE'LL TORTURE THE DRUID. HE'LL TALK!
YOU'RE TALKING, RIGHT?
NO, YOU ARE!
LATER ON...
COME ON, DRUID, THIS ISN'T FAIR! WE'VE BEEN TORTURING YOU FOR HOURS, AND IT HAS NO EFFECT ON YOU.
YES, IT DOES. IT'S WHILING AWAY THE TIME FOR ME.
DRUID, IF YOU SPEAK, I'LL MAKE A RICH, POWERFUL MAN OUT OF YOU!
NO!
YOU'LL GET SESTERCES! PILES OF SESTERCES!
NO!
ARE YOU GOING TO TORTURE ME MUCH LONGER? I'VE GOT THINGS TO DO!
THIS DRUID'S MAGICAL POWERS ARE TOO STRONG FOR ME... AND HE'S STUBBORN!
MEAN-WHILE...
WHAT'S GOING ON, ASTERIX? YOU LOOK WORRIED...
THE DRUID LEFT TO GET MISTLETOE IN THE FOREST AND HASN'T COME BACK...
I'LL GO LOOK FOR HIM!
CAREFUL, ASTERIX. IT'S BEEN A LONG TIME SINCE YOU DRANK ANY POTION!
BAH! I'LL TRUST MY WITS TO FIND THE DRUID!
1.60
20

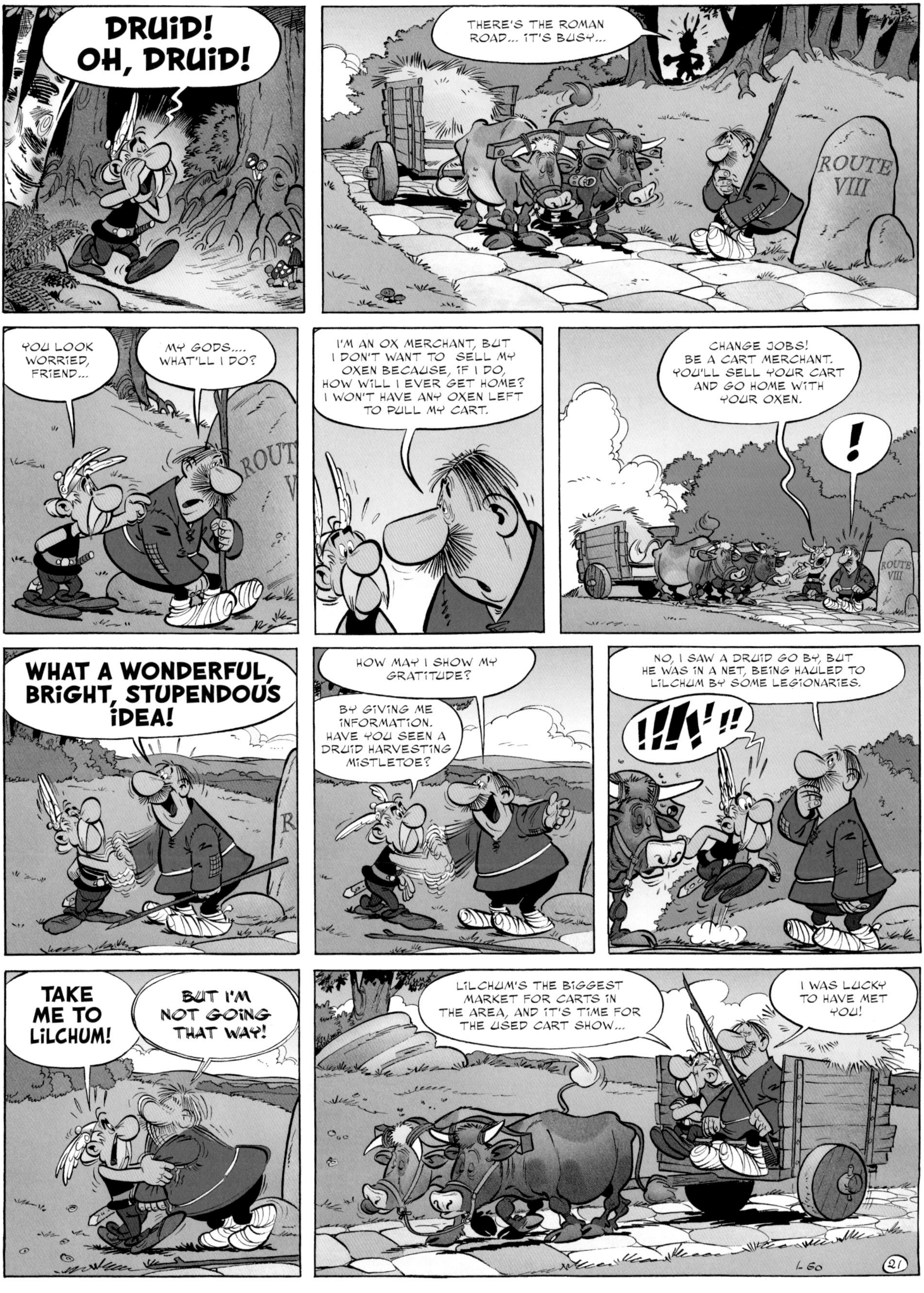
DRUID! OH, DRUID!
THERE'S THE ROMAN ROAD... IT'S BUSY...
ROUTE VIII
YOU LOOK WORRIED, FRIEND...
MY GODS.... WHAT'LL I DO?
I'M AN OX MERCHANT, BUT I DON'T WANT TO SELL MY OXEN BECAUSE, IF I DO, HOW WILL I EVER GET HOME? I WON'T HAVE ANY OXEN LEFT TO PULL MY CART.
CHANGE JOBS! BE A CART MERCHANT. YOU'LL SELL YOUR CART AND GO HOME WITH YOUR OXEN.
!
WHAT A WONDERFUL, BRIGHT, STUPENDOUS IDEA!
HOW MAY I SHOW MY GRATITUDE?
BY GIVING ME INFORMATION. HAVE YOU SEEN A DRUID HARVESTING MISTLETOE?
NO, I SAW A DRUID GO BY, BUT HE WAS IN A NET, BEING HAULED TO LILCHUM BY SOME LEGIONARIES.
TAKE ME TO LILCHUM!
BUT I'M NOT GOING THAT WAY!
LILCHUM'S THE BIGGEST MARKET FOR CARTS IN THE AREA, AND IT'S TIME FOR THE USED CART SHOW...
I WAS LUCKY TO HAVE MET YOU!
21

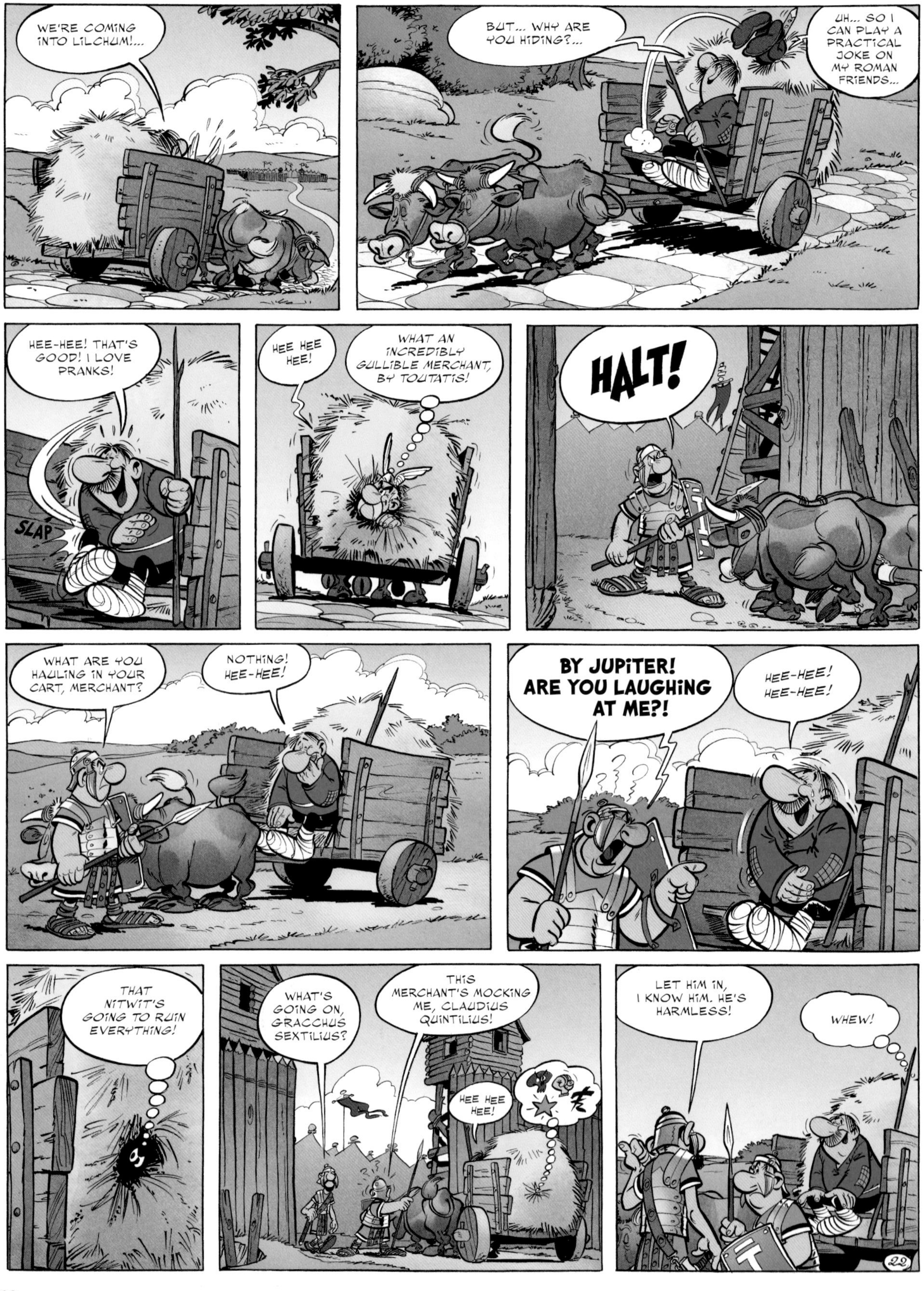

WE'RE COMING INTO LILCHUM!...
BUT... WHY ARE YOU HIDING?...
UH... SO I CAN PLAY A PRACTICAL JOKE ON MY ROMAN FRIENDS...
HEE-HEE! THAT'S GOOD! I LOVE PRANKS!
SLAP
HEE HEE HEE!
WHAT AN INCREDIBLY GULLIBLE MERCHANT, BY TOUTATIS!
HALT!
WHAT ARE YOU HAULING IN YOUR CART, MERCHANT?
NOTHING! HEE-HEE!
BY JUPITER! ARE YOU LAUGHING AT ME?!
HEE-HEE! HEE-HEE!
THAT NITWIT'S GOING TO RUIN EVERYTHING!
WHAT'S GOING ON, GRACCHUS SEXTILIUS?
THIS MERCHANT'S MOCKING ME, CLAUDIUS QUINTILIUS!
HEE HEE HEE!
LET HIM IN, I KNOW HIM. HE'S HARMLESS!
WHEW!
22

WE'RE IN THE ENCAMPMENT! YOU GOING TO PLAY YOUR PRANK NOW?...

NO, NIGHT'S FALLING. I'LL WAIT TILL MORNING, IT'LL BE FUNNIER!

OH? OKAY...

GOODNIGHT!...

SOON AFTER...

LET'S TRY TO FIND WHERE THE DRUID'S LOCKED UP...

ZZZZZ

LET'S LOOK OVER HERE...

LIE DOWN AND EAT, O MARCUS DONTMESSWITHUS, MY TRUSTY NUMBER TWO. WE HAVE TO TALK.

THANKS, O CRISMUS BONUS!

WE MUST GET THAT FORMULA FOR THE DRUID'S POTION. WE'LL BE INVINCIBLE WITH IT. WE'LL GO TO ROME AND TAKE POWER FROM CAESAR.

JULIUS CAESAR?!

CERTAINLY, JULIUS! AND TOGETHER, WE'LL FORM A TRIUMVIRATE!

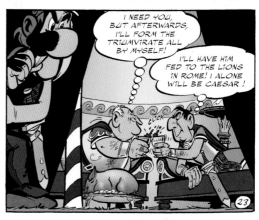

I NEED YOU, BUT AFTERWARDS, I'LL FORM THE TRIUMVIRATE ALL BY MYSELF!

I'LL HAVE HIM FED TO THE LIONS IN ROME! I ALONE WILL BE CAESAR!

23

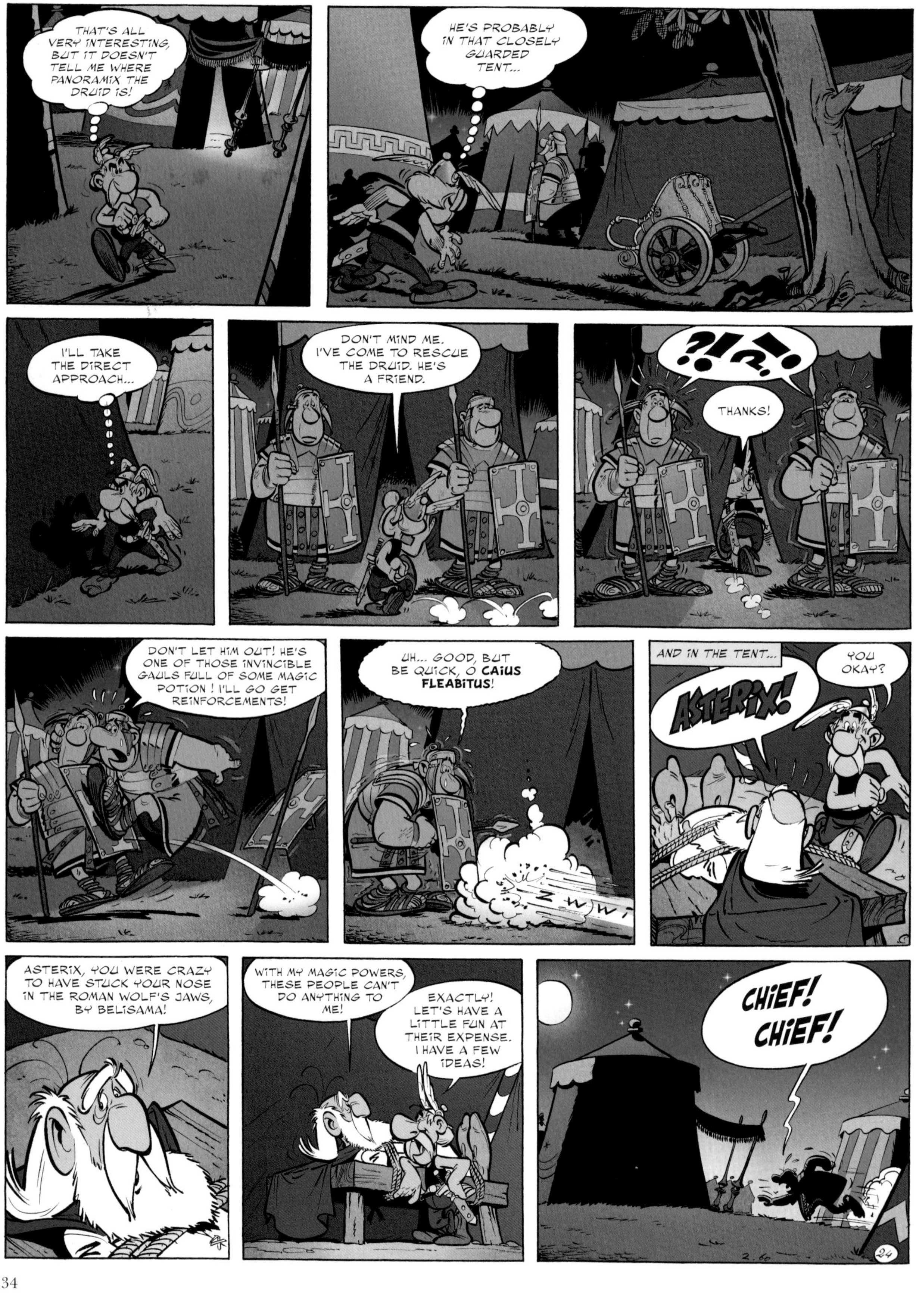

THAT'S ALL VERY INTERESTING, BUT IT DOESN'T TELL ME WHERE PANORAMIX THE DRUID IS!
HE'S PROBABLY IN THAT CLOSELY GUARDED TENT...
I'LL TAKE THE DIRECT APPROACH...
DON'T MIND ME. I'VE COME TO RESCUE THE DRUID. HE'S A FRIEND.
?!?!
THANKS!
DON'T LET HIM OUT! HE'S ONE OF THOSE INVINCIBLE GAULS FULL OF SOME MAGIC POTION ! I'LL GO GET REINFORCEMENTS!
UH... GOOD, BUT BE QUICK, O CAIUS FLEABITUS!
ZWWI
AND IN THE TENT...
ASTERIX!
YOU OKAY?
ASTERIX, YOU WERE CRAZY TO HAVE STUCK YOUR NOSE IN THE ROMAN WOLF'S JAWS, BY BELISAMA!
WITH MY MAGIC POWERS, THESE PEOPLE CAN'T DO ANYTHING TO ME!
EXACTLY! LET'S HAVE A LITTLE FUN AT THEIR EXPENSE. I HAVE A FEW IDEAS!
CHIEF! CHIEF!
24

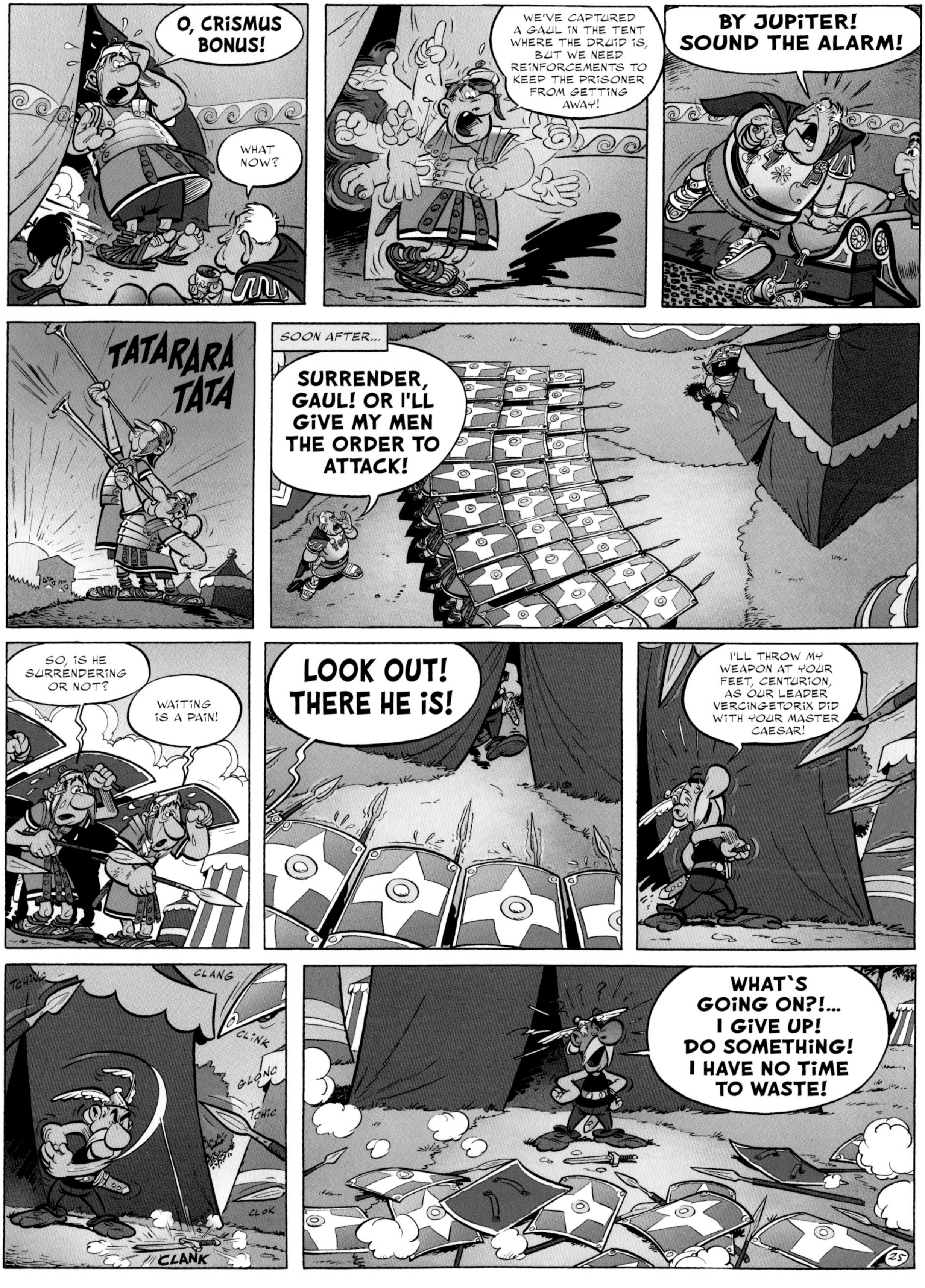
O, CRISMUS BONUS!
WHAT NOW?
WE'VE CAPTURED A GAUL IN THE TENT WHERE THE DRUID IS, BUT WE NEED REINFORCEMENTS TO KEEP THE PRISONER FROM GETTING AWAY!
BY JUPITER! SOUND THE ALARM!
TATARARA TATA
SOON AFTER...
SURRENDER, GAUL! OR I'LL GIVE MY MEN THE ORDER TO ATTACK!
SO, IS HE SURRENDERING OR NOT?
WAITING IS A PAIN!
LOOK OUT! THERE HE IS!
I'LL THROW MY WEAPON AT YOUR FEET, CENTURION, AS OUR LEADER VERCINGETORIX DID WITH YOUR MASTER CAESAR!
TCHING
CLANG
CLINK
GLONC
TCHIC
CLOK
CLANK
WHAT'S GOING ON?!... I GIVE UP! DO SOMETHING! I HAVE NO TIME TO WASTE!
25

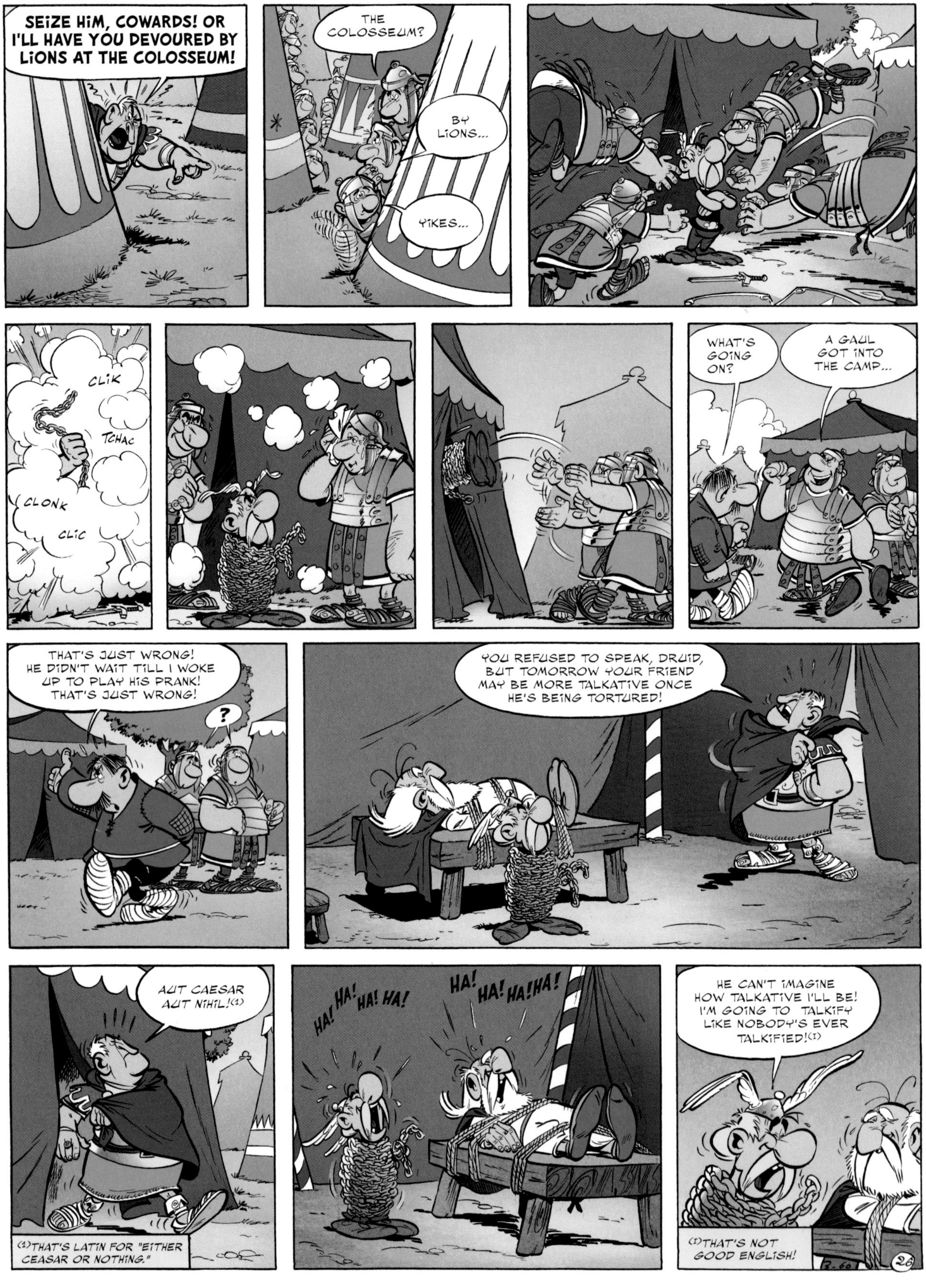
SEIZE HIM, COWARDS! OR I'LL HAVE YOU DEVOURED BY LIONS AT THE COLOSSEUM!
THE COLOSSEUM?
BY LIONS...
YIKES...
CLIK
TCHAC
CLONK
CLIC
WHAT'S GOING ON?
A GAUL GOT INTO THE CAMP...
THAT'S JUST WRONG! HE DIDN'T WAIT TILL I WOKE UP TO PLAY HIS PRANK! THAT'S JUST WRONG!
?
YOU REFUSED TO SPEAK, DRUID, BUT TOMORROW YOUR FRIEND MAY BE MORE TALKATIVE ONCE HE'S BEING TORTURED!
AUT CAESAR AUT NIHIL!(1)
(1)THAT'S LATIN FOR "EITHER CEASAR OR NOTHING."
HA! HA! HA! HA!
HA! HA! HA! HA!
HE CAN'T IMAGINE HOW TALKATIVE I'LL BE! I'M GOING TO TALKIFY LIKE NOBODY'S EVER TALKIFIED!(1)
(1)THAT'S NOT GOOD ENGLISH!
26

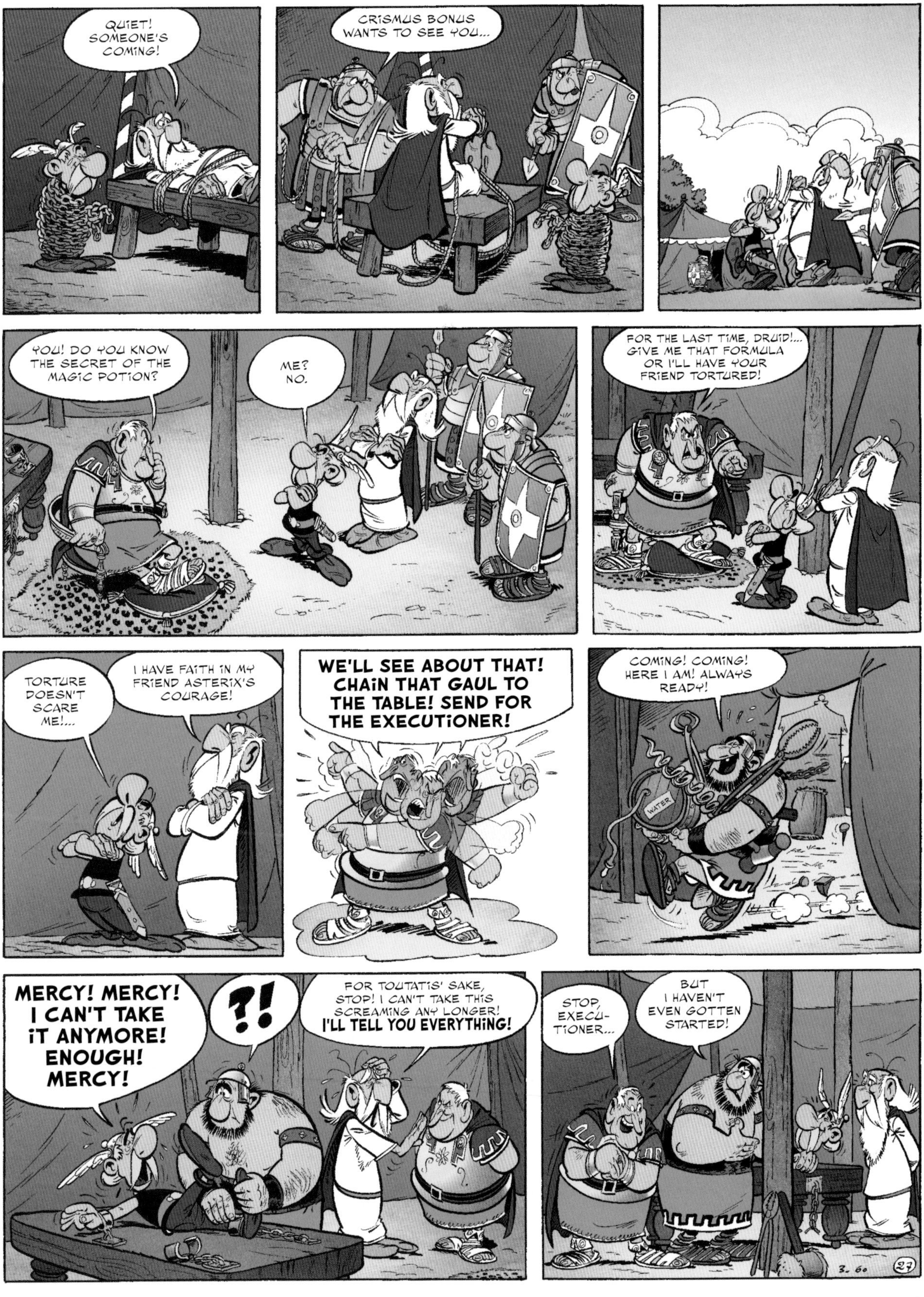

QUIET! SOMEONE'S COMING!
CRISMUS BONUS WANTS TO SEE YOU...
YOU! DO YOU KNOW THE SECRET OF THE MAGIC POTION?
ME? NO.
FOR THE LAST TIME, DRUID!... GIVE ME THAT FORMULA OR I'LL HAVE YOUR FRIEND TORTURED!
TORTURE DOESN'T SCARE ME!...
I HAVE FAITH IN MY FRIEND ASTERIX'S COURAGE!
WE'LL SEE ABOUT THAT! CHAIN THAT GAUL TO THE TABLE! SEND FOR THE EXECUTIONER!
COMING! COMING! HERE I AM! ALWAYS READY!
WATER
MERCY! MERCY! I CAN'T TAKE IT ANYMORE! ENOUGH! MERCY!
?!
FOR TOUTATIS' SAKE, STOP! I CAN'T TAKE THIS SCREAMING ANY LONGER! I'LL TELL YOU EVERYTHING!
STOP, EXECU-TIONER...
BUT I HAVEN'T EVEN GOTTEN STARTED!
3. 60
27

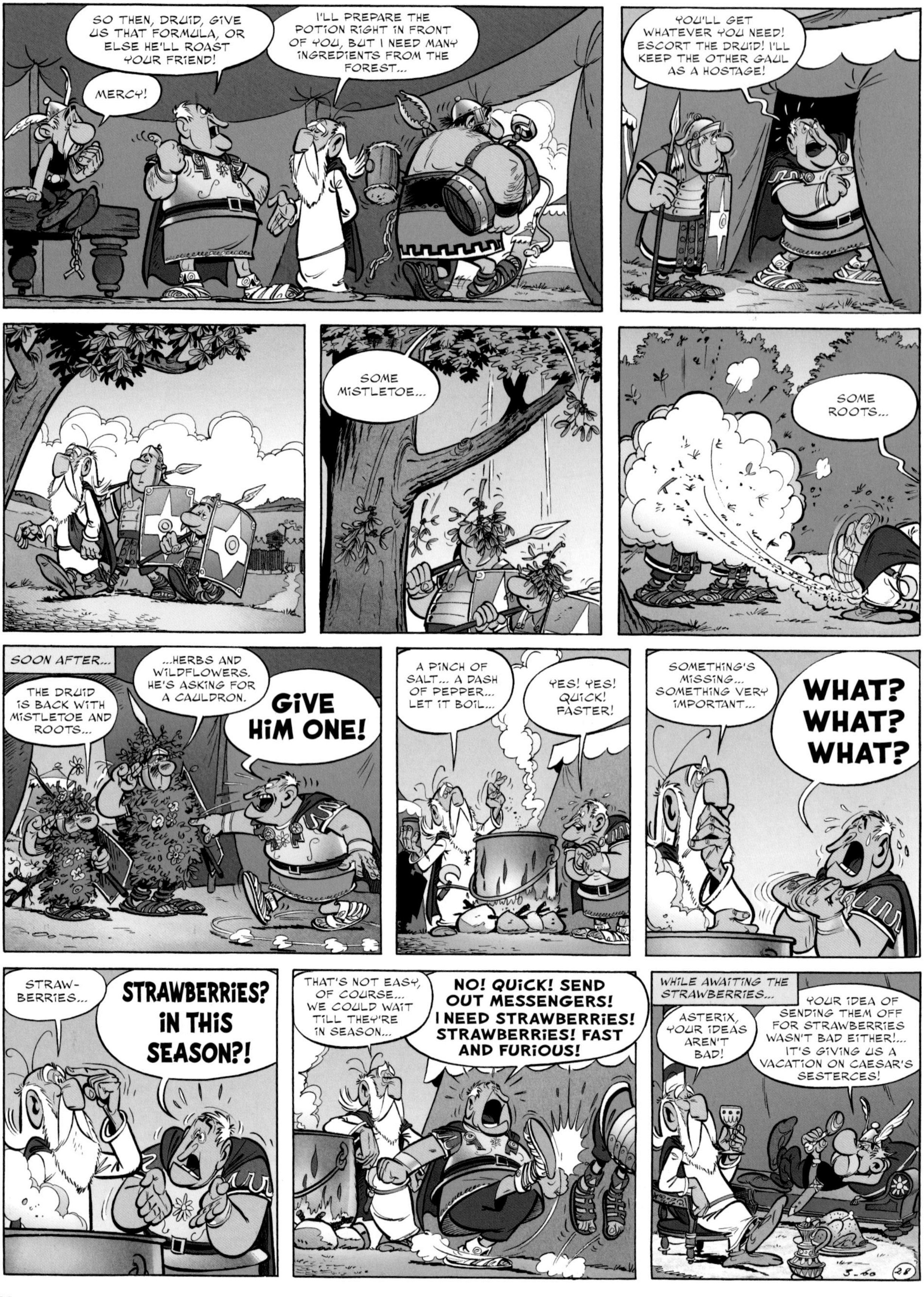
SO THEN, DRUID, GIVE US THAT FORMULA, OR ELSE HE'LL ROAST YOUR FRIEND!
MERCY!
I'LL PREPARE THE POTION RIGHT IN FRONT OF YOU, BUT I NEED MANY INGREDIENTS FROM THE FOREST...
YOU'LL GET WHATEVER YOU NEED! ESCORT THE DRUID! I'LL KEEP THE OTHER GAUL AS A HOSTAGE!
SOME MISTLETOE...
SOME ROOTS...
SOON AFTER...
THE DRUID IS BACK WITH MISTLETOE AND ROOTS...
...HERBS AND WILDFLOWERS. HE'S ASKING FOR A CAULDRON.
GIVE HIM ONE!
A PINCH OF SALT... A DASH OF PEPPER... LET IT BOIL...
YES! YES! QUICK! FASTER!
SOMETHING'S MISSING... SOMETHING VERY IMPORTANT...
WHAT? WHAT? WHAT?
STRAW-BERRIES...
STRAWBERRIES? IN THIS SEASON?!
THAT'S NOT EASY, OF COURSE... WE COULD WAIT TILL THEY'RE IN SEASON...
NO! QUICK! SEND OUT MESSENGERS! I NEED STRAWBERRIES! STRAWBERRIES! FAST AND FURIOUS!
WHILE AWAITING THE STRAWBERRIES...
ASTERIX, YOUR IDEAS AREN'T BAD!
YOUR IDEA OF SENDING THEM OFF FOR STRAWBERRIES WASN'T BAD EITHER!... IT'S GIVING US A VACATION ON CAESAR'S SESTERCES!
5-60
28

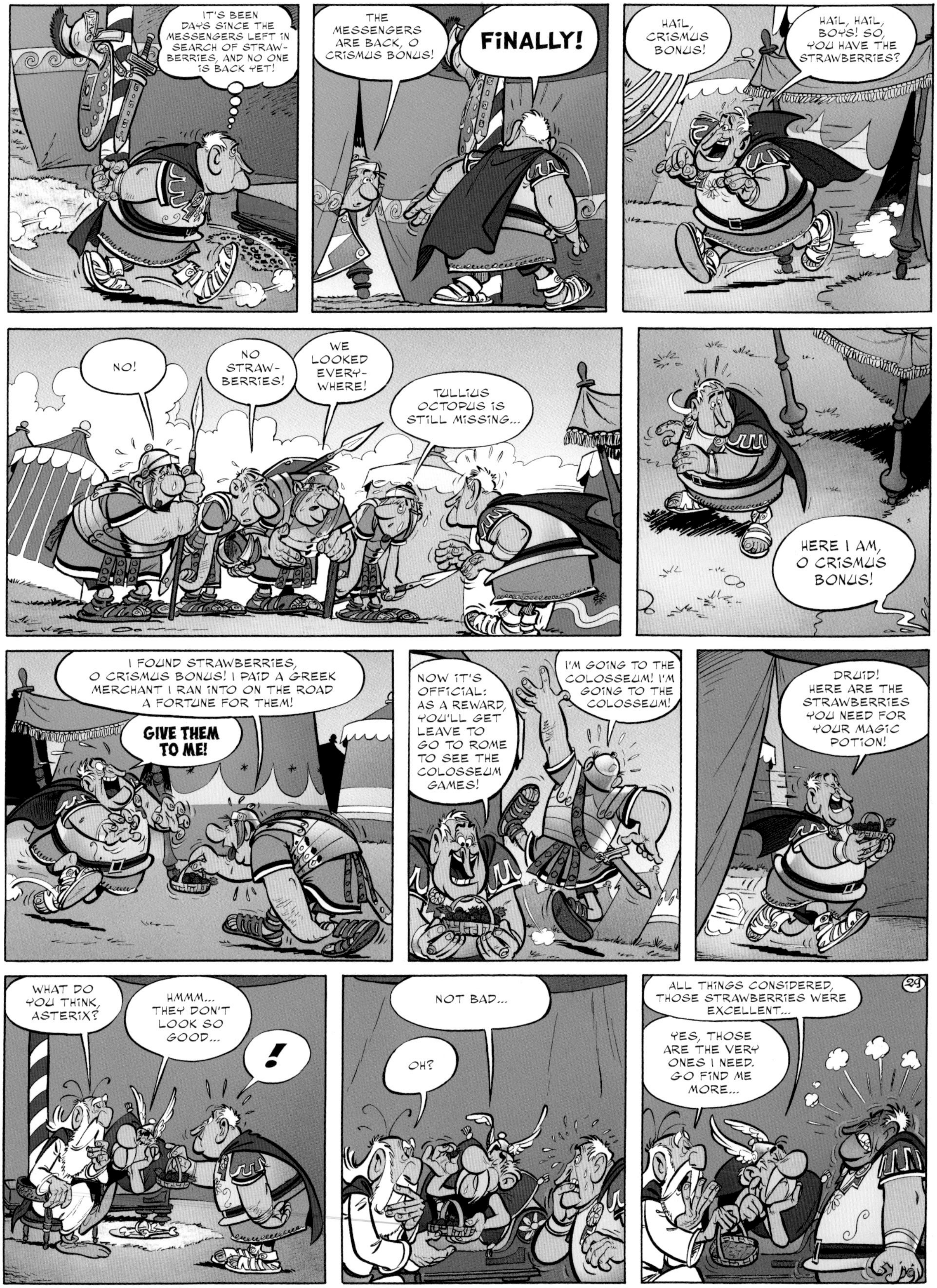
IT'S BEEN DAYS SINCE THE MESSENGERS LEFT IN SEARCH OF STRAWBERRIES, AND NO ONE IS BACK YET!
THE MESSENGERS ARE BACK, O CRISMUS BONUS!
FiNALLY!
HAIL, CRISMUS BONUS!
HAIL, HAIL, BOYS! SO, YOU HAVE THE STRAWBERRIES?
NO!
NO STRAWBERRIES!
WE LOOKED EVERYWHERE!
TULLIUS OCTOPUS IS STILL MISSING...
HERE I AM, O CRISMUS BONUS!
I FOUND STRAWBERRIES, O CRISMUS BONUS! I PAID A GREEK MERCHANT I RAN INTO ON THE ROAD A FORTUNE FOR THEM!
GIVE THEM TO ME!
NOW IT'S OFFICIAL: AS A REWARD, YOU'LL GET LEAVE TO GO TO ROME TO SEE THE COLOSSEUM GAMES!
I'M GOING TO THE COLOSSEUM! I'M GOING TO THE COLOSSEUM!
DRUID! HERE ARE THE STRAWBERRIES YOU NEED FOR YOUR MAGIC POTION!
WHAT DO YOU THINK, ASTERIX?
HMMM... THEY DON'T LOOK SO GOOD...
!
NOT BAD...
OH?
ALL THINGS CONSIDERED, THOSE STRAWBERRIES WERE EXCELLENT...
YES, THOSE ARE THE VERY ONES I NEED. GO FIND ME MORE...
29

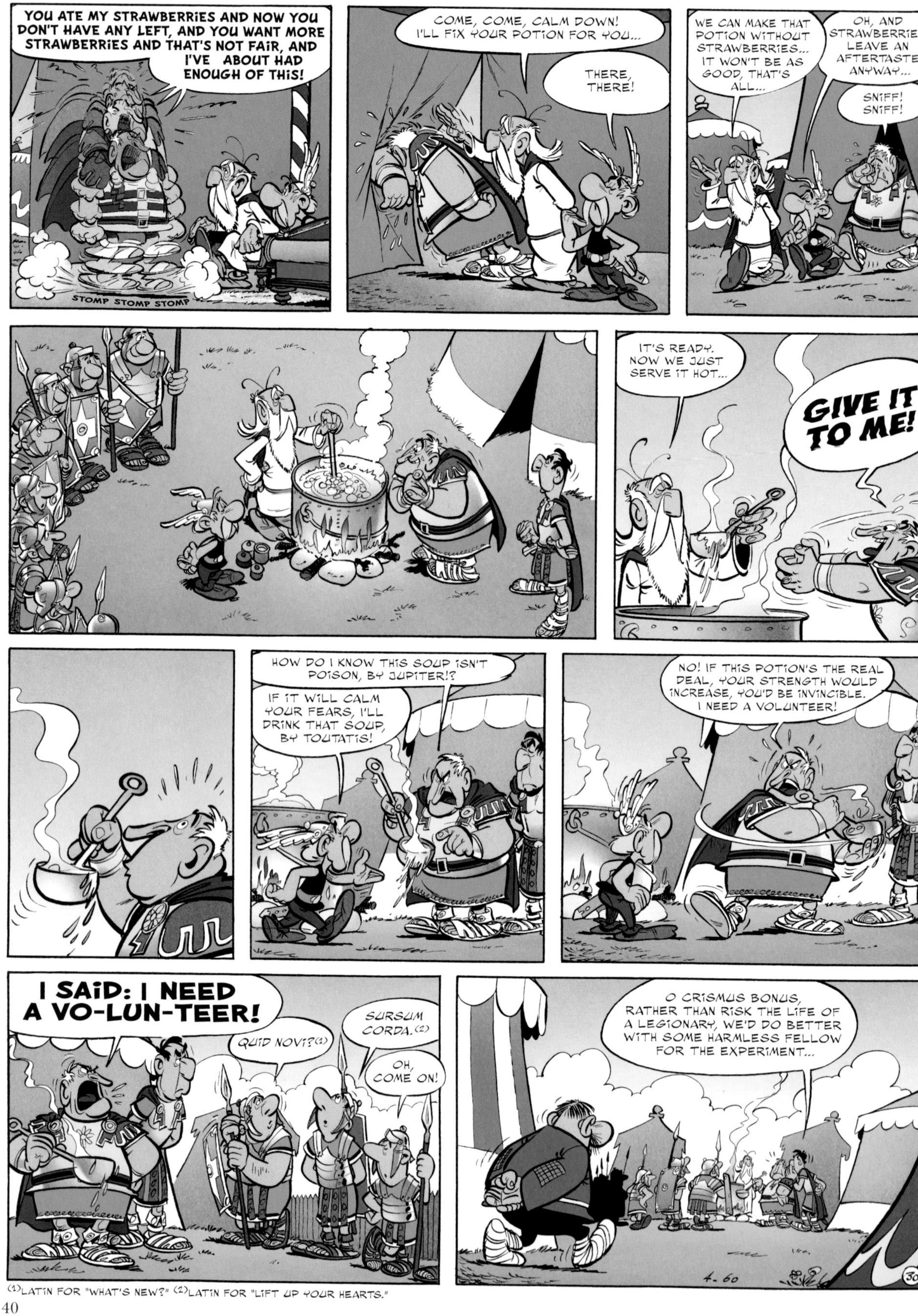
YOU ATE MY STRAWBERRIES AND NOW YOU DON'T HAVE ANY LEFT, AND YOU WANT MORE STRAWBERRIES AND THAT'S NOT FAIR, AND I'VE ABOUT HAD ENOUGH OF THIS!
STOMP STOMP STOMP
COME, COME, CALM DOWN! I'LL FIX YOUR POTION FOR YOU...
THERE, THERE!
WE CAN MAKE THAT POTION WITHOUT STRAWBERRIES... IT WON'T BE AS GOOD, THAT'S ALL...
OH, AND STRAWBERRIES LEAVE AN AFTERTASTE ANYWAY...
SNIFF! SNIFF!
IT'S READY. NOW WE JUST SERVE IT HOT...
GIVE IT TO ME!
HOW DO I KNOW THIS SOUP ISN'T POISON, BY JUPITER!?
IF IT WILL CALM YOUR FEARS, I'LL DRINK THAT SOUP, BY TOUTATIS!
NO! IF THIS POTION'S THE REAL DEAL, YOUR STRENGTH WOULD INCREASE, YOU'D BE INVINCIBLE. I NEED A VOLUNTEER!
I SAID: I NEED A VO-LUN-TEER!
QUID NOVI?(1)
SURSUM CORDA.(2)
OH, COME ON!
O CRISMUS BONUS, RATHER THAN RISK THE LIFE OF A LEGIONARY, WE'D DO BETTER WITH SOME HARMLESS FELLOW FOR THE EXPERIMENT...
30

(1)LATIN FOR "WHAT'S NEW?" (2)LATIN FOR "LIFT UP YOUR HEARTS."

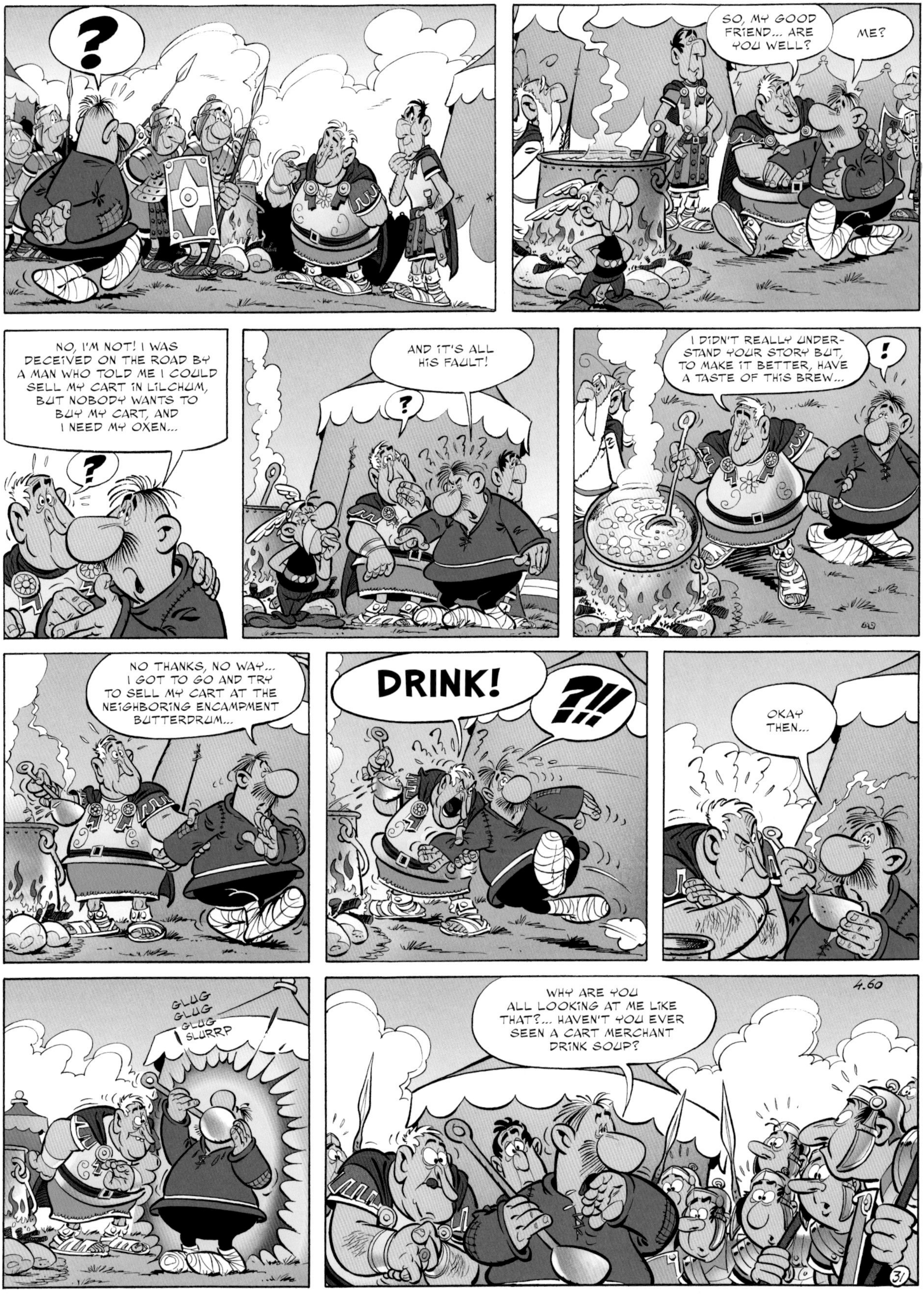
?
SO, MY GOOD FRIEND... ARE YOU WELL?
ME?
NO, I'M NOT! I WAS DECEIVED ON THE ROAD BY A MAN WHO TOLD ME I COULD SELL MY CART IN LILCHUM, BUT NOBODY WANTS TO BUY MY CART, AND I NEED MY OXEN...
?
AND IT'S ALL HIS FAULT!
?
I DIDN'T REALLY UNDERSTAND YOUR STORY BUT, TO MAKE IT BETTER, HAVE A TASTE OF THIS BREW...
!
NO THANKS, NO WAY... I GOT TO GO AND TRY TO SELL MY CART AT THE NEIGHBORING ENCAMPMENT BUTTERDRUM...
DRINK!
?!!
OKAY THEN...
GLUG GLUG GLUG SLURRP
WHY ARE YOU ALL LOOKING AT ME LIKE THAT?... HAVEN'T YOU EVER SEEN A CART MERCHANT DRINK SOUP?
31

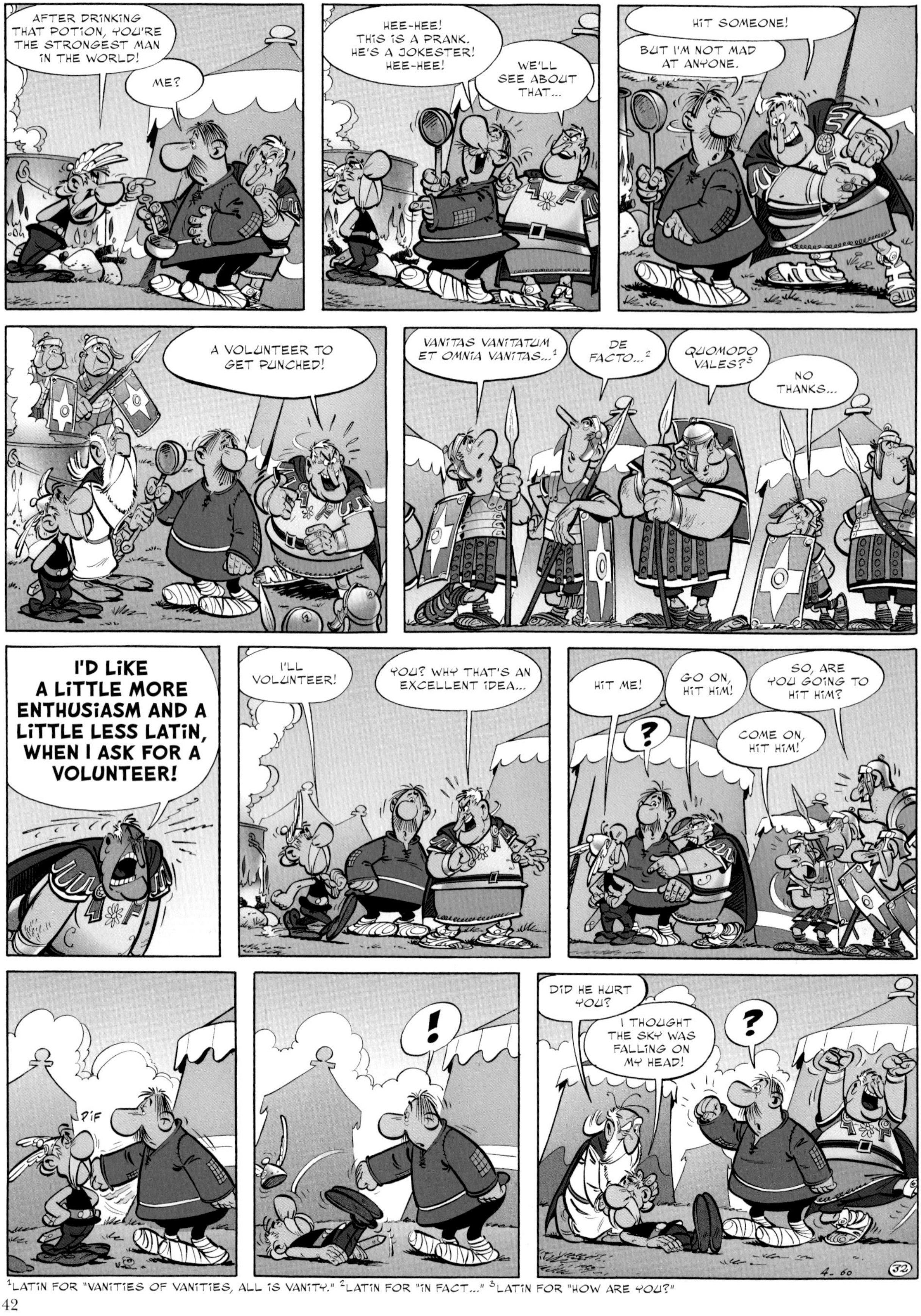
AFTER DRINKING THAT POTION, YOU'RE THE STRONGEST MAN IN THE WORLD!
ME?
HEE-HEE! THIS IS A PRANK. HE'S A JOKESTER! HEE-HEE!
WE'LL SEE ABOUT THAT...
HIT SOMEONE!
BUT I'M NOT MAD AT ANYONE.
A VOLUNTEER TO GET PUNCHED!
VANITAS VANITATUM ET OMNIA VANITAS...1
DE FACTO...2
QUOMODO VALES?3
NO THANKS...
I'D LIKE A LITTLE MORE ENTHUSIASM AND A LITTLE LESS LATIN, WHEN I ASK FOR A VOLUNTEER!
I'LL VOLUNTEER!
YOU? WHY THAT'S AN EXCELLENT IDEA...
HIT ME!
?
GO ON, HIT HIM!
SO, ARE YOU GOING TO HIT HIM?
COME ON, HIT HIM!
DIF
!
DID HE HURT YOU?
I THOUGHT THE SKY WAS FALLING ON MY HEAD!
?
4-60
32

[1] LATIN FOR "VANITIES OF VANITIES, ALL IS VANITY." [2] LATIN FOR "IN FACT..." [3] LATIN FOR "HOW ARE YOU?"

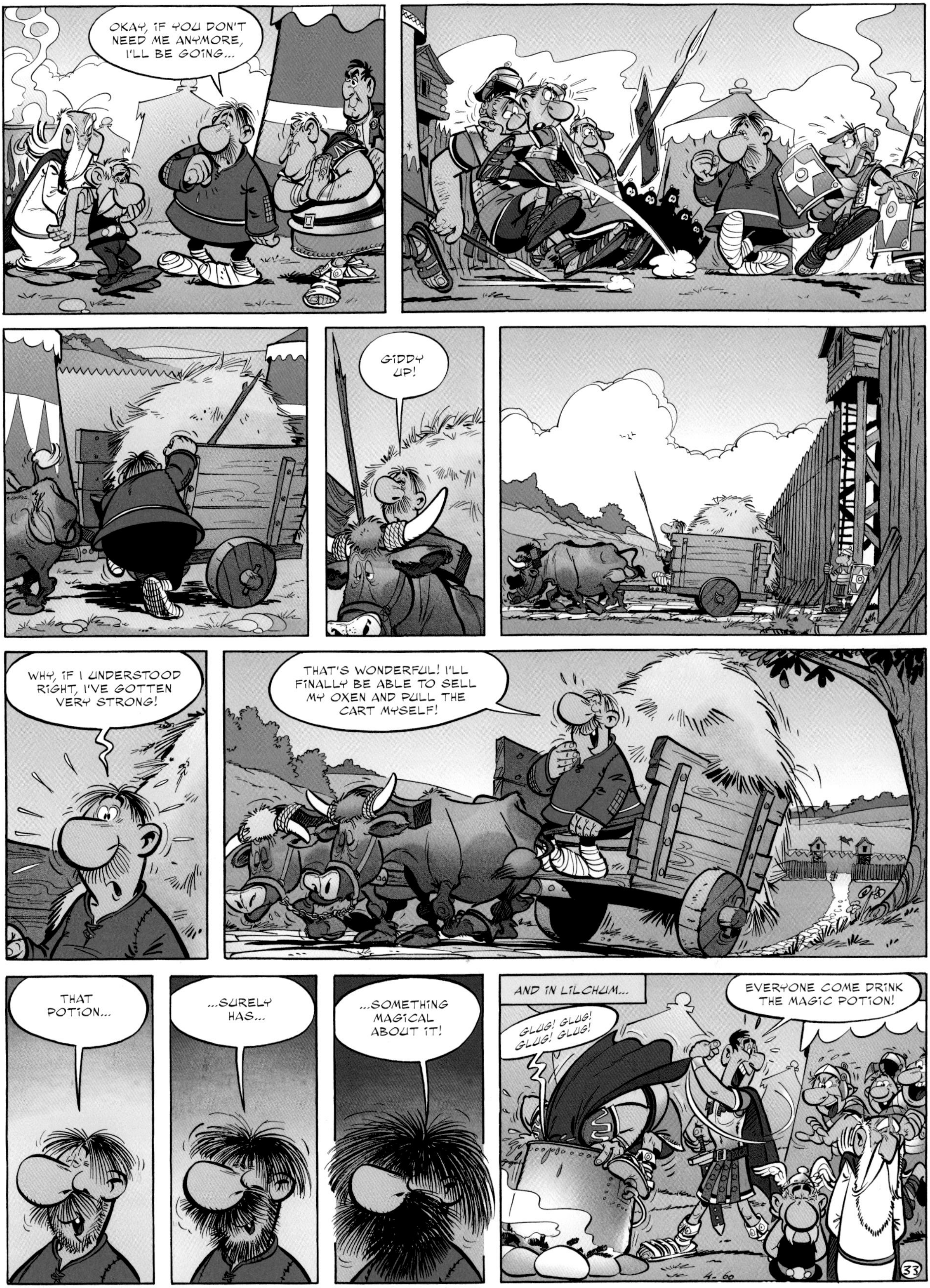
OKAY, IF YOU DON'T NEED ME ANYMORE, I'LL BE GOING...
GIDDY UP!
WHY, IF I UNDERSTOOD RIGHT, I'VE GOTTEN VERY STRONG!
THAT'S WONDERFUL! I'LL FINALLY BE ABLE TO SELL MY OXEN AND PULL THE CART MYSELF!
THAT POTION...
...SURELY HAS...
...SOMETHING MAGICAL ABOUT IT!
AND IN LILCHUM...
GLUG! GLUG! GLUG! GLUG!
EVERYONE COME DRINK THE MAGIC POTION!
33

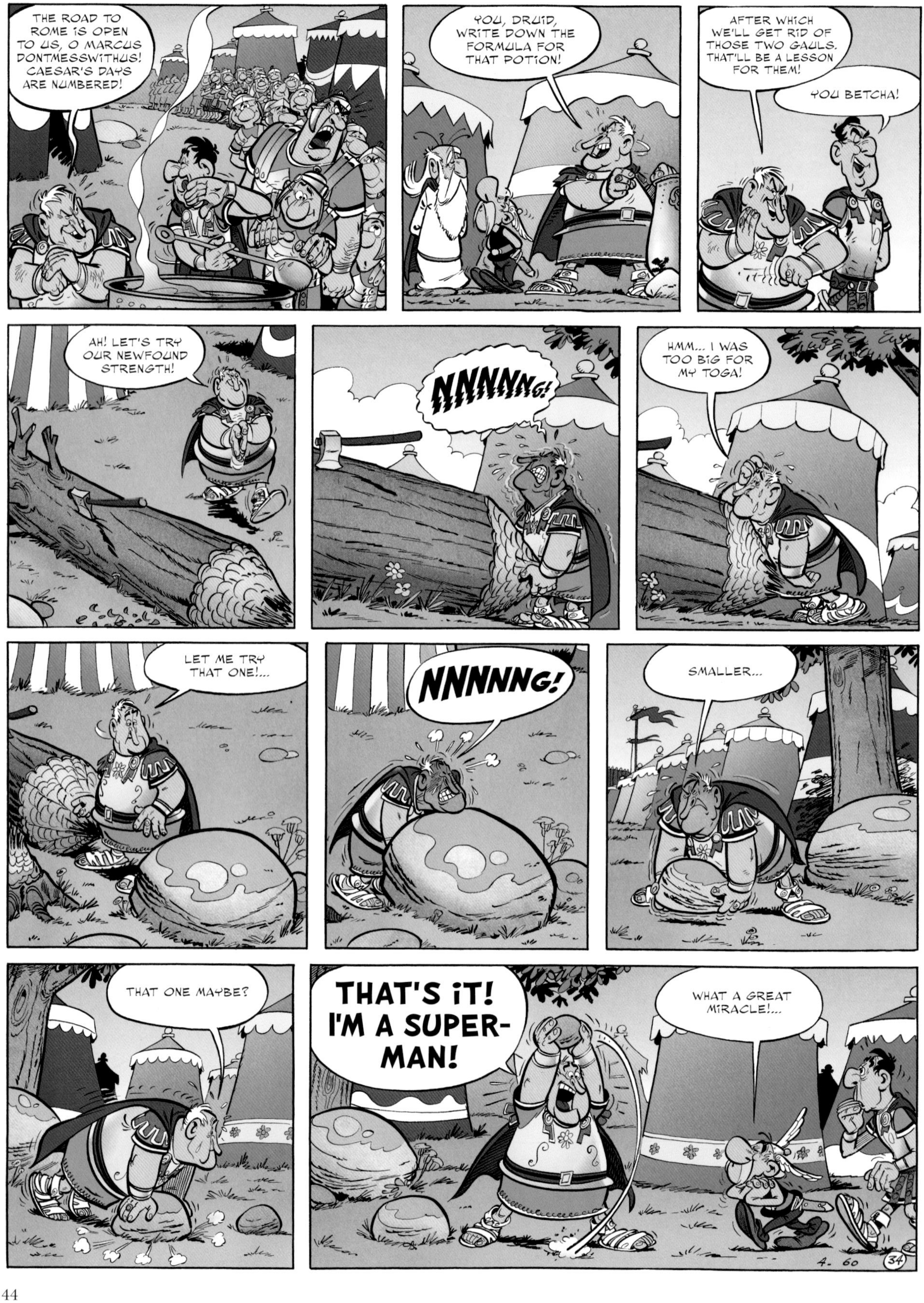
THE ROAD TO ROME IS OPEN TO US, O MARCUS DONTMESSWITHUS! CAESAR'S DAYS ARE NUMBERED!
YOU, DRUID, WRITE DOWN THE FORMULA FOR THAT POTION!
AFTER WHICH WE'LL GET RID OF THOSE TWO GAULS. THAT'LL BE A LESSON FOR THEM!
YOU BETCHA!
AH! LET'S TRY OUR NEWFOUND STRENGTH!
NNNNNG!
HMM... I WAS TOO BIG FOR MY TOGA!
LET ME TRY THAT ONE!...
NNNNG!
SMALLER...
THAT ONE MAYBE?
THAT'S IT! I'M A SUPER-MAN!
WHAT A GREAT MIRACLE!...
4. 60
34

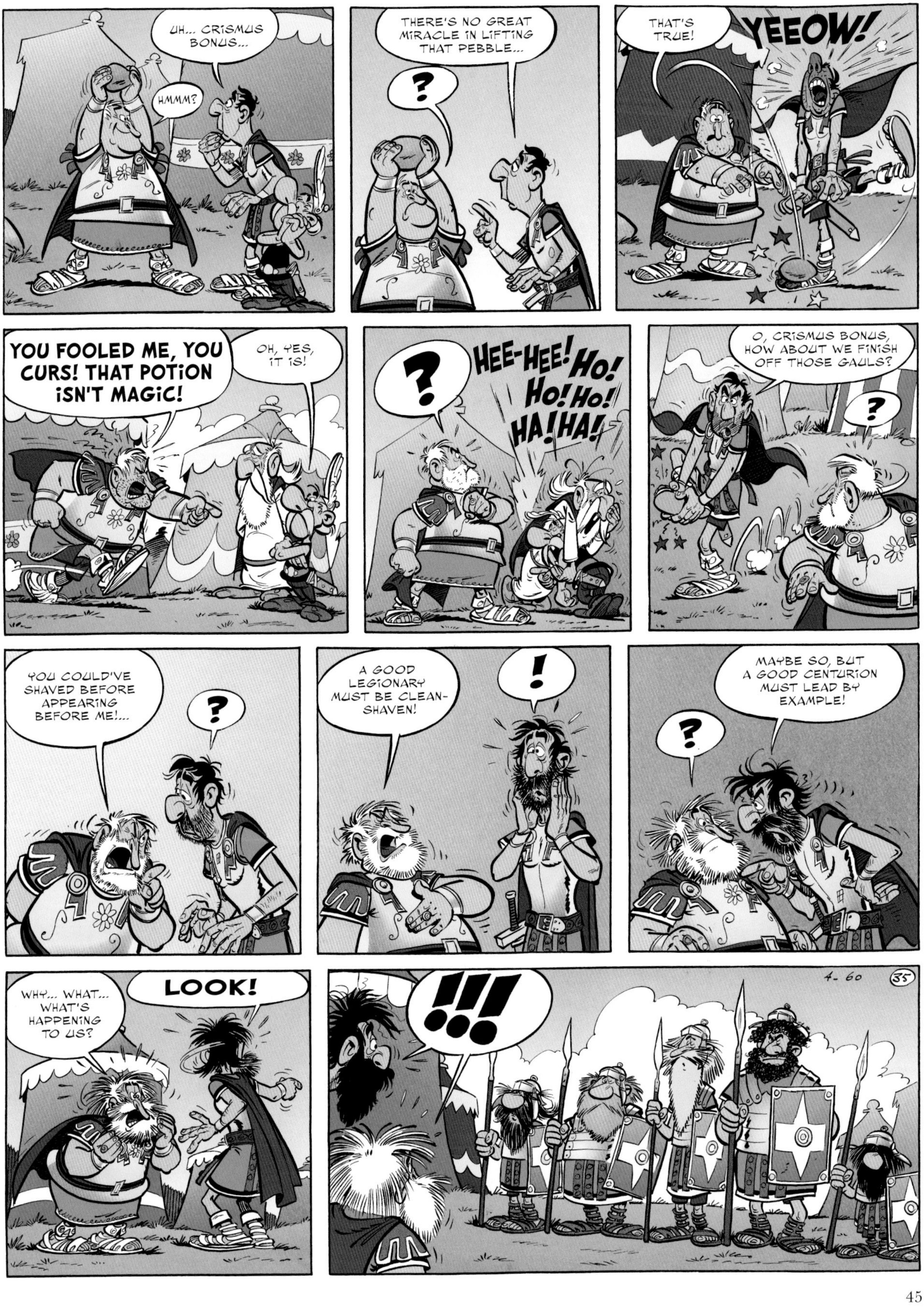

UH... CRISMUS BONUS...
HMMM?
THERE'S NO GREAT MIRACLE IN LIFTING THAT PEBBLE...
?
THAT'S TRUE!
YEEOW!
YOU FOOLED ME, YOU CURS! THAT POTION ISN'T MAGIC!
OH, YES, IT IS!
?
HEE-HEE! HO! HO! HO! HA! HA!
O, CRISMUS BONUS, HOW ABOUT WE FINISH OFF THOSE GAULS?
?
YOU COULD'VE SHAVED BEFORE APPEARING BEFORE ME!...
?
A GOOD LEGIONARY MUST BE CLEAN-SHAVEN!
!
?
MAYBE SO, BUT A GOOD CENTURION MUST LEAD BY EXAMPLE!
WHY... WHAT... WHAT'S HAPPENING TO US?
LOOK!
!!!
4-60
35

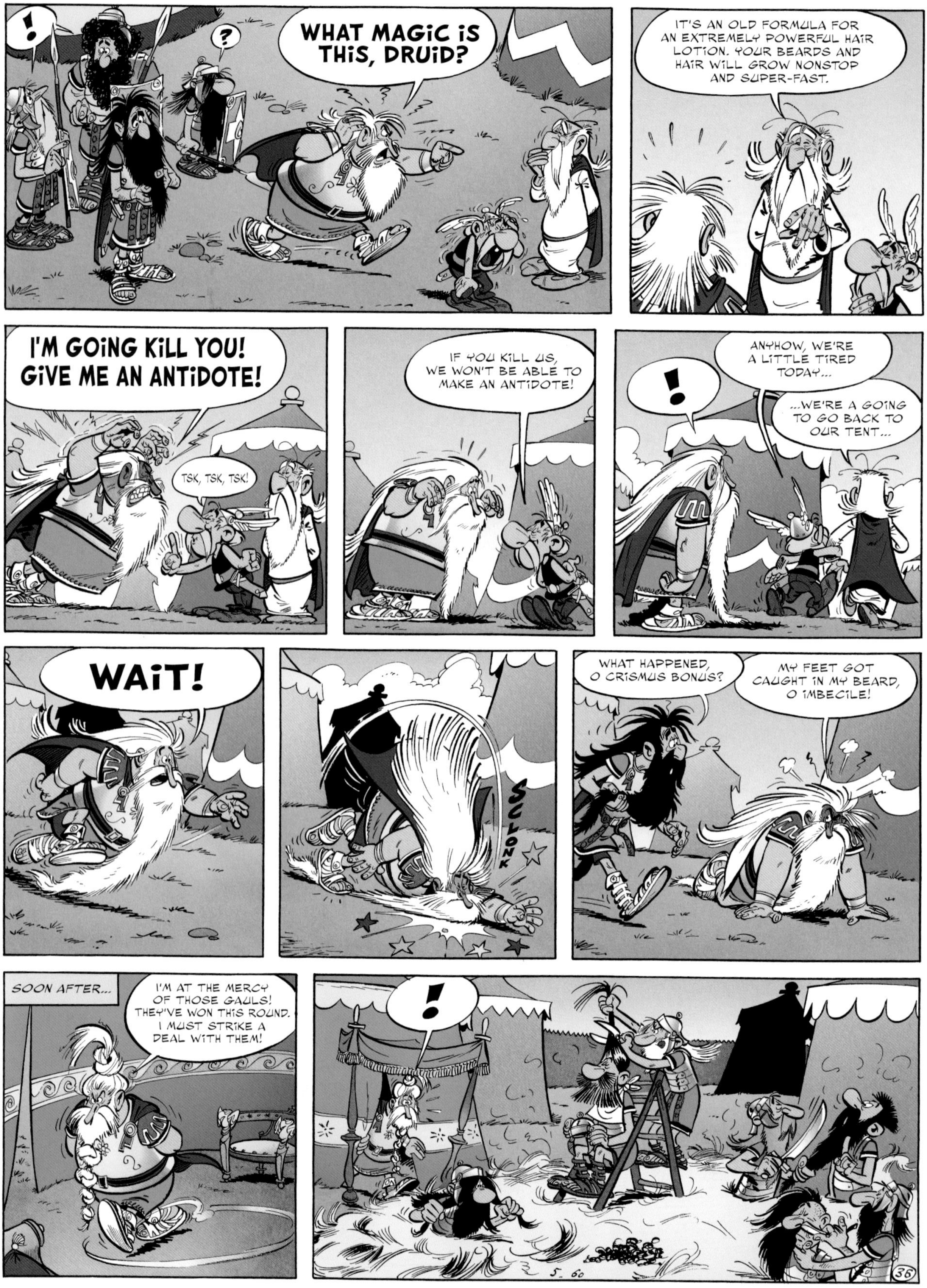
!
?
WHAT MAGIC IS THIS, DRUID?
IT'S AN OLD FORMULA FOR AN EXTREMELY POWERFUL HAIR LOTION. YOUR BEARDS AND HAIR WILL GROW NONSTOP AND SUPER-FAST.
I'M GOING KILL YOU! GIVE ME AN ANTIDOTE!
TSK, TSK, TSK!
IF YOU KILL US, WE WON'T BE ABLE TO MAKE AN ANTIDOTE!
!
ANYHOW, WE'RE A LITTLE TIRED TODAY...
...WE'RE A GOING TO GO BACK TO OUR TENT...
WAIT!
SCLONK
WHAT HAPPENED, O CRISMUS BONUS?
MY FEET GOT CAUGHT IN MY BEARD, O IMBECILE!
SOON AFTER...
I'M AT THE MERCY OF THOSE GAULS! THEY'VE WON THIS ROUND. I MUST STRIKE A DEAL WITH THEM!
!
5. 60
36

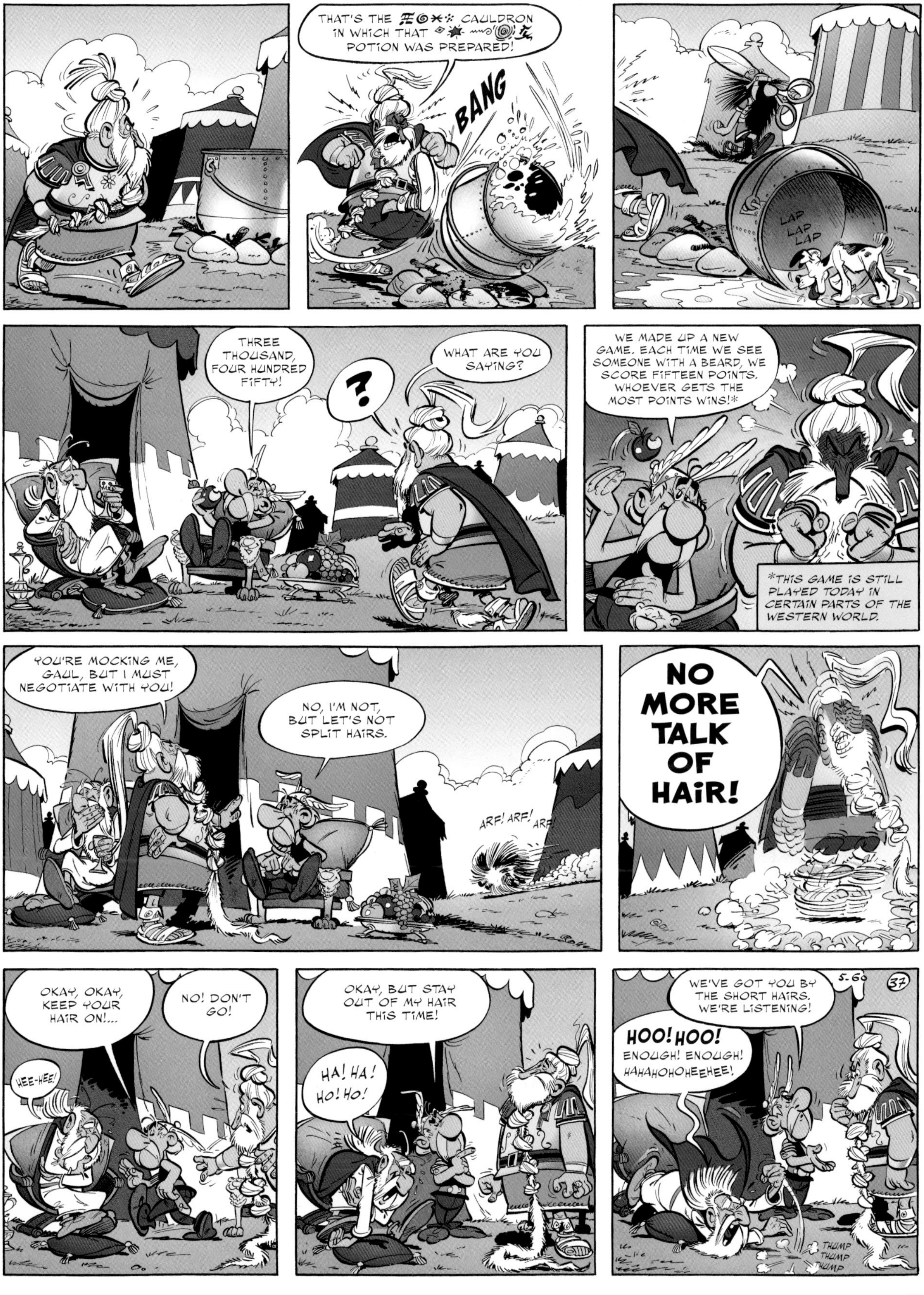

THAT'S THE CAULDRON IN WHICH THAT POTION WAS PREPARED!
BANG
LAP LAP LAP
THREE THOUSAND, FOUR HUNDRED FIFTY!
?
WHAT ARE YOU SAYING?
WE MADE UP A NEW GAME. EACH TIME WE SEE SOMEONE WITH A BEARD, WE SCORE FIFTEEN POINTS. WHOEVER GETS THE MOST POINTS WINS!*
*THIS GAME IS STILL PLAYED TODAY IN CERTAIN PARTS OF THE WESTERN WORLD.
YOU'RE MOCKING ME, GAUL, BUT I MUST NEGOTIATE WITH YOU!
NO, I'M NOT, BUT LET'S NOT SPLIT HAIRS.
ARF! ARF! ARF!
NO MORE TALK OF HAIR!
OKAY, OKAY, KEEP YOUR HAIR ON!...
HEE-HEE!
NO! DON'T GO!
OKAY, BUT STAY OUT OF MY HAIR THIS TIME!
HA! HA! HO! HO!
5.60
37
WE'VE GOT YOU BY THE SHORT HAIRS. WE'RE LISTENING!
HOO! HOO! ENOUGH! ENOUGH! HAHAHOHOHEEHEE!
THUMP THUMP THUMP

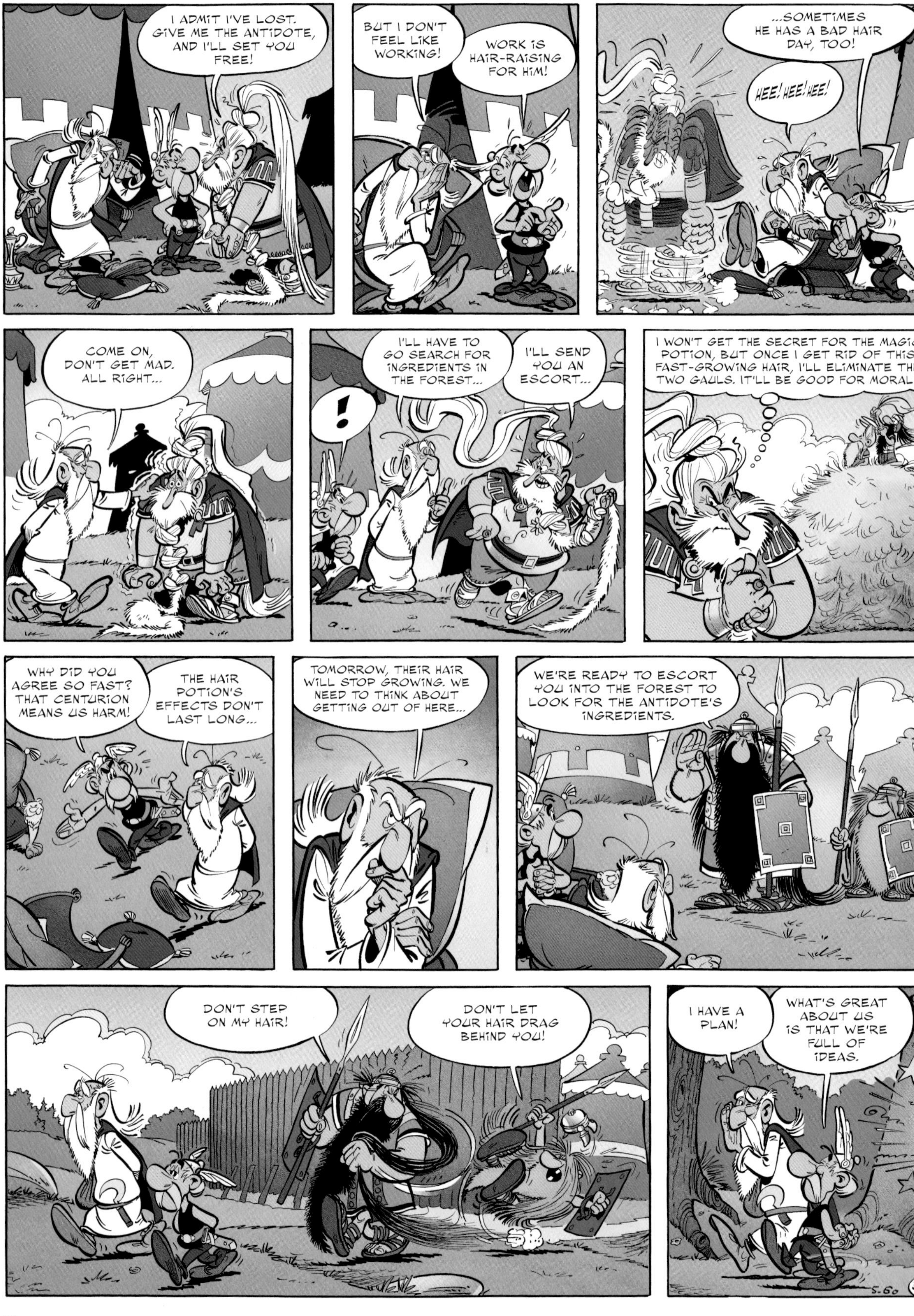
I ADMIT I'VE LOST. GIVE ME THE ANTIDOTE, AND I'LL SET YOU FREE!
BUT I DON'T FEEL LIKE WORKING!
WORK IS HAIR-RAISING FOR HIM!
...SOMETIMES HE HAS A BAD HAIR DAY, TOO!
HEE! HEE! HEE!
COME ON, DON'T GET MAD. ALL RIGHT...
I'LL HAVE TO GO SEARCH FOR INGREDIENTS IN THE FOREST...
!
I'LL SEND YOU AN ESCORT...
I WON'T GET THE SECRET FOR THE MAGIC POTION, BUT ONCE I GET RID OF THIS FAST-GROWING HAIR, I'LL ELIMINATE THE TWO GAULS. IT'LL BE GOOD FOR MORALE!
WHY DID YOU AGREE SO FAST? THAT CENTURION MEANS US HARM!
THE HAIR POTION'S EFFECTS DON'T LAST LONG...
TOMORROW, THEIR HAIR WILL STOP GROWING. WE NEED TO THINK ABOUT GETTING OUT OF HERE...
WE'RE READY TO ESCORT YOU INTO THE FOREST TO LOOK FOR THE ANTIDOTE'S INGREDIENTS.
DON'T STEP ON MY HAIR!
DON'T LET YOUR HAIR DRAG BEHIND YOU!
I HAVE A PLAN!
WHAT'S GREAT ABOUT US IS THAT WE'RE FULL OF IDEAS.
S.60
38

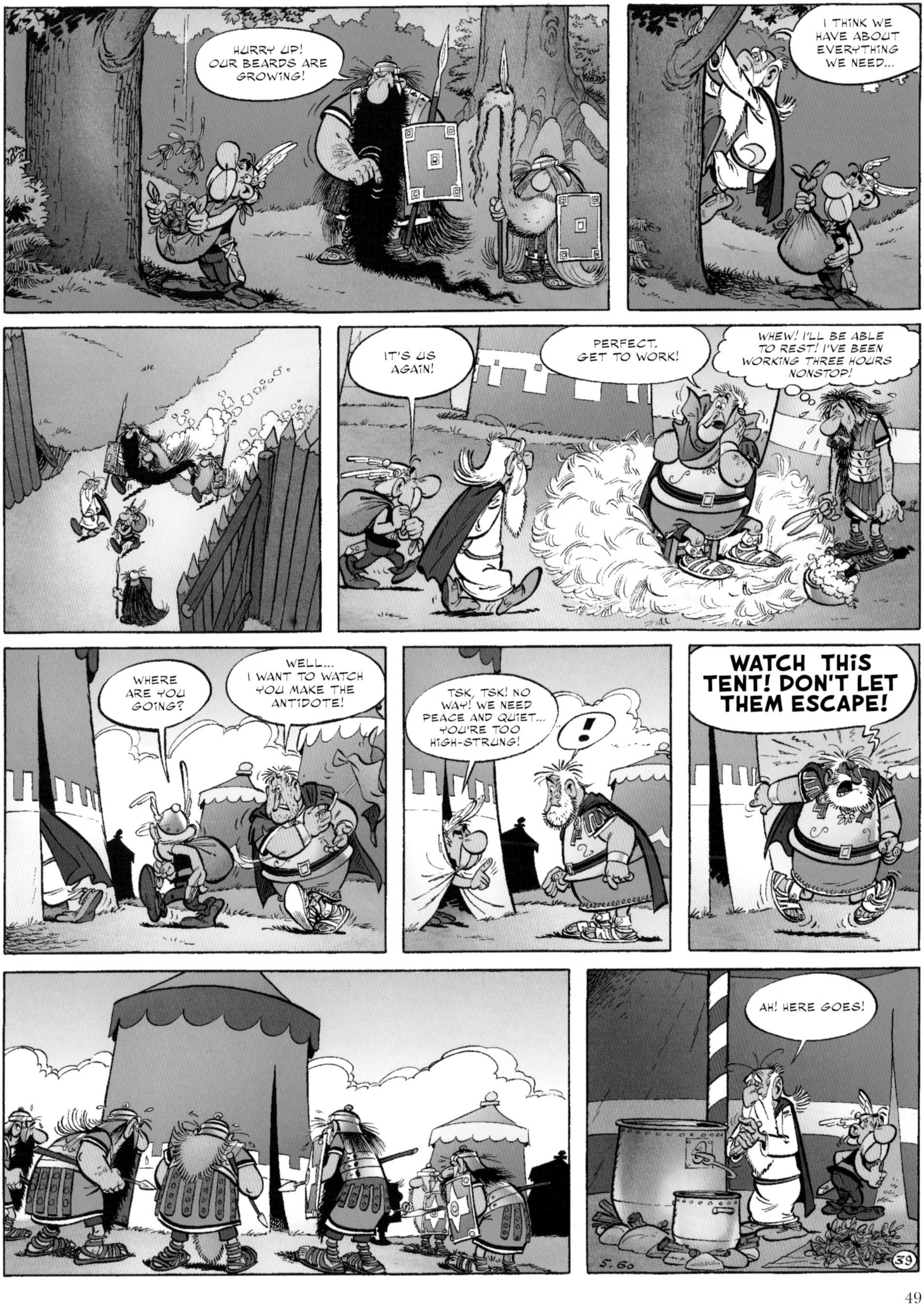
HURRY UP! OUR BEARDS ARE GROWING!
I THINK WE HAVE ABOUT EVERYTHING WE NEED...
IT'S US AGAIN!
PERFECT. GET TO WORK!
WHEW! I'LL BE ABLE TO REST! I'VE BEEN WORKING THREE HOURS NONSTOP!
WHERE ARE YOU GOING?
WELL... I WANT TO WATCH YOU MAKE THE ANTIDOTE!
TSK, TSK! NO WAY! WE NEED PEACE AND QUIET... YOU'RE TOO HIGH-STRUNG!
!
WATCH THIS TENT! DON'T LET THEM ESCAPE!
AH! HERE GOES!
5.60
39

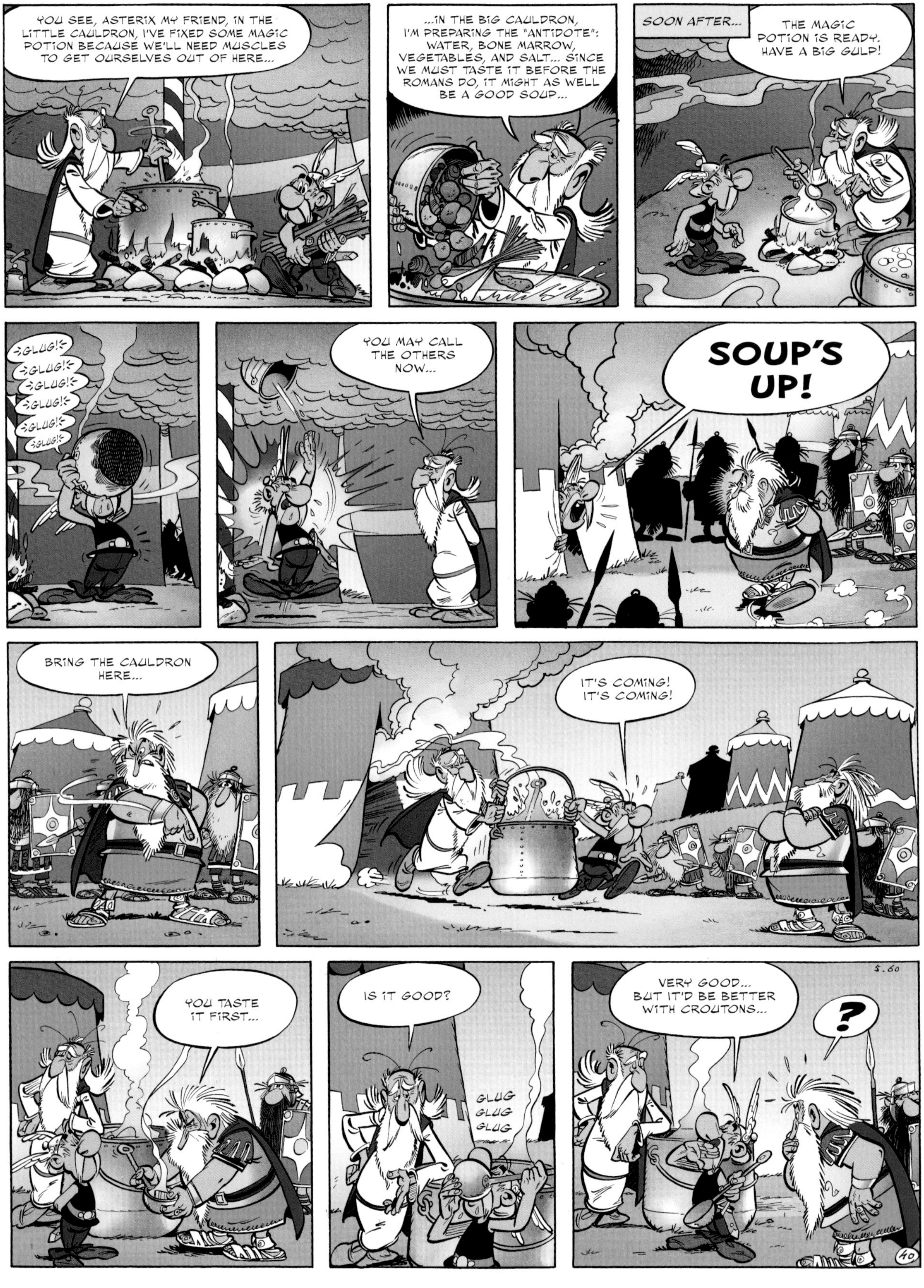
YOU SEE, ASTERIX MY FRIEND, IN THE LITTLE CAULDRON, I'VE FIXED SOME MAGIC POTION BECAUSE WE'LL NEED MUSCLES TO GET OURSELVES OUT OF HERE...
...IN THE BIG CAULDRON, I'M PREPARING THE "ANTIDOTE": WATER, BONE MARROW, VEGETABLES, AND SALT... SINCE WE MUST TASTE IT BEFORE THE ROMANS DO, IT MIGHT AS WELL BE A GOOD SOUP...
SOON AFTER...
THE MAGIC POTION IS READY. HAVE A BIG GULP!
GLUG! GLUG! GLUG! GLUG! GLUG! GLUG!
YOU MAY CALL THE OTHERS NOW...
SOUP'S UP!
BRING THE CAULDRON HERE...
IT'S COMING! IT'S COMING!
YOU TASTE IT FIRST...
IS IT GOOD?
GLUG GLUG GLUG
VERY GOOD... BUT IT'D BE BETTER WITH CROUTONS...
?

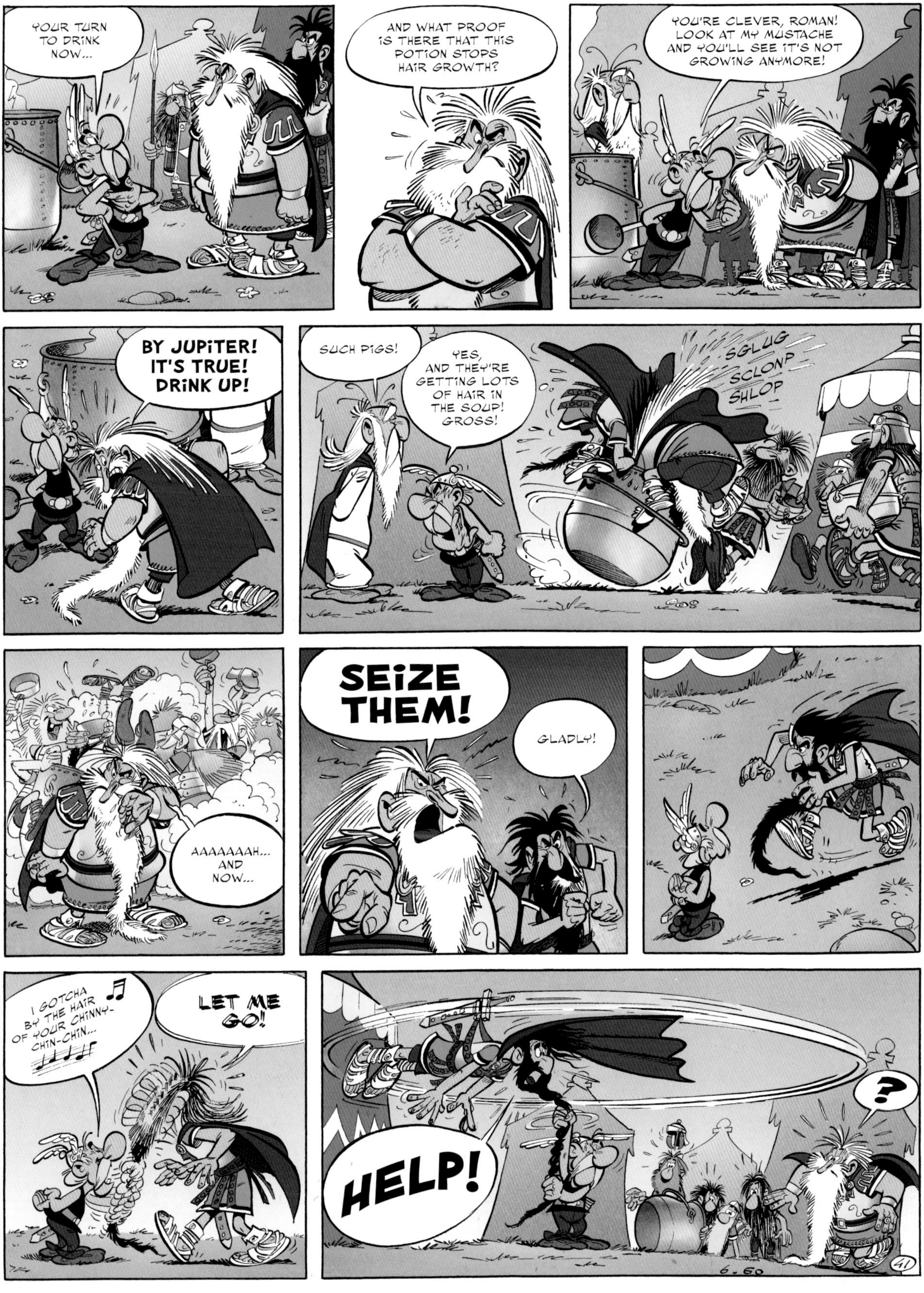
YOUR TURN TO DRINK NOW...
AND WHAT PROOF IS THERE THAT THIS POTION STOPS HAIR GROWTH?
YOU'RE CLEVER, ROMAN! LOOK AT MY MUSTACHE AND YOU'LL SEE IT'S NOT GROWING ANYMORE!
BY JUPITER! IT'S TRUE! DRINK UP!
SUCH PIGS!
YES, AND THEY'RE GETTING LOTS OF HAIR IN THE SOUP! GROSS!
SGLUG
SCLONP
SHLOP
AAAAAAAH... AND NOW...
SEIZE THEM!
GLADLY!
I GOTCHA BY THE HAIR OF YOUR CHINNY-CHIN-CHIN...
LET ME GO!
HELP!
?
41
6.60

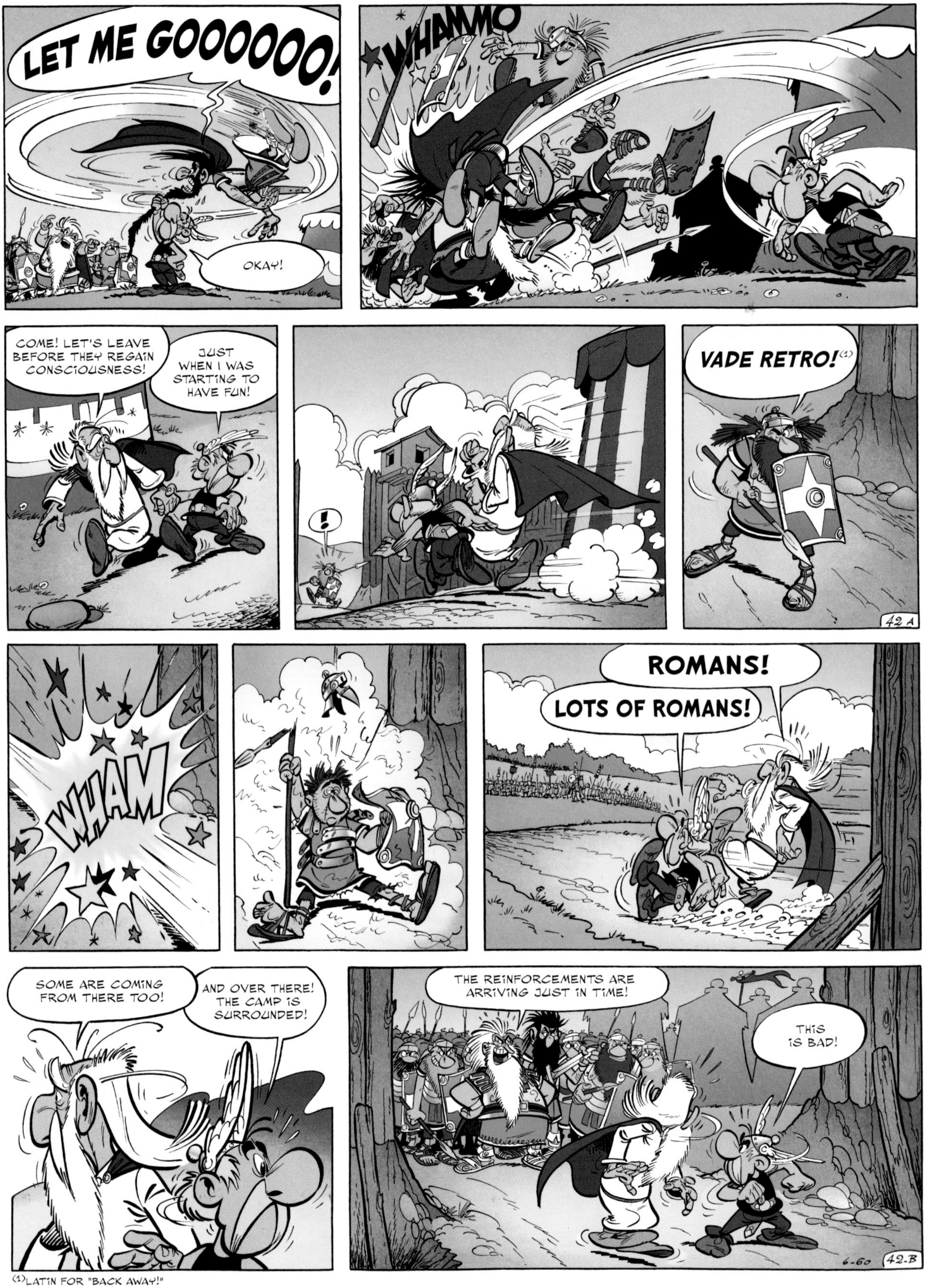
LET ME GOOOOOO!
OKAY!
WHAMMO
COME! LET'S LEAVE BEFORE THEY REGAIN CONSCIOUSNESS!
JUST WHEN I WAS STARTING TO HAVE FUN!
!
VADE RETRO!(1)
42 A
WHAM
ROMANS!
LOTS OF ROMANS!
SOME ARE COMING FROM THERE TOO!
AND OVER THERE! THE CAMP IS SURROUNDED!
THE REINFORCEMENTS ARE ARRIVING JUST IN TIME!
THIS IS BAD!
6-60
42-B

(1) LATIN FOR "BACK AWAY!"

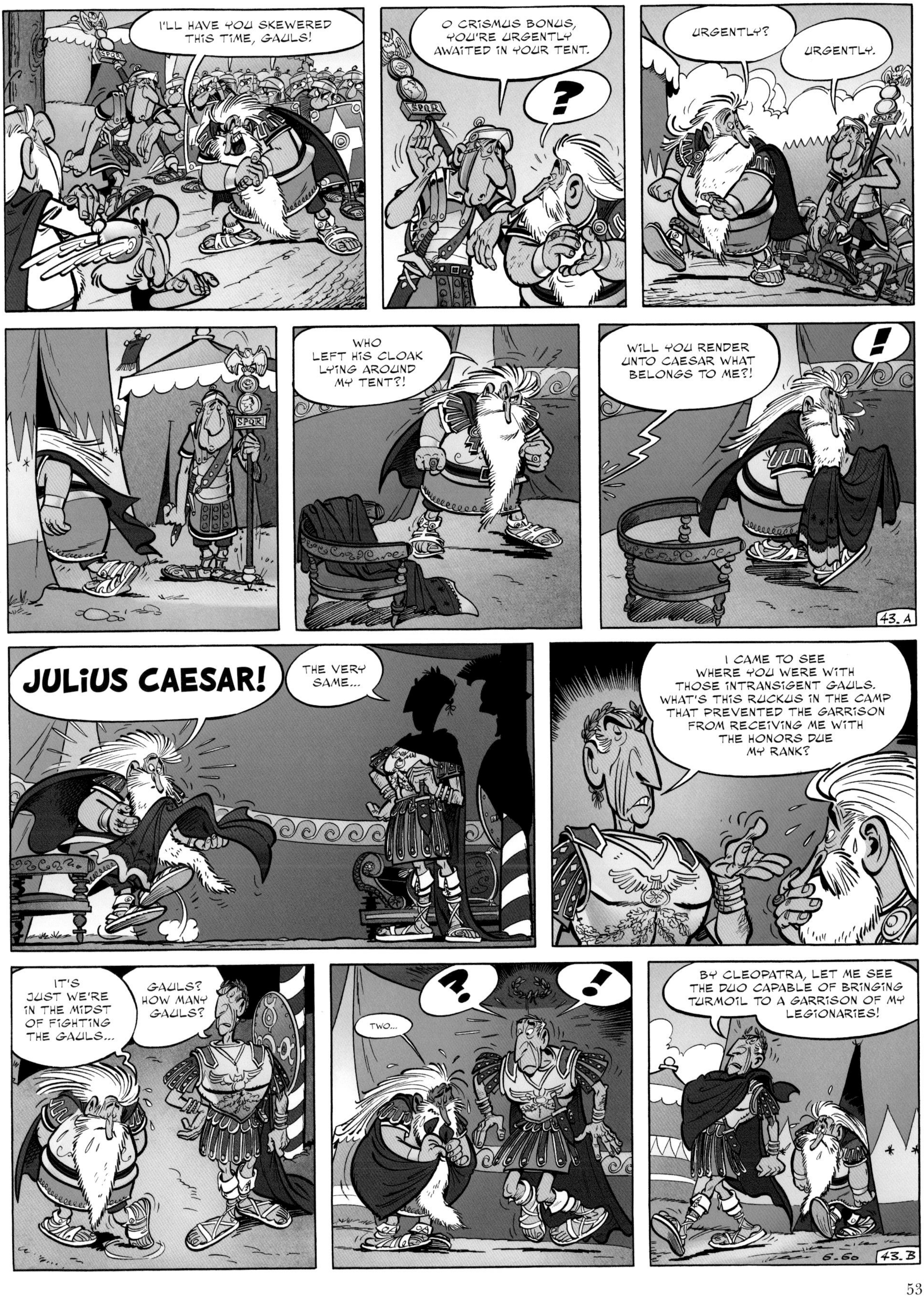
I'LL HAVE YOU SKEWERED THIS TIME, GAULS!
SPQR
O CRISMUS BONUS, YOU'RE URGENTLY AWAITED IN YOUR TENT.
?
URGENTLY?
URGENTLY.
WHO LEFT HIS CLOAK LYING AROUND MY TENT?!
WILL YOU RENDER UNTO CAESAR WHAT BELONGS TO ME?!
!
43.A
JULIUS CAESAR!
THE VERY SAME...
I CAME TO SEE WHERE YOU WERE WITH THOSE INTRANSIGENT GAULS. WHAT'S THIS RUCKUS IN THE CAMP THAT PREVENTED THE GARRISON FROM RECEIVING ME WITH THE HONORS DUE MY RANK?
IT'S JUST WE'RE IN THE MIDST OF FIGHTING THE GAULS...
GAULS? HOW MANY GAULS?
?
!
TWO...
BY CLEOPATRA, LET ME SEE THE DUO CAPABLE OF BRINGING TURMOIL TO A GARRISON OF MY LEGIONARIES!
6.60
43.B

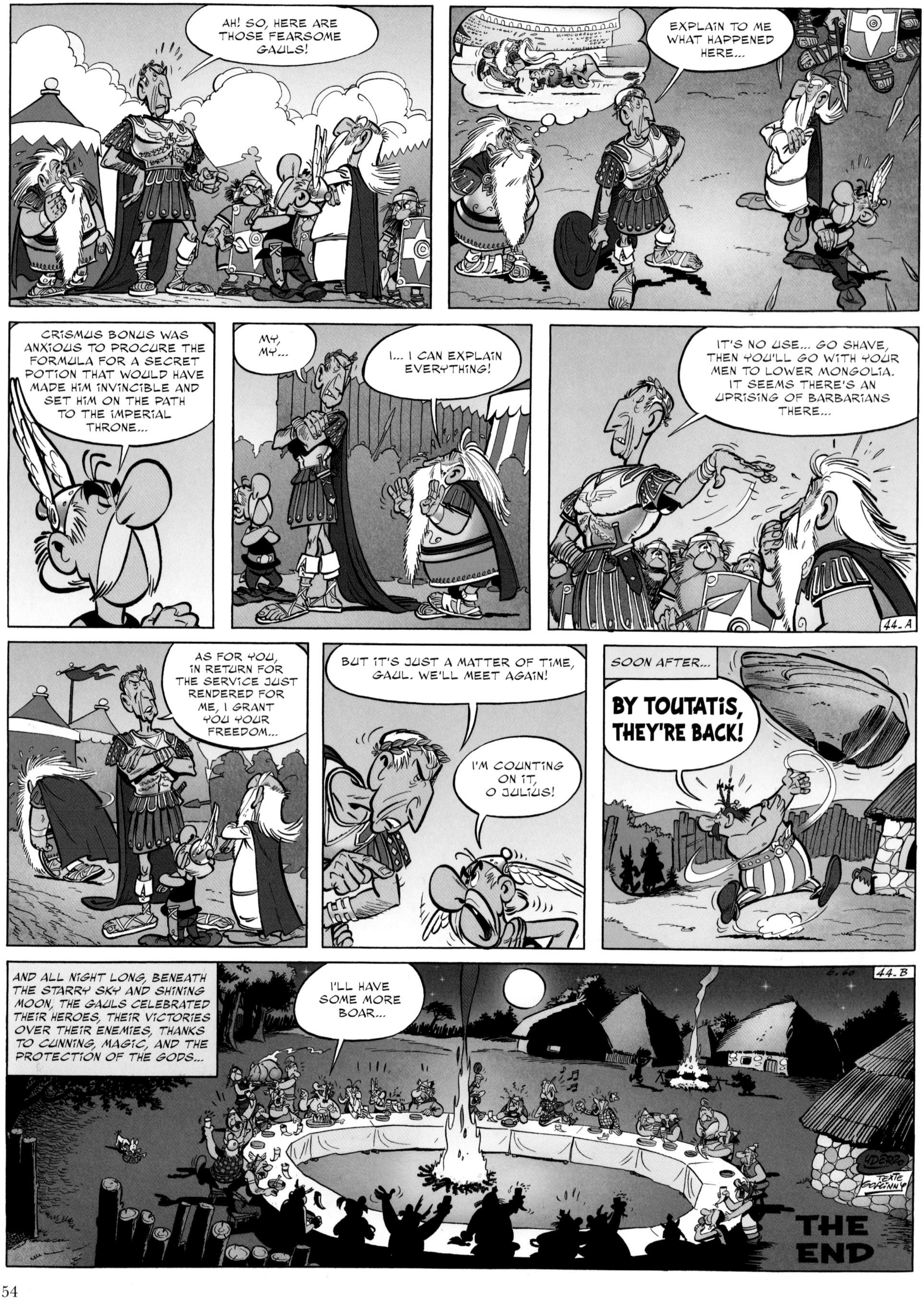
AH! SO, HERE ARE THOSE FEARSOME GAULS!
EXPLAIN TO ME WHAT HAPPENED HERE...
CRISMUS BONUS WAS ANXIOUS TO PROCURE THE FORMULA FOR A SECRET POTION THAT WOULD HAVE MADE HIM INVINCIBLE AND SET HIM ON THE PATH TO THE IMPERIAL THRONE...
MY, MY...
I... I CAN EXPLAIN EVERYTHING!
IT'S NO USE... GO SHAVE, THEN YOU'LL GO WITH YOUR MEN TO LOWER MONGOLIA. IT SEEMS THERE'S AN UPRISING OF BARBARIANS THERE...
44_A
AS FOR YOU, IN RETURN FOR THE SERVICE JUST RENDERED FOR ME, I GRANT YOU YOUR FREEDOM...
BUT IT'S JUST A MATTER OF TIME, GAUL. WE'LL MEET AGAIN!
I'M COUNTING ON IT, O JULIUS!
SOON AFTER...
BY TOUTATIS, THEY'RE BACK!
AND ALL NIGHT LONG, BENEATH THE STARRY SKY AND SHINING MOON, THE GAULS CELEBRATED THEIR HEROES, THEIR VICTORIES OVER THEIR ENEMIES, THANKS TO CUNNING, MAGIC, AND THE PROTECTION OF THE GODS...
I'LL HAVE SOME MORE BOAR...
44_B
THE END

R. GOSCINNY Asterix A. UDERZO

Asterix and the Golden Sickle

RENÉ GOSCINNY
Writer

ALBERT UDERZO
Illustrator

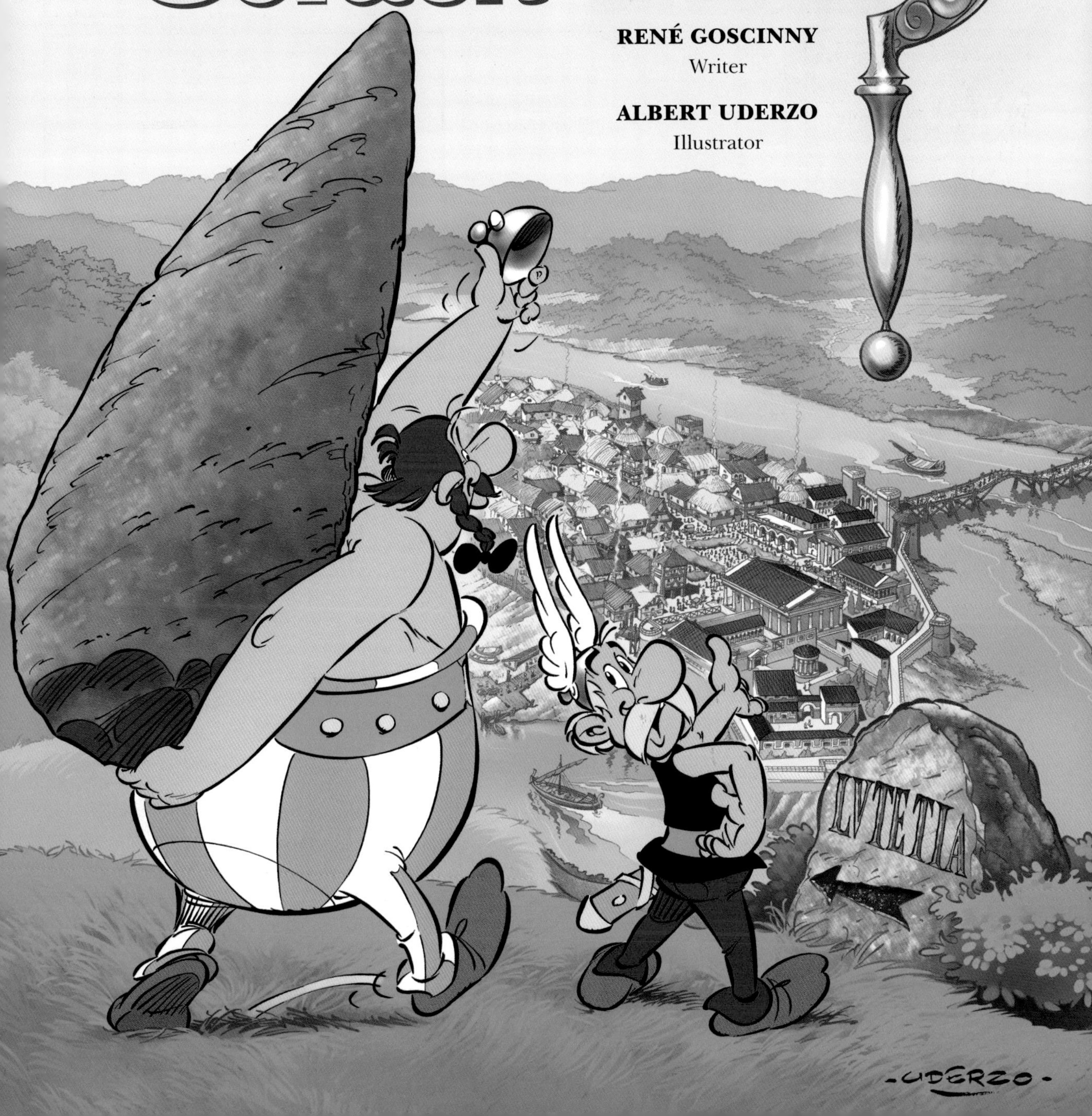
LVTETIA
UDERZO

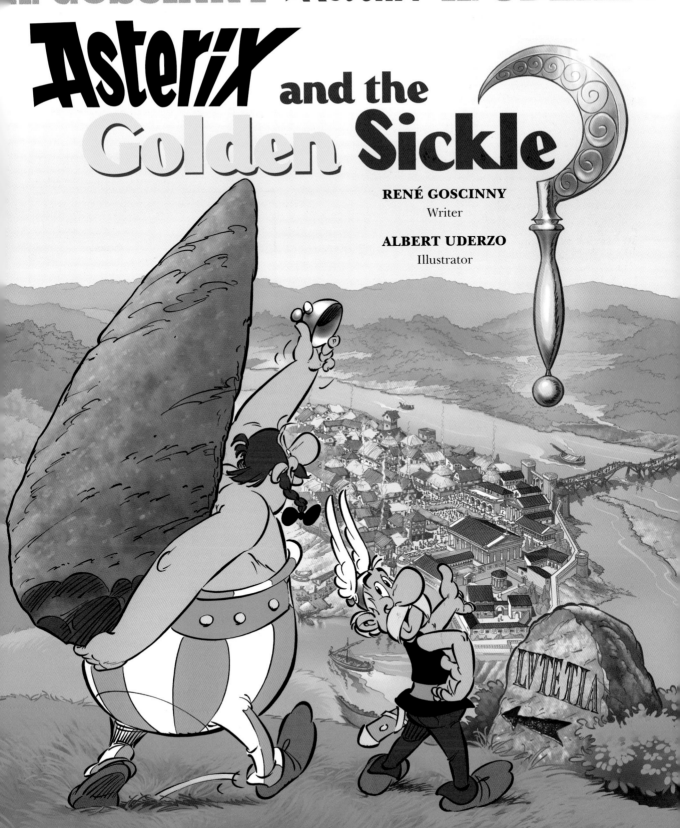

ASTERIX AND THE GOLDEN SICKLE

Written by RENÉ GOSCINNY *and illustrated by* ALBERT UDERZO

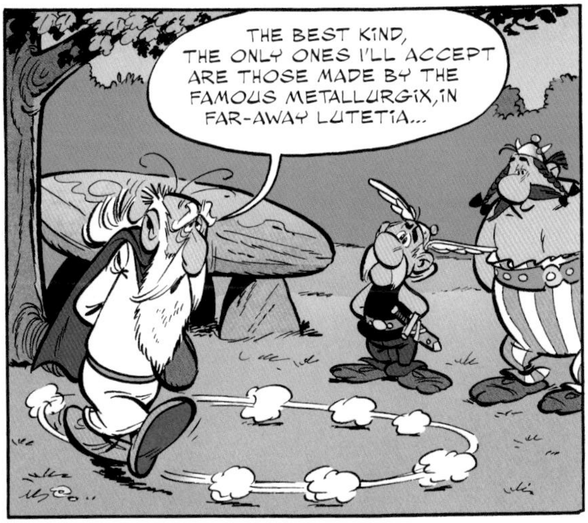
THE BEST KIND, THE ONLY ONES I'LL ACCEPT ARE THOSE MADE BY THE FAMOUS METALLURGIX, IN FAR-AWAY LUTETIA...

THE FIERCELY INDEPENDENT LITTLE VILLAGE WHERE ASTERIX, THE GAULISH WARRIOR, LIVES PEACEFULLY...

Gaulish Wine

GOOD HUNTING, ASTERIX?

NAH, NOT SO MUCH TODAY...

1 A

OBELIX, THE MENHIR SCULPTOR AND DELIVERYMAN, IS WORKING JOYFULLY...

ROCK ON... ♪♫

CACOFONIX THE BARD IS GIVING A LESSON...

SO, YOUNG MAN, WHO WERE OUR ANCESTORS?

$VIII \times V = XL$

$\begin{array}{r} III \\ + I \\ \hline = IV \end{array}$

?

IN SHORT, EVERYONE IS LIVING PEACEFULLY IN PEACE AND PROSPERITY...

ANOTHER BOAR, OBELIX?

MMMM! YES!

WHEN SUDDENLY...

BY TOUTATIS!

??

?

?

1 B

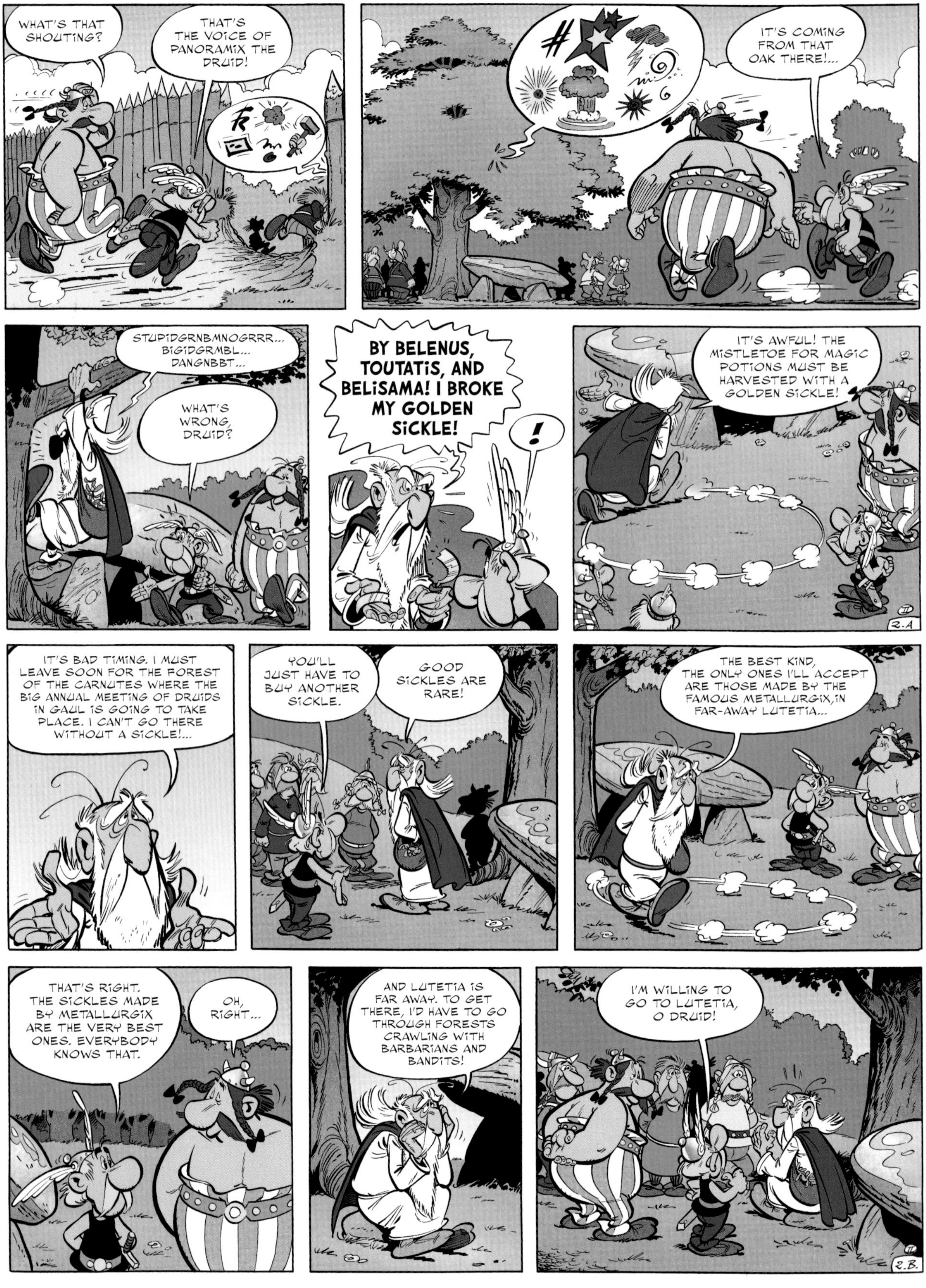

WHAT'S THAT SHOUTING?
THAT'S THE VOICE OF PANORAMIX THE DRUID!
IT'S COMING FROM THAT OAK THERE!...
STUPIDGRNBMNOGRRR... BIGIDGRMBL... DANGNBBT...
WHAT'S WRONG, DRUID?
BY BELENUS, TOUTATIS, AND BELISAMA! I BROKE MY GOLDEN SICKLE!
!
IT'S AWFUL! THE MISTLETOE FOR MAGIC POTIONS MUST BE HARVESTED WITH A GOLDEN SICKLE!
IT'S BAD TIMING. I MUST LEAVE SOON FOR THE FOREST OF THE CARNUTES WHERE THE BIG ANNUAL MEETING OF DRUIDS IN GAUL IS GOING TO TAKE PLACE. I CAN'T GO THERE WITHOUT A SICKLE!...
YOU'LL JUST HAVE TO BUY ANOTHER SICKLE.
GOOD SICKLES ARE RARE!
THE BEST KIND, THE ONLY ONES I'LL ACCEPT ARE THOSE MADE BY THE FAMOUS METALLURGIX,IN FAR-AWAY LUTETIA...
THAT'S RIGHT. THE SICKLES MADE BY METALLURGIX ARE THE VERY BEST ONES. EVERYBODY KNOWS THAT.
OH, RIGHT...
AND LUTETIA IS FAR AWAY. TO GET THERE, I'D HAVE TO GO THROUGH FORESTS CRAWLING WITH BARBARIANS AND BANDITS!
I'M WILLING TO GO TO LUTETIA, O DRUID!

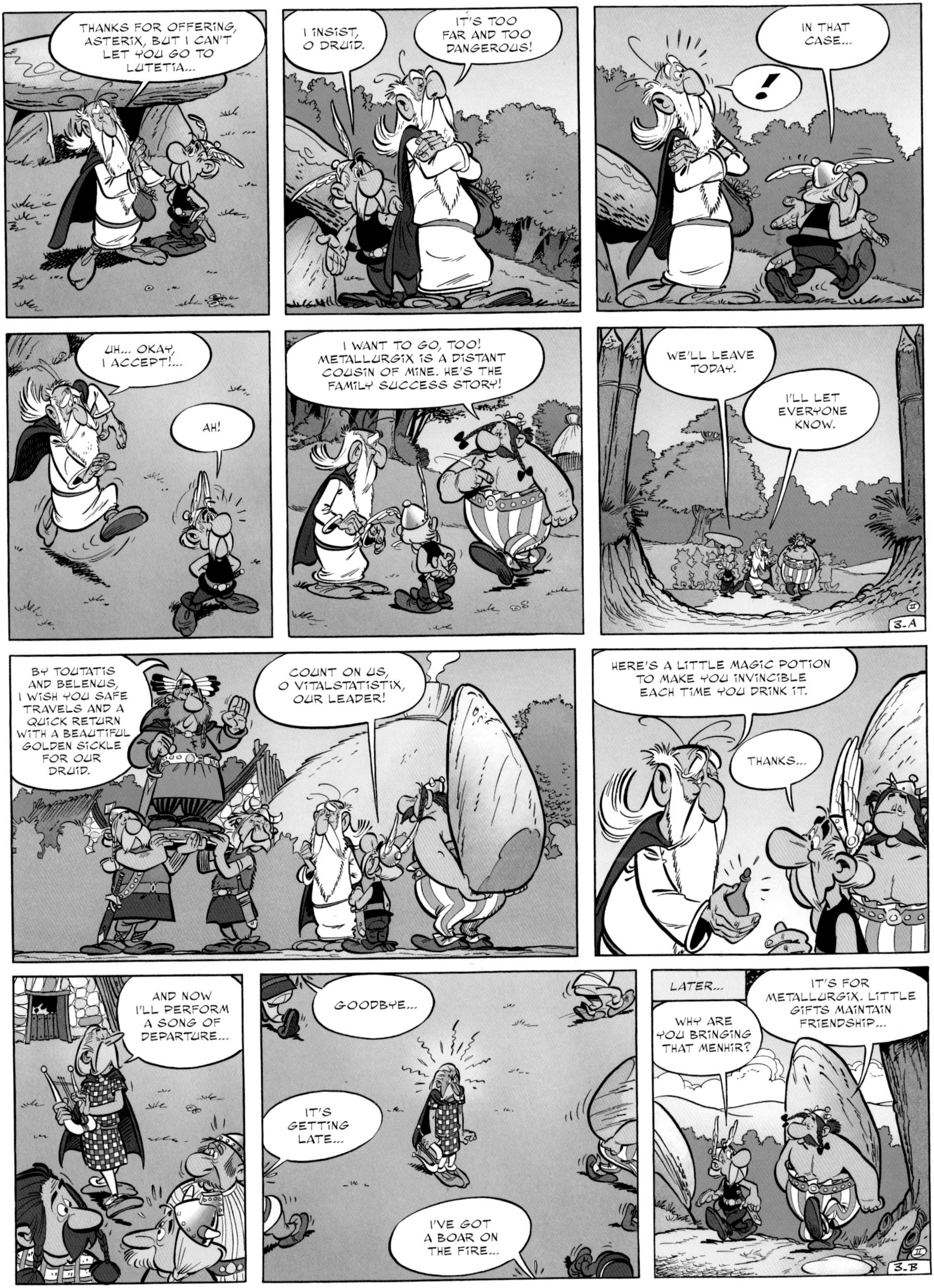
THANKS FOR OFFERING, ASTERIX, BUT I CAN'T LET YOU GO TO LUTETIA...
I INSIST, O DRUID.
IT'S TOO FAR AND TOO DANGEROUS!
!
IN THAT CASE...
UH... OKAY, I ACCEPT!...
AH!
I WANT TO GO, TOO! METALLURGIX IS A DISTANT COUSIN OF MINE. HE'S THE FAMILY SUCCESS STORY!
WE'LL LEAVE TODAY.
I'LL LET EVERYONE KNOW.
3-A
BY TOUTATIS AND BELENUS, I WISH YOU SAFE TRAVELS AND A QUICK RETURN WITH A BEAUTIFUL GOLDEN SICKLE FOR OUR DRUID.
COUNT ON US, O VITALSTATISTIX, OUR LEADER!
HERE'S A LITTLE MAGIC POTION TO MAKE YOU INVINCIBLE EACH TIME YOU DRINK IT.
THANKS...
AND NOW I'LL PERFORM A SONG OF DEPARTURE...
GOODBYE...
IT'S GETTING LATE...
I'VE GOT A BOAR ON THE FIRE...
LATER...
WHY ARE YOU BRINGING THAT MENHIR?
IT'S FOR METALLURGIX. LITTLE GIFTS MAINTAIN FRIENDSHIP...
3-B

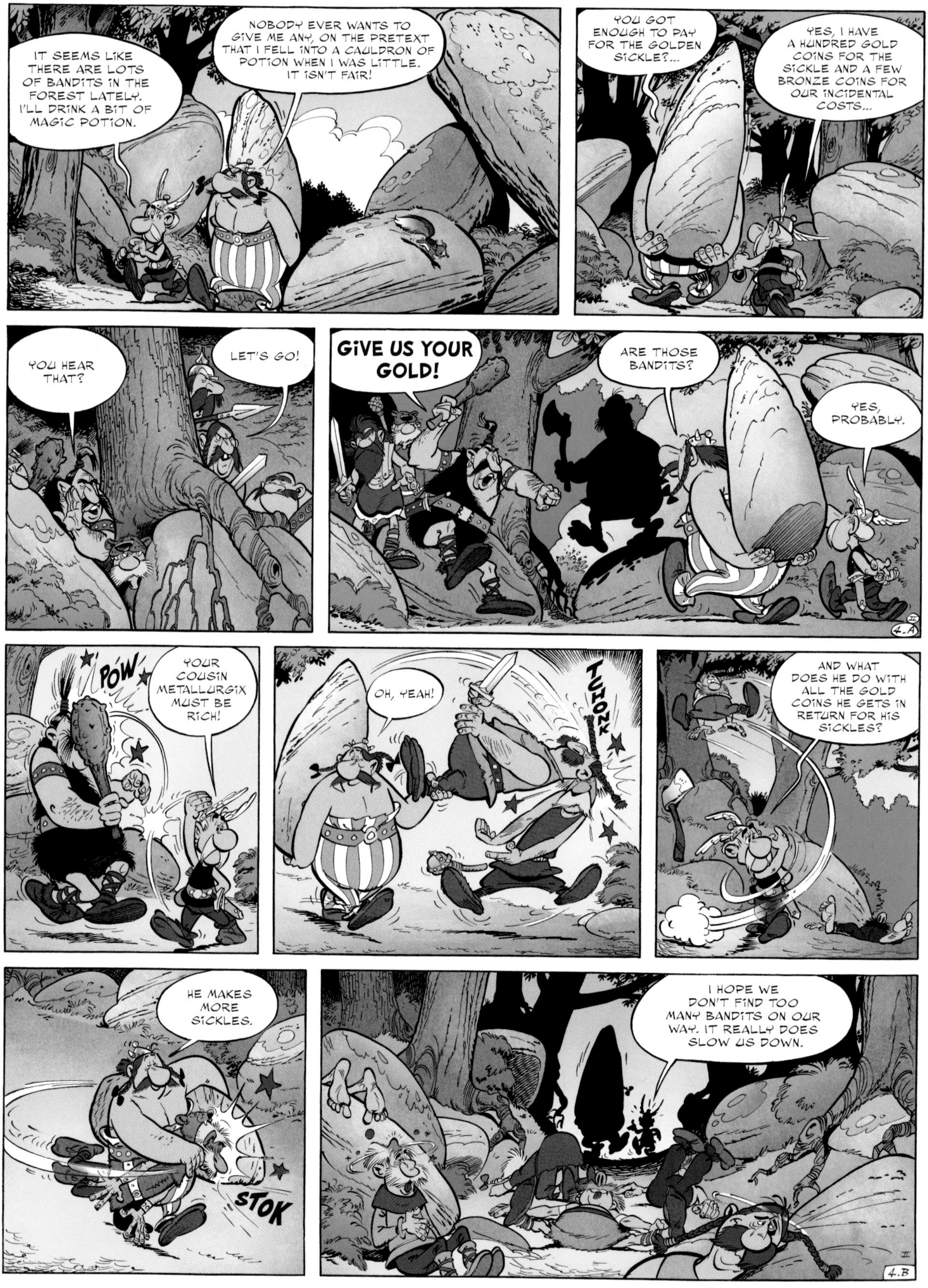
IT SEEMS LIKE THERE ARE LOTS OF BANDITS IN THE FOREST LATELY. I'LL DRINK A BIT OF MAGIC POTION.
NOBODY EVER WANTS TO GIVE ME ANY, ON THE PRETEXT THAT I FELL INTO A CAULDRON OF POTION WHEN I WAS LITTLE. IT ISN'T FAIR!
YOU GOT ENOUGH TO PAY FOR THE GOLDEN SICKLE?...
YES, I HAVE A HUNDRED GOLD COINS FOR THE SICKLE AND A FEW BRONZE COINS FOR OUR INCIDENTAL COSTS...
YOU HEAR THAT?
LET'S GO!
GIVE US YOUR GOLD!
ARE THOSE BANDITS?
YES, PROBABLY.
4-A
POW
YOUR COUSIN METALLURGIX MUST BE RICH!
OH, YEAH!
TCHONK
AND WHAT DOES HE DO WITH ALL THE GOLD COINS HE GETS IN RETURN FOR HIS SICKLES?
HE MAKES MORE SICKLES.
STOK
I HOPE WE DON'T FIND TOO MANY BANDITS ON OUR WAY. IT REALLY DOES SLOW US DOWN.
4.B

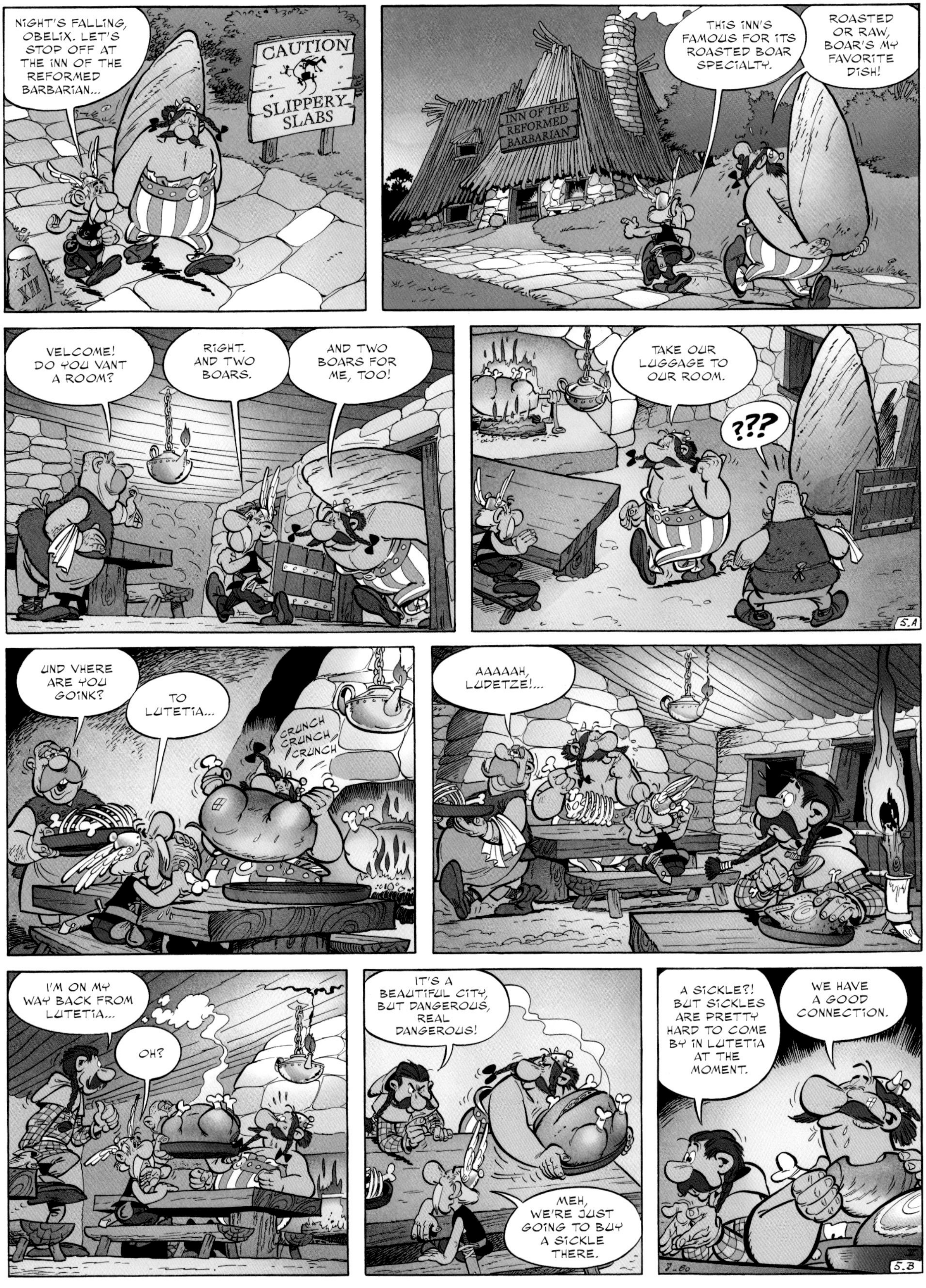
NIGHT'S FALLING, OBELIX. LET'S STOP OFF AT THE INN OF THE REFORMED BARBARIAN...
CAUTION
SLIPPERY SLABS
N XIII
THIS INN'S FAMOUS FOR ITS ROASTED BOAR SPECIALTY.
ROASTED OR RAW, BOAR'S MY FAVORITE DISH!
INN OF THE REFORMED BARBARIAN
VELCOME! DO YOU VANT A ROOM?
RIGHT. AND TWO BOARS.
AND TWO BOARS FOR ME, TOO!
TAKE OUR LUGGAGE TO OUR ROOM.
???
UND VHERE ARE YOU GOINK?
TO LUTETIA...
CRUNCH CRUNCH CRUNCH
AAAAAH, LUDETZE!...
I'M ON MY WAY BACK FROM LUTETIA...
OH?
IT'S A BEAUTIFUL CITY, BUT DANGEROUS, REAL DANGEROUS!
MEH, WE'RE JUST GOING TO BUY A SICKLE THERE.
A SICKLE?! BUT SICKLES ARE PRETTY HARD TO COME BY IN LUTETIA AT THE MOMENT.
WE HAVE A GOOD CONNECTION.

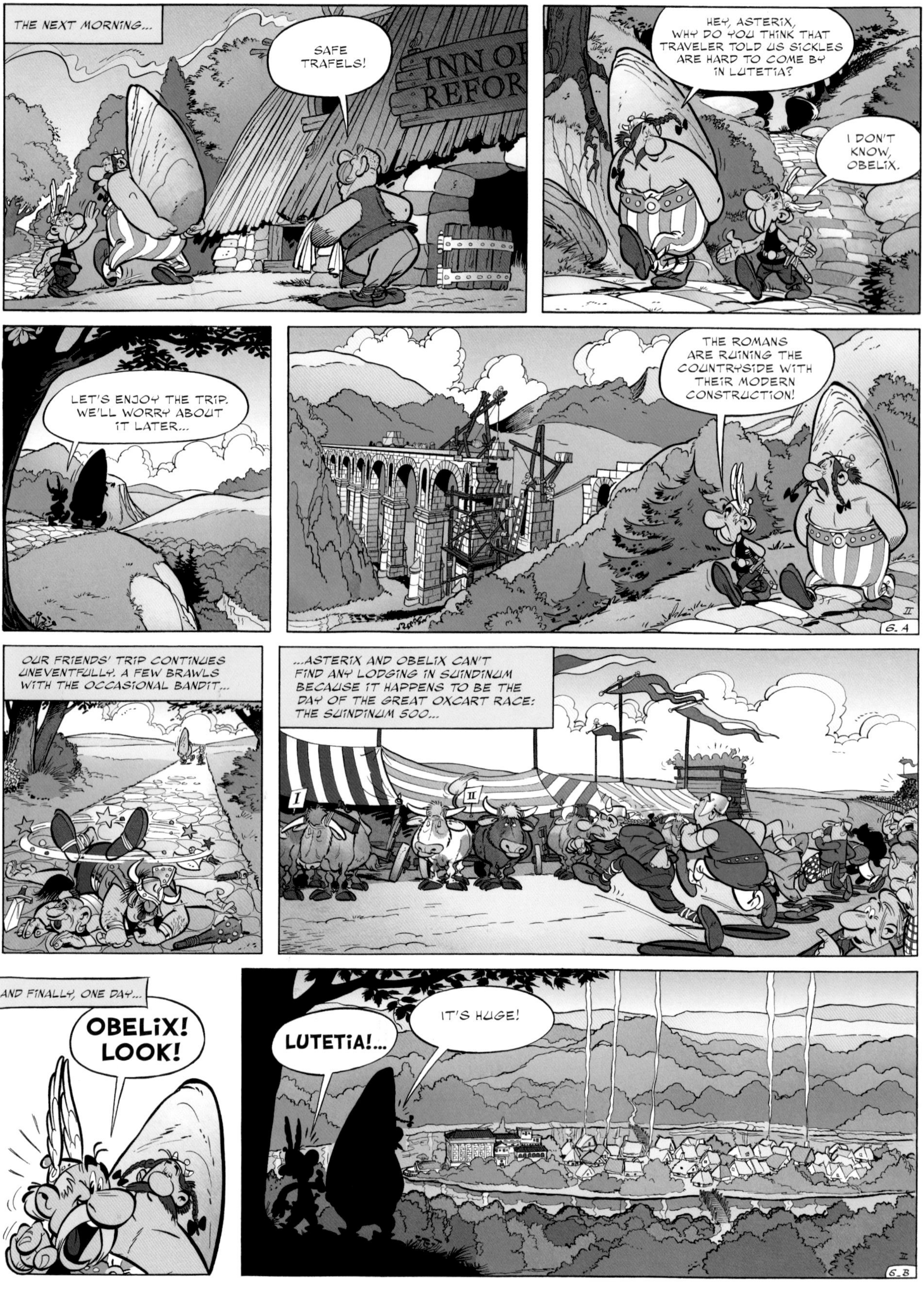
THE NEXT MORNING...
SAFE TRAFELS!
INN OF REFOR
HEY, ASTERIX, WHY DO YOU THINK THAT TRAVELER TOLD US SICKLES ARE HARD TO COME BY IN LUTETIA?
I DON'T KNOW, OBELIX.
LET'S ENJOY THE TRIP. WE'LL WORRY ABOUT IT LATER...
THE ROMANS ARE RUINING THE COUNTRYSIDE WITH THEIR MODERN CONSTRUCTION!
OUR FRIENDS' TRIP CONTINUES UNEVENTFULLY. A FEW BRAWLS WITH THE OCCASIONAL BANDIT...
...ASTERIX AND OBELIX CAN'T FIND ANY LODGING IN SUINDINUM BECAUSE IT HAPPENS TO BE THE DAY OF THE GREAT OXCART RACE: THE SUINDINUM 500...
AND FINALLY, ONE DAY...
OBELIX! LOOK!
LUTETIA!...
IT'S HUGE!

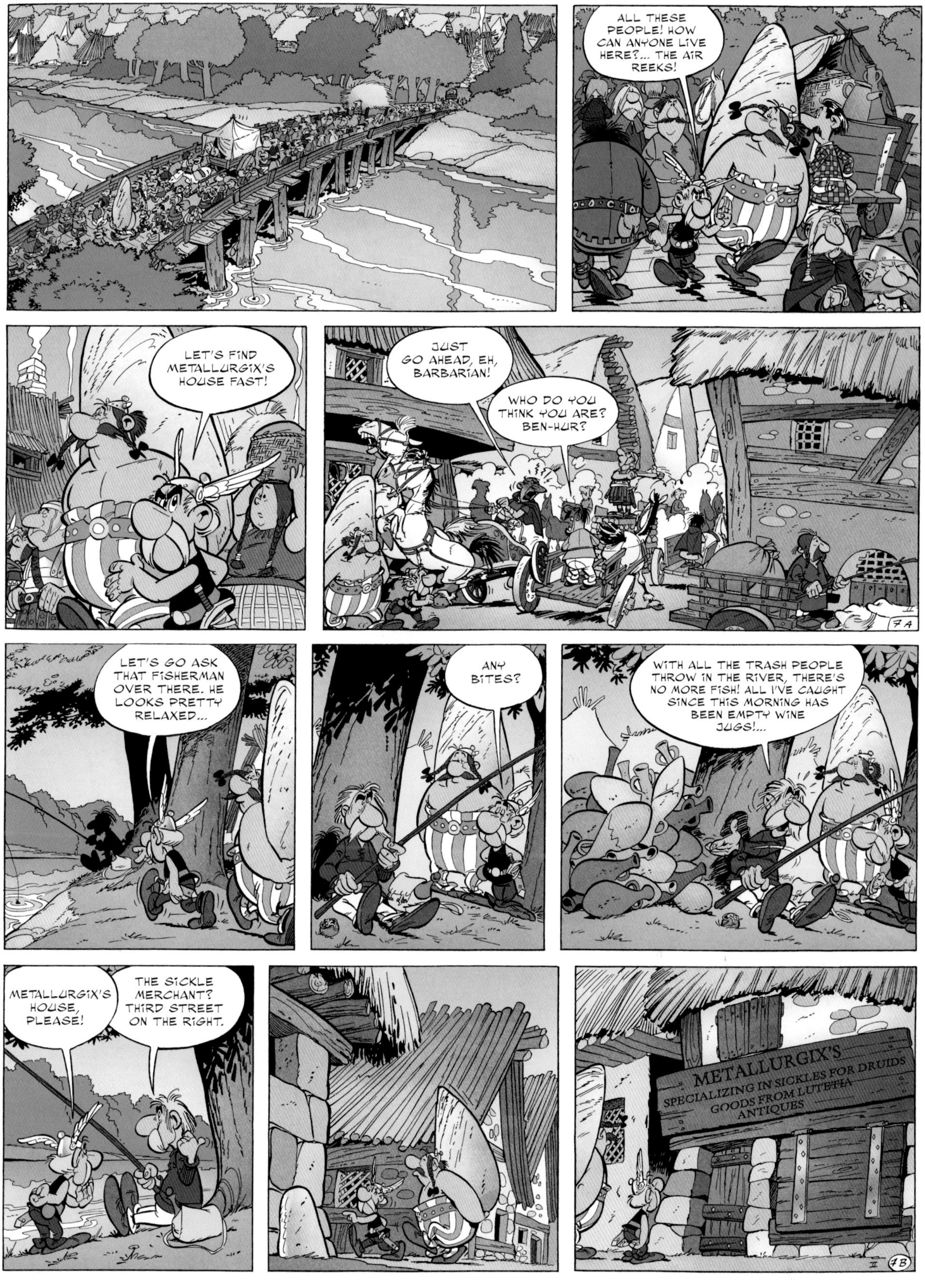
ALL THESE PEOPLE! HOW CAN ANYONE LIVE HERE?... THE AIR REEKS!
LET'S FIND METALLURGIX'S HOUSE FAST!
JUST GO AHEAD, EH, BARBARIAN!
WHO DO YOU THINK YOU ARE? BEN-HUR?
LET'S GO ASK THAT FISHERMAN OVER THERE. HE LOOKS PRETTY RELAXED...
ANY BITES?
WITH ALL THE TRASH PEOPLE THROW IN THE RIVER, THERE'S NO MORE FISH! ALL I'VE CAUGHT SINCE THIS MORNING HAS BEEN EMPTY WINE JUGS!...
METALLURGIX'S HOUSE, PLEASE!
THE SICKLE MERCHANT? THIRD STREET ON THE RIGHT.
METALLURGIX'S
SPECIALIZING IN SICKLES FOR DRUIDS
GOODS FROM LUTETIA
ANTIQUES

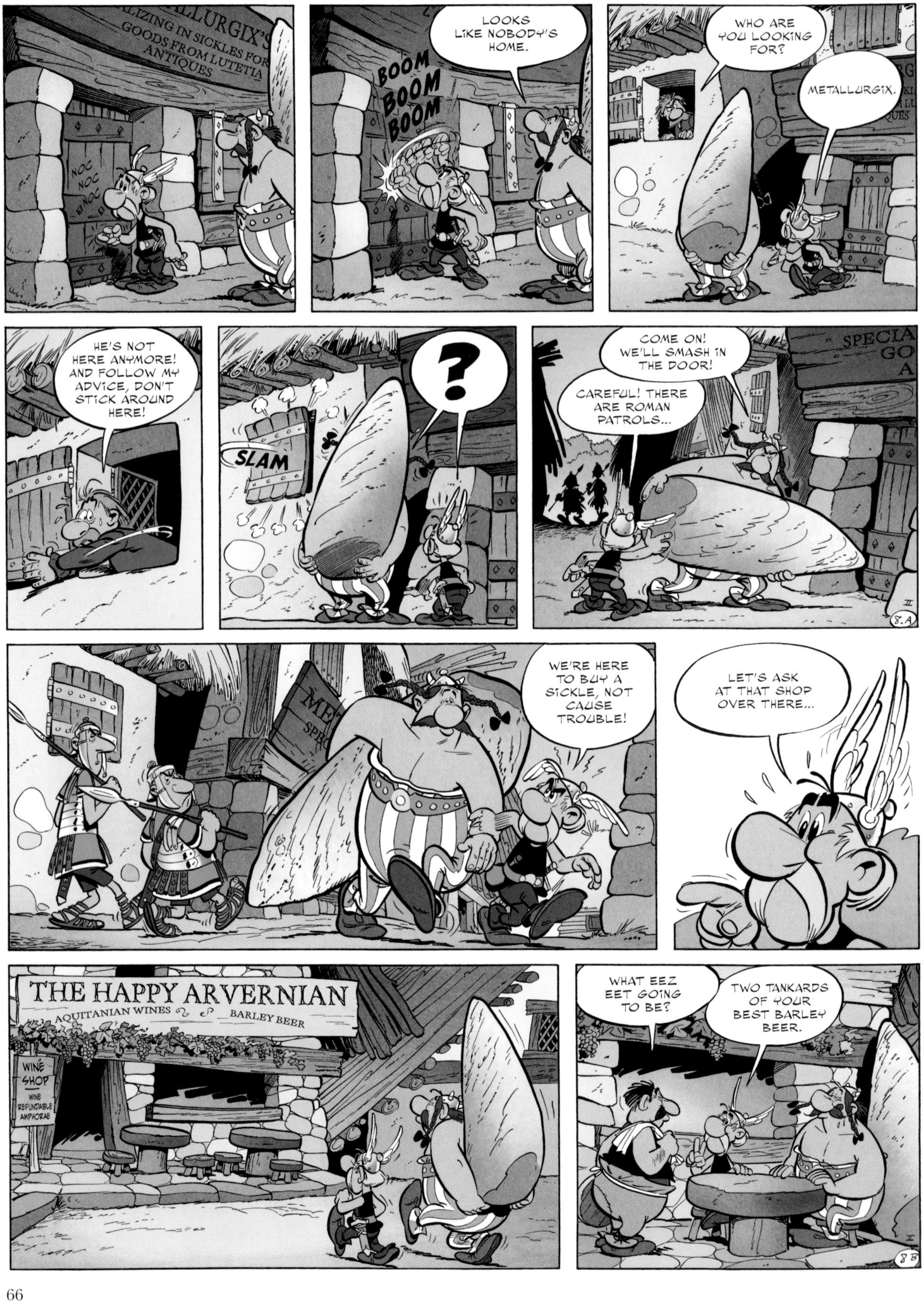
ALLURGIX'S
LIZING IN SICKLES FOR
GOODS FROM LUTETIA
ANTIQUES
NOC
NOC
NOC
LOOKS LIKE NOBODY'S HOME.
BOOM
BOOM
BOOM
WHO ARE YOU LOOKING FOR?
METALLURGIX.
HE'S NOT HERE ANYMORE! AND FOLLOW MY ADVICE, DON'T STICK AROUND HERE!
SLAM
?
COME ON! WE'LL SMASH IN THE DOOR!
CAREFUL! THERE ARE ROMAN PATROLS...
WE'RE HERE TO BUY A SICKLE, NOT CAUSE TROUBLE!
LET'S ASK AT THAT SHOP OVER THERE...
THE HAPPY ARVERNIAN
AQUITANIAN WINES
BARLEY BEER
WINE SHOP
WINE REFUNDABLE AMPHORAE
WHAT EEZ EET GOING TO BE?
TWO TANKARDS OF YOUR BEST BARLEY BEER.

SO YOU ARE FROM ZE PROVEENCES NEAR ZE BEEG SEA?

HOW CAN YOU TELL?

FROM YOUR MENHIR ZAT I ZEE OVER YONDER... I AHM VEREE OBSERVANT!

BARLEY BEER

I AM AN ARVERNIAN, FROM NEAR SHERGOVIE.

SHERGOVIE?

GERGOVIA!

THE HAPPY ARVERNIAN
AQUITANIAN WINES · BARLEY BEER

TELL ME, FRIEND... DO YOU KNOW METALLURGIX, THE SICKLE MERCHANT?

METALLURSHEEX?!

I DO NOT KNOW EEN-YONE BY ZAT NAME! BOTTOMZ UP, I 'AVE GOT TO CLOSE!

?

!

THE HAPPY ARVERNIAN
AQUITANIAN WINES · BARLEY BEER

SLAM

CLOSED DUE TO ILLNESS

CLOSED DUE TO ILLNESS

CREEE

THE HAPPY A
AQUITANIAN WINES

BOOM BOOM

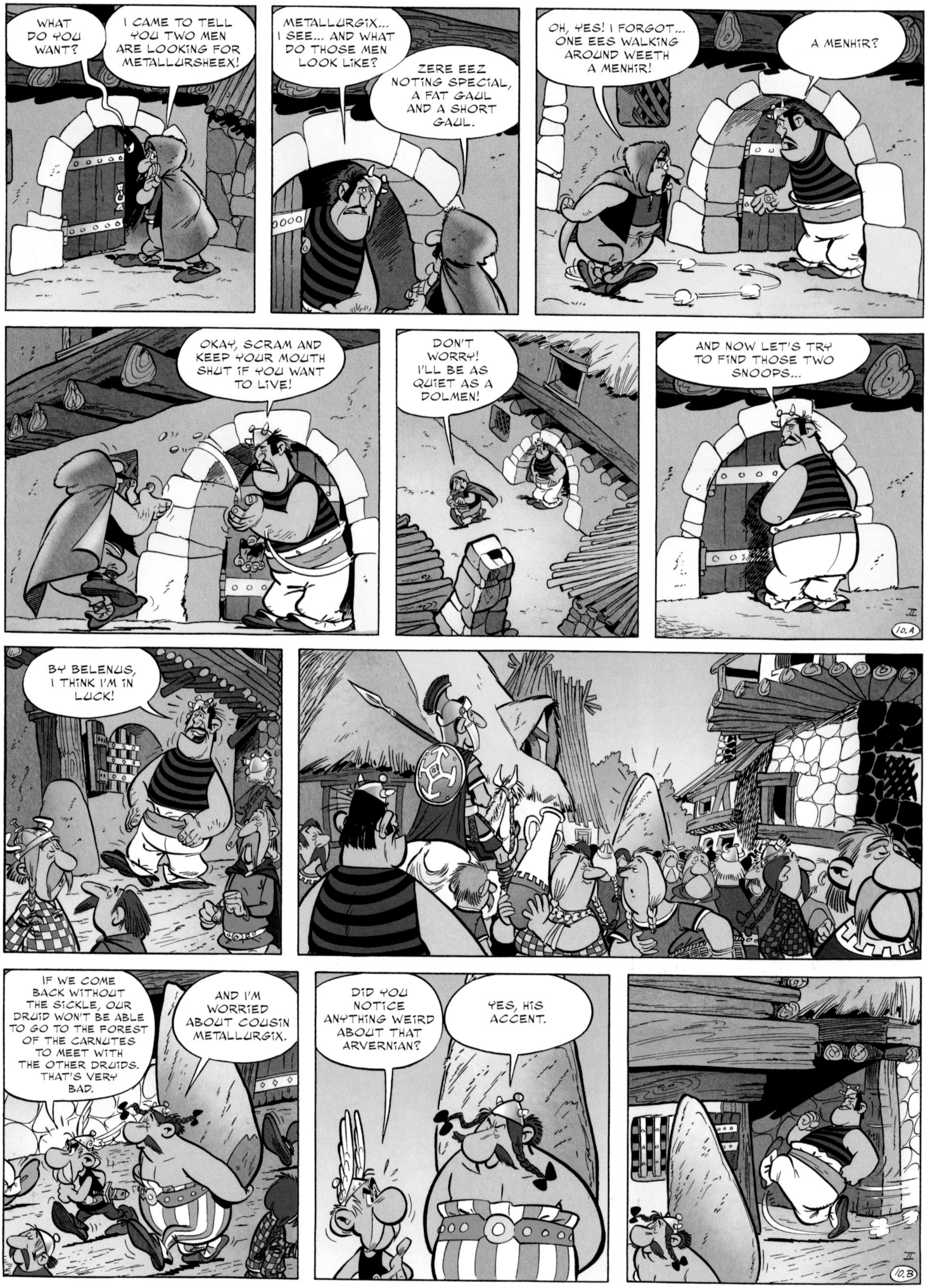
WHAT DO YOU WANT?
I CAME TO TELL YOU TWO MEN ARE LOOKING FOR METALLURSHEEX!
METALLURGIX... I SEE... AND WHAT DO THOSE MEN LOOK LIKE?
ZERE EEZ NOTING SPECIAL, A FAT GAUL AND A SHORT GAUL.
OH, YES! I FORGOT... ONE EES WALKING AROUND WEETH A MENHIR!
A MENHIR?
OKAY, SCRAM AND KEEP YOUR MOUTH SHUT IF YOU WANT TO LIVE!
DON'T WORRY! I'LL BE AS QUIET AS A DOLMEN!
AND NOW LET'S TRY TO FIND THOSE TWO SNOOPS...
10.A
BY BELENUS, I THINK I'M IN LUCK!
IF WE COME BACK WITHOUT THE SICKLE, OUR DRUID WON'T BE ABLE TO GO TO THE FOREST OF THE CARNUTES TO MEET WITH THE OTHER DRUIDS. THAT'S VERY BAD.
AND I'M WORRIED ABOUT COUSIN METALLURGIX.
DID YOU NOTICE ANYTHING WEIRD ABOUT THAT ARVERNIAN?
YES, HIS ACCENT.
10.B

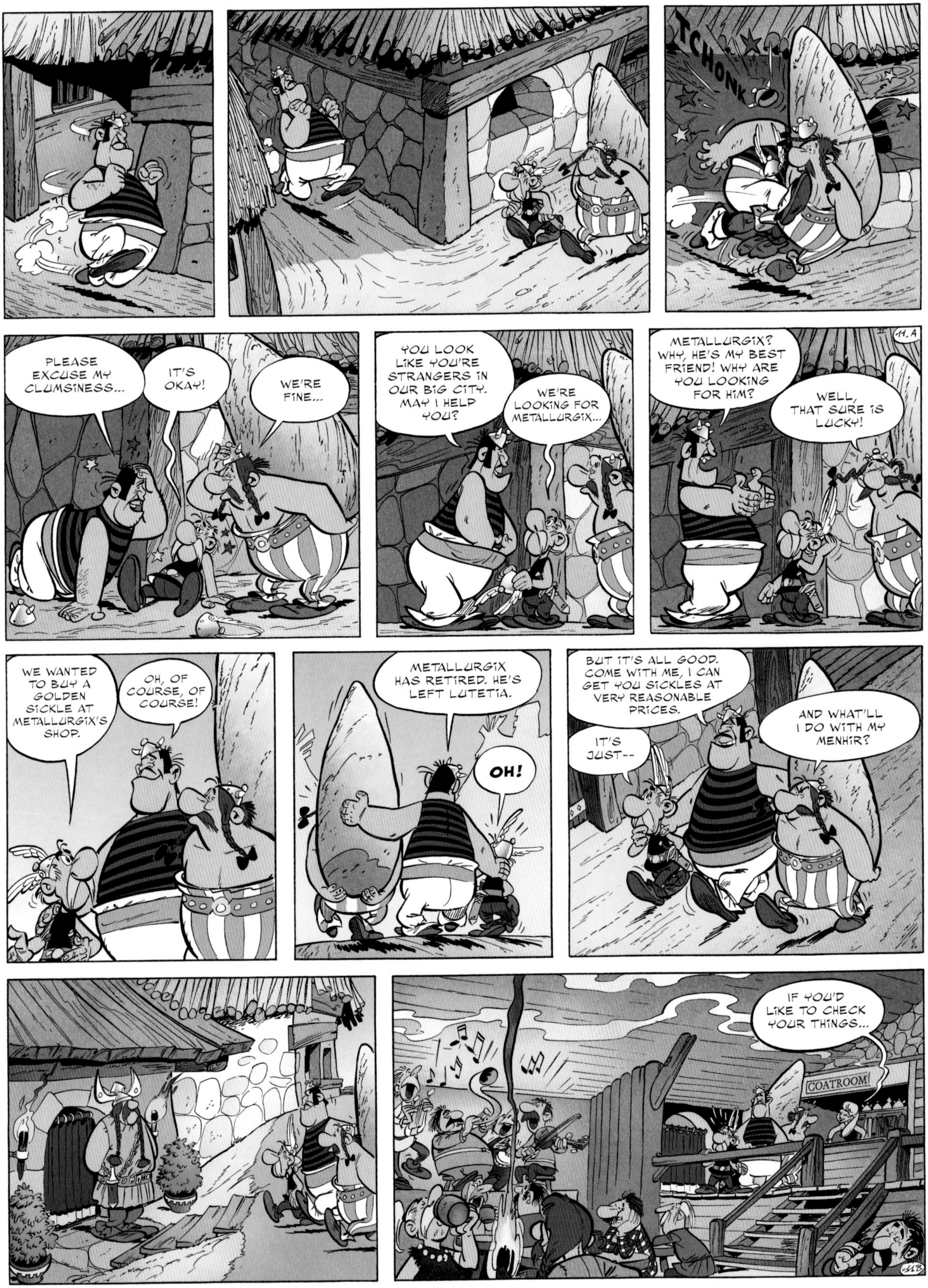
TCHONK
PLEASE EXCUSE MY CLUMSINESS...
IT'S OKAY!
WE'RE FINE...
YOU LOOK LIKE YOU'RE STRANGERS IN OUR BIG CITY. MAY I HELP YOU?
WE'RE LOOKING FOR METALLURGIX...
METALLURGIX? WHY, HE'S MY BEST FRIEND! WHY ARE YOU LOOKING FOR HIM?
WELL, THAT SURE IS LUCKY!
WE WANTED TO BUY A GOLDEN SICKLE AT METALLURGIX'S SHOP.
OH, OF COURSE, OF COURSE!
METALLURGIX HAS RETIRED. HE'S LEFT LUTETIA.
OH!
BUT IT'S ALL GOOD. COME WITH ME, I CAN GET YOU SICKLES AT VERY REASONABLE PRICES.
IT'S JUST--
AND WHAT'LL I DO WITH MY MENHIR?
COATROOM
IF YOU'D LIKE TO CHECK YOUR THINGS...

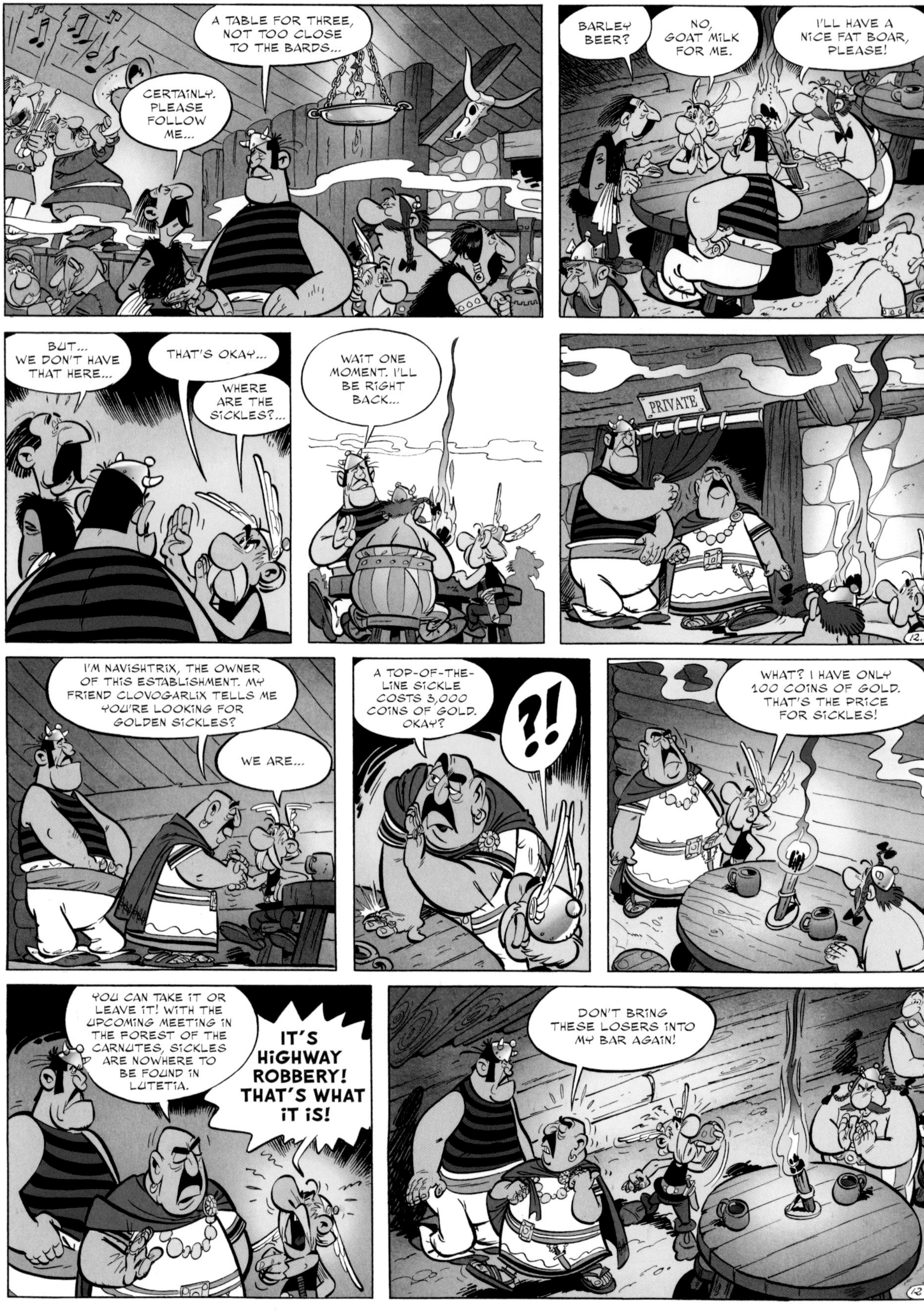
A TABLE FOR THREE, NOT TOO CLOSE TO THE BARDS...
CERTAINLY. PLEASE FOLLOW ME...
BARLEY BEER?
NO, GOAT MILK FOR ME.
I'LL HAVE A NICE FAT BOAR, PLEASE!
BUT... WE DON'T HAVE THAT HERE...
THAT'S OKAY...
WHERE ARE THE SICKLES?...
WAIT ONE MOMENT. I'LL BE RIGHT BACK...
PRIVATE
I'M NAVISHTRIX, THE OWNER OF THIS ESTABLISHMENT. MY FRIEND CLOVOGARLIX TELLS ME YOU'RE LOOKING FOR GOLDEN SICKLES?
WE ARE...
A TOP-OF-THE-LINE SICKLE COSTS 3,000 COINS OF GOLD. OKAY?
?!
WHAT? I HAVE ONLY 100 COINS OF GOLD. THAT'S THE PRICE FOR SICKLES!
YOU CAN TAKE IT OR LEAVE IT! WITH THE UPCOMING MEETING IN THE FOREST OF THE CARNUTES, SICKLES ARE NOWHERE TO BE FOUND IN LUTETIA.
IT'S HIGHWAY ROBBERY! THAT'S WHAT IT IS!
DON'T BRING THESE LOSERS INTO MY BAR AGAIN!

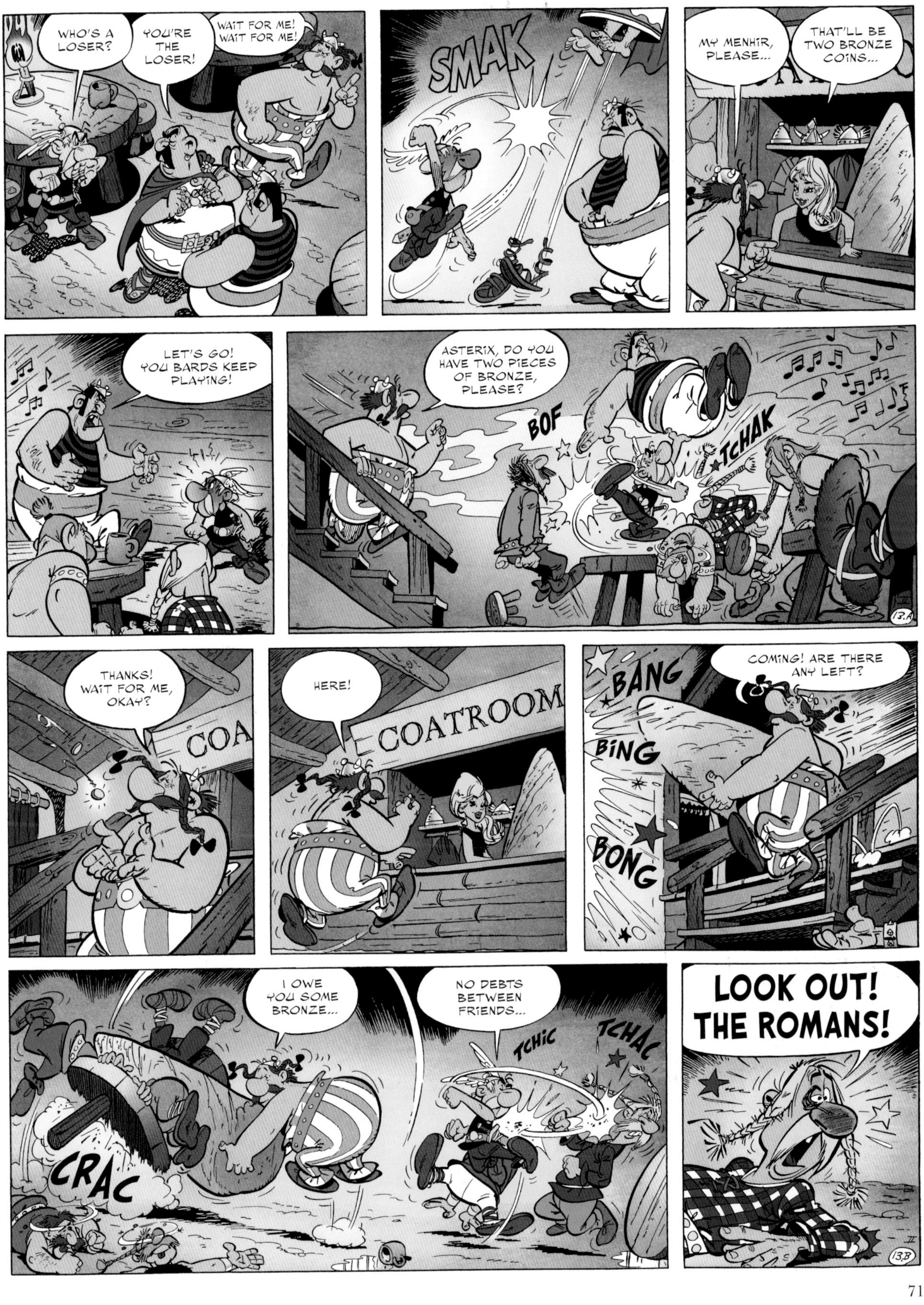
WHO'S A LOSER?
YOU'RE THE LOSER!
WAIT FOR ME! WAIT FOR ME!
SMAK
MY MENHIR, PLEASE...
THAT'LL BE TWO BRONZE COINS...
LET'S GO! YOU BARDS KEEP PLAYING!
ASTERIX, DO YOU HAVE TWO PIECES OF BRONZE, PLEASE?
BOF
TCHAK
THANKS! WAIT FOR ME, OKAY?
COA
HERE!
COATROOM
BANG
BING
BONG
COMING! ARE THERE ANY LEFT?
I OWE YOU SOME BRONZE...
NO DEBTS BETWEEN FRIENDS...
TCHIC
TCHAC
CRAC
LOOK OUT! THE ROMANS!

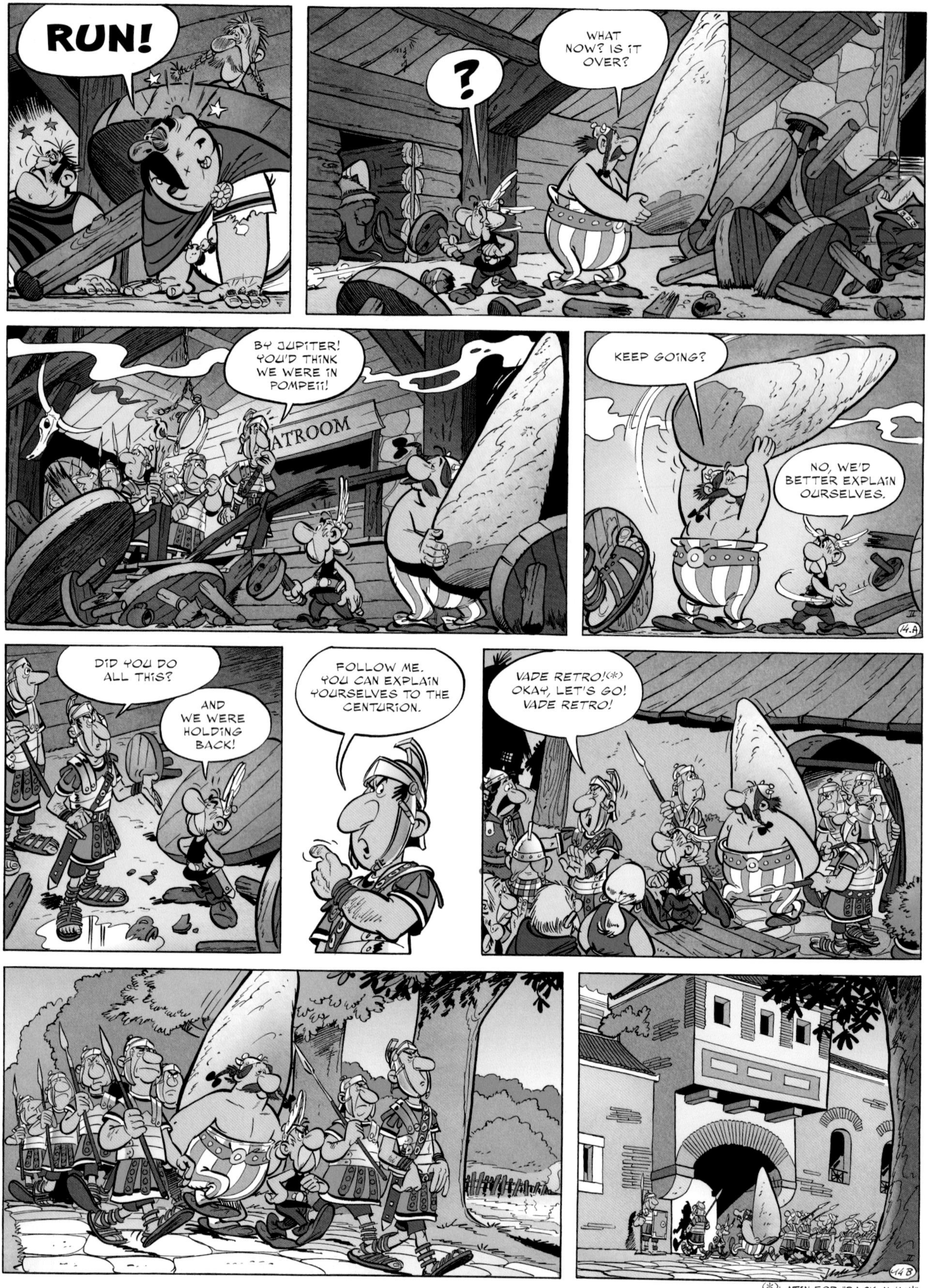
RUN!
?
WHAT NOW? IS IT OVER?
BY JUPITER! YOU'D THINK WE WERE IN POMPEII!
ATROOM
KEEP GOING?
NO, WE'D BETTER EXPLAIN OURSELVES.
DID YOU DO ALL THIS?
AND WE WERE HOLDING BACK!
FOLLOW ME. YOU CAN EXPLAIN YOURSELVES TO THE CENTURION.
VADE RETRO!(*) OKAY, LET'S GO! VADE RETRO!

(*)LATIN FOR "BACK AWAY!"

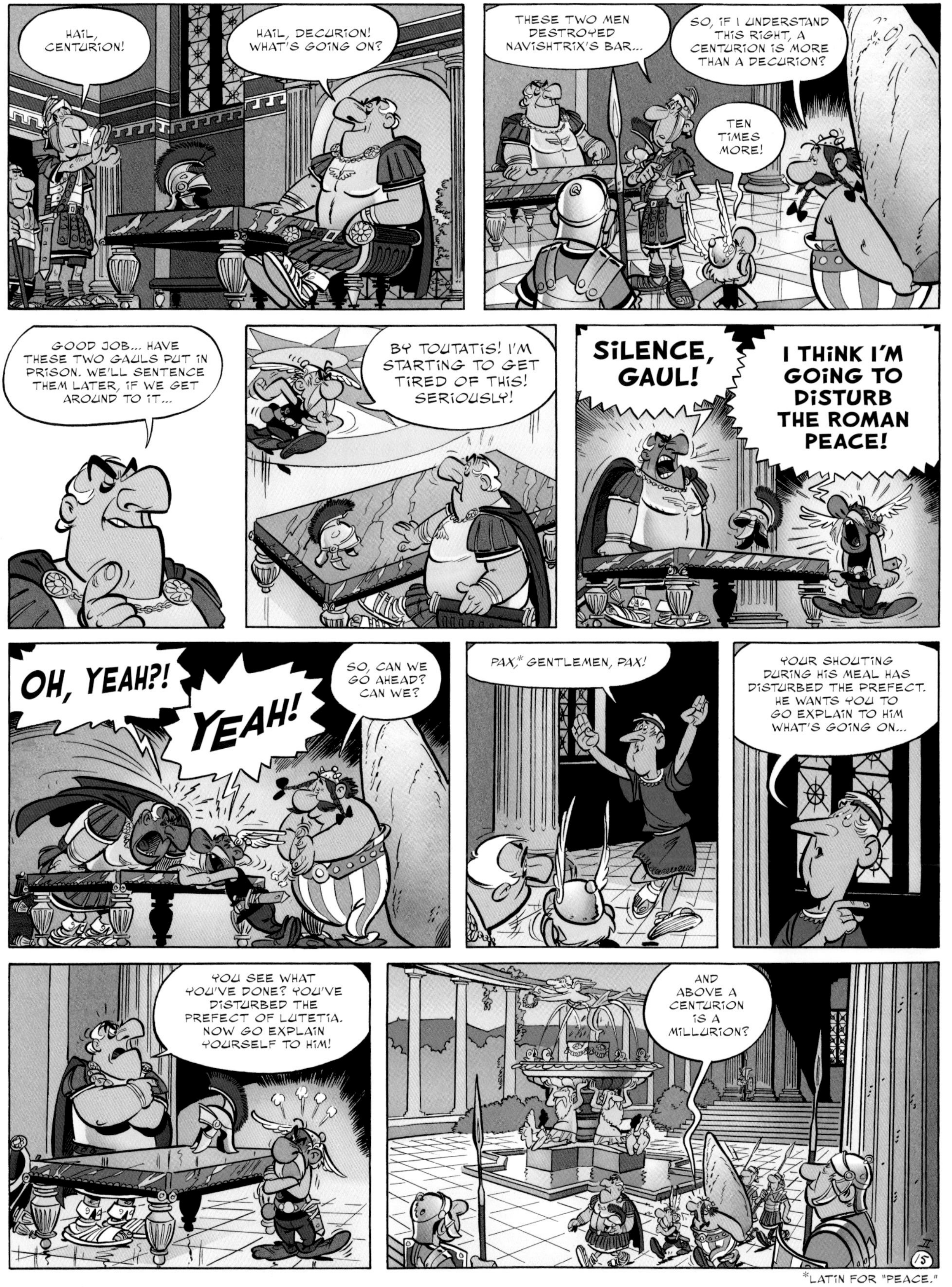
HAIL, CENTURION!
HAIL, DECURION! WHAT'S GOING ON?
THESE TWO MEN DESTROYED NAVISHTRIX'S BAR...
SO, IF I UNDERSTAND THIS RIGHT, A CENTURION IS MORE THAN A DECURION?
TEN TIMES MORE!
GOOD JOB... HAVE THESE TWO GAULS PUT IN PRISON. WE'LL SENTENCE THEM LATER, IF WE GET AROUND TO IT...
BY TOUTATIS! I'M STARTING TO GET TIRED OF THIS! SERIOUSLY!
SILENCE, GAUL!
I THINK I'M GOING TO DISTURB THE ROMAN PEACE!
OH, YEAH?!
YEAH!
SO, CAN WE GO AHEAD? CAN WE?
PAX,* GENTLEMEN, PAX!
YOUR SHOUTING DURING HIS MEAL HAS DISTURBED THE PREFECT. HE WANTS YOU TO GO EXPLAIN TO HIM WHAT'S GOING ON...
YOU SEE WHAT YOU'VE DONE? YOU'VE DISTURBED THE PREFECT OF LUTETIA. NOW GO EXPLAIN YOURSELF TO HIM!
AND ABOVE A CENTURION IS A MILLURION?
II 15

*LATIN FOR "PEACE."

HAIL, O SURPLUS DAIRYPRODUS.

HAIL, MY FRIEND, HAIL...

WHO ARE THESE PEOPLE DISTURBING MY MEAL?

TWO GAULS! IT WAS A GAUL BRAWL.

I'M WEARY OF THE GAULS. THEY FIGHT ALL THE TIME. IT'S SO TIRESOME...

THESE TWO GAULS DESTROYED NAVISHTRIX'S BAR.

DID YOU DRINK TOO MUCH BARLEY BEER?

NO, WE JUST WANTED TO BUY A GOLDEN SICKLE FOR OUR DRUID.

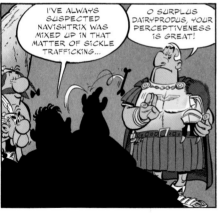

I'VE ALWAYS SUSPECTED NAVISHTRIX WAS MIXED UP IN THAT MATTER OF SICKLE TRAFFICKING...

O SURPLUS DAIRYPRODUS, YOUR PERCEPTIVENESS IS GREAT!

OH, ALL RIGHT... RELEASE THESE GAULS. THEY BORE ME... THIS IS SO LALALA...

WHAT'S THAT ABOUT SICKLE TRAFFICK-ING?

THERE'S A GANG OF SICKLE TRAFFICKERS IN LUTETIA. SICKLES ARE IN HIGH DEMAND BECAUSE OF THE MEETING IN THE FOREST OF THE CARNUTES.

WHAT DOES "SO LALALA" MEAN?

YOU CAN ONLY GET SICKLES FROM THE TRAFFICKERS, ESPECIALLY SINCE METALLURGIX THE SICKLE-MAKER DISAPPEARED WITHOUT A TRACE...

BUT THEN... MAYBE METALLURGIX WAS ABDUCTED BY THE TRAFFICKERS?

ABDUCTED OR KILLED. ANYHOW, GOOD RIDDANCE AND DON'T COME BACK...

WAAAAAAAH! MY POOR COUSIN METALLURGIX!

16

WAAAAAAAH! MY POOR COUSIN METALLURGIX!

WE'LL FIND HIM, OBELIX... FOR STARTERS, WHAT DOES YOUR COUSIN LOOK LIKE?

WHAT DOES HE LOOK LIKE? I DON'T KNOW. I'VE NEVER SEEN HIM.

!

LET'S GO TO HIS PLACE. MAYBE WE'LL FIND SOMETHING THERE...

THAT'S RIGHT. HOW DOES HE EXPECT ME TO KNOW WHAT HE LOOKS LIKE, IF I'VE NEVER SEEN HIM? ASTERIX ISN'T THINKING!

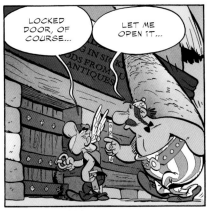
LOCKED DOOR, OF COURSE...

LET ME OPEN IT...

CRRRAAK

THERE YOU GO!

WHAT A MESS! THAT'S FUNNY, IN MY FAMILY WE'RE USUALLY MORE ORDERLY...

THERE WAS A FIGHT HERE. LOOK, METALLURGIX LEFT HIS STUFF AND HIS COOKING UTENSILS...

ON THE OTHER HAND, HIS TOOLS, SICKLES, AND GOLD ARE MISSING. YOUR COUSIN WAS ABDUCTED BY THE SICKLE TRAFFICKERS!

WAAAAAAAAH! POOR METALLURGIX!

THAT PROVES METALLURGIX IS ALIVE! WE'LL FIND HIM, BY TOUTATIS!

COOL!

WE'LL STAY HERE. AND TO START WITH, WE'RE GOING TO DO OUR SHOPPING.

THAT'S A GOOD IDEA.

LATER...

BOAR IS OVERPRICED IN LUTETIA!

AND THE MERCHANT SAID PRICES WERE GOING TO KEEP GOING UP! POOR GAUL!

17

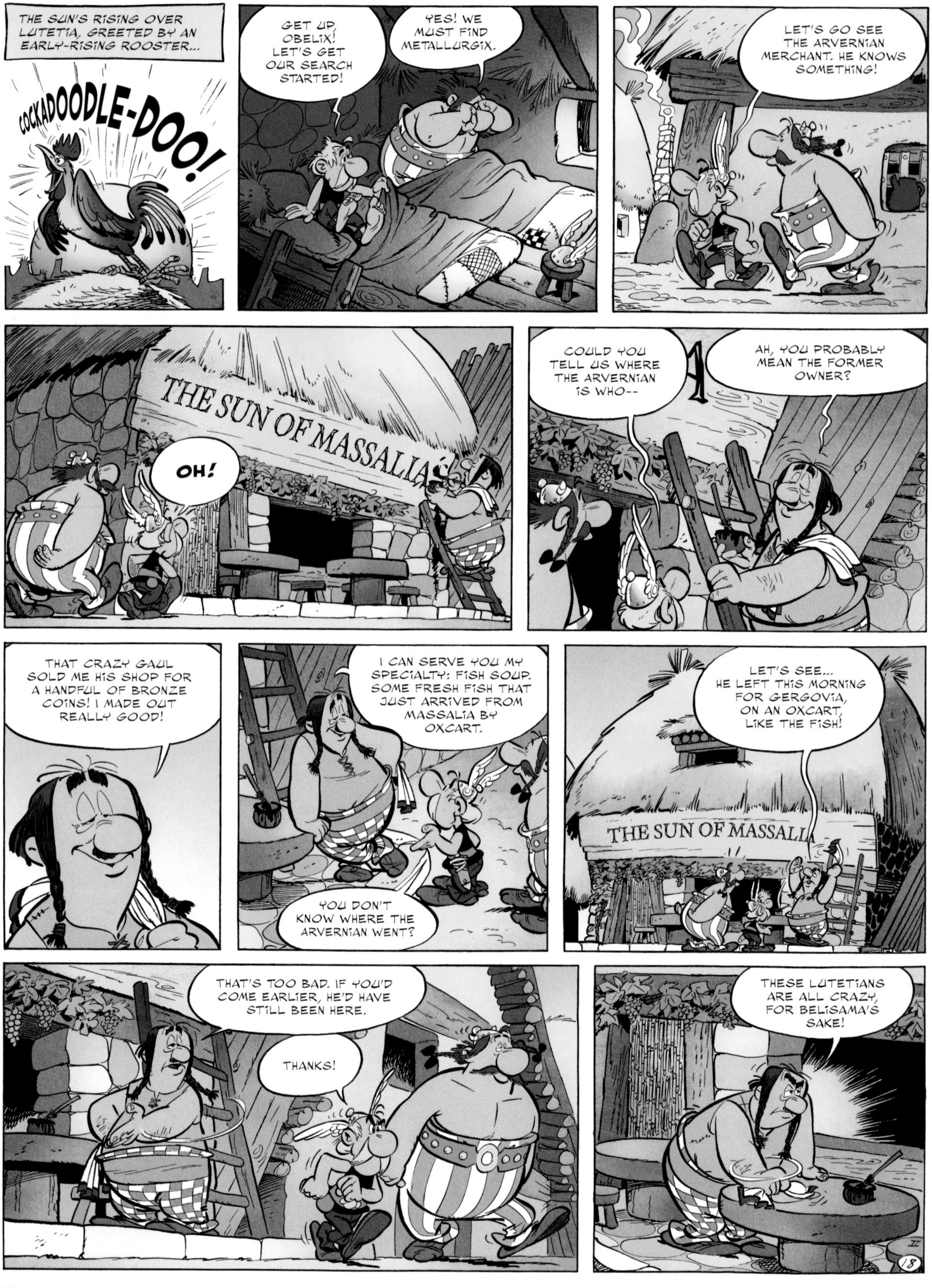
THE SUN'S RISING OVER LUTETIA, GREETED BY AN EARLY-RISING ROOSTER...
COCKADOODLE-DOO!
GET UP, OBELIX! LET'S GET OUR SEARCH STARTED!
YES! WE MUST FIND METALLURGIX.
LET'S GO SEE THE ARVERNIAN MERCHANT. HE KNOWS SOMETHING!
THE SUN OF MASSALIA
OH!
COULD YOU TELL US WHERE THE ARVERNIAN IS WHO--
AH, YOU PROBABLY MEAN THE FORMER OWNER?
THAT CRAZY GAUL SOLD ME HIS SHOP FOR A HANDFUL OF BRONZE COINS! I MADE OUT REALLY GOOD!
I CAN SERVE YOU MY SPECIALTY: FISH SOUP. SOME FRESH FISH THAT JUST ARRIVED FROM MASSALIA BY OXCART.
YOU DON'T KNOW WHERE THE ARVERNIAN WENT?
LET'S SEE... HE LEFT THIS MORNING FOR GERGOVIA, ON AN OXCART, LIKE THE FISH!
THE SUN OF MASSALIA
THAT'S TOO BAD. IF YOU'D COME EARLIER, HE'D HAVE STILL BEEN HERE.
THANKS!
THESE LUTETIANS ARE ALL CRAZY, FOR BELISAMA'S SAKE!
18

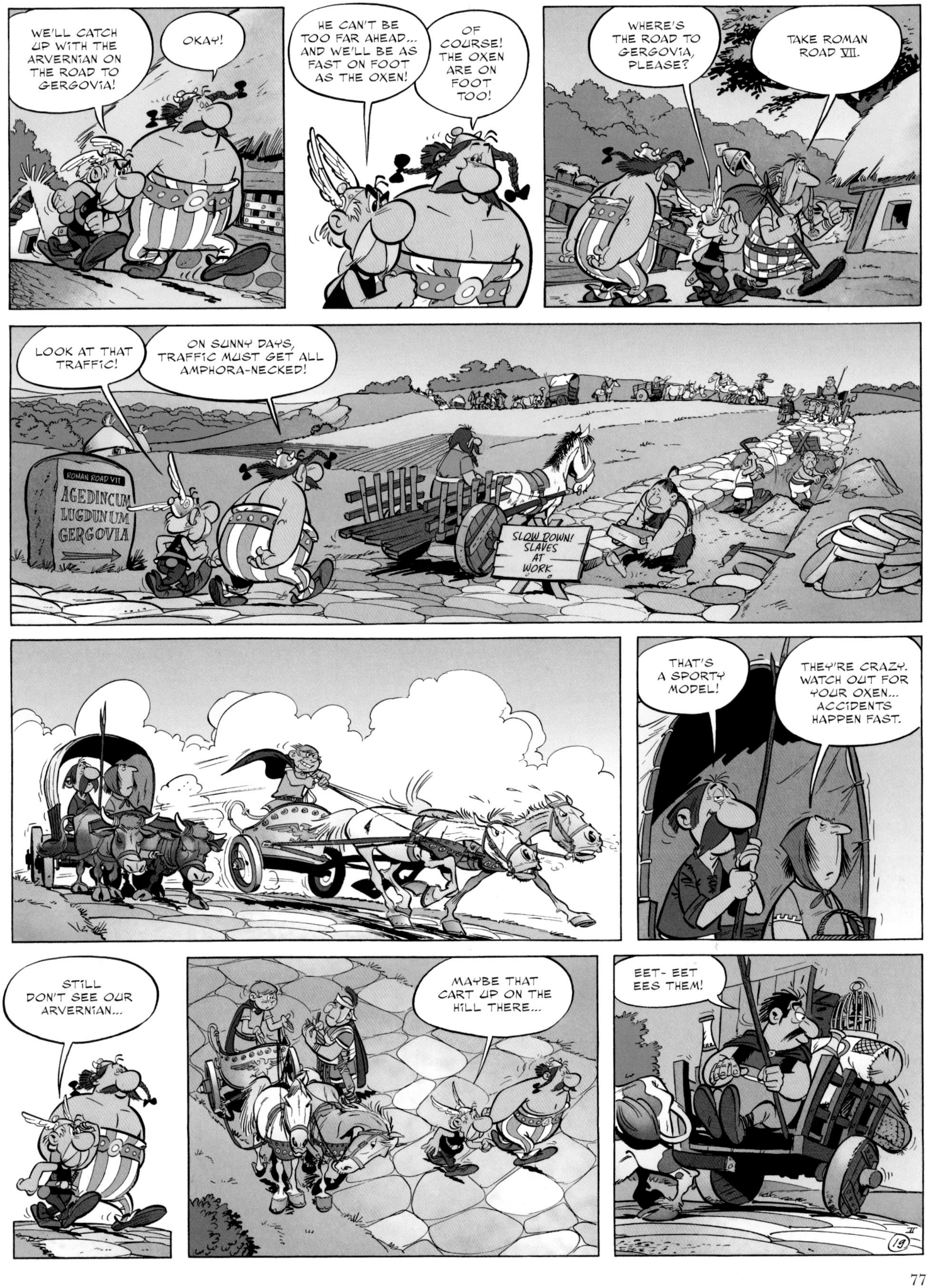
WE'LL CATCH UP WITH THE ARVERNIAN ON THE ROAD TO GERGOVIA!
OKAY!
HE CAN'T BE TOO FAR AHEAD... AND WE'LL BE AS FAST ON FOOT AS THE OXEN!
OF COURSE! THE OXEN ARE ON FOOT TOO!
WHERE'S THE ROAD TO GERGOVIA, PLEASE?
TAKE ROMAN ROAD VII.
LOOK AT THAT TRAFFIC!
ON SUNNY DAYS, TRAFFIC MUST GET ALL AMPHORA-NECKED!
ROMAN ROAD VII
AGEDINCUM
LUGDUNUM
GERGOVIA
SLOW DOWN! SLAVES AT WORK
THAT'S A SPORTY MODEL!
THEY'RE CRAZY. WATCH OUT FOR YOUR OXEN... ACCIDENTS HAPPEN FAST.
STILL DON'T SEE OUR ARVERNIAN...
MAYBE THAT CART UP ON THE HILL THERE...
EET- EET EES THEM!
II
19

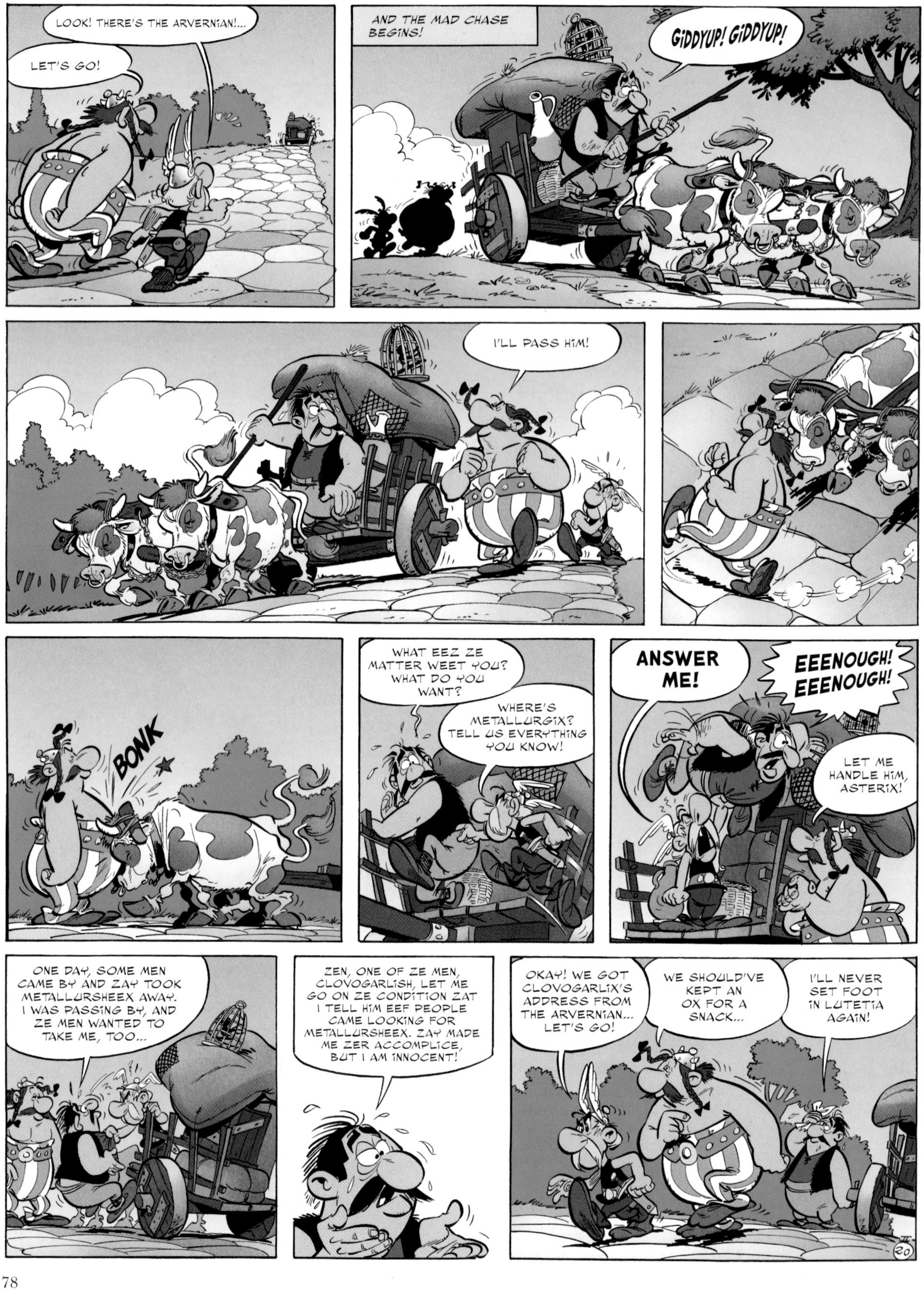
LOOK! THERE'S THE ARVERNIAN!...
LET'S GO!
AND THE MAD CHASE BEGINS!
GIDDYUP! GIDDYUP!
I'LL PASS HIM!
BONK
WHAT EEZ ZE MATTER WEET YOU? WHAT DO YOU WANT?
WHERE'S METALLURGIX? TELL US EVERYTHING YOU KNOW!
ANSWER ME!
EEENOUGH! EEENOUGH!
LET ME HANDLE HIM, ASTERIX!
ONE DAY, SOME MEN CAME BY AND ZAY TOOK METALLURSHEEX AWAY. I WAS PASSING BY, AND ZE MEN WANTED TO TAKE ME, TOO...
ZEN, ONE OF ZE MEN, CLOVOGARLISH, LET ME GO ON ZE CONDITION ZAT I TELL HIM EEF PEOPLE CAME LOOKING FOR METALLURSHEEX. ZAY MADE ME ZER ACCOMPLICE, BUT I AM INNOCENT!
OKAY! WE GOT CLOVOGARLIX'S ADDRESS FROM THE ARVERNIAN... LET'S GO!
WE SHOULD'VE KEPT AN OX FOR A SNACK...
I'LL NEVER SET FOOT IN LUTETIA AGAIN!
20

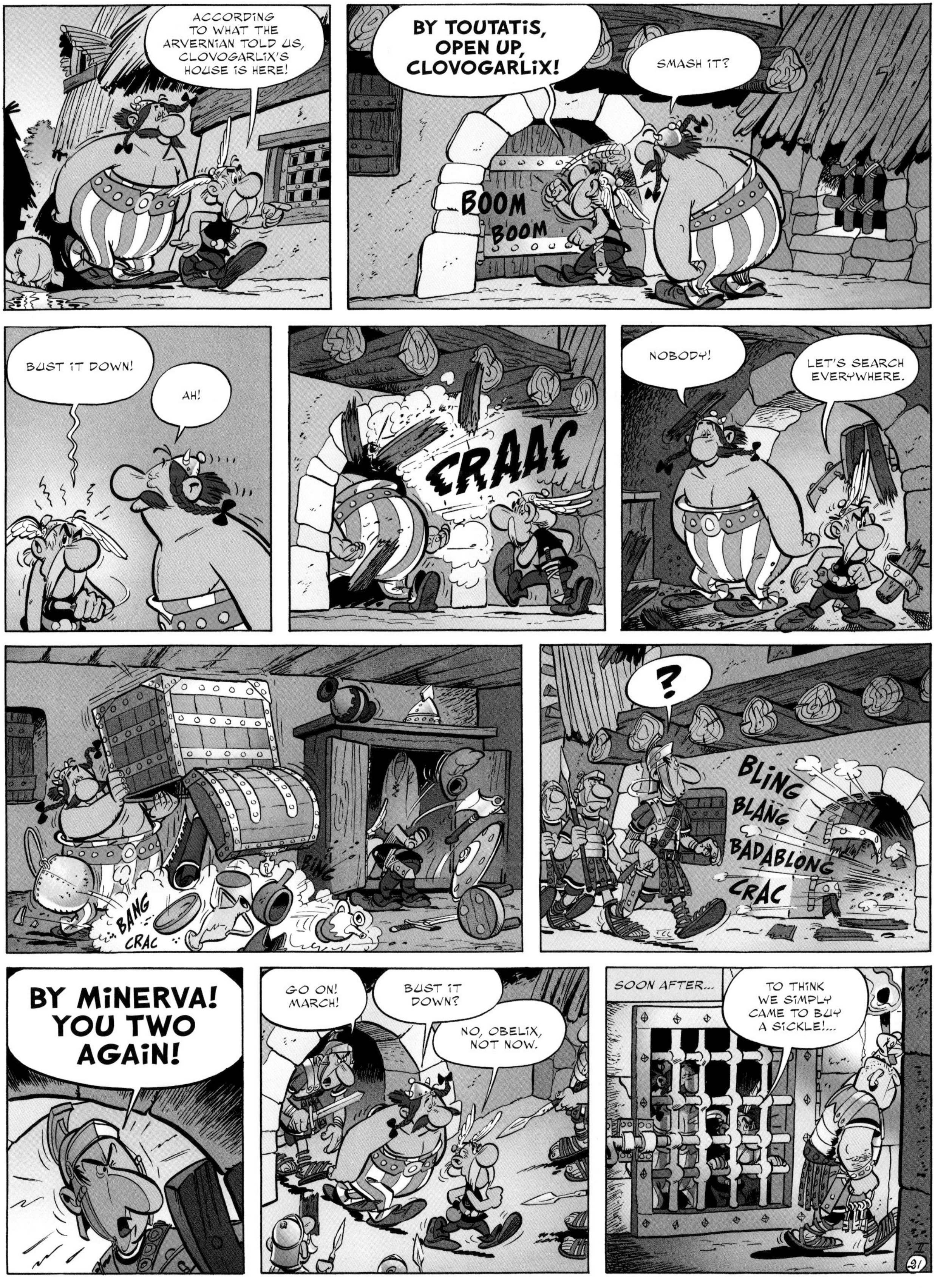
ACCORDING TO WHAT THE ARVERNIAN TOLD US, CLOVOGARLIX'S HOUSE IS HERE!
BY TOUTATIS, OPEN UP, CLOVOGARLIX!
SMASH IT?
BOOM
BOOM
BUST IT DOWN!
AH!
CRAAC
NOBODY!
LET'S SEARCH EVERYWHERE.
BING
BANG
CRAC
?
BLING
BLANG
BADABLONG
CRAC
BY MINERVA! YOU TWO AGAIN!
GO ON! MARCH!
BUST IT DOWN?
NO, OBELIX, NOT NOW.
SOON AFTER...
TO THINK WE SIMPLY CAME TO BUY A SICKLE!...
21

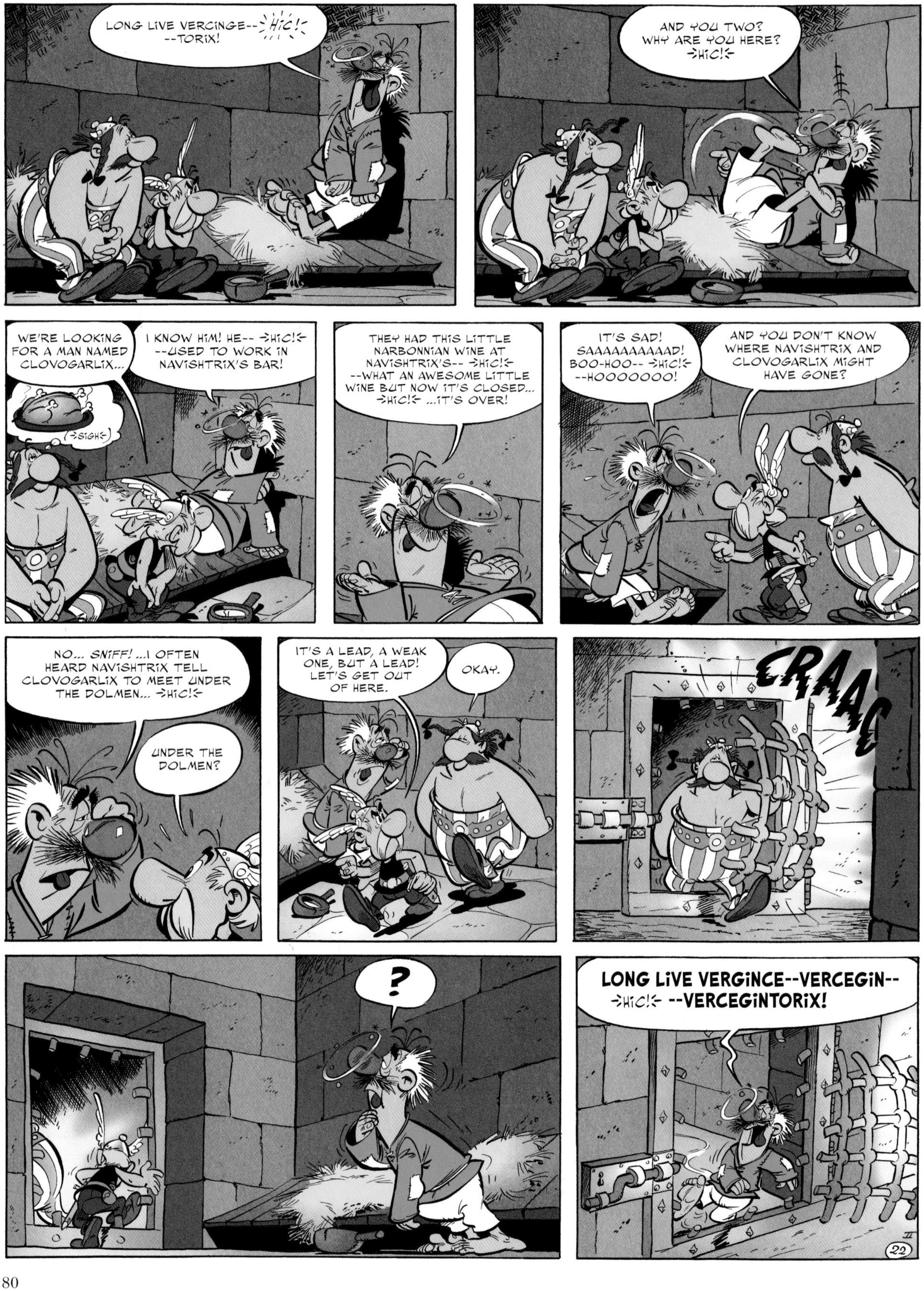

LONG LIVE VERCINGE-- HIC! --TORIX!
AND YOU TWO? WHY ARE YOU HERE? HIC!
WE'RE LOOKING FOR A MAN NAMED CLOVOGARLIX...
I KNOW HIM! HE-- HIC! --USED TO WORK IN NAVISHTRIX'S BAR!
(SIGH)
THEY HAD THIS LITTLE NARBONNIAN WINE AT NAVISHTRIX'S-- HIC! --WHAT AN AWESOME LITTLE WINE BUT NOW IT'S CLOSED... HIC! ...IT'S OVER!
IT'S SAD! SAAAAAAAAAAD! BOO-HOO-- HIC! --HOOOOOOO!
AND YOU DON'T KNOW WHERE NAVISHTRIX AND CLOVOGARLIX MIGHT HAVE GONE?
NO... SNIFF! ...I OFTEN HEARD NAVISHTRIX TELL CLOVOGARLIX TO MEET UNDER THE DOLMEN... HIC!
UNDER THE DOLMEN?
IT'S A LEAD, A WEAK ONE, BUT A LEAD! LET'S GET OUT OF HERE.
OKAY.
CRAAAC
?
LONG LIVE VERGINCE--VERCEGIN-- HIC! --VERCEGINTORIX!
22

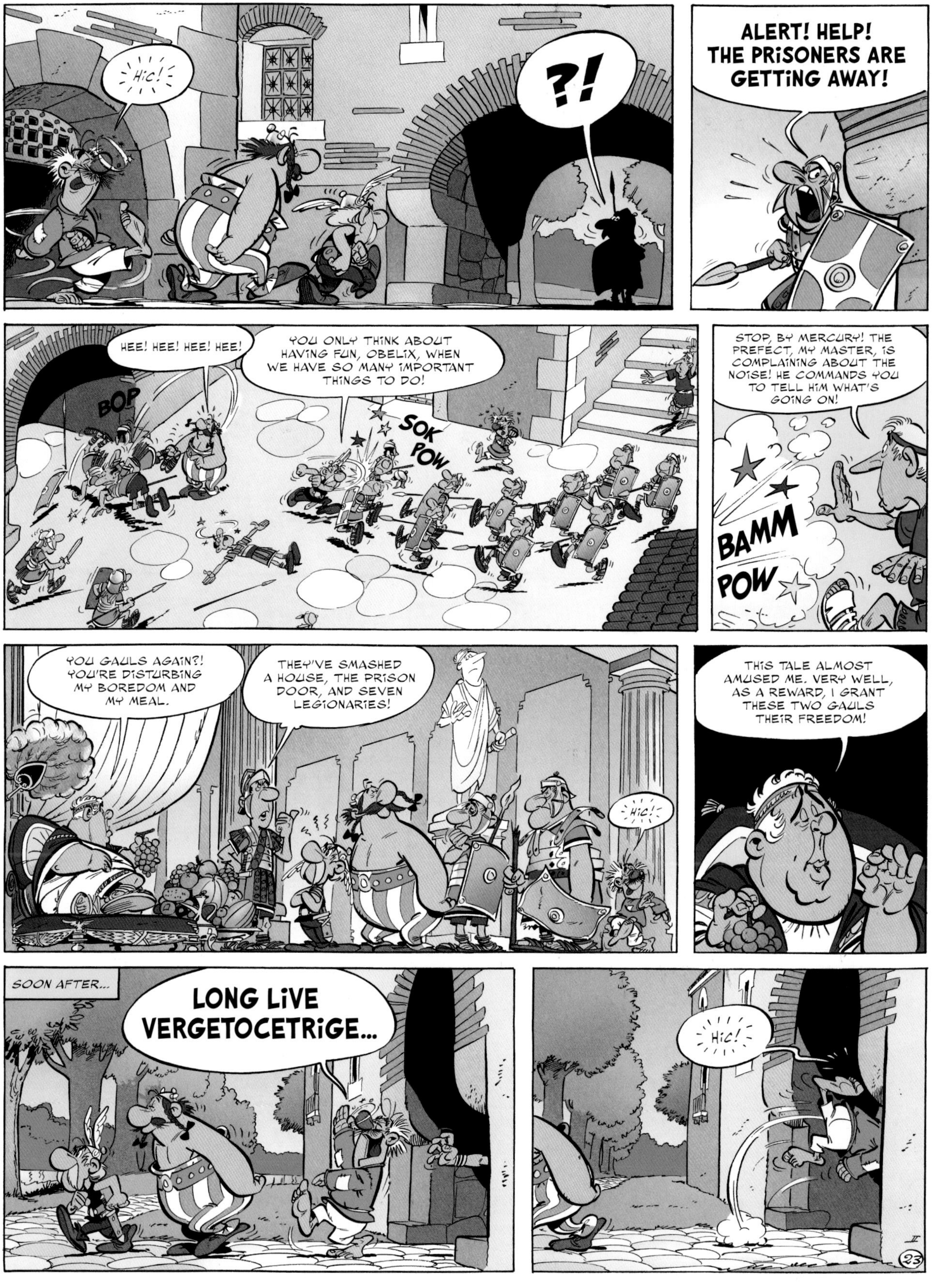

Hic!
?!
ALERT! HELP! THE PRISONERS ARE GETTING AWAY!
HEE! HEE! HEE! HEE!
YOU ONLY THINK ABOUT HAVING FUN, OBELIX, WHEN WE HAVE SO MANY IMPORTANT THINGS TO DO!
BOP
SOK
POW
STOP, BY MERCURY! THE PREFECT, MY MASTER, IS COMPLAINING ABOUT THE NOISE! HE COMMANDS YOU TO TELL HIM WHAT'S GOING ON!
BAMM
POW
YOU GAULS AGAIN?! YOU'RE DISTURBING MY BOREDOM AND MY MEAL.
THEY'VE SMASHED A HOUSE, THE PRISON DOOR, AND SEVEN LEGIONARIES!
Hic!
THIS TALE ALMOST AMUSED ME. VERY WELL, AS A REWARD, I GRANT THESE TWO GAULS THEIR FREEDOM!
SOON AFTER...
LONG LIVE VERGETOCETRIGE...
Hic!
II
23

WE'VE GOT TO FIND THE DOLMEN THAT SERVES AS CLOVOGARLIX AND NAVISHTRIX'S MEETING PLACE!

IT WON'T BE EASY...

Aquitanian Wipes GRAPEYMIX

WHO KNOWS? LUTETIANS MUST NOT HAVE MANY DOLMENS...

THE POOR THINGS!

I THINK WE CAN GET DIRECTIONS OVER THERE...

visit Lutetia

CLAUDIUS CITIBUS GUIDE

WE SPEAK LATIN
WE SPEAK CELTIC
WE SPEAK GERMANIC

YOU WANT TO TOUR OUR LOVELY CITY?

NO, WE WANT TO SEE DOLMENS!

LUTETIAN NIGHTS
THE CITY LIGHTS
NIGHTLIFE
PLEASURES
3 Sesterces

BUT WE DON'T HAVE ANY DOLMENS HERE!

(SIGH.) THE POOR THINGS!

I'M SURE THERE'S AT LEAST ONE!

TIAN NIGHTS
CITY LIGHTS
NIGHTLIFE
EASURES
Sesterces

WAIT... ACTUALLY ... I'VE HEARD ABOUT A DOLMEN THAT'D BE IN THE FOREST... THE FOREST OVER TOWARDS THE SETTING SUN...

PERFECT! LEAD US TO THAT FOREST!

NO! THERE ARE WOLVES AND BANDITS IN THAT FOREST!

WOULDN'T YOU PREFER A TOUR OF LUTETIA BY NIGHT? THREE SESTERCES, ALL THE BARLEY BEER YOU CAN DRINK!

AUDIUS ... IBUS GUIDE

NO THANKS...

LET'S GO SEARCH IN THAT FOREST OVER TOWARDS THE SETTING SUN!

ONLY ONE DOLMEN... THE POOR THINGS!

visit Lutetia CLAUDIUS CITIBUS GUIDE

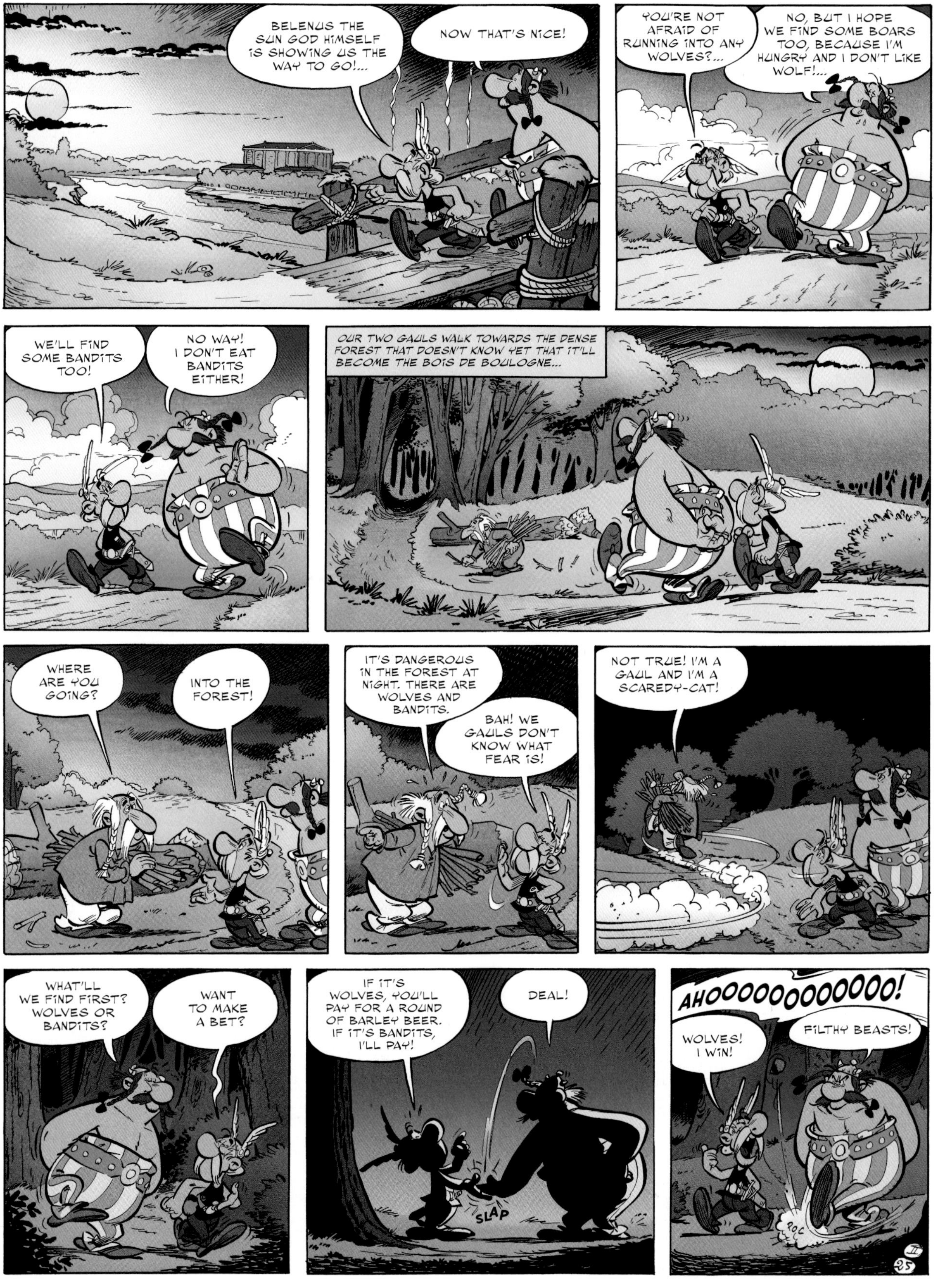

BELENUS THE SUN GOD HIMSELF IS SHOWING US THE WAY TO GO!...
NOW THAT'S NICE!
YOU'RE NOT AFRAID OF RUNNING INTO ANY WOLVES?...
NO, BUT I HOPE WE FIND SOME BOARS TOO, BECAUSE I'M HUNGRY AND I DON'T LIKE WOLF!...
WE'LL FIND SOME BANDITS TOO!
NO WAY! I DON'T EAT BANDITS EITHER!
OUR TWO GAULS WALK TOWARDS THE DENSE FOREST THAT DOESN'T KNOW YET THAT IT'LL BECOME THE BOIS DE BOULOGNE...
WHERE ARE YOU GOING?
INTO THE FOREST!
IT'S DANGEROUS IN THE FOREST AT NIGHT. THERE ARE WOLVES AND BANDITS.
BAH! WE GAULS DON'T KNOW WHAT FEAR IS!
NOT TRUE! I'M A GAUL AND I'M A SCAREDY-CAT!
WHAT'LL WE FIND FIRST? WOLVES OR BANDITS?
WANT TO MAKE A BET?
IF IT'S WOLVES, YOU'LL PAY FOR A ROUND OF BARLEY BEER. IF IT'S BANDITS, I'LL PAY!
DEAL!
SLAP
AHOOOOOOOOOOOO!
WOLVES! I WIN!
FILTHY BEASTS!
POC

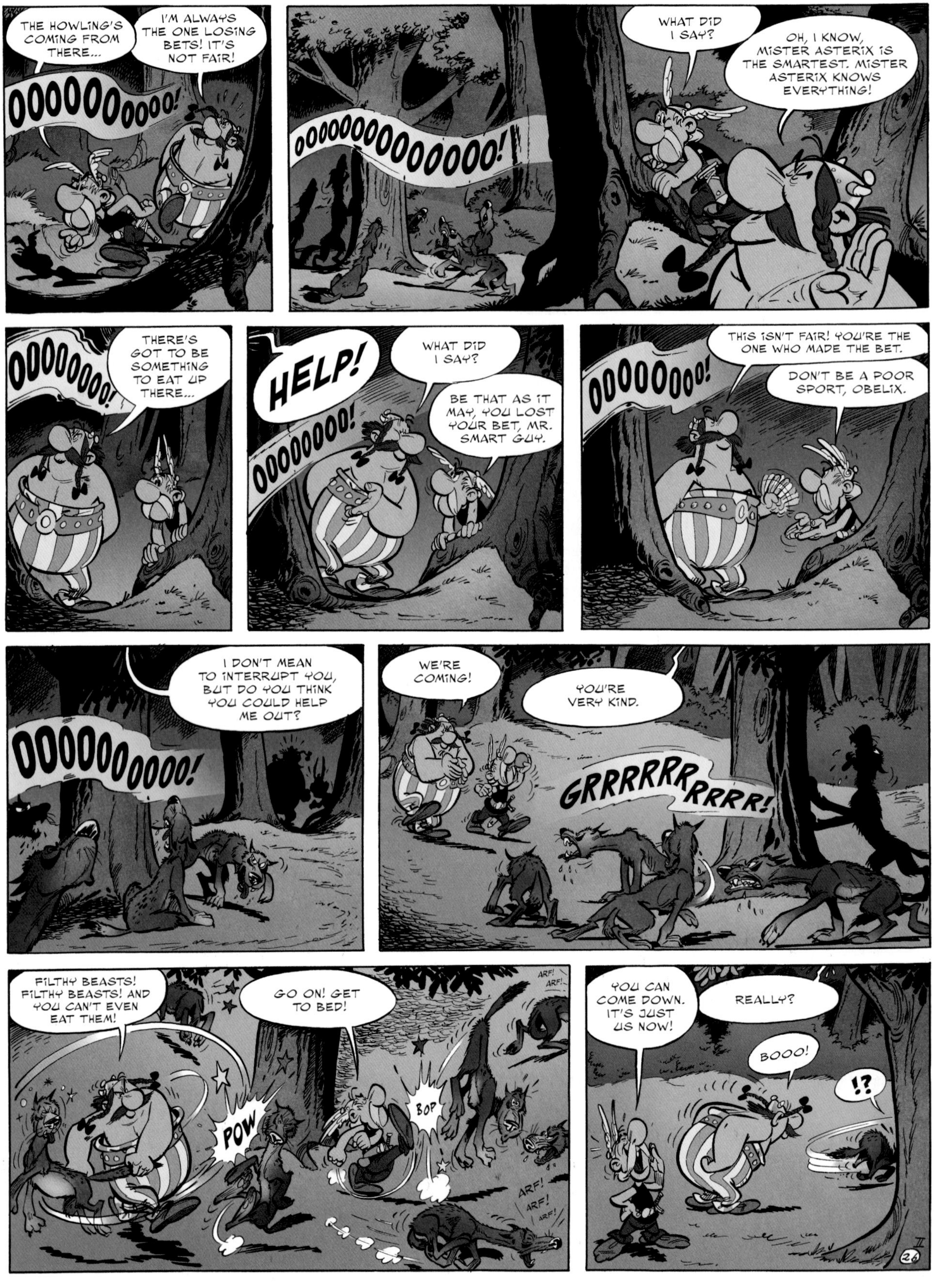
THE HOWLING'S COMING FROM THERE...
I'M ALWAYS THE ONE LOSING BETS! IT'S NOT FAIR!
OOOOOOoooo!
oOOOOOOOOOOOOO!
WHAT DID I SAY?
OH, I KNOW, MISTER ASTERIX IS THE SMARTEST. MISTER ASTERIX KNOWS EVERYTHING!
OOOOOOOOo!
THERE'S GOT TO BE SOMETHING TO EAT UP THERE...
HELP!
WHAT DID I SAY?
OOOOOOOO!
BE THAT AS IT MAY, YOU LOST YOUR BET, MR. SMART GUY.
OOOOOOOoo!
THIS ISN'T FAIR! YOU'RE THE ONE WHO MADE THE BET.
DON'T BE A POOR SPORT, OBELIX.
I DON'T MEAN TO INTERRUPT YOU, BUT DO YOU THINK YOU COULD HELP ME OUT?
OOOOOOOoooo!
WE'RE COMING!
YOU'RE VERY KIND.
GRRRRRRRRRR!
FILTHY BEASTS! FILTHY BEASTS! AND YOU CAN'T EVEN EAT THEM!
GO ON! GET TO BED!
ARF! ARF!
POW
BOP
ARF! ARF! ARF!
YOU CAN COME DOWN. IT'S JUST US NOW!
REALLY?
BOOO!
!?
26

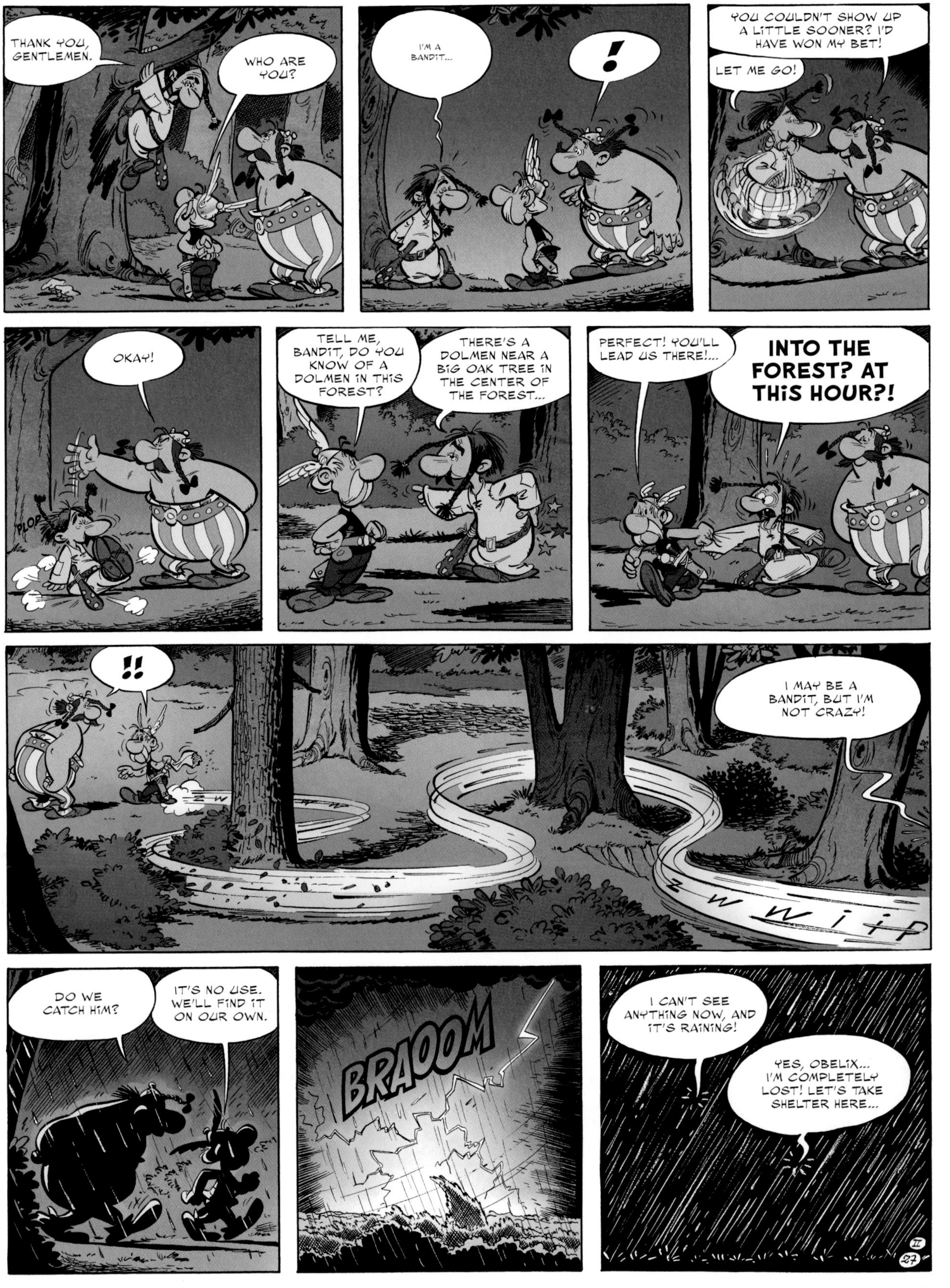

THANK YOU, GENTLEMEN.
WHO ARE YOU?
I'M A BANDIT...
!
YOU COULDN'T SHOW UP A LITTLE SOONER? I'D HAVE WON MY BET!
LET ME GO!
OKAY!
PLOP
TELL ME, BANDIT, DO YOU KNOW OF A DOLMEN IN THIS FOREST?
THERE'S A DOLMEN NEAR A BIG OAK TREE IN THE CENTER OF THE FOREST...
PERFECT! YOU'LL LEAD US THERE!...
INTO THE FOREST? AT THIS HOUR?!
!!
I MAY BE A BANDIT, BUT I'M NOT CRAZY!
ZWWIT
DO WE CATCH HIM?
IT'S NO USE. WE'LL FIND IT ON OUR OWN.
BRAOOM
I CAN'T SEE ANYTHING NOW, AND IT'S RAINING!
YES, OBELIX... I'M COMPLETELY LOST! LET'S TAKE SHELTER HERE...
II 27

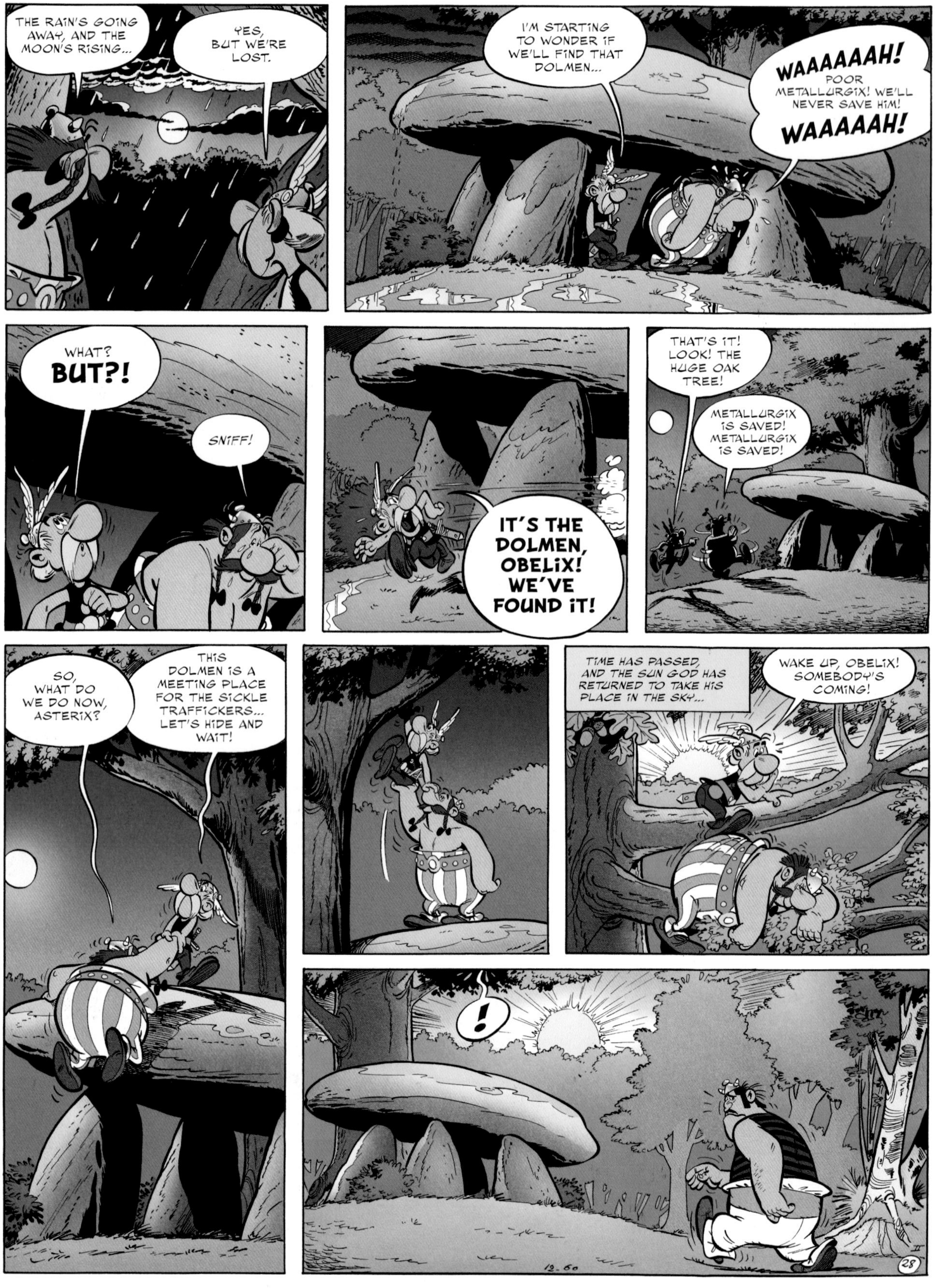
THE RAIN'S GOING AWAY, AND THE MOON'S RISING...
YES, BUT WE'RE LOST.
I'M STARTING TO WONDER IF WE'LL FIND THAT DOLMEN...
WAAAAAAH! POOR METALLURGIX! WE'LL NEVER SAVE HIM! WAAAAAH!
WHAT? BUT?!
SNIFF!
IT'S THE DOLMEN, OBELIX! WE'VE FOUND IT!
THAT'S IT! LOOK! THE HUGE OAK TREE!
METALLURGIX IS SAVED! METALLURGIX IS SAVED!
SO, WHAT DO WE DO NOW, ASTERIX?
THIS DOLMEN IS A MEETING PLACE FOR THE SICKLE TRAFFICKERS... LET'S HIDE AND WAIT!
TIME HAS PASSED, AND THE SUN GOD HAS RETURNED TO TAKE HIS PLACE IN THE SKY...
WAKE UP, OBELIX! SOMEBODY'S COMING!
!
28

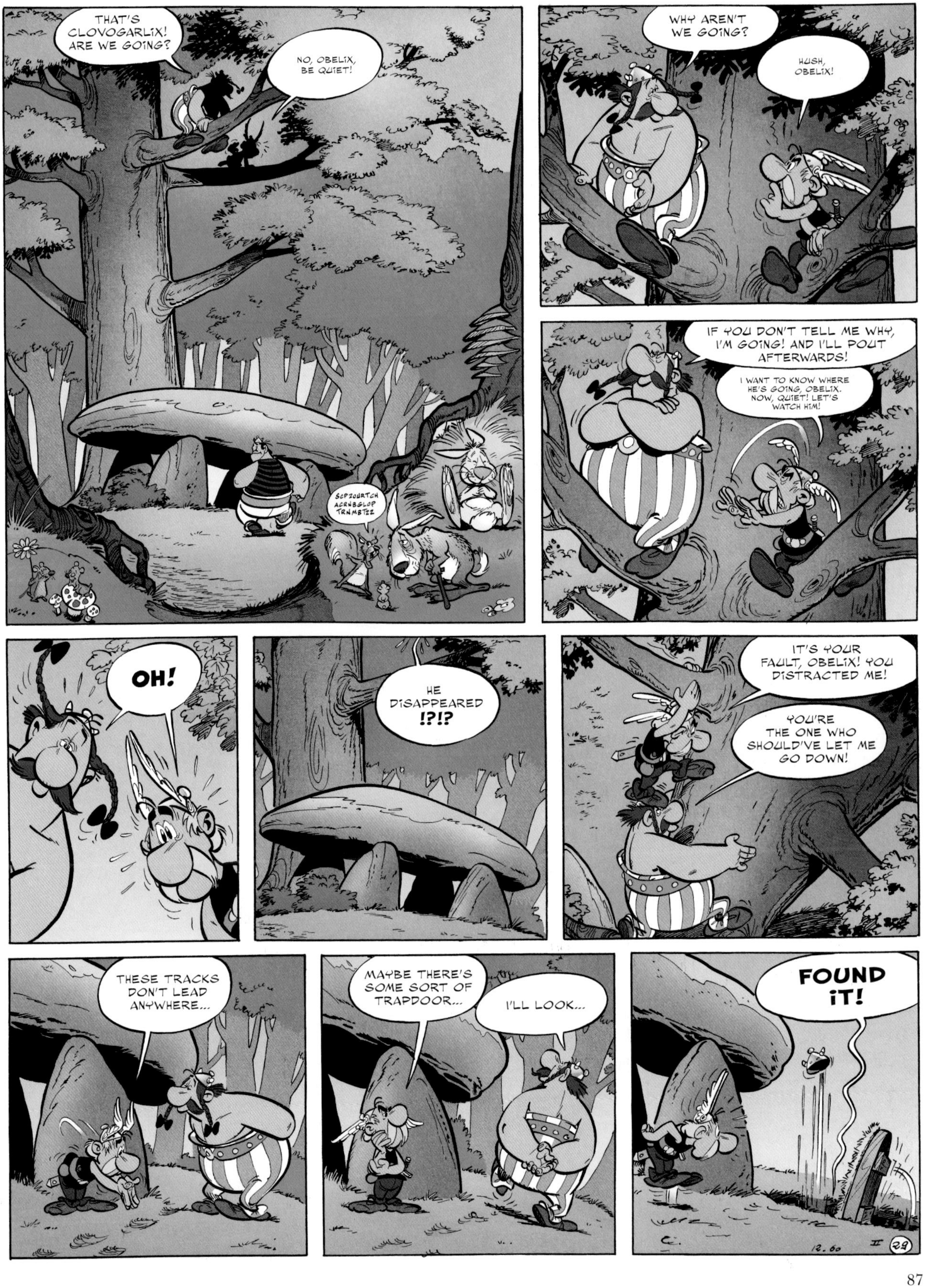

THAT'S CLOVOGARLIX! ARE WE GOING?
NO, OBELIX, BE QUIET!
SCPZOURTCH ACRNBGLOP TRNMBTZZ
WHY AREN'T WE GOING?
HUSH, OBELIX!
IF YOU DON'T TELL ME WHY, I'M GOING! AND I'LL POUT AFTERWARDS!
I WANT TO KNOW WHERE HE'S GOING, OBELIX. NOW, QUIET! LET'S WATCH HIM!
OH!
HE DISAPPEARED !?!?
IT'S YOUR FAULT, OBELIX! YOU DISTRACTED ME!
YOU'RE THE ONE WHO SHOULD'VE LET ME GO DOWN!
THESE TRACKS DON'T LEAD ANYWHERE...
MAYBE THERE'S SOME SORT OF TRAPDOOR...
I'LL LOOK...
FOUND IT!
12.60
II 29

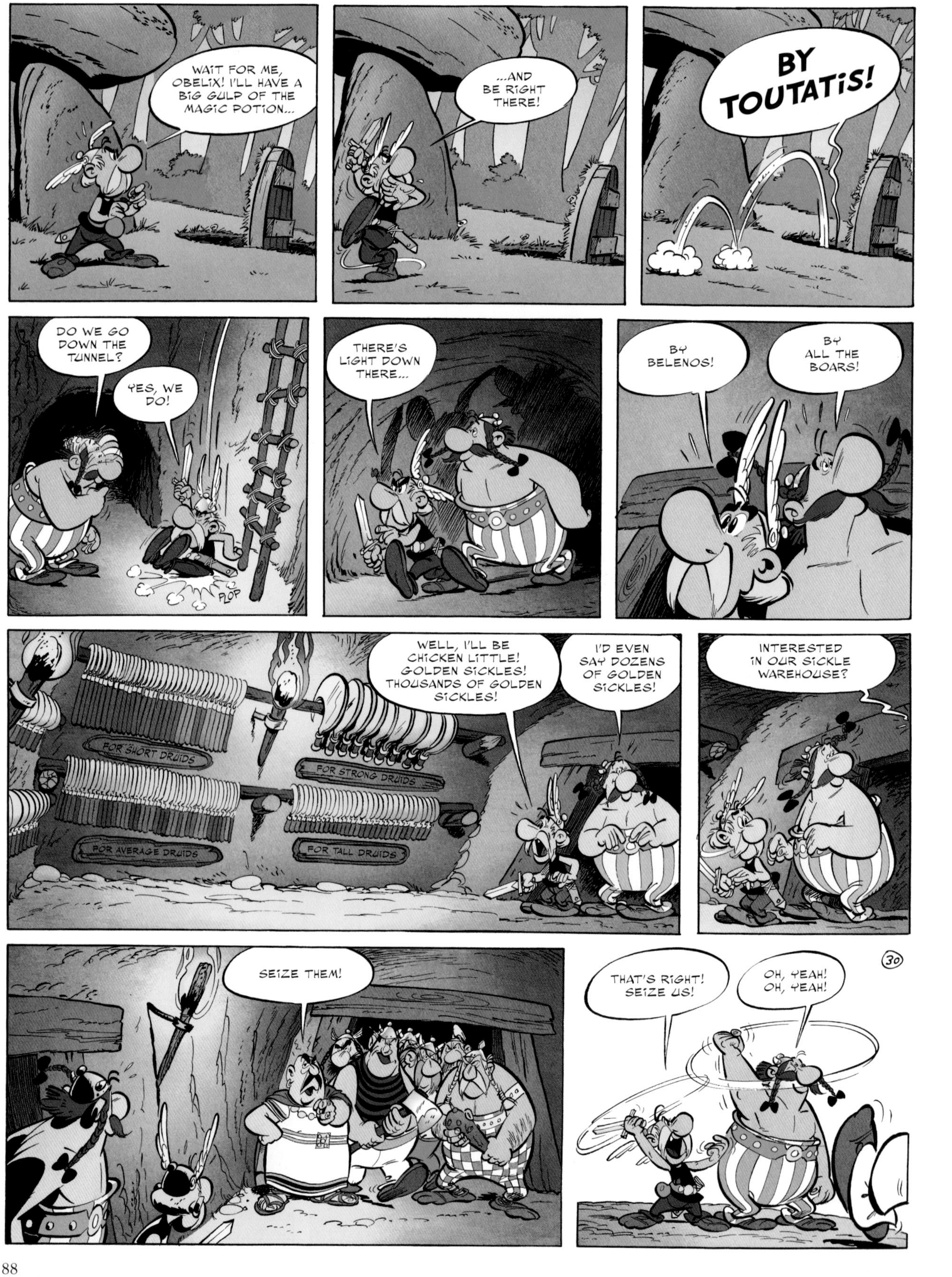
WAIT FOR ME, OBELIX! I'LL HAVE A BIG GULP OF THE MAGIC POTION...
...AND BE RIGHT THERE!
BY TOUTATIS!
DO WE GO DOWN THE TUNNEL?
YES, WE DO!
PLOP
THERE'S LIGHT DOWN THERE...
BY BELENOS!
BY ALL THE BOARS!
FOR SHORT DRUIDS
FOR STRONG DRUIDS
FOR AVERAGE DRUIDS
FOR TALL DRUIDS
WELL, I'LL BE CHICKEN LITTLE! GOLDEN SICKLES! THOUSANDS OF GOLDEN SICKLES!
I'D EVEN SAY DOZENS OF GOLDEN SICKLES!
INTERESTED IN OUR SICKLE WAREHOUSE?
SEIZE THEM!
30
THAT'S RIGHT! SEIZE US!
OH, YEAH! OH, YEAH!

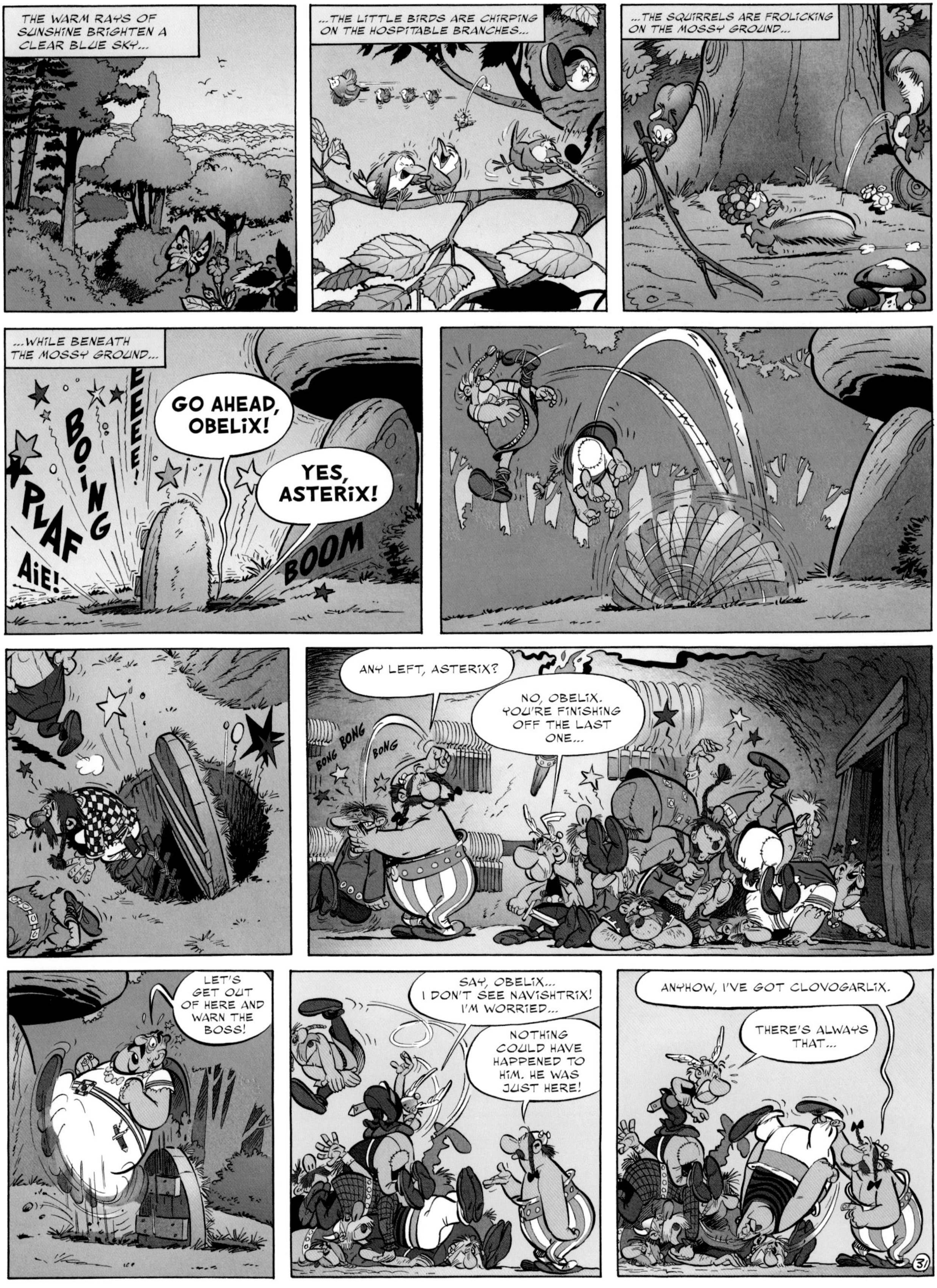
THE WARM RAYS OF SUNSHINE BRIGHTEN A CLEAR BLUE SKY...
...THE LITTLE BIRDS ARE CHIRPING ON THE HOSPITABLE BRANCHES...
...THE SQUIRRELS ARE FROLICKING ON THE MOSSY GROUND...
...WHILE BENEATH THE MOSSY GROUND...
EEEE!
GO AHEAD, OBELIX!
YES, ASTERIX!
BOING
PLAF
AIE!
BOOM
ANY LEFT, ASTERIX?
NO, OBELIX. YOU'RE FINISHING OFF THE LAST ONE...
BONG BONG BONG
LET'S GET OUT OF HERE AND WARN THE BOSS!
SAY, OBELIX... I DON'T SEE NAVISHTRIX! I'M WORRIED...
NOTHING COULD HAVE HAPPENED TO HIM. HE WAS JUST HERE!
ANYHOW, I'VE GOT CLOVOGARLIX.
THERE'S ALWAYS THAT...
31

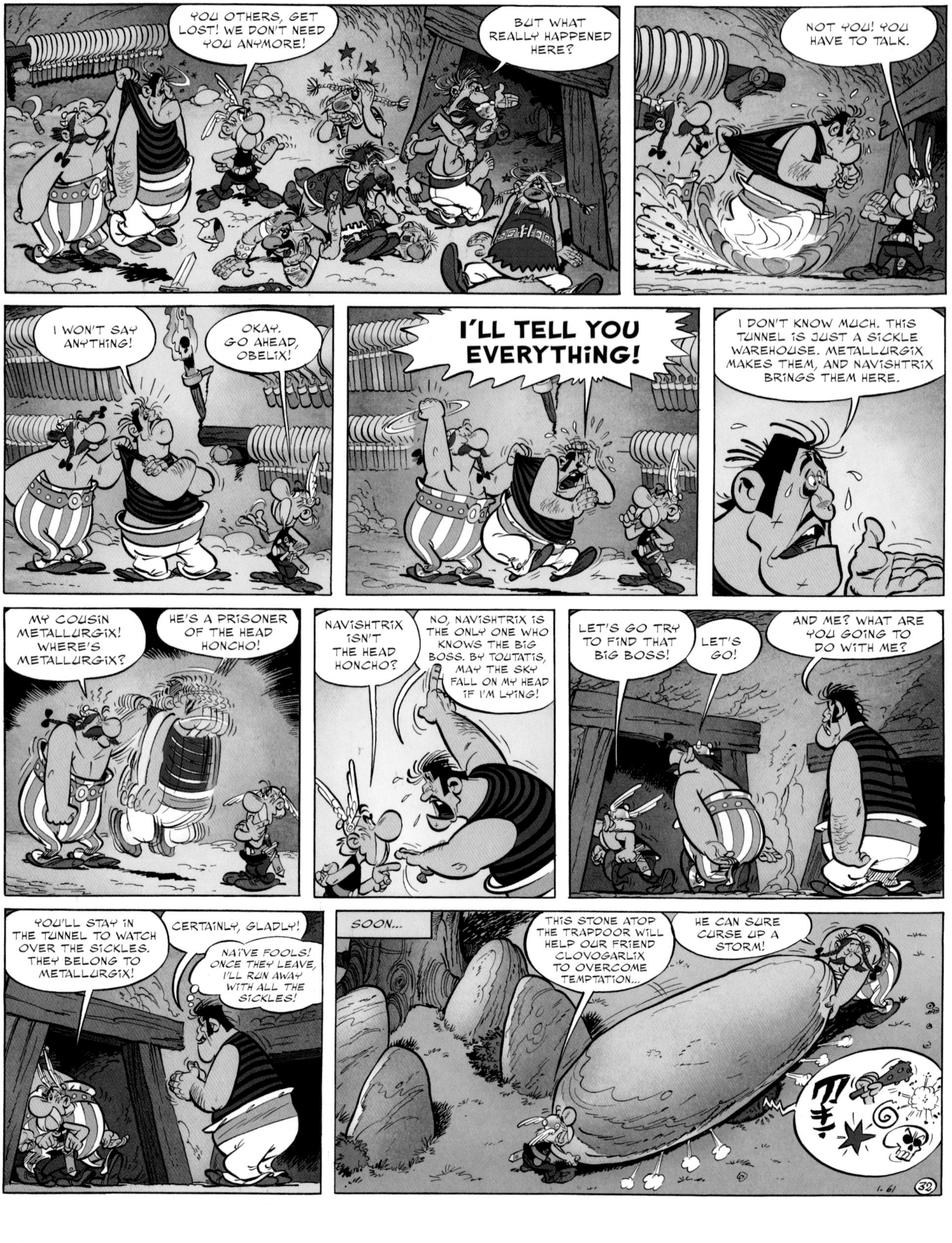

YOU OTHERS, GET LOST! WE DON'T NEED YOU ANYMORE!
BUT WHAT REALLY HAPPENED HERE?
NOT YOU! YOU HAVE TO TALK.
I WON'T SAY ANYTHING!
OKAY. GO AHEAD, OBELIX!
I'LL TELL YOU EVERYTHING!
I DON'T KNOW MUCH. THIS TUNNEL IS JUST A SICKLE WAREHOUSE. METALLURGIX MAKES THEM, AND NAVISHTRIX BRINGS THEM HERE.
MY COUSIN METALLURGIX! WHERE'S METALLURGIX?
HE'S A PRISONER OF THE HEAD HONCHO!
NAVISHTRIX ISN'T THE HEAD HONCHO?
NO, NAVISHTRIX IS THE ONLY ONE WHO KNOWS THE BIG BOSS. BY TOUTATIS, MAY THE SKY FALL ON MY HEAD IF I'M LYING!
LET'S GO TRY TO FIND THAT BIG BOSS!
LET'S GO!
AND ME? WHAT ARE YOU GOING TO DO WITH ME?
YOU'LL STAY IN THE TUNNEL TO WATCH OVER THE SICKLES. THEY BELONG TO METALLURGIX!
CERTAINLY, GLADLY!
NAÏVE FOOLS! ONCE THEY LEAVE, I'LL RUN AWAY WITH ALL THE SICKLES!
SOON...
THIS STONE ATOP THE TRAPDOOR WILL HELP OUR FRIEND CLOVOGARLIX TO OVERCOME TEMPTATION...
HE CAN SURE CURSE UP A STORM!
1.61
32

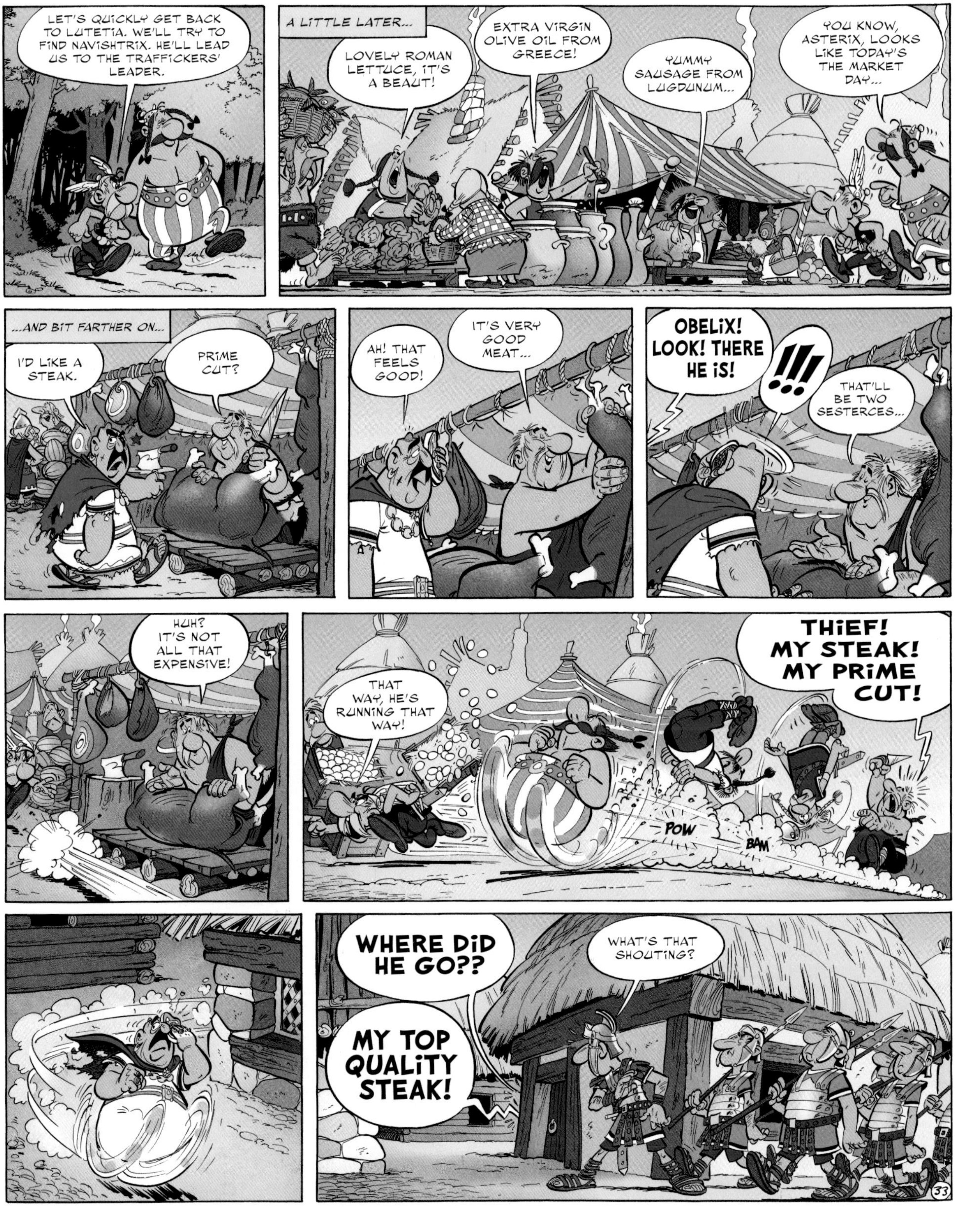

LET'S QUICKLY GET BACK TO LUTETIA. WE'LL TRY TO FIND NAVISHTRIX. HE'LL LEAD US TO THE TRAFFICKERS' LEADER.
A LITTLE LATER...
LOVELY ROMAN LETTUCE, IT'S A BEAUT!
EXTRA VIRGIN OLIVE OIL FROM GREECE!
YUMMY SAUSAGE FROM LUGDUNUM...
YOU KNOW, ASTERIX, LOOKS LIKE TODAY'S THE MARKET DAY...
...AND BIT FARTHER ON...
I'D LIKE A STEAK.
PRIME CUT?
AH! THAT FEELS GOOD!
IT'S VERY GOOD MEAT...
OBELIX! LOOK! THERE HE IS!
!!!
THAT'LL BE TWO SESTERCES...
HUH? IT'S NOT ALL THAT EXPENSIVE!
THAT WAY, HE'S RUNNING THAT WAY!
THIEF! MY STEAK! MY PRIME CUT!
POW
BAM
WHERE DID HE GO??
MY TOP QUALITY STEAK!
WHAT'S THAT SHOUTING?
33

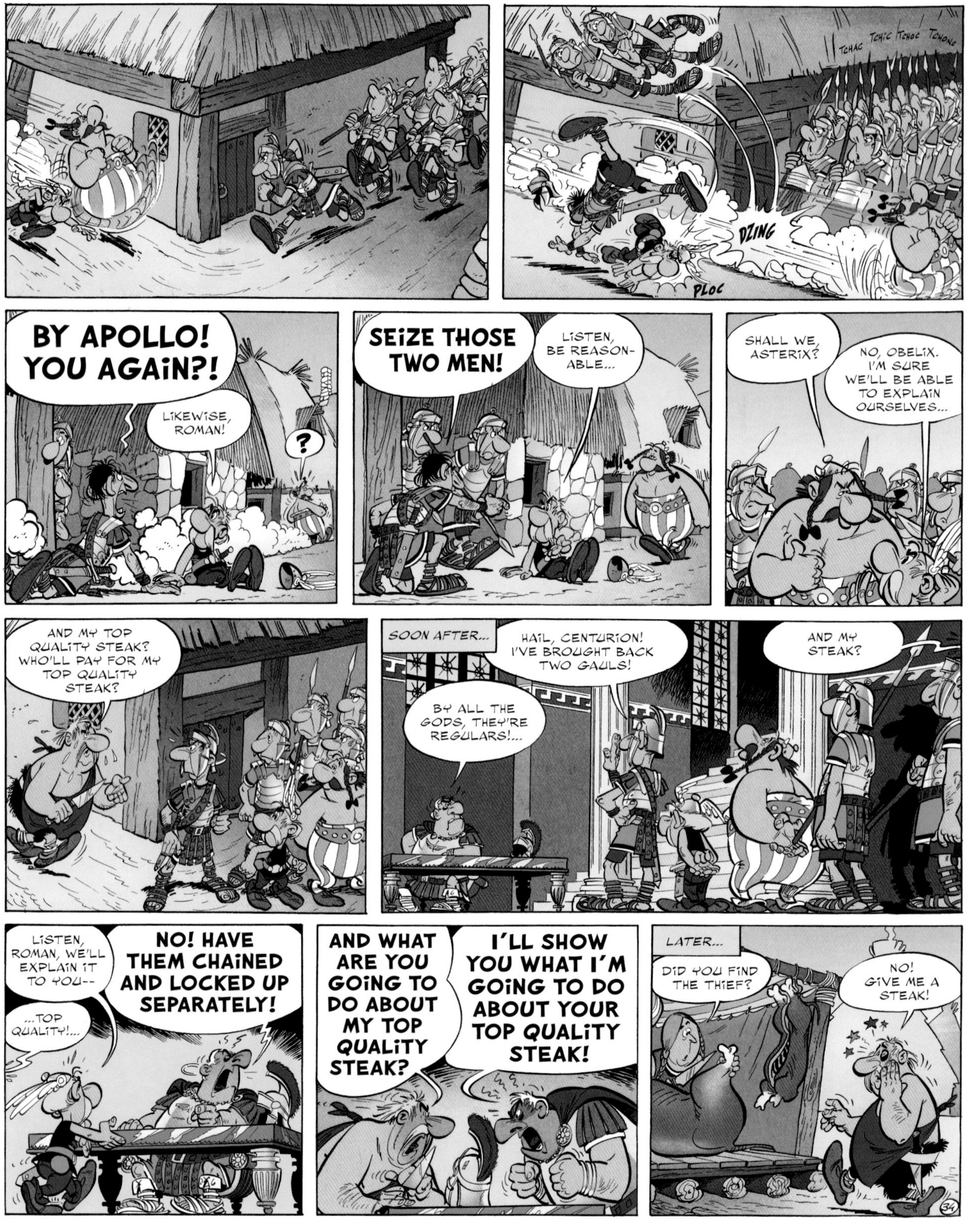

TCHAC TCHIC TCHOC TCHONG
DZING
PLOC
BY APOLLO! YOU AGAIN?!
LIKEWISE, ROMAN!
?
SEIZE THOSE TWO MEN!
LISTEN, BE REASON-ABLE...
SHALL WE, ASTERIX?
NO, OBELIX. I'M SURE WE'LL BE ABLE TO EXPLAIN OURSELVES...
AND MY TOP QUALITY STEAK? WHO'LL PAY FOR MY TOP QUALITY STEAK?
SOON AFTER...
HAIL, CENTURION! I'VE BROUGHT BACK TWO GAULS!
AND MY STEAK?
BY ALL THE GODS, THEY'RE REGULARS!...
LISTEN, ROMAN, WE'LL EXPLAIN IT TO YOU--
NO! HAVE THEM CHAINED AND LOCKED UP SEPARATELY!
...TOP QUALITY!...
AND WHAT ARE YOU GOING TO DO ABOUT MY TOP QUALITY STEAK?
I'LL SHOW YOU WHAT I'M GOING TO DO ABOUT YOUR TOP QUALITY STEAK!
LATER...
DID YOU FIND THE THIEF?
NO! GIVE ME A STEAK!
34

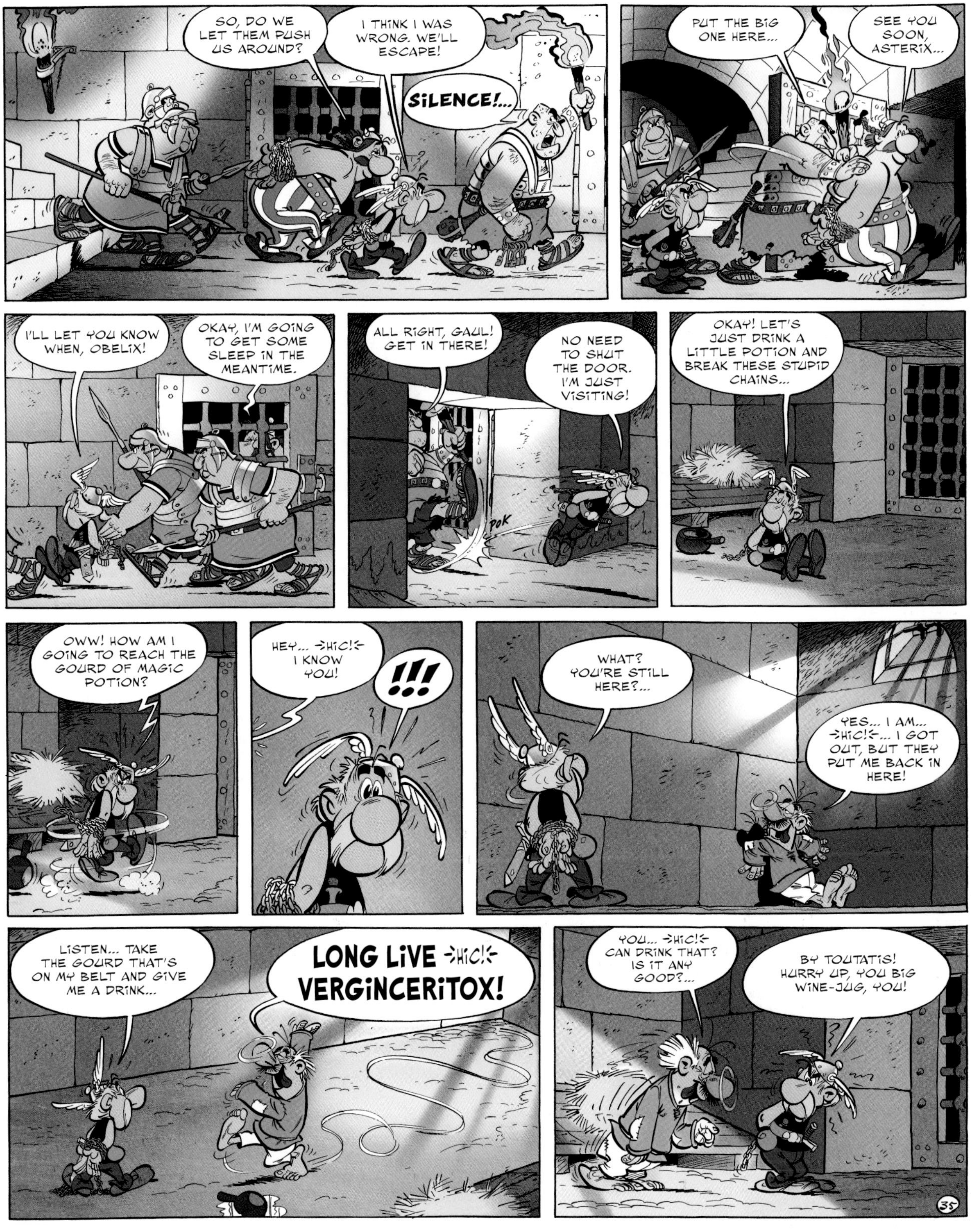

SO, DO WE LET THEM PUSH US AROUND?
I THINK I WAS WRONG. WE'LL ESCAPE!
SILENCE!...
PUT THE BIG ONE HERE...
SEE YOU SOON, ASTERIX...
I'LL LET YOU KNOW WHEN, OBELIX!
OKAY, I'M GOING TO GET SOME SLEEP IN THE MEANTIME.
ALL RIGHT, GAUL! GET IN THERE!
NO NEED TO SHUT THE DOOR. I'M JUST VISITING!
POK
OKAY! LET'S JUST DRINK A LITTLE POTION AND BREAK THESE STUPID CHAINS...
OWW! HOW AM I GOING TO REACH THE GOURD OF MAGIC POTION?
HEY... HIC! I KNOW YOU!
!!!
WHAT? YOU'RE STILL HERE?...
YES... I AM... HIC!... I GOT OUT, BUT THEY PUT ME BACK IN HERE!
LISTEN... TAKE THE GOURD THAT'S ON MY BELT AND GIVE ME A DRINK...
LONG LIVE HIC! VERGINCERITOX!
YOU... HIC! CAN DRINK THAT? IS IT ANY GOOD?...
BY TOUTATIS! HURRY UP, YOU BIG WINE-JUG, YOU!
35

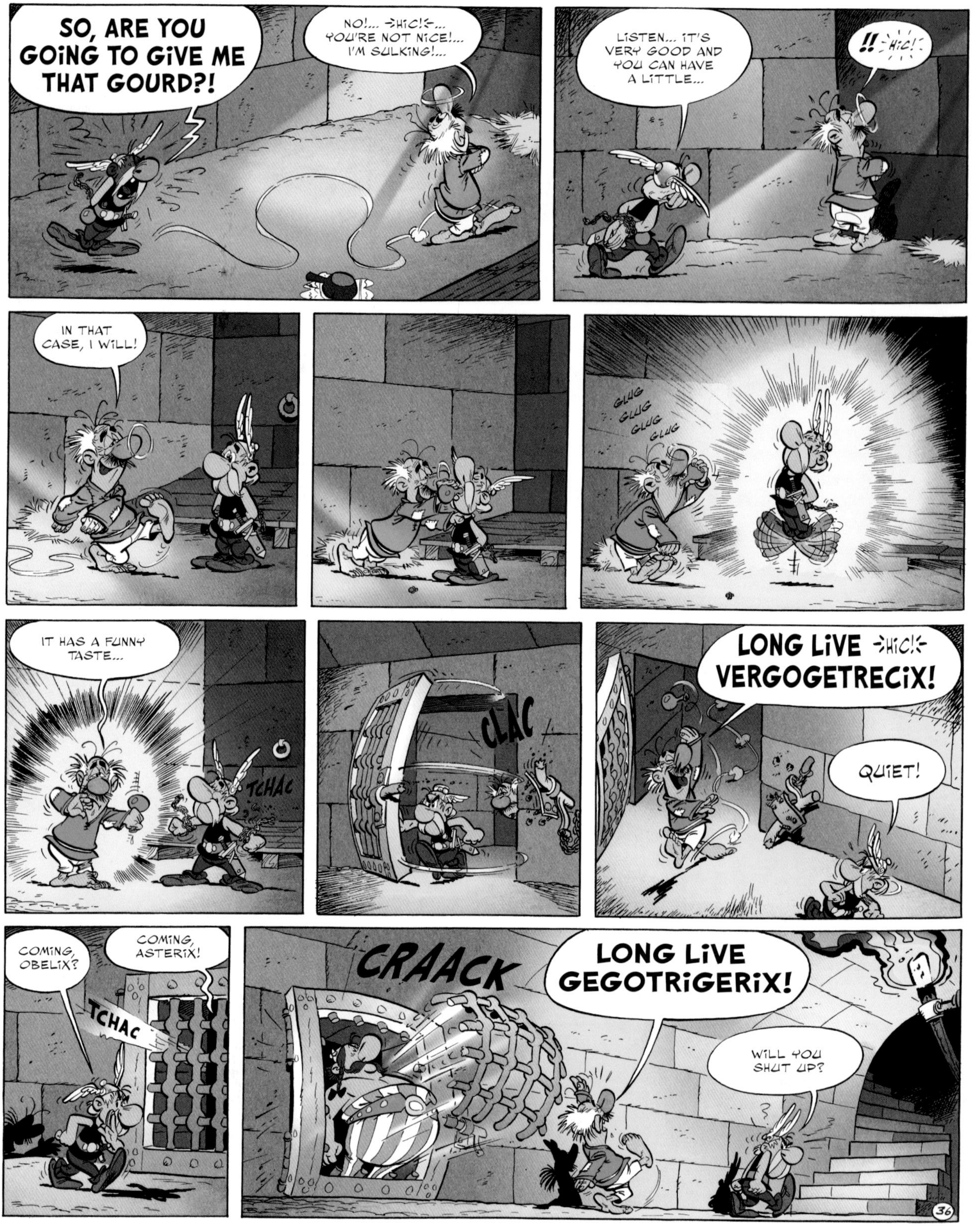
SO, ARE YOU GOING TO GIVE ME THAT GOURD?!
NO!... HIC!... YOU'RE NOT NICE!... I'M SULKING!...
LISTEN... IT'S VERY GOOD AND YOU CAN HAVE A LITTLE...
!! HIC!
IN THAT CASE, I WILL!
GLUG GLUG GLUG GLUG
IT HAS A FUNNY TASTE...
TCHAC
CLAC
LONG LIVE HIC! VERGOGETRECIX!
QUIET!
COMING, OBELIX?
COMING, ASTERIX!
TCHAC
CRAACK
LONG LIVE GEGOTRIGERIX!
WILL YOU SHUT UP?
36

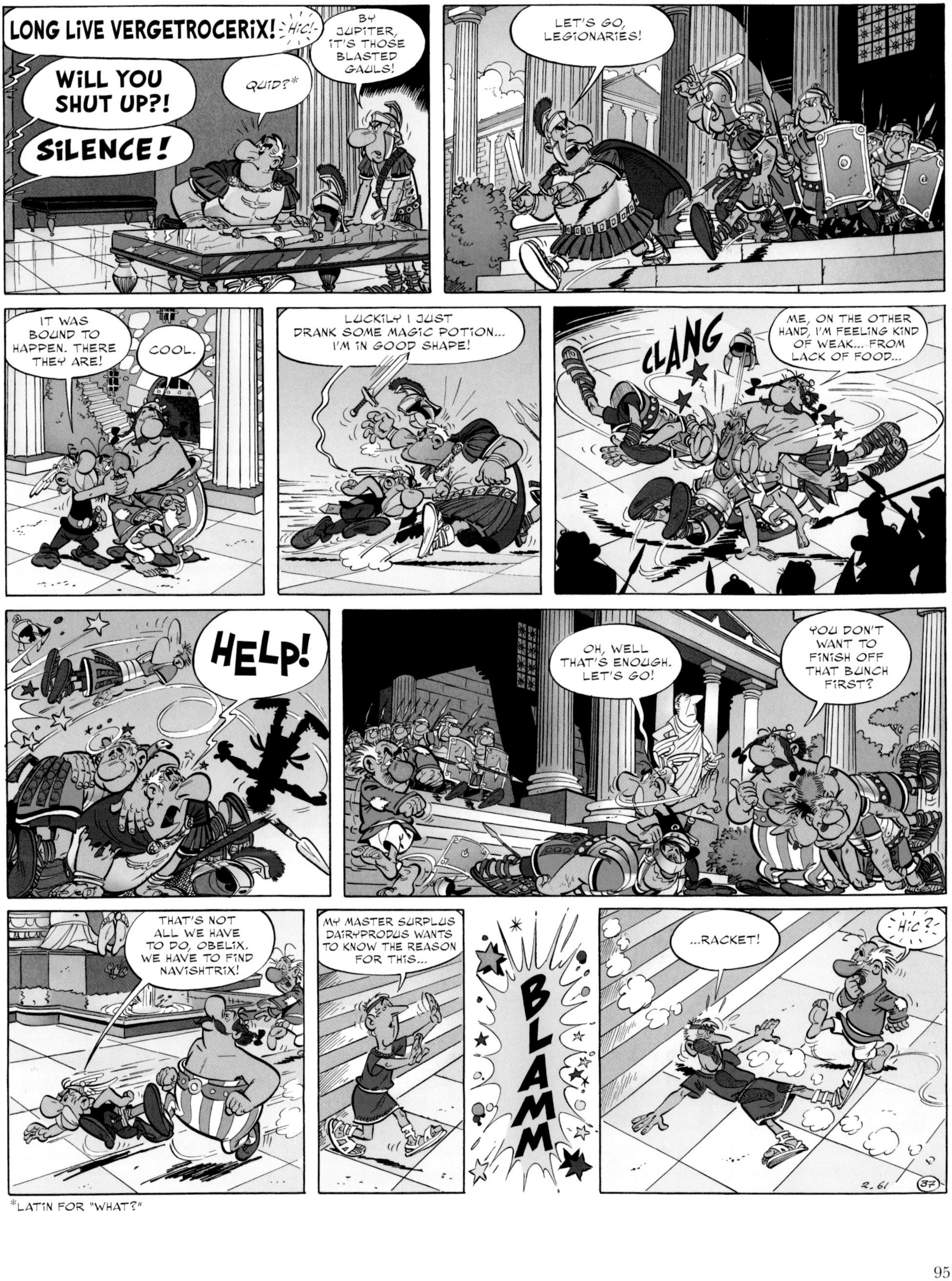
LONG LIVE VERGETROCERIX!
HIC!
WILL YOU SHUT UP?!
SILENCE!
QUID?*
BY JUPITER, IT'S THOSE BLASTED GAULS!
LET'S GO, LEGIONARIES!
IT WAS BOUND TO HAPPEN. THERE THEY ARE!
COOL.
LUCKILY I JUST DRANK SOME MAGIC POTION... I'M IN GOOD SHAPE!
CLANG
ME, ON THE OTHER HAND, I'M FEELING KIND OF WEAK... FROM LACK OF FOOD...
HELP!
OH, WELL THAT'S ENOUGH. LET'S GO!
YOU DON'T WANT TO FINISH OFF THAT BUNCH FIRST?
THAT'S NOT ALL WE HAVE TO DO, OBELIX. WE HAVE TO FIND NAVISHTRIX!
MY MASTER SURPLUS DAIRYPRODUS WANTS TO KNOW THE REASON FOR THIS...
BLAMM
...RACKET!
HIC?
2.61
37

*LATIN FOR "WHAT?"

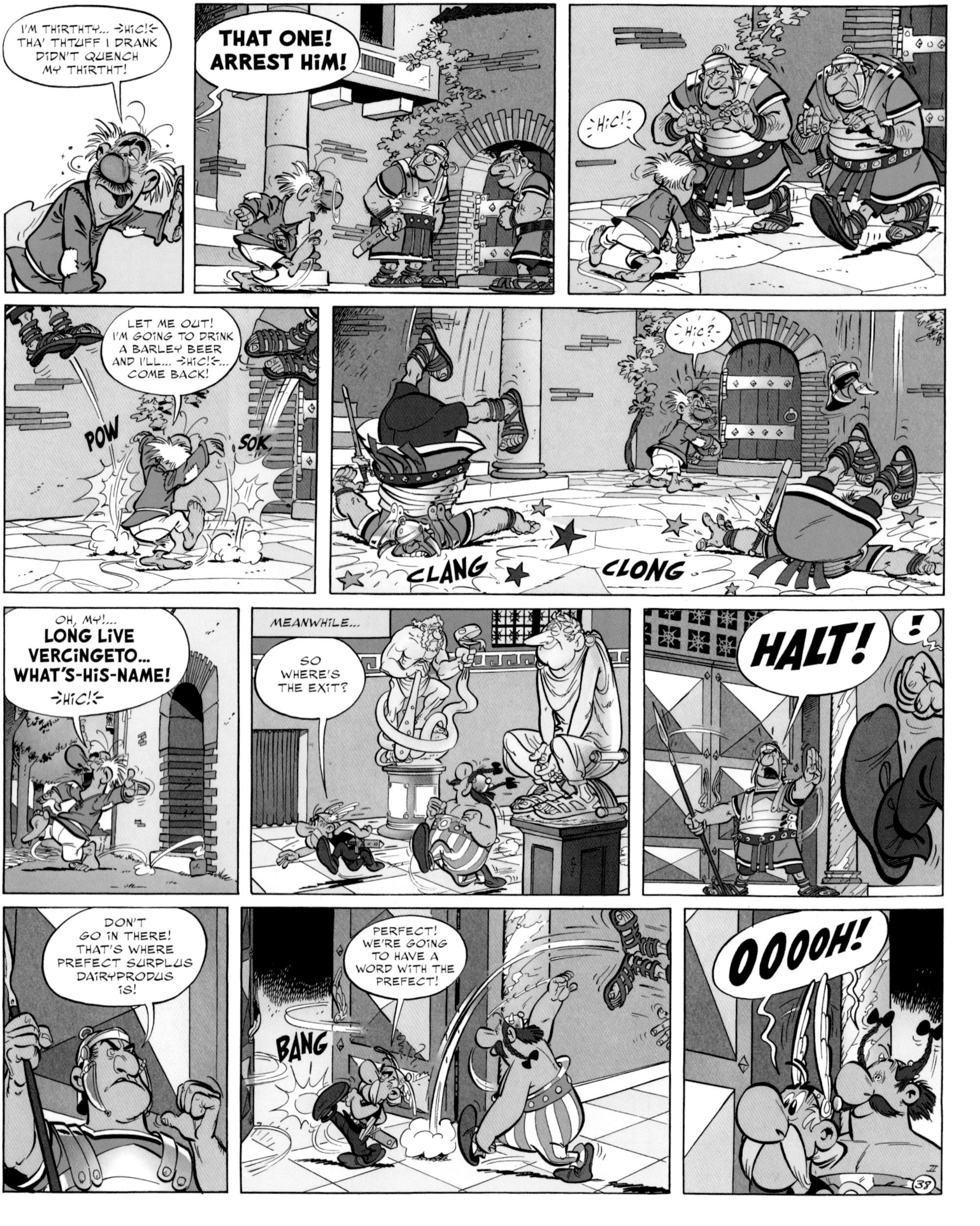
I'M THIRTHTY... HIC! THA' THTUFF I DRANK DIDN'T QUENCH MY THIRTHT!
THAT ONE! ARREST HIM!
HIC!
LET ME OUT! I'M GOING TO DRINK A BARLEY BEER AND I'LL... HIC!... COME BACK!
POW
SOK
HIC?
CLANG
CLONG
OH, MY!... LONG LIVE VERCINGETO... WHAT'S-HIS-NAME!
HIC!
MEANWHILE...
SO WHERE'S THE EXIT?
HALT!
!
DON'T GO IN THERE! THAT'S WHERE PREFECT SURPLUS DAIRYPRODUS IS!
PERFECT! WE'RE GOING TO HAVE A WORD WITH THE PREFECT!
BANG
OOOOH!
38

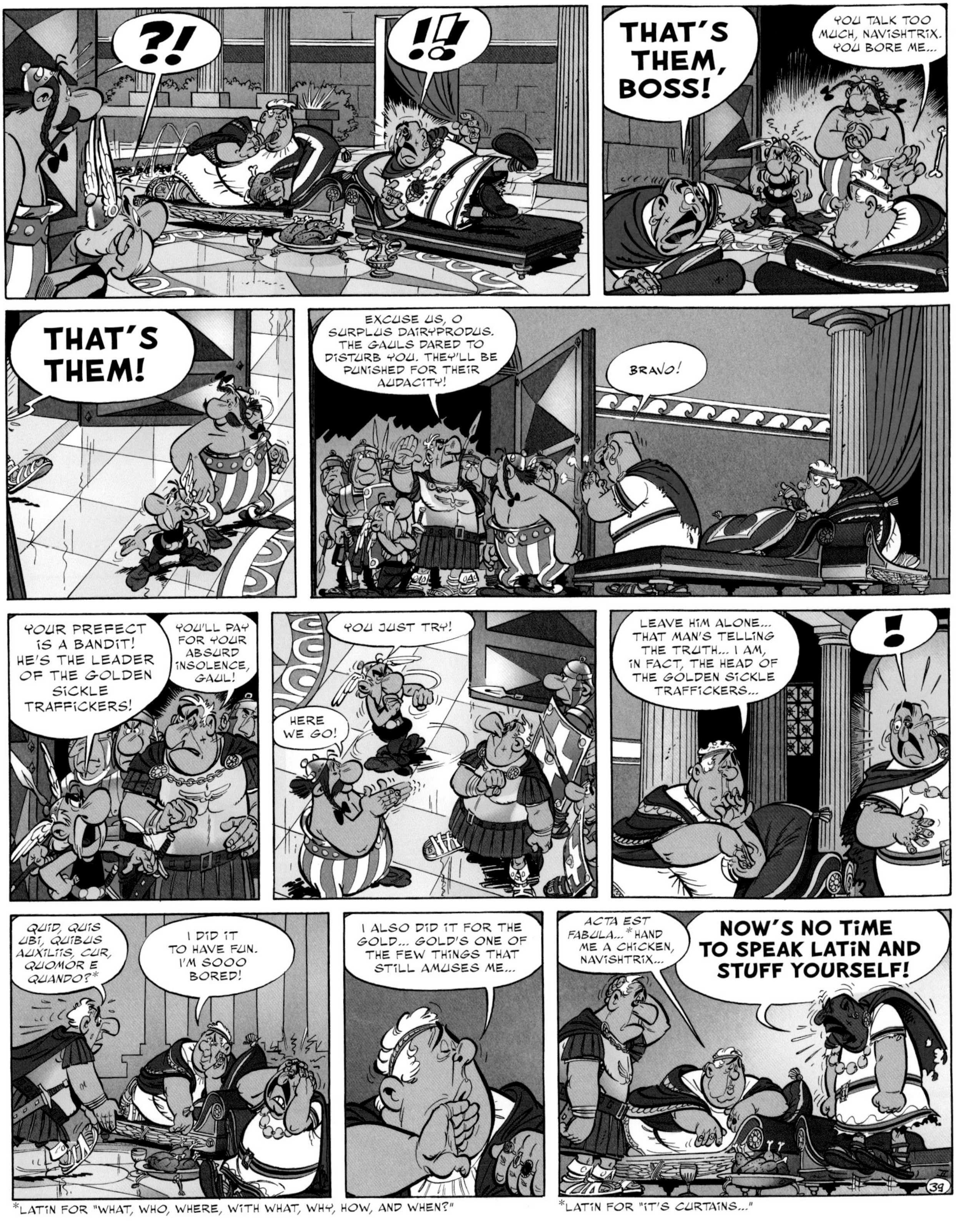
?!
!!
THAT'S THEM, BOSS!
YOU TALK TOO MUCH, NAVISHTRIX. YOU BORE ME...
THAT'S THEM!
EXCUSE US, O SURPLUS DAIRYPRODUS. THE GAULS DARED TO DISTURB YOU. THEY'LL BE PUNISHED FOR THEIR AUDACITY!
BRAVO!
YOUR PREFECT IS A BANDIT! HE'S THE LEADER OF THE GOLDEN SICKLE TRAFFICKERS!
YOU'LL PAY FOR YOUR ABSURD INSOLENCE, GAUL!
YOU JUST TRY!
HERE WE GO!
LEAVE HIM ALONE... THAT MAN'S TELLING THE TRUTH... I AM, IN FACT, THE HEAD OF THE GOLDEN SICKLE TRAFFICKERS...
!
QUID, QUIS UBI, QUIBUS AUXILIIS, CUR, QUOMOR E QUANDO?*
I DID IT TO HAVE FUN. I'M SOOO BORED!
I ALSO DID IT FOR THE GOLD... GOLD'S ONE OF THE FEW THINGS THAT STILL AMUSES ME...
ACTA EST FABULA...* HAND ME A CHICKEN, NAVISHTRIX...
NOW'S NO TIME TO SPEAK LATIN AND STUFF YOURSELF!
39

*LATIN FOR "WHAT, WHO, WHERE, WITH WHAT, WHY, HOW, AND WHEN?"

*LATIN FOR "IT'S CURTAINS..."

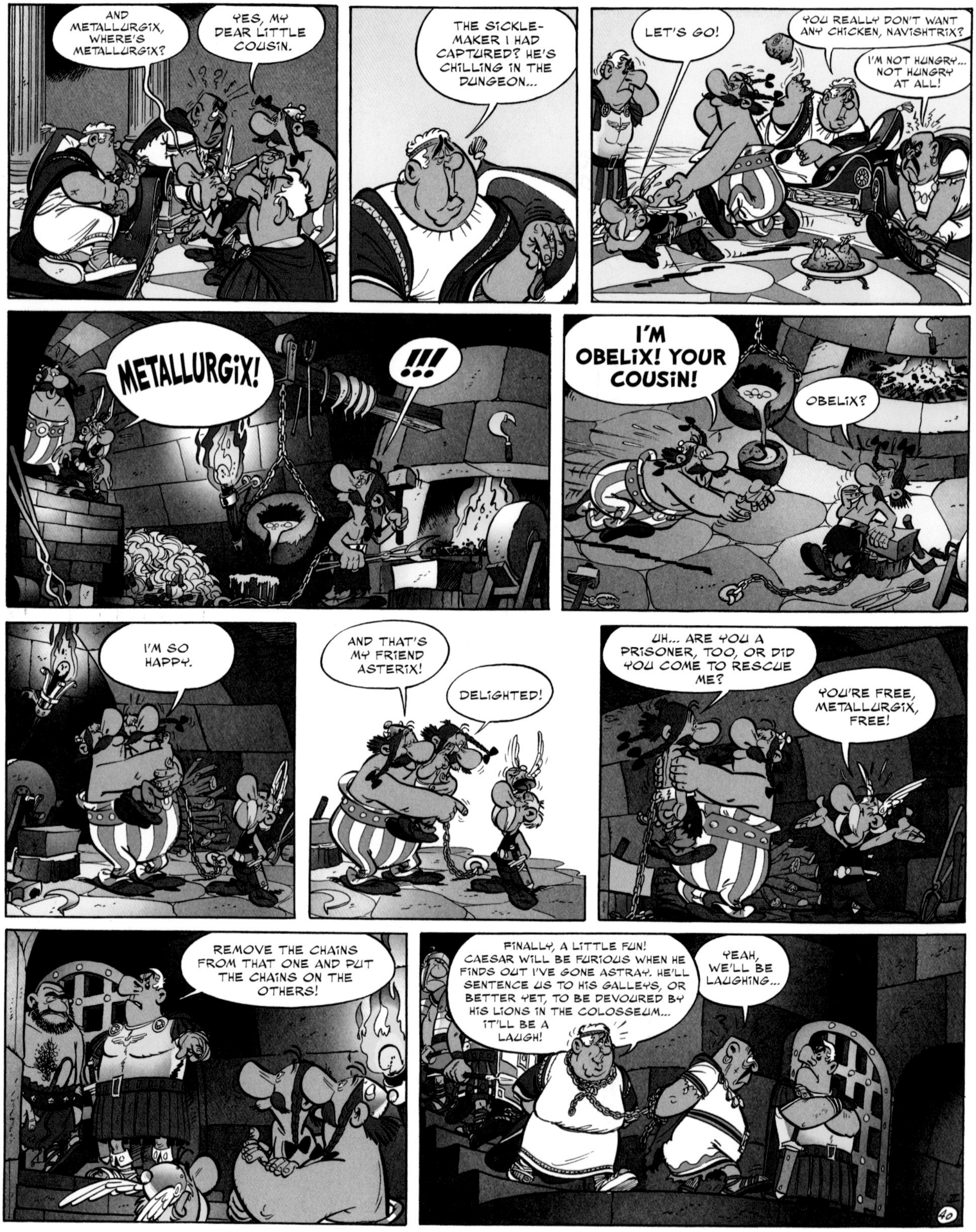
AND METALLURGIX, WHERE'S METALLURGIX?
YES, MY DEAR LITTLE COUSIN.
THE SICKLE-MAKER I HAD CAPTURED? HE'S CHILLING IN THE DUNGEON...
LET'S GO!
YOU REALLY DON'T WANT ANY CHICKEN, NAVISHTRIX?
I'M NOT HUNGRY... NOT HUNGRY AT ALL!
METALLURGIX!
!!!
I'M OBELIX! YOUR COUSIN!
OBELIX?
I'M SO HAPPY.
AND THAT'S MY FRIEND ASTERIX!
DELIGHTED!
UH... ARE YOU A PRISONER, TOO, OR DID YOU COME TO RESCUE ME?
YOU'RE FREE, METALLURGIX, FREE!
REMOVE THE CHAINS FROM THAT ONE AND PUT THE CHAINS ON THE OTHERS!
FINALLY, A LITTLE FUN! CAESAR WILL BE FURIOUS WHEN HE FINDS OUT I'VE GONE ASTRAY. HE'LL SENTENCE US TO HIS GALLEYS, OR BETTER YET, TO BE DEVOURED BY HIS LIONS IN THE COLOSSEUM... IT'LL BE A LAUGH!
YEAH, WE'LL BE LAUGHING...
40

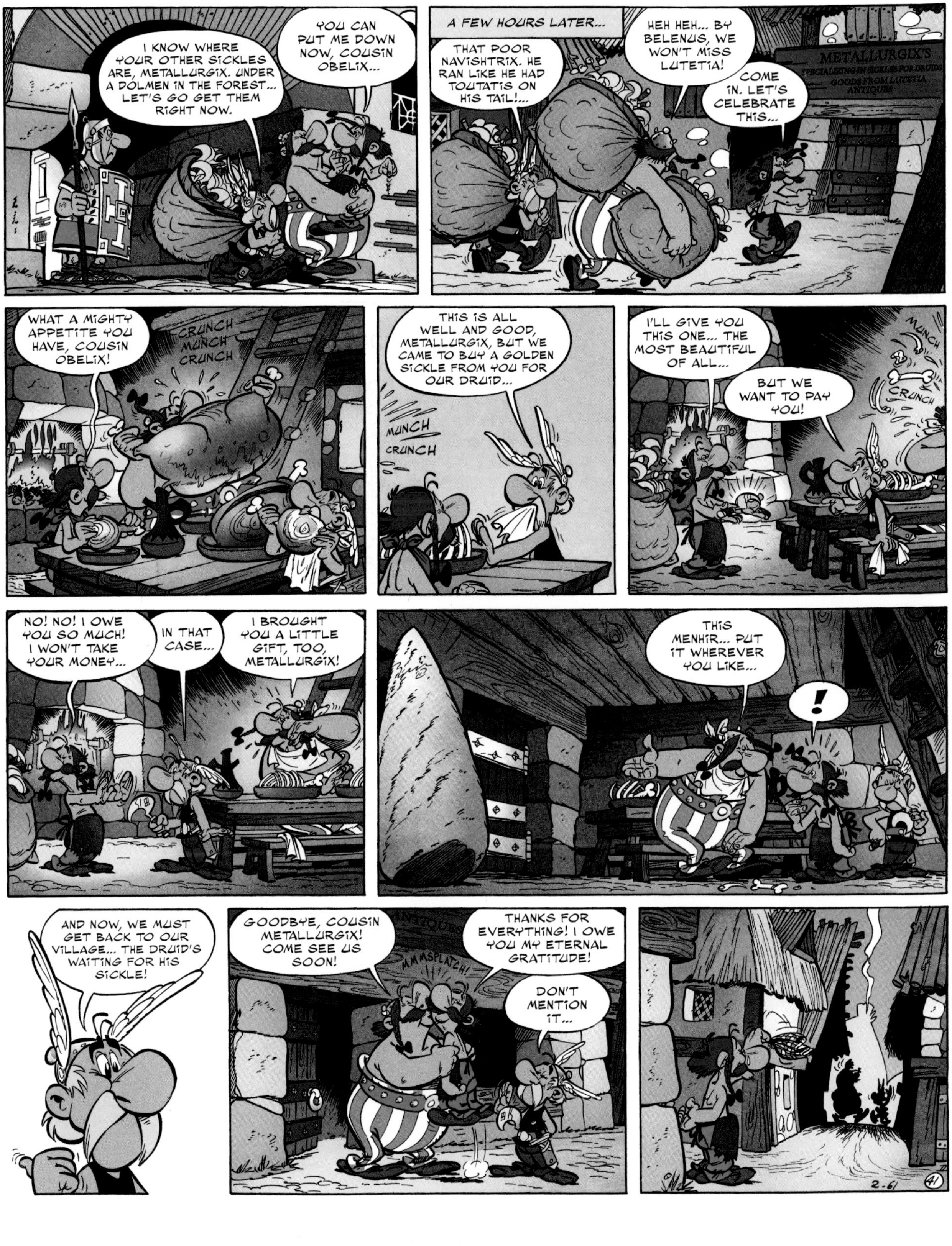
I KNOW WHERE YOUR OTHER SICKLES ARE, METALLURGIX. UNDER A DOLMEN IN THE FOREST... LET'S GO GET THEM RIGHT NOW.
YOU CAN PUT ME DOWN NOW, COUSIN OBELIX...
A FEW HOURS LATER...
THAT POOR NAVISHTRIX. HE RAN LIKE HE HAD TOUTATIS ON HIS TAIL!...
HEH HEH... BY BELENUS, WE WON'T MISS LUTETIA!
METALLURGIX'S
SPECIALISING IN SICKLES FOR DRUIDS
GOODS FROM LUTETIA
ANTIQUES
COME IN. LET'S CELEBRATE THIS...
WHAT A MIGHTY APPETITE YOU HAVE, COUSIN OBELIX!
CRUNCH MUNCH CRUNCH
THIS IS ALL WELL AND GOOD, METALLURGIX, BUT WE CAME TO BUY A GOLDEN SICKLE FROM YOU FOR OUR DRUID...
MUNCH
CRUNCH
I'LL GIVE YOU THIS ONE... THE MOST BEAUTIFUL OF ALL...
BUT WE WANT TO PAY YOU!
MUNCH
CRUNCH
NO! NO! I OWE YOU SO MUCH! I WON'T TAKE YOUR MONEY...
IN THAT CASE...
I BROUGHT YOU A LITTLE GIFT, TOO, METALLURGIX!
THIS MENHIR... PUT IT WHEREVER YOU LIKE...
!
AND NOW, WE MUST GET BACK TO OUR VILLAGE... THE DRUID'S WAITING FOR HIS SICKLE!
GOODBYE, COUSIN METALLURGIX! COME SEE US SOON!
MMMSPLATCH!
THANKS FOR EVERYTHING! I OWE YOU MY ETERNAL GRATITUDE!
DON'T MENTION IT...

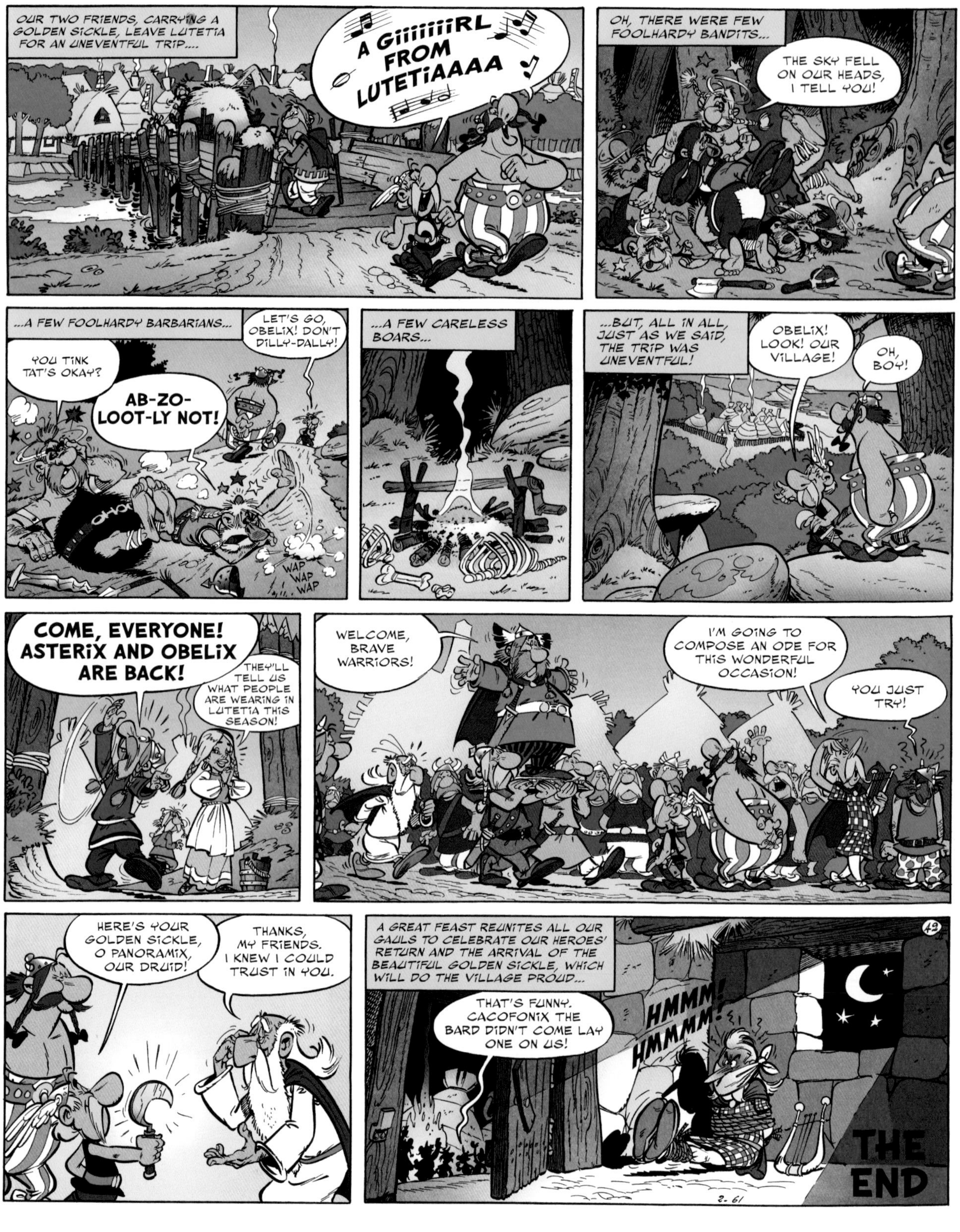

OUR TWO FRIENDS, CARRYING A GOLDEN SICKLE, LEAVE LUTETIA FOR AN UNEVENTFUL TRIP....
A GiiiiiiiRL FROM LUTETiAAAA
OH, THERE WERE FEW FOOLHARDY BANDITS...
THE SKY FELL ON OUR HEADS, I TELL YOU!
...A FEW FOOLHARDY BARBARIANS...
LET'S GO, OBELIX! DON'T DILLY-DALLY!
YOU TINK TAT'S OKAY?
AB-ZO-LOOT-LY NOT!
WAP WAP WAP
...A FEW CARELESS BOARS...
...BUT, ALL IN ALL, JUST AS WE SAID, THE TRIP WAS UNEVENTFUL!
OBELIX! LOOK! OUR VILLAGE!
OH, BOY!
COME, EVERYONE! ASTERIX AND OBELIX ARE BACK!
THEY'LL TELL US WHAT PEOPLE ARE WEARING IN LUTETIA THIS SEASON!
WELCOME, BRAVE WARRIORS!
I'M GOING TO COMPOSE AN ODE FOR THIS WONDERFUL OCCASION!
YOU JUST TRY!
HERE'S YOUR GOLDEN SICKLE, O PANORAMIX, OUR DRUID!
THANKS, MY FRIENDS. I KNEW I COULD TRUST IN YOU.
A GREAT FEAST REUNITES ALL OUR GAULS TO CELEBRATE OUR HEROES' RETURN AND THE ARRIVAL OF THE BEAUTIFUL GOLDEN SICKLE, WHICH WILL DO THE VILLAGE PROUD...
49
THAT'S FUNNY. CACOFONIX THE BARD DIDN'T COME LAY ONE ON US!
HMMM! HMMMM!
THE END
2-61

R. GOSCINNY **Asterix** A. UDERZO

Asterix and the Goths

RENÉ GOSCINNY
Writer

ALBERT UDERZO
Illustrator

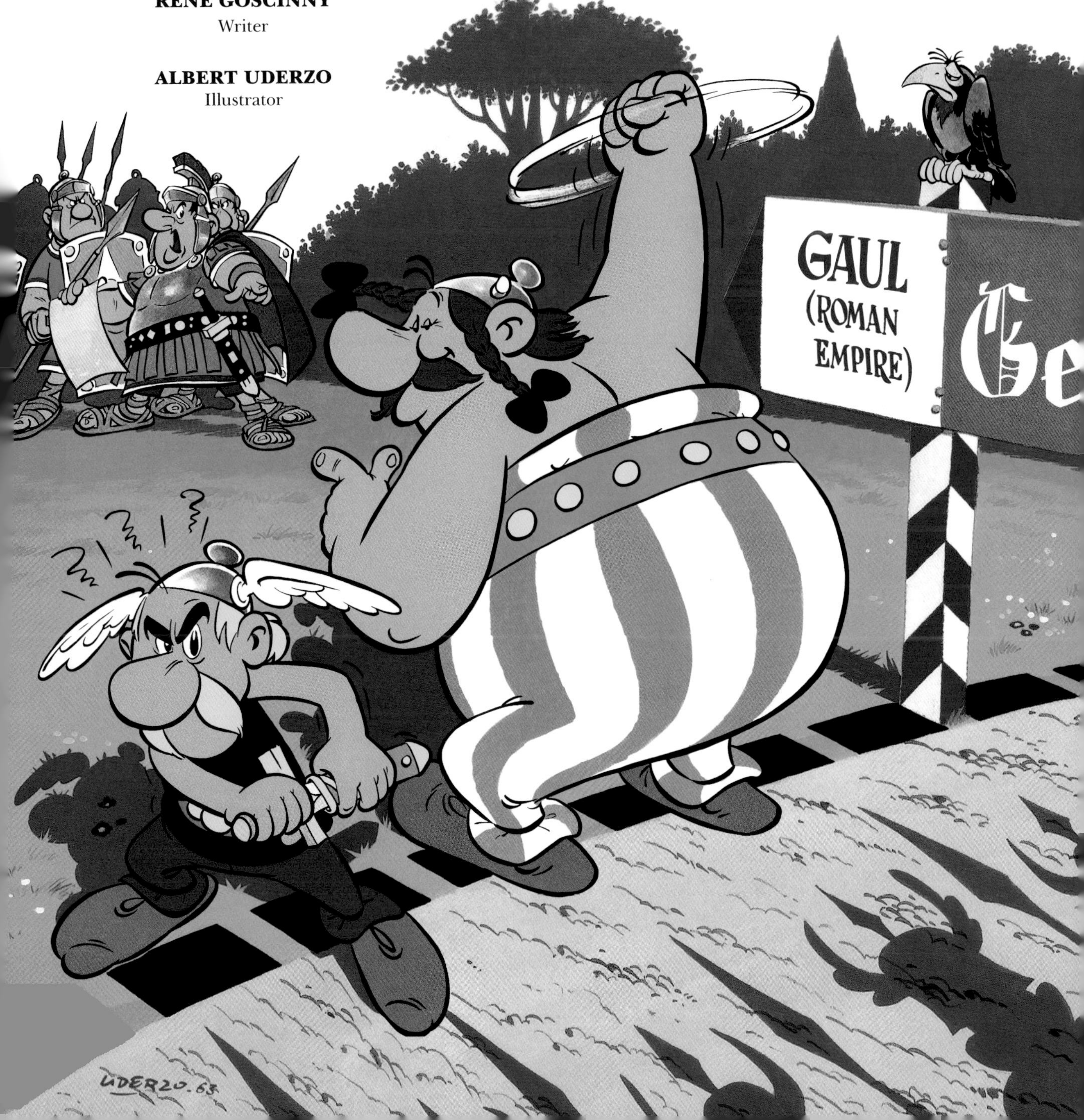
GAUL (ROMAN EMPIRE)
UDERZO.63

ASTERIX AND THE GOTHS

Written by RENÉ GOSCINNY *and illustrated by* ALBERT UDERZO

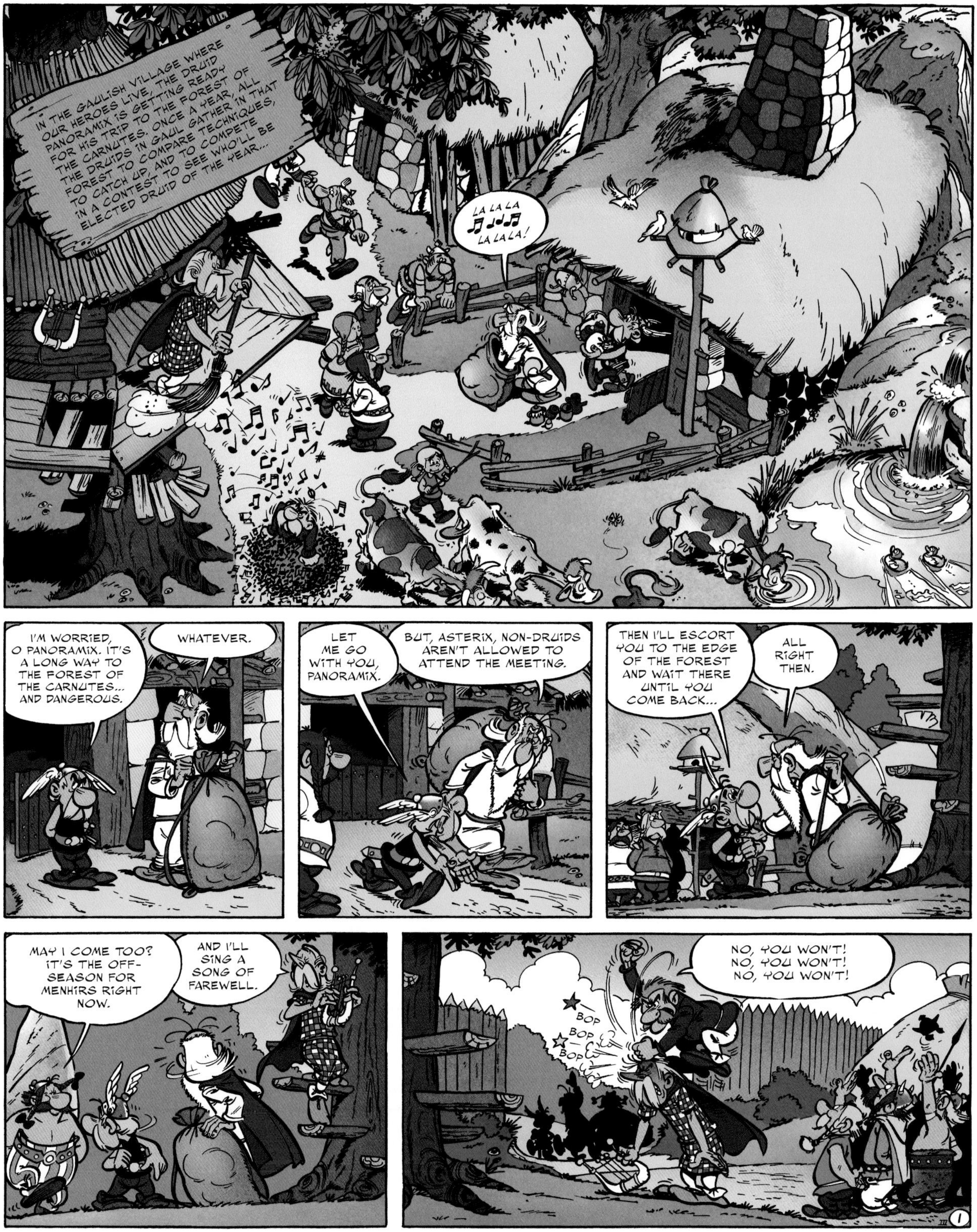

IN THE GAULISH VILLAGE WHERE OUR HEROES LIVE, THE DRUID PANORAMIX IS GETTING READY FOR HIS TRIP TO THE FOREST OF THE CARNUTES. ONCE A YEAR, ALL THE DRUIDS IN GAUL GATHER IN THAT FOREST TO COMPARE TECHNIQUES, TO CATCH UP, AND TO COMPETE IN A CONTEST TO SEE WHO'LL BE ELECTED DRUID OF THE YEAR...
LA LA LA LA LA LA!
I'M WORRIED, O PANORAMIX. IT'S A LONG WAY TO THE FOREST OF THE CARNUTES... AND DANGEROUS.
WHATEVER.
LET ME GO WITH YOU, PANORAMIX.
BUT, ASTERIX, NON-DRUIDS AREN'T ALLOWED TO ATTEND THE MEETING.
THEN I'LL ESCORT YOU TO THE EDGE OF THE FOREST AND WAIT THERE UNTIL YOU COME BACK...
ALL RIGHT THEN.
MAY I COME TOO? IT'S THE OFF-SEASON FOR MENHIRS RIGHT NOW.
AND I'LL SING A SONG OF FAREWELL.
NO, YOU WON'T! NO, YOU WON'T! NO, YOU WON'T!
BOP
BOP
BOP
1

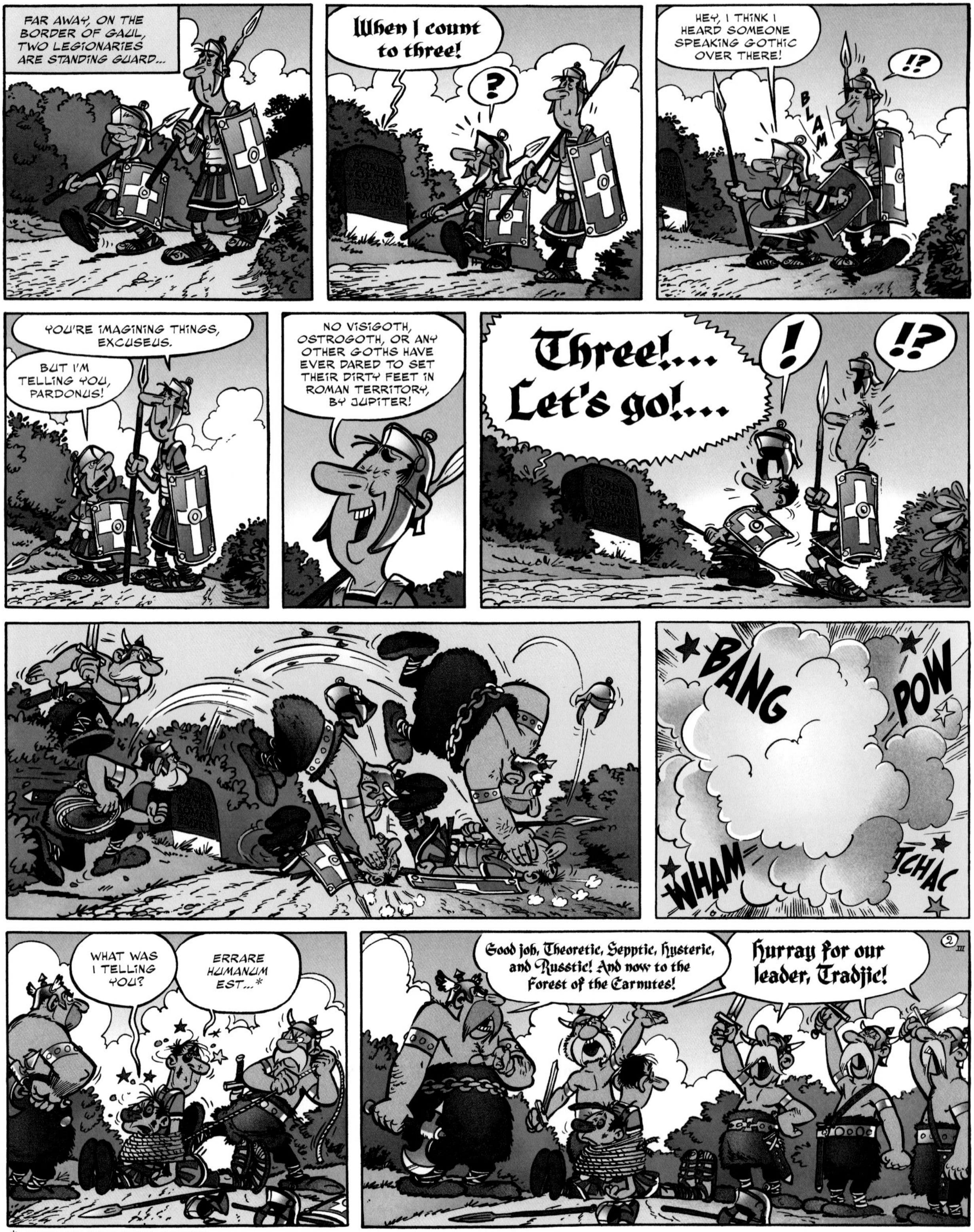
FAR AWAY, ON THE BORDER OF GAUL, TWO LEGIONARIES ARE STANDING GUARD...
When I count to three!
?
HEY, I THINK I HEARD SOMEONE SPEAKING GOTHIC OVER THERE!
BLAM
!?
YOU'RE IMAGINING THINGS, EXCUSEUS.
BUT I'M TELLING YOU, PARDONUS!
NO VISIGOTH, OSTROGOTH, OR ANY OTHER GOTHS HAVE EVER DARED TO SET THEIR DIRTY FEET IN ROMAN TERRITORY, BY JUPITER!
Three!... Let's go!...
!
!?
BANG
POW
WHAM
TCHAC
WHAT WAS I TELLING YOU?
ERRARE HUMANUM EST...*
Good job, Theoretic, Sepptic, Hysteric, and Russtic! And now to the Forest of the Carnutes!
Hurray for our leader, Tradjic!

*LATIN FOR "TO ERR IS HUMAN."

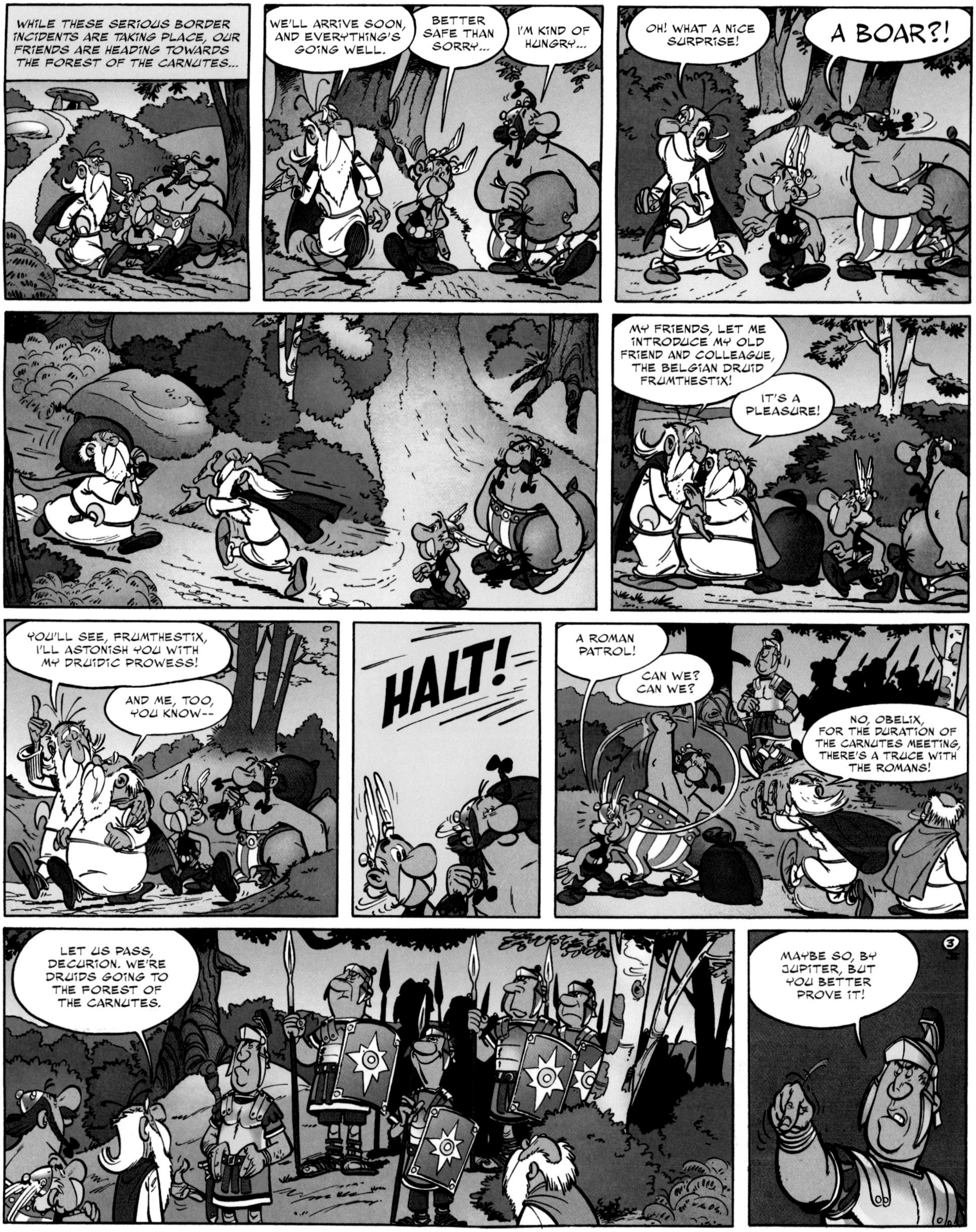

WHILE THESE SERIOUS BORDER INCIDENTS ARE TAKING PLACE, OUR FRIENDS ARE HEADING TOWARDS THE FOREST OF THE CARNUTES...
WE'LL ARRIVE SOON, AND EVERYTHING'S GOING WELL.
BETTER SAFE THAN SORRY...
I'M KIND OF HUNGRY...
OH! WHAT A NICE SURPRISE!
A BOAR?!
MY FRIENDS, LET ME INTRODUCE MY OLD FRIEND AND COLLEAGUE, THE BELGIAN DRUID FRUMTHESTIX!
IT'S A PLEASURE!
YOU'LL SEE, FRUMTHESTIX, I'LL ASTONISH YOU WITH MY DRUIDIC PROWESS!
AND ME, TOO, YOU KNOW--
HALT!
A ROMAN PATROL!
CAN WE? CAN WE?
NO, OBELIX, FOR THE DURATION OF THE CARNUTES MEETING, THERE'S A TRUCE WITH THE ROMANS!
LET US PASS, DECURION. WE'RE DRUIDS GOING TO THE FOREST OF THE CARNUTES.
MAYBE SO, BY JUPITER, BUT YOU BETTER PROVE IT!
3

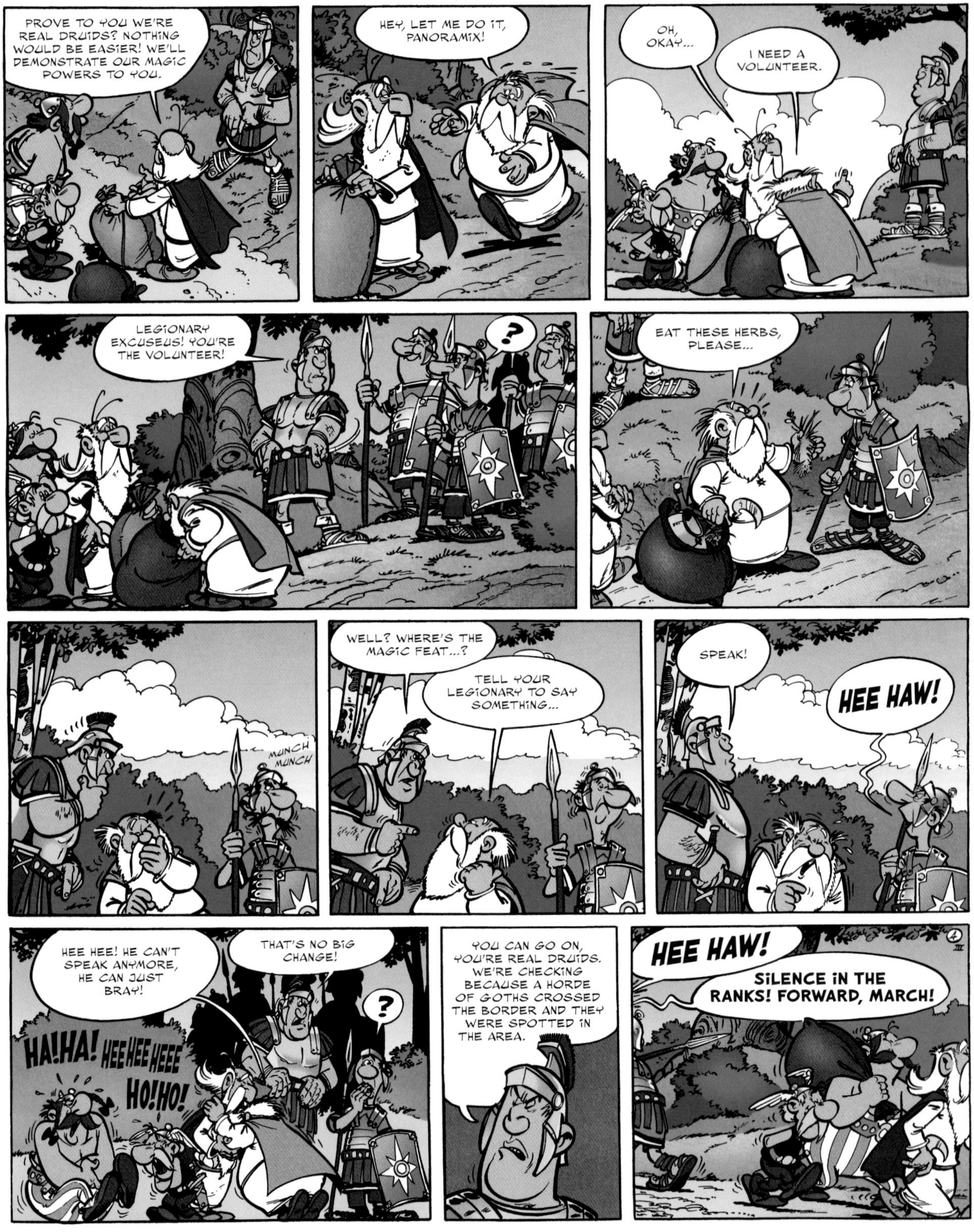
PROVE TO YOU WE'RE REAL DRUIDS? NOTHING WOULD BE EASIER! WE'LL DEMONSTRATE OUR MAGIC POWERS TO YOU.
HEY, LET ME DO IT, PANORAMIX!
OH, OKAY...
I NEED A VOLUNTEER.
LEGIONARY EXCUSEUS! YOU'RE THE VOLUNTEER!
?
EAT THESE HERBS, PLEASE...
MUNCH MUNCH
WELL? WHERE'S THE MAGIC FEAT...?
TELL YOUR LEGIONARY TO SAY SOMETHING...
SPEAK!
HEE HAW!
HEE HEE! HE CAN'T SPEAK ANYMORE, HE CAN JUST BRAY!
THAT'S NO BIG CHANGE!
?
HA!HA! HEEHEEHEEE HO!HO!
YOU CAN GO ON, YOU'RE REAL DRUIDS. WE'RE CHECKING BECAUSE A HORDE OF GOTHS CROSSED THE BORDER AND THEY WERE SPOTTED IN THE AREA.
HEE HAW!
SILENCE IN THE RANKS! FORWARD, MARCH!

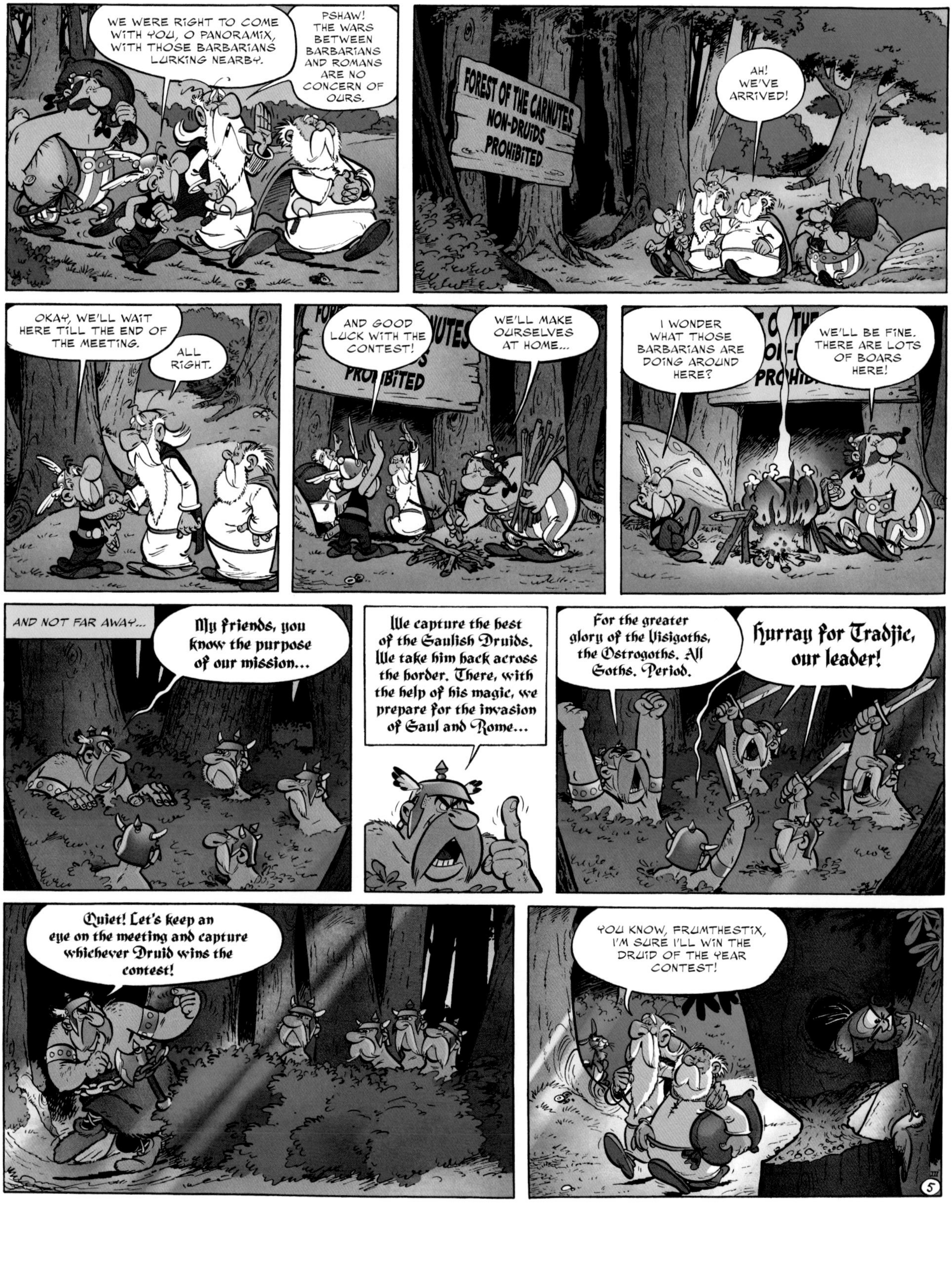

WE WERE RIGHT TO COME WITH YOU, O PANORAMIX, WITH THOSE BARBARIANS LURKING NEARBY.
PSHAW! THE WARS BETWEEN BARBARIANS AND ROMANS ARE NO CONCERN OF OURS.
FOREST OF THE CARNUTES NON-DRUIDS PROHIBITED
AH! WE'VE ARRIVED!
OKAY, WE'LL WAIT HERE TILL THE END OF THE MEETING.
ALL RIGHT.
AND GOOD LUCK WITH THE CONTEST!
WE'LL MAKE OURSELVES AT HOME...
I WONDER WHAT THOSE BARBARIANS ARE DOING AROUND HERE?
WE'LL BE FINE. THERE ARE LOTS OF BOARS HERE!
AND NOT FAR AWAY...
My friends, you know the purpose of our mission...
We capture the best of the Gaulish Druids. We take him back across the border. There, with the help of his magic, we prepare for the invasion of Gaul and Rome...
For the greater glory of the Visigoths, the Ostrogoths. All Goths. Period.
Hurray for Tradjic, our leader!
Quiet! Let's keep an eye on the meeting and capture whichever Druid wins the contest!
YOU KNOW, FRUMTHESTIX, I'M SURE I'LL WIN THE DRUID OF THE YEAR CONTEST!
5

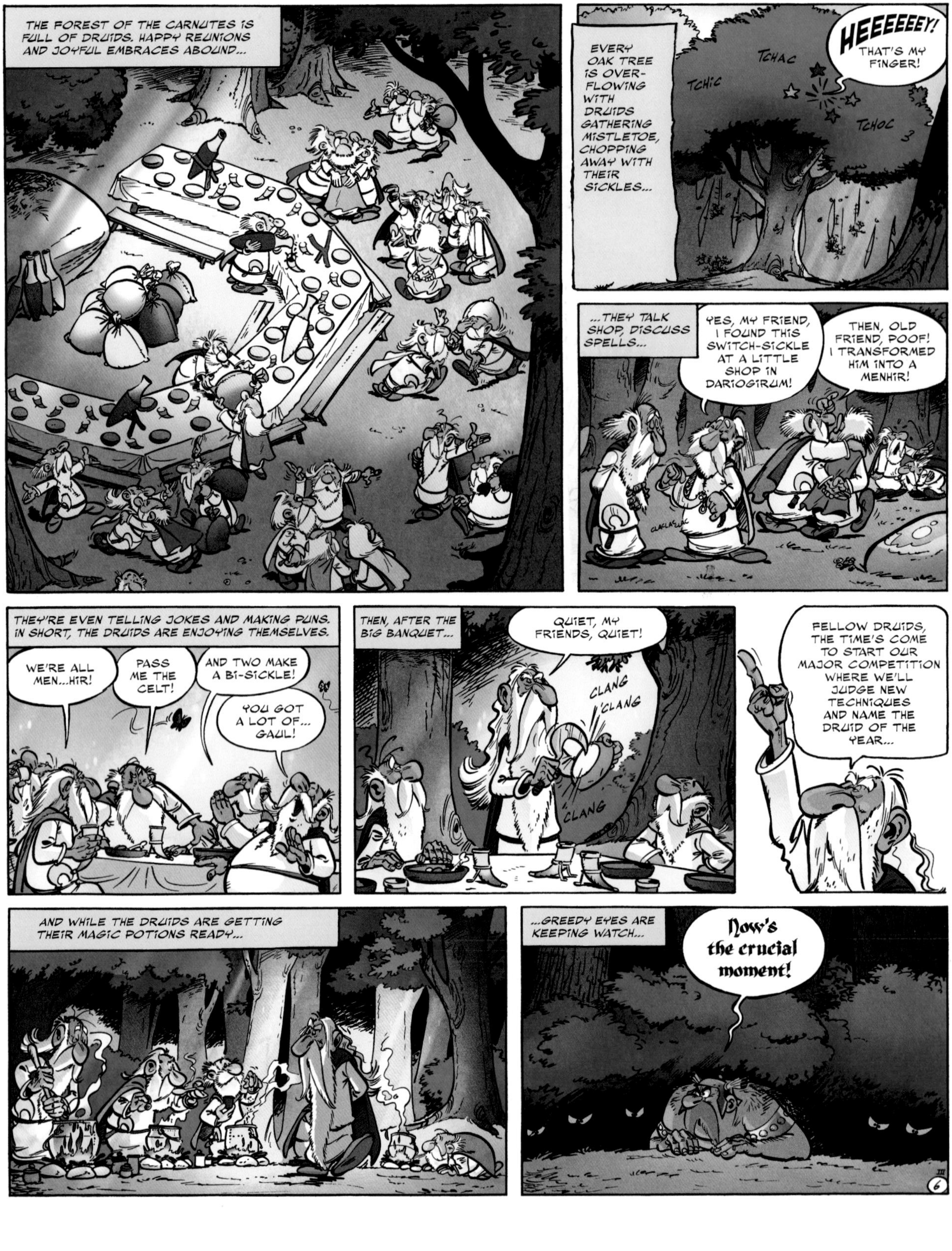
THE FOREST OF THE CARNUTES IS FULL OF DRUIDS. HAPPY REUNIONS AND JOYFUL EMBRACES ABOUND...
EVERY OAK TREE IS OVER-FLOWING WITH DRUIDS GATHERING MISTLETOE, CHOPPING AWAY WITH THEIR SICKLES...
TCHIC
TCHAC
TCHOC
HEEEEEEY! THAT'S MY FINGER!
...THEY TALK SHOP, DISCUSS SPELLS...
YES, MY FRIEND, I FOUND THIS SWITCH-SICKLE AT A LITTLE SHOP IN DARIOGIRUM!
THEN, OLD FRIEND, POOF! I TRANSFORMED HIM INTO A MENHIR!
THEY'RE EVEN TELLING JOKES AND MAKING PUNS. IN SHORT, THE DRUIDS ARE ENJOYING THEMSELVES.
WE'RE ALL MEN...HIR!
PASS ME THE CELT!
AND TWO MAKE A BI-SICKLE!
YOU GOT A LOT OF... GAUL!
THEN, AFTER THE BIG BANQUET...
QUIET, MY FRIENDS, QUIET!
CLANG
CLANG
CLANG
FELLOW DRUIDS, THE TIME'S COME TO START OUR MAJOR COMPETITION WHERE WE'LL JUDGE NEW TECHNIQUES AND NAME THE DRUID OF THE YEAR...
AND WHILE THE DRUIDS ARE GETTING THEIR MAGIC POTIONS READY...
...GREEDY EYES ARE KEEPING WATCH...
Now's the crucial moment!
6

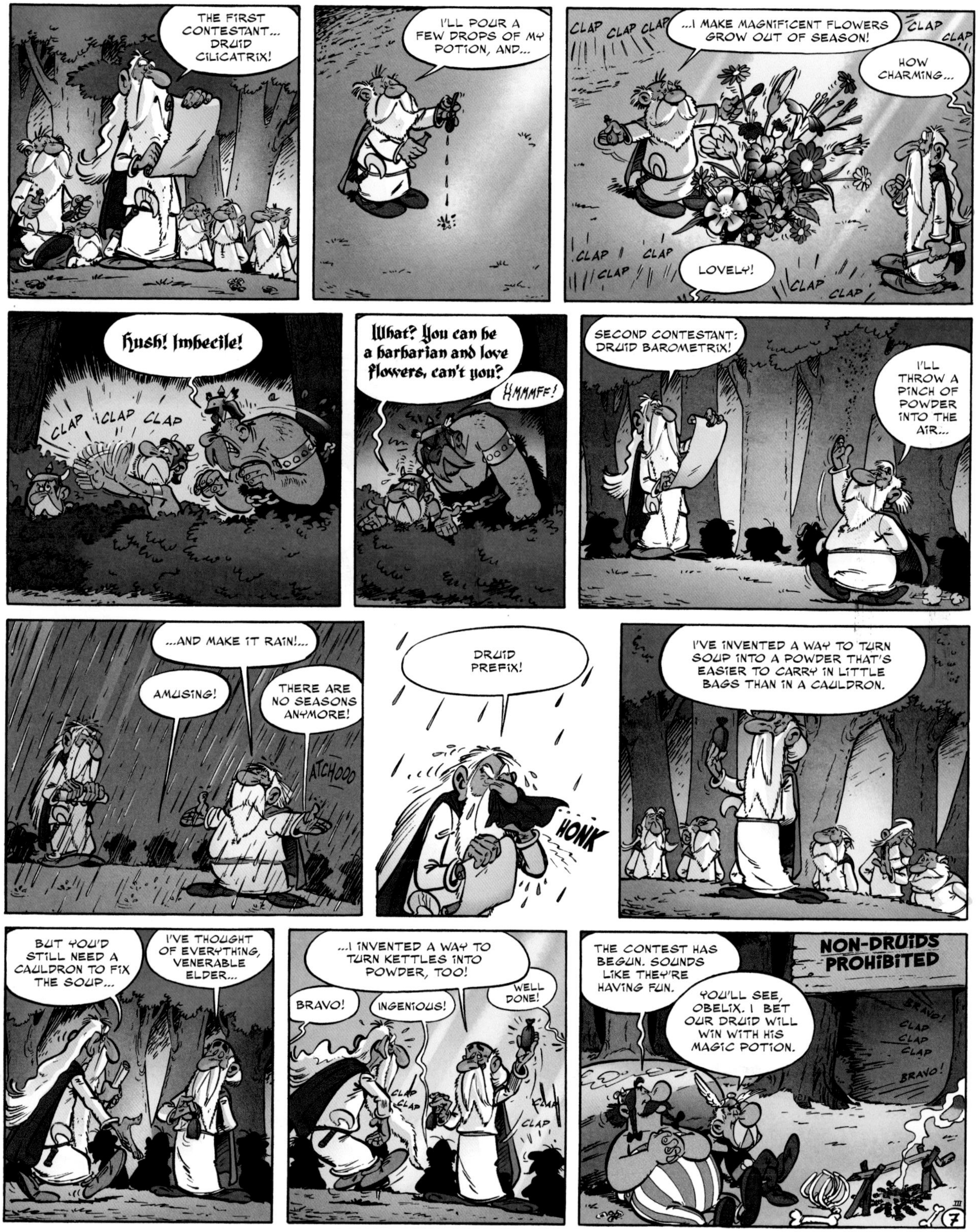
THE FIRST CONTESTANT... DRUID CILICATRIX!
I'LL POUR A FEW DROPS OF MY POTION, AND...
CLAP CLAP CLAP
...I MAKE MAGNIFICENT FLOWERS GROW OUT OF SEASON!
CLAP CLAP
HOW CHARMING...
CLAP CLAP CLAP
LOVELY!
CLAP CLAP
Hush! Imbecile!
CLAP CLAP CLAP
What? You can be a barbarian and love flowers, can't you?
HMMMFF!
SECOND CONTESTANT: DRUID BAROMETRIX!
I'LL THROW A PINCH OF POWDER INTO THE AIR...
...AND MAKE IT RAIN!...
AMUSING!
THERE ARE NO SEASONS ANYMORE!
ATCHOOO
DRUID PREFIX!
HONK
I'VE INVENTED A WAY TO TURN SOUP INTO A POWDER THAT'S EASIER TO CARRY IN LITTLE BAGS THAN IN A CAULDRON.
BUT YOU'D STILL NEED A CAULDRON TO FIX THE SOUP...
I'VE THOUGHT OF EVERYTHING, VENERABLE ELDER...
...I INVENTED A WAY TO TURN KETTLES INTO POWDER, TOO!
BRAVO!
INGENIOUS!
WELL DONE!
CLAP CLAP
CLAP
NON-DRUIDS PROHIBITED
THE CONTEST HAS BEGUN. SOUNDS LIKE THEY'RE HAVING FUN.
YOU'LL SEE, OBELIX. I BET OUR DRUID WILL WIN WITH HIS MAGIC POTION.
BRAVO!
CLAP CLAP CLAP
BRAVO!
7

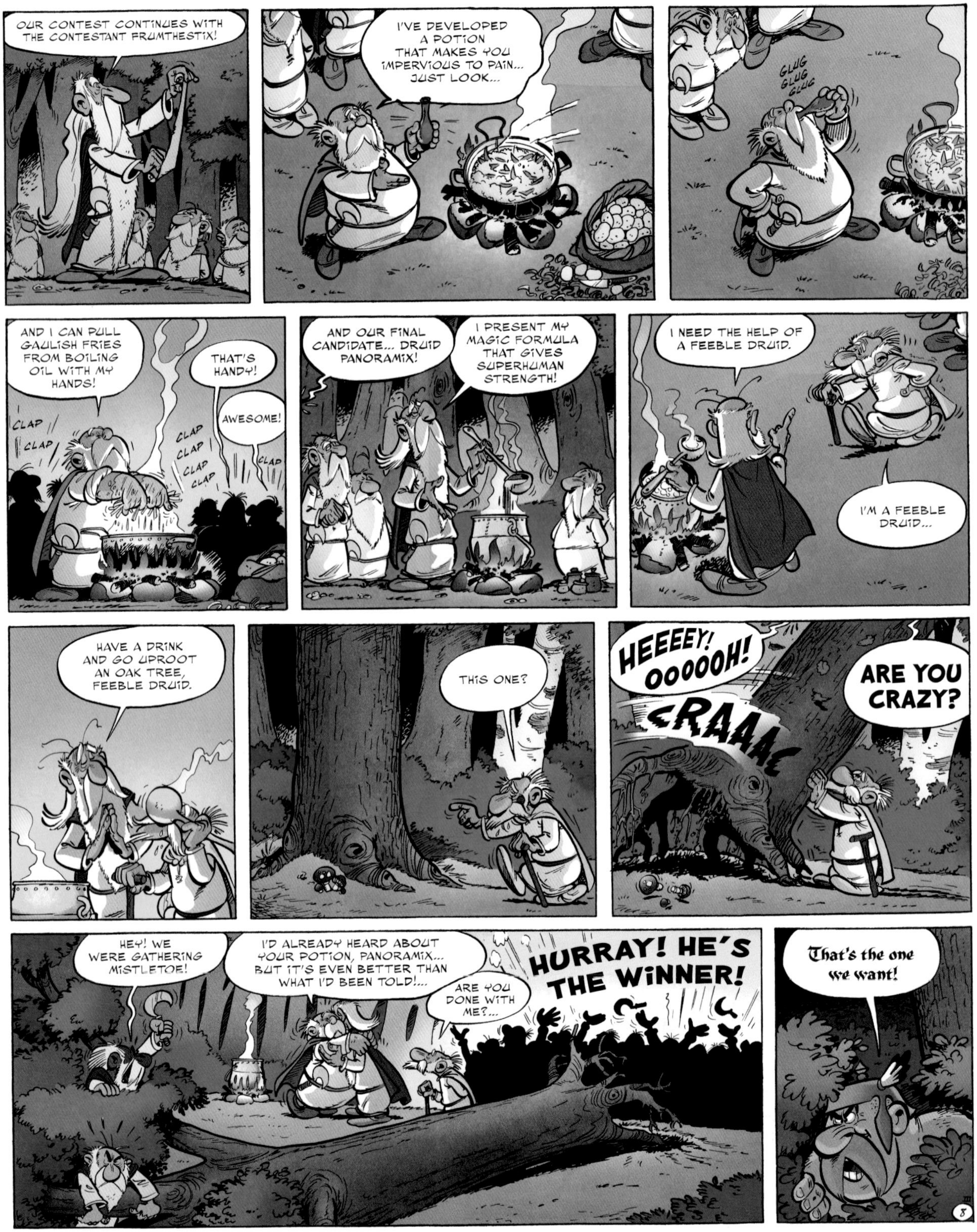
OUR CONTEST CONTINUES WITH THE CONTESTANT FRUMTHESTIX!
I'VE DEVELOPED A POTION THAT MAKES YOU IMPERVIOUS TO PAIN... JUST LOOK...
GLUG GLUG GLUG
AND I CAN PULL GAULISH FRIES FROM BOILING OIL WITH MY HANDS!
THAT'S HANDY!
AWESOME!
CLAP CLAP
CLAP CLAP CLAP CLAP
CLAP
AND OUR FINAL CANDIDATE... DRUID PANORAMIX!
I PRESENT MY MAGIC FORMULA THAT GIVES SUPERHUMAN STRENGTH!
I NEED THE HELP OF A FEEBLE DRUID.
I'M A FEEBLE DRUID...
HAVE A DRINK AND GO UPROOT AN OAK TREE, FEEBLE DRUID.
THIS ONE?
HEEEEY! OOOOOH!
CRAAAC
ARE YOU CRAZY?
HEY! WE WERE GATHERING MISTLETOE!
I'D ALREADY HEARD ABOUT YOUR POTION, PANORAMIX... BUT IT'S EVEN BETTER THAN WHAT I'D BEEN TOLD!...
ARE YOU DONE WITH ME?...
HURRAY! HE'S THE WINNER!
That's the one we want!
8

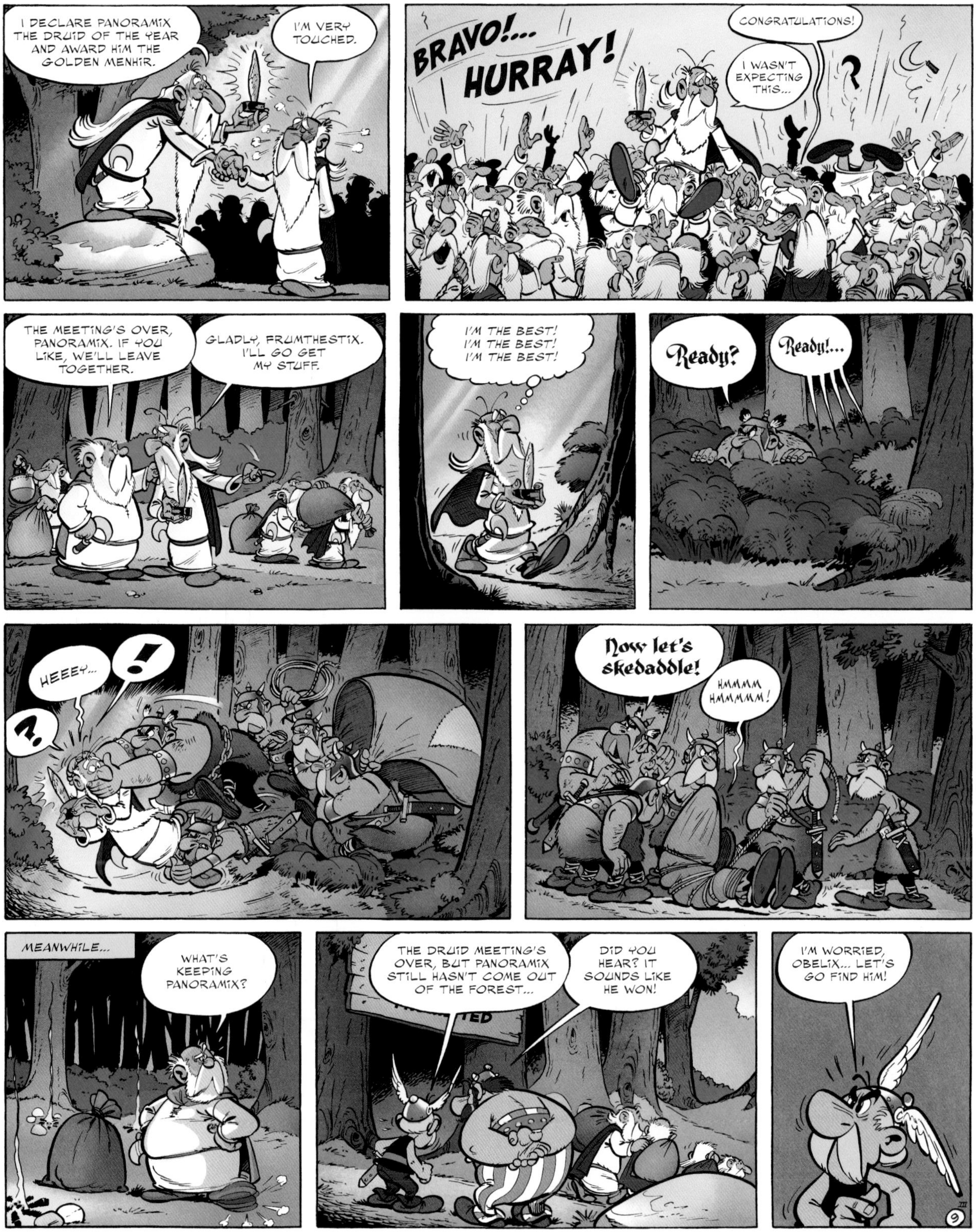
I DECLARE PANORAMIX THE DRUID OF THE YEAR AND AWARD HIM THE GOLDEN MENHIR.
I'M VERY TOUCHED.
BRAVO!... HURRAY!
CONGRATULATIONS!
I WASN'T EXPECTING THIS...
THE MEETING'S OVER, PANORAMIX. IF YOU LIKE, WE'LL LEAVE TOGETHER.
GLADLY, FRUMTHESTIX. I'LL GO GET MY STUFF.
I'M THE BEST! I'M THE BEST! I'M THE BEST!
Ready?
Ready!...
HEEEY...
!
?
Now let's skedaddle!
HMMMM HMMMMM!
MEANWHILE...
WHAT'S KEEPING PANORAMIX?
THE DRUID MEETING'S OVER, BUT PANORAMIX STILL HASN'T COME OUT OF THE FOREST...
DID YOU HEAR? IT SOUNDS LIKE HE WON!
I'M WORRIED, OBELIX... LET'S GO FIND HIM!
9

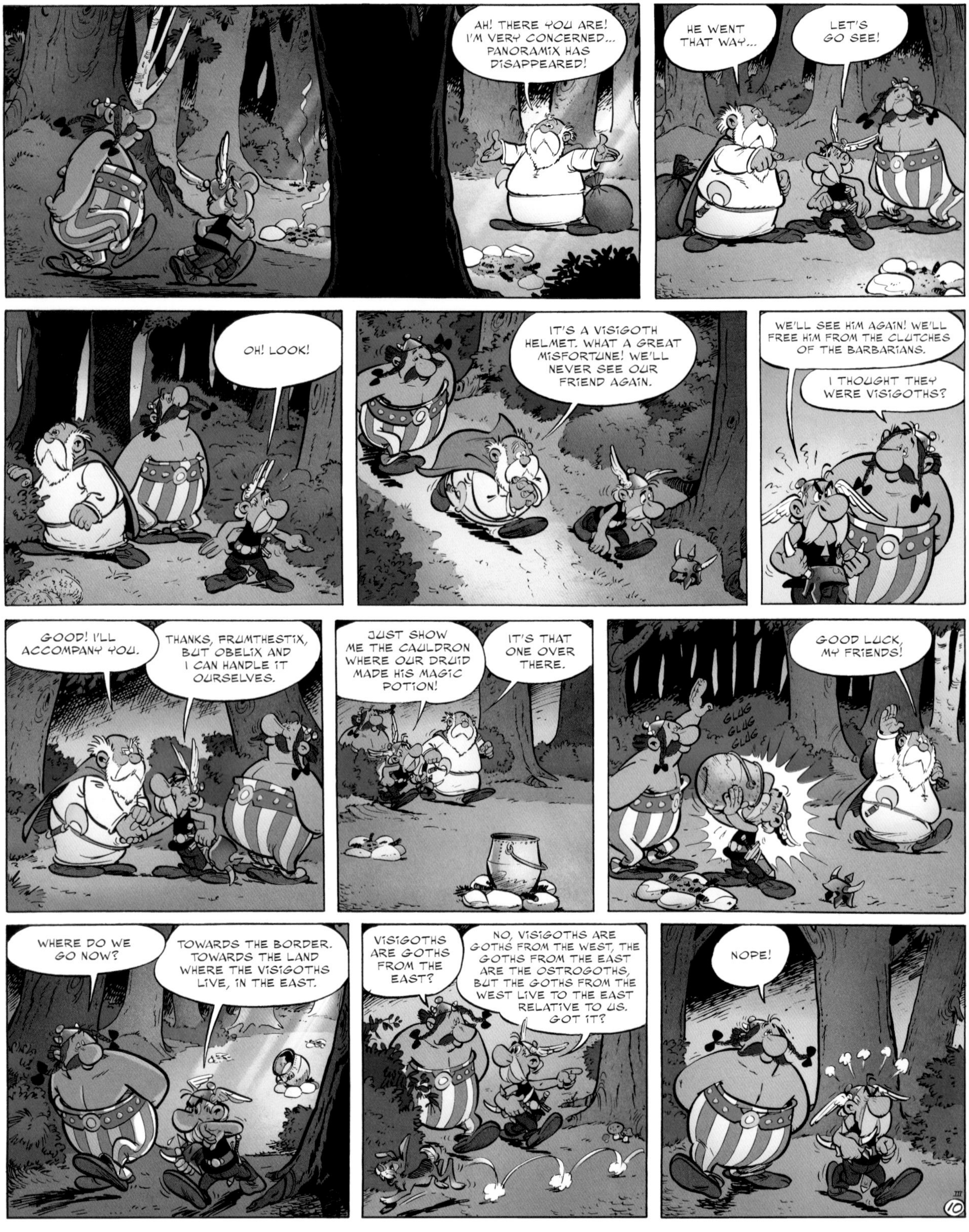
AH! THERE YOU ARE! I'M VERY CONCERNED... PANORAMIX HAS DISAPPEARED!
HE WENT THAT WAY...
LET'S GO SEE!
OH! LOOK!
IT'S A VISIGOTH HELMET. WHAT A GREAT MISFORTUNE! WE'LL NEVER SEE OUR FRIEND AGAIN.
WE'LL SEE HIM AGAIN! WE'LL FREE HIM FROM THE CLUTCHES OF THE BARBARIANS.
I THOUGHT THEY WERE VISIGOTHS?
GOOD! I'LL ACCOMPANY YOU.
THANKS, FRUMTHESTIX, BUT OBELIX AND I CAN HANDLE IT OURSELVES.
JUST SHOW ME THE CAULDRON WHERE OUR DRUID MADE HIS MAGIC POTION!
IT'S THAT ONE OVER THERE.
GOOD LUCK, MY FRIENDS!
GLUG GLUG GLUG
WHERE DO WE GO NOW?
TOWARDS THE BORDER. TOWARDS THE LAND WHERE THE VISIGOTHS LIVE, IN THE EAST.
VISIGOTHS ARE GOTHS FROM THE EAST?
NO, VISIGOTHS ARE GOTHS FROM THE WEST, THE GOTHS FROM THE EAST ARE THE OSTROGOTHS, BUT THE GOTHS FROM THE WEST LIVE TO THE EAST RELATIVE TO US. GOT IT?
NOPE!
10

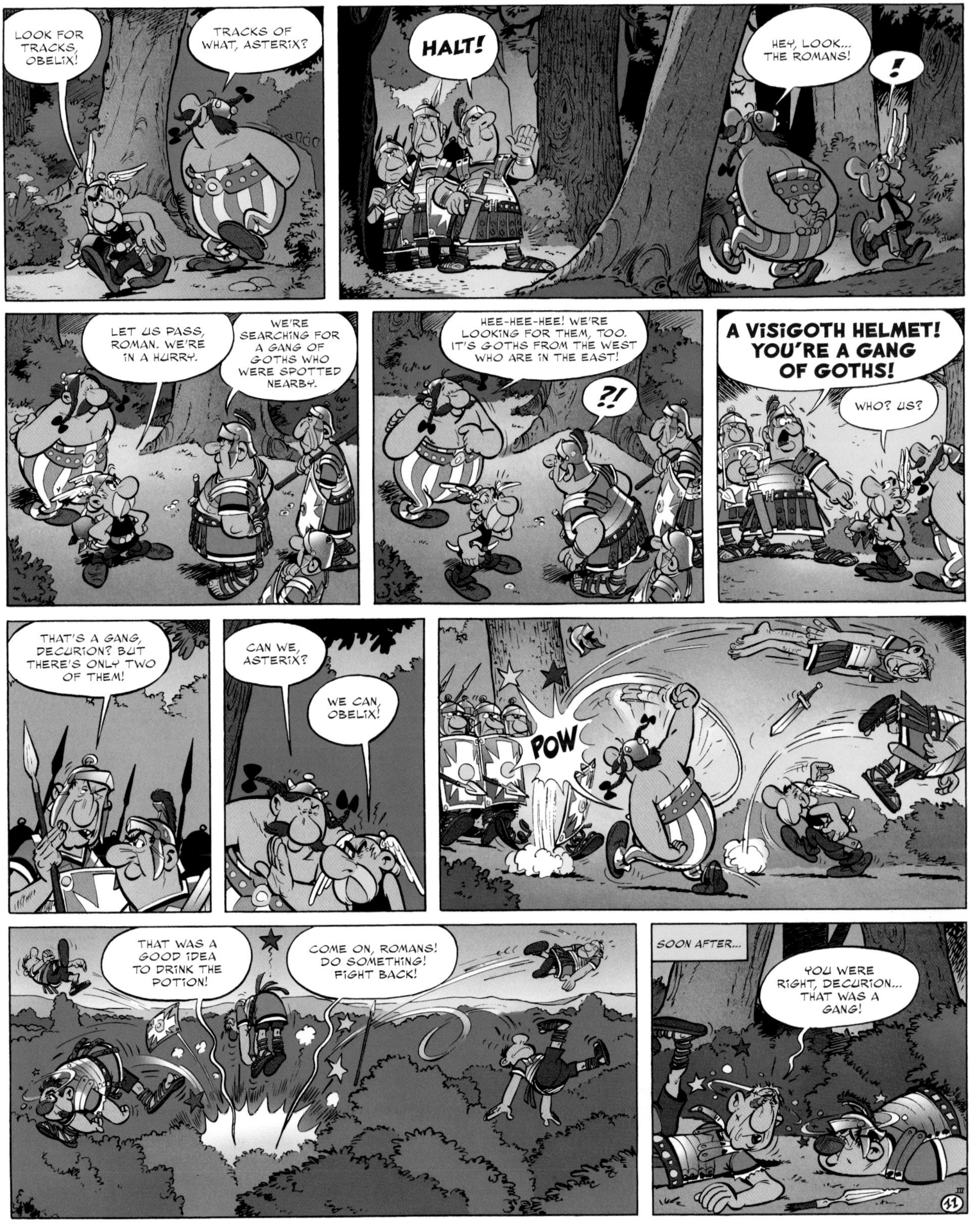
LOOK FOR TRACKS, OBELIX!
TRACKS OF WHAT, ASTERIX?
HALT!
HEY, LOOK... THE ROMANS!
!
LET US PASS, ROMAN. WE'RE IN A HURRY.
WE'RE SEARCHING FOR A GANG OF GOTHS WHO WERE SPOTTED NEARBY.
HEE-HEE-HEE! WE'RE LOOKING FOR THEM, TOO. IT'S GOTHS FROM THE WEST WHO ARE IN THE EAST!
?!
A VISIGOTH HELMET! YOU'RE A GANG OF GOTHS!
WHO? US?
THAT'S A GANG, DECURION? BUT THERE'S ONLY TWO OF THEM!
CAN WE, ASTERIX?
WE CAN, OBELIX!
POW
THAT WAS A GOOD IDEA TO DRINK THE POTION!
COME ON, ROMANS! DO SOMETHING! FIGHT BACK!
SOON AFTER...
YOU WERE RIGHT, DECURION... THAT WAS A GANG!
11

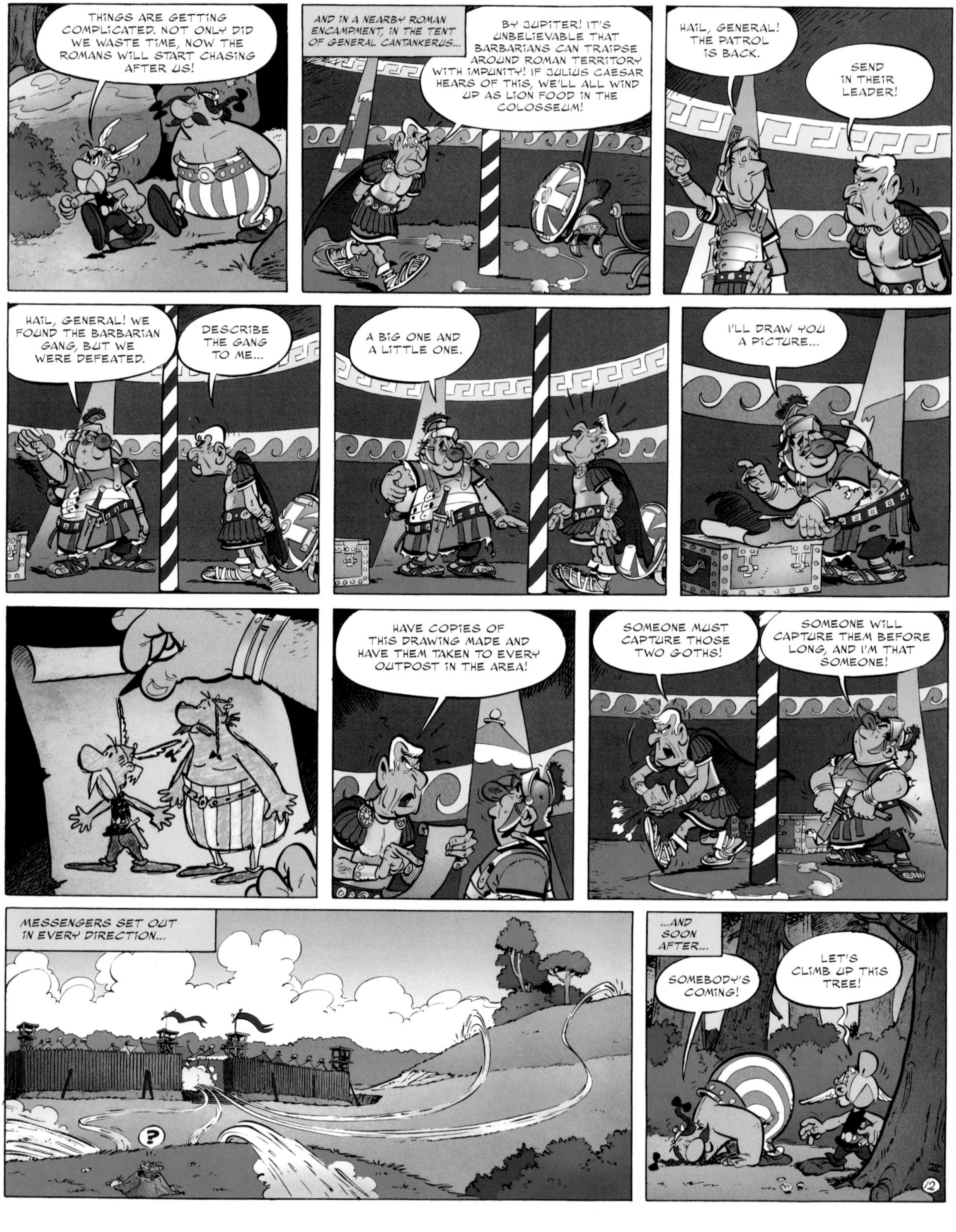
THINGS ARE GETTING COMPLICATED. NOT ONLY DID WE WASTE TIME, NOW THE ROMANS WILL START CHASING AFTER US!
AND IN A NEARBY ROMAN ENCAMPMENT, IN THE TENT OF GENERAL CANTANKERUS...
BY JUPITER! IT'S UNBELIEVABLE THAT BARBARIANS CAN TRAIPSE AROUND ROMAN TERRITORY WITH IMPUNITY! IF JULIUS CAESAR HEARS OF THIS, WE'LL ALL WIND UP AS LION FOOD IN THE COLOSSEUM!
HAIL, GENERAL! THE PATROL IS BACK.
SEND IN THEIR LEADER!
HAIL, GENERAL! WE FOUND THE BARBARIAN GANG, BUT WE WERE DEFEATED.
DESCRIBE THE GANG TO ME...
A BIG ONE AND A LITTLE ONE.
I'LL DRAW YOU A PICTURE...
HAVE COPIES OF THIS DRAWING MADE AND HAVE THEM TAKEN TO EVERY OUTPOST IN THE AREA!
SOMEONE MUST CAPTURE THOSE TWO GOTHS!
SOMEONE WILL CAPTURE THEM BEFORE LONG, AND I'M THAT SOMEONE!
MESSENGERS SET OUT IN EVERY DIRECTION...
?
...AND SOON AFTER...
SOMEBODY'S COMING!
LET'S CLIMB UP THIS TREE!
12

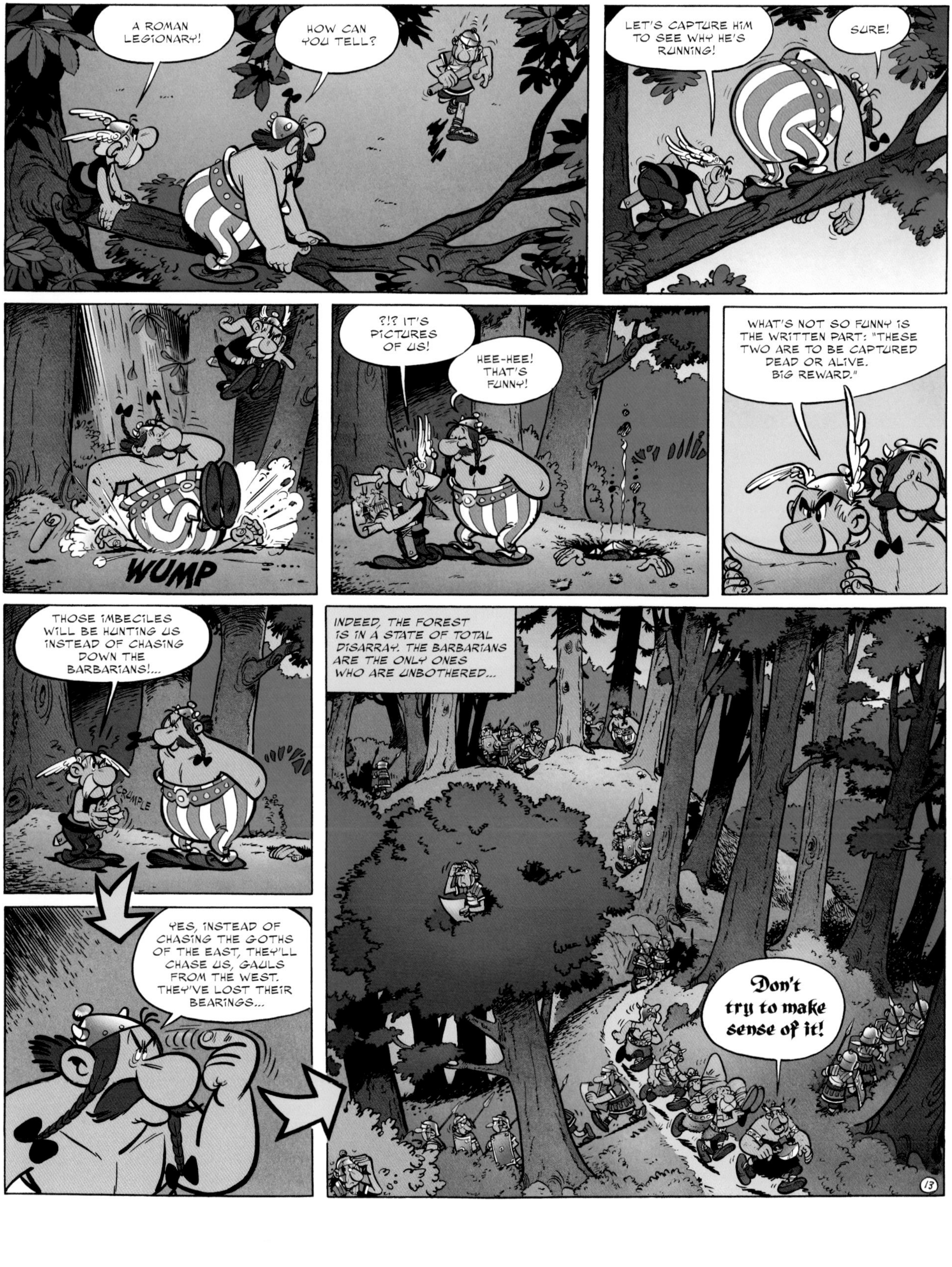
A ROMAN LEGIONARY!
HOW CAN YOU TELL?
LET'S CAPTURE HIM TO SEE WHY HE'S RUNNING!
SURE!
WUMP
?!? IT'S PICTURES OF US!
HEE-HEE! THAT'S FUNNY!
WHAT'S NOT SO FUNNY IS THE WRITTEN PART: "THESE TWO ARE TO BE CAPTURED DEAD OR ALIVE. BIG REWARD."
THOSE IMBECILES WILL BE HUNTING US INSTEAD OF CHASING DOWN THE BARBARIANS!...
CRUMPLE
YES, INSTEAD OF CHASING THE GOTHS OF THE EAST, THEY'LL CHASE US, GAULS FROM THE WEST. THEY'VE LOST THEIR BEARINGS...
INDEED, THE FOREST IS IN A STATE OF TOTAL DISARRAY. THE BARBARIANS ARE THE ONLY ONES WHO ARE UNBOTHERED...
Don't try to make sense of it!
13

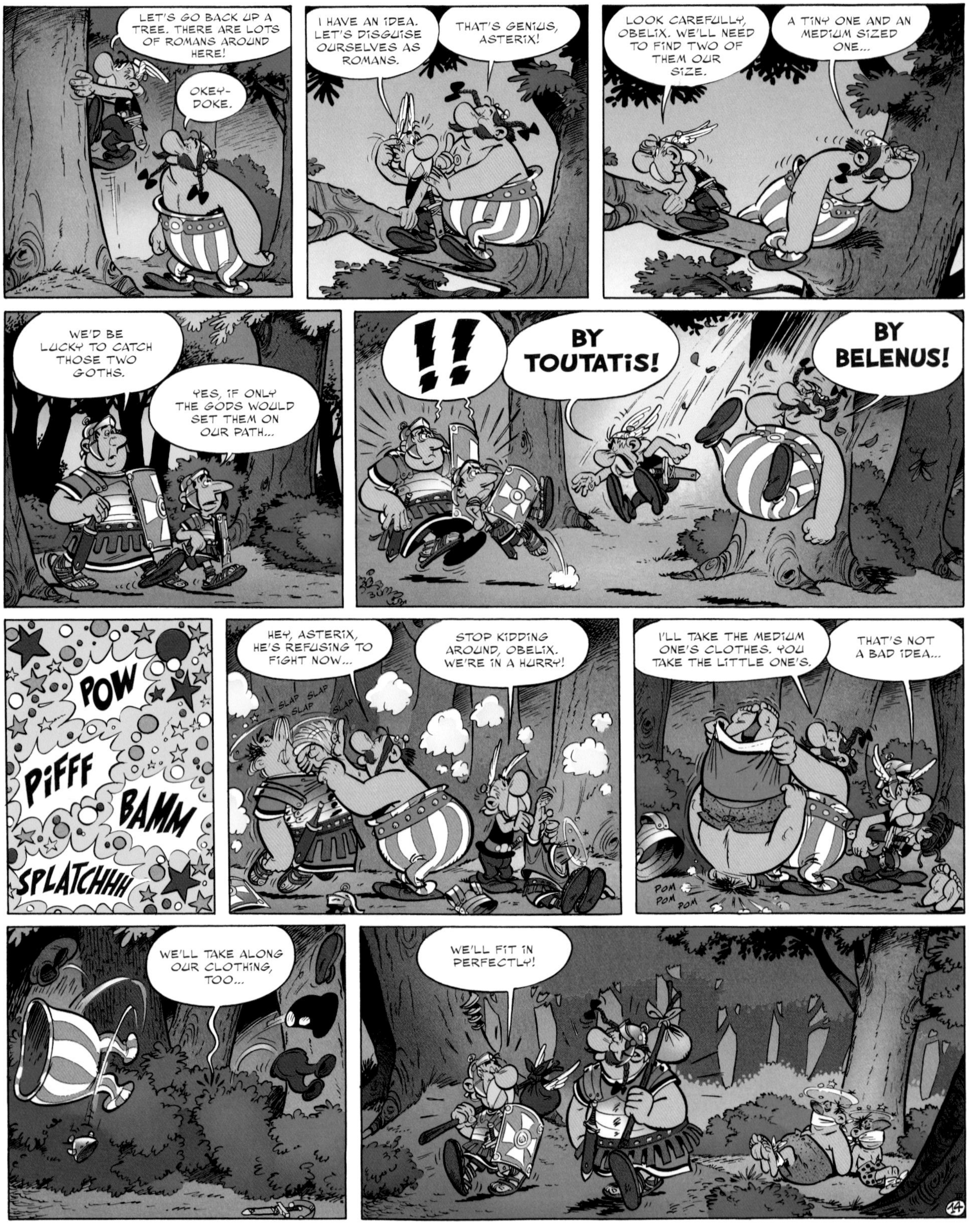

LET'S GO BACK UP A TREE. THERE ARE LOTS OF ROMANS AROUND HERE!
OKEY-DOKE.
I HAVE AN IDEA. LET'S DISGUISE OURSELVES AS ROMANS.
THAT'S GENIUS, ASTERIX!
LOOK CAREFULLY, OBELIX. WE'LL NEED TO FIND TWO OF THEM OUR SIZE.
A TINY ONE AND AN MEDIUM SIZED ONE...
WE'D BE LUCKY TO CATCH THOSE TWO GOTHS.
YES, IF ONLY THE GODS WOULD SET THEM ON OUR PATH...
!!
BY TOUTATIS!
BY BELENUS!
POW
PIFFF
BAMM
SPLATCHHH
HEY, ASTERIX, HE'S REFUSING TO FIGHT NOW...
SLAP SLAP SLAP SLAP
STOP KIDDING AROUND, OBELIX. WE'RE IN A HURRY!
I'LL TAKE THE MEDIUM ONE'S CLOTHES. YOU TAKE THE LITTLE ONE'S.
THAT'S NOT A BAD IDEA...
POM POM POM
WE'LL TAKE ALONG OUR CLOTHING, TOO...
WE'LL FIT IN PERFECTLY!
14

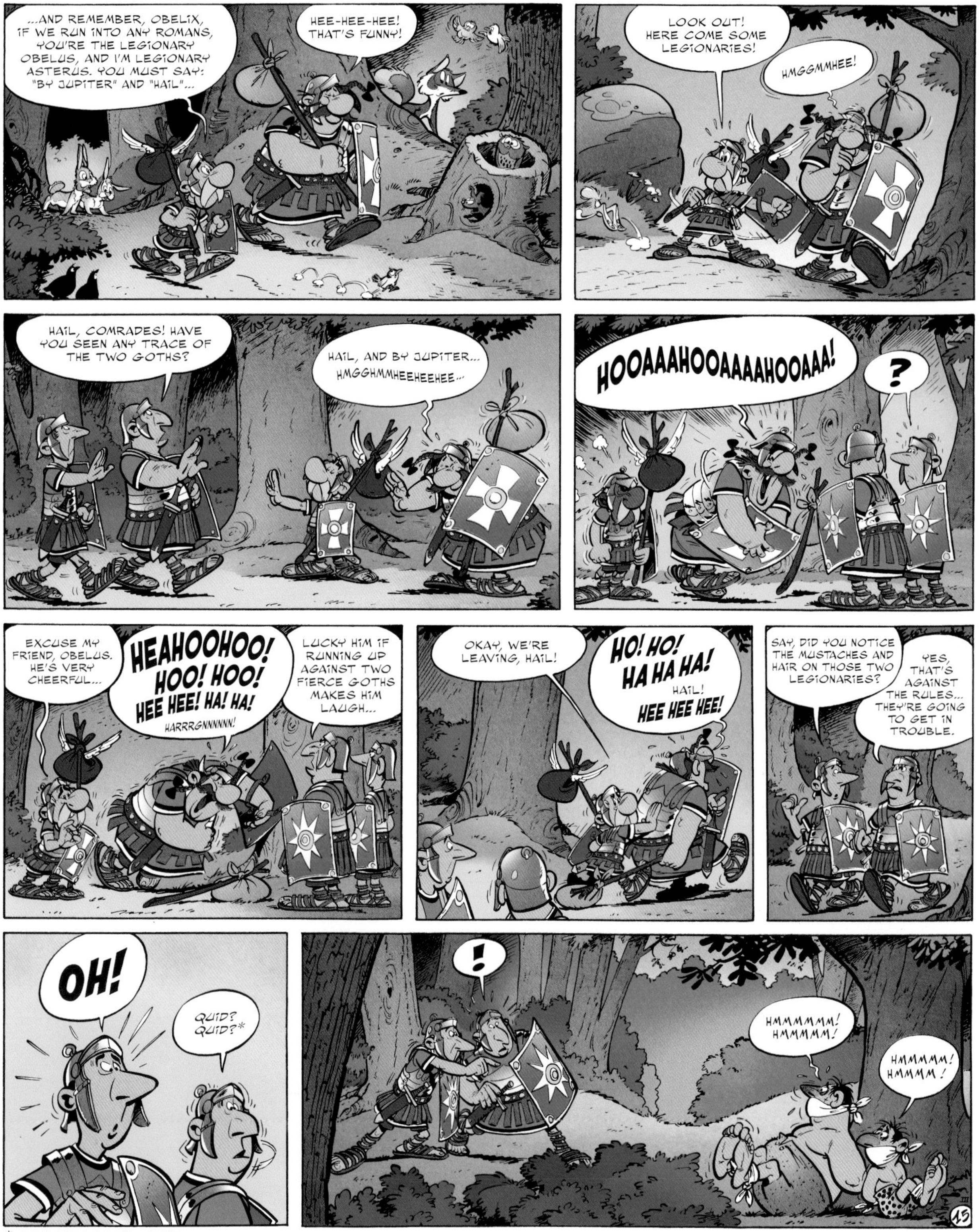
...AND REMEMBER, OBELIX, IF WE RUN INTO ANY ROMANS, YOU'RE THE LEGIONARY OBELUS, AND I'M LEGIONARY ASTERUS. YOU MUST SAY: "BY JUPITER" AND "HAIL"...
HEE-HEE-HEE! THAT'S FUNNY!
LOOK OUT! HERE COME SOME LEGIONARIES!
HMGGMMHEE!
HAIL, COMRADES! HAVE YOU SEEN ANY TRACE OF THE TWO GOTHS?
HAIL, AND BY JUPITER... HMGGHMMHEEHEEHEE...
HOOAAAHOOAAAAHOOAAA!
?
EXCUSE MY FRIEND, OBELUS. HE'S VERY CHEERFUL...
HEAHOOHOO! HOO! HOO! HEE HEE! HA! HA! HARRRGNNNNNN!
LUCKY HIM IF RUNNING UP AGAINST TWO FIERCE GOTHS MAKES HIM LAUGH...
OKAY, WE'RE LEAVING, HAIL!
HO! HO! HA HA HA! HAIL! HEE HEE HEE!
SAY, DID YOU NOTICE THE MUSTACHES AND HAIR ON THOSE TWO LEGIONARIES?
YES, THAT'S AGAINST THE RULES... THEY'RE GOING TO GET IN TROUBLE.
OH!
QUID? QUID?*
!
HMMMMMM! HMMMMM!
HMMMMM! HMMMM!
15

*LATIN FOR "WHAT? WHAT?"

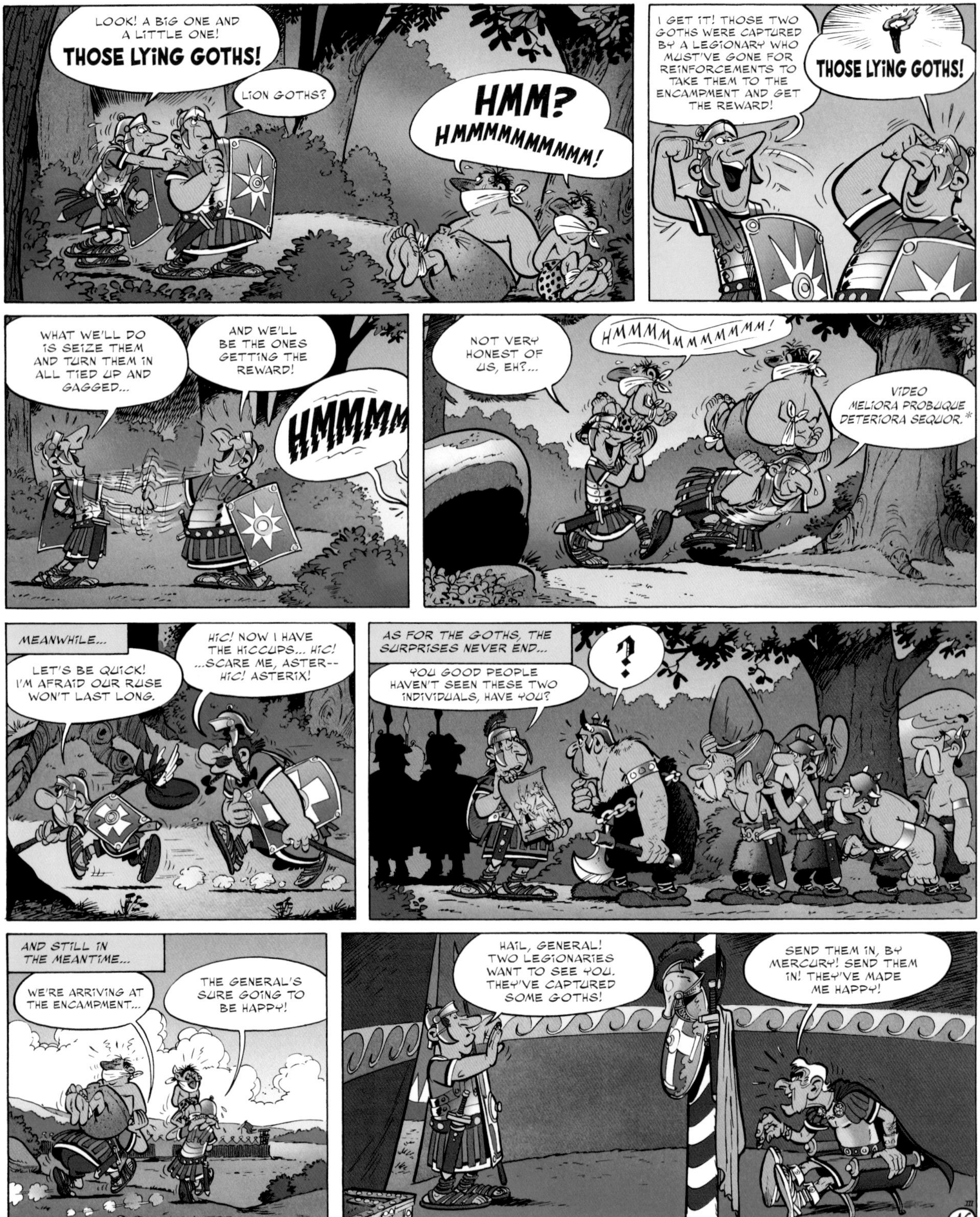

LOOK! A BIG ONE AND A LITTLE ONE! THOSE LYING GOTHS!
LION GOTHS?
HMM? HMMMMMMMMMM!
I GET IT! THOSE TWO GOTHS WERE CAPTURED BY A LEGIONARY WHO MUST'VE GONE FOR REINFORCEMENTS TO TAKE THEM TO THE ENCAMPMENT AND GET THE REWARD!
THOSE LYING GOTHS!
WHAT WE'LL DO IS SEIZE THEM AND TURN THEM IN ALL TIED UP AND GAGGED...
AND WE'LL BE THE ONES GETTING THE REWARD!
HMMMM
NOT VERY HONEST OF US, EH?...
HMMMMMMMMMMM!
VIDEO MELIORA PROBUQUE DETERIORA SEQUOR.*
MEANWHILE...
LET'S BE QUICK! I'M AFRAID OUR RUSE WON'T LAST LONG.
HIC! NOW I HAVE THE HICCUPS... HIC! ...SCARE ME, ASTER-- HIC! ASTERIX!
AS FOR THE GOTHS, THE SURPRISES NEVER END...
YOU GOOD PEOPLE HAVEN'T SEEN THESE TWO INDIVIDUALS, HAVE YOU?
?
AND STILL IN THE MEANTIME...
WE'RE ARRIVING AT THE ENCAMPMENT...
THE GENERAL'S SURE GOING TO BE HAPPY!
HAIL, GENERAL! TWO LEGIONARIES WANT TO SEE YOU. THEY'VE CAPTURED SOME GOTHS!
SEND THEM IN, BY MERCURY! SEND THEM IN! THEY'VE MADE ME HAPPY!
16

*LATIN FOR "I SEE AND APPROVE OF THE BETTER PATH, BUT I FOLLOW THE WORSE." IN OTHER WORDS, "DISHONESTY IS THE BEST POLICY."

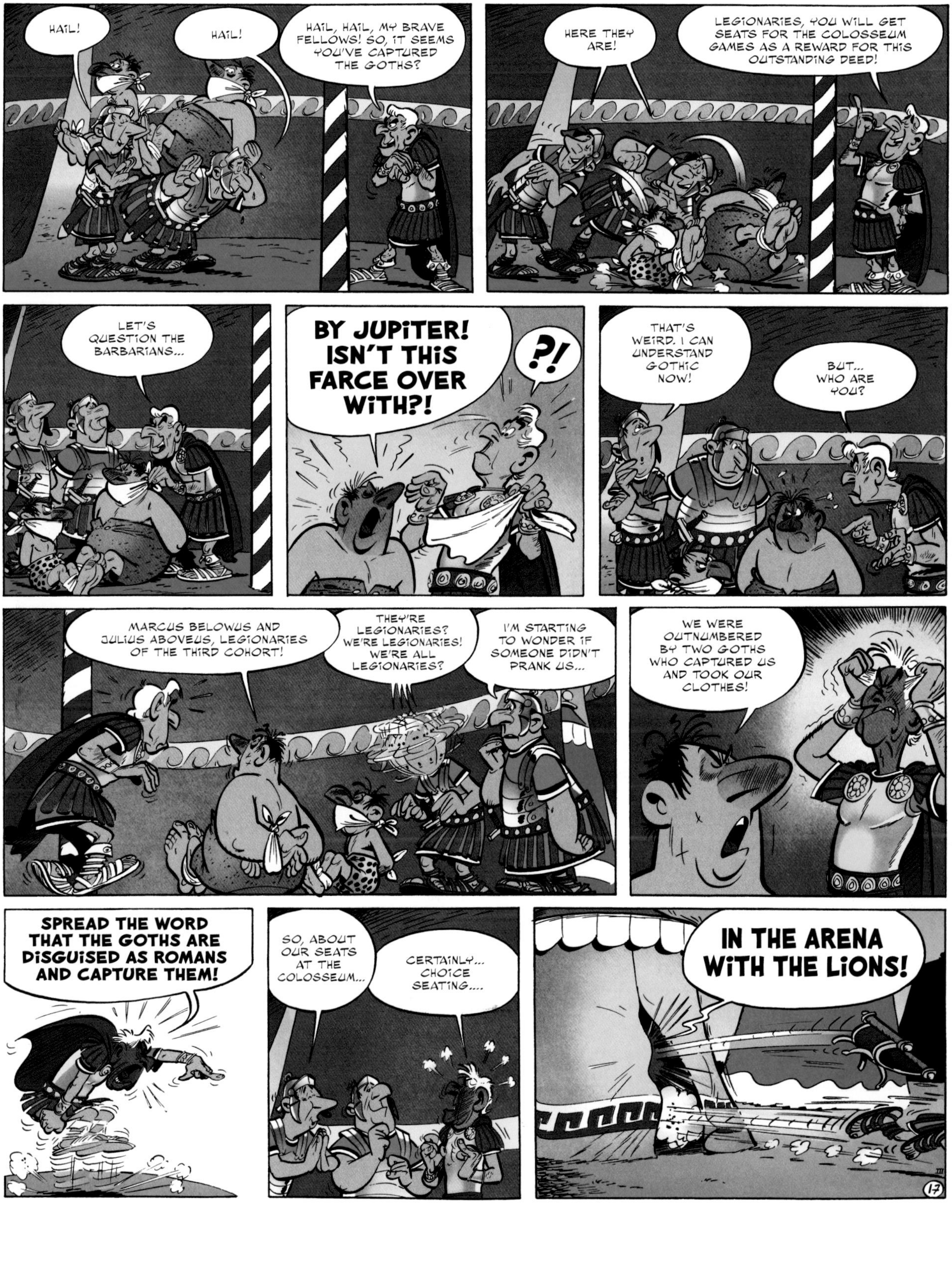
HAIL!
HAIL!
HAIL, HAIL, MY BRAVE FELLOWS! SO, IT SEEMS YOU'VE CAPTURED THE GOTHS?
HERE THEY ARE!
LEGIONARIES, YOU WILL GET SEATS FOR THE COLOSSEUM GAMES AS A REWARD FOR THIS OUTSTANDING DEED!
LET'S QUESTION THE BARBARIANS...
BY JUPITER! ISN'T THIS FARCE OVER WITH?!
?!
THAT'S WEIRD. I CAN UNDERSTAND GOTHIC NOW!
BUT... WHO ARE YOU?
MARCUS BELOWUS AND JULIUS ABOVEUS, LEGIONARIES OF THE THIRD COHORT!
THEY'RE LEGIONARIES? WE'RE LEGIONARIES! WE'RE ALL LEGIONARIES?
I'M STARTING TO WONDER IF SOMEONE DIDN'T PRANK US...
WE WERE OUTNUMBERED BY TWO GOTHS WHO CAPTURED US AND TOOK OUR CLOTHES!
SPREAD THE WORD THAT THE GOTHS ARE DISGUISED AS ROMANS AND CAPTURE THEM!
SO, ABOUT OUR SEATS AT THE COLOSSEUM...
CERTAINLY... CHOICE SEATING....
IN THE ARENA WITH THE LIONS!
17

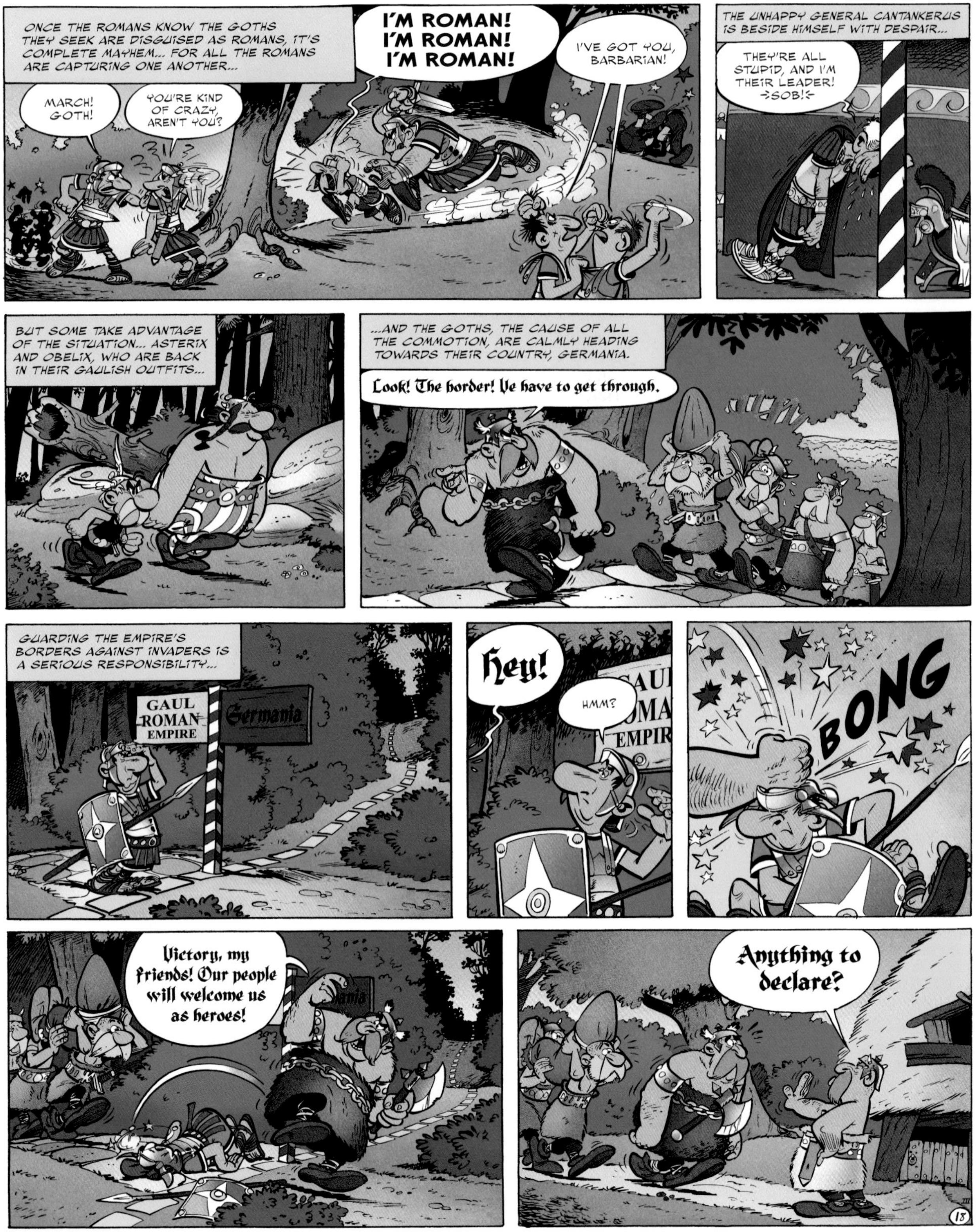
ONCE THE ROMANS KNOW THE GOTHS THEY SEEK ARE DISGUISED AS ROMANS, IT'S COMPLETE MAYHEM... FOR ALL THE ROMANS ARE CAPTURING ONE ANOTHER...
MARCH! GOTH!
YOU'RE KIND OF CRAZY, AREN'T YOU?
I'M ROMAN! I'M ROMAN! I'M ROMAN!
I'VE GOT YOU, BARBARIAN!
THE UNHAPPY GENERAL CANTANKERUS IS BESIDE HIMSELF WITH DESPAIR...
THEY'RE ALL STUPID, AND I'M THEIR LEADER! >SOB!<
BUT SOME TAKE ADVANTAGE OF THE SITUATION... ASTERIX AND OBELIX, WHO ARE BACK IN THEIR GAULISH OUTFITS...
...AND THE GOTHS, THE CAUSE OF ALL THE COMMOTION, ARE CALMLY HEADING TOWARDS THEIR COUNTRY, GERMANIA.
Look! The border! Ve have to get through.
GUARDING THE EMPIRE'S BORDERS AGAINST INVADERS IS A SERIOUS RESPONSIBILITY...
GAUL ROMAN EMPIRE
Germania
Hey!
HMM?
BONG
Victory, my friends! Our people will welcome us as heroes!
Anything to declare?
18

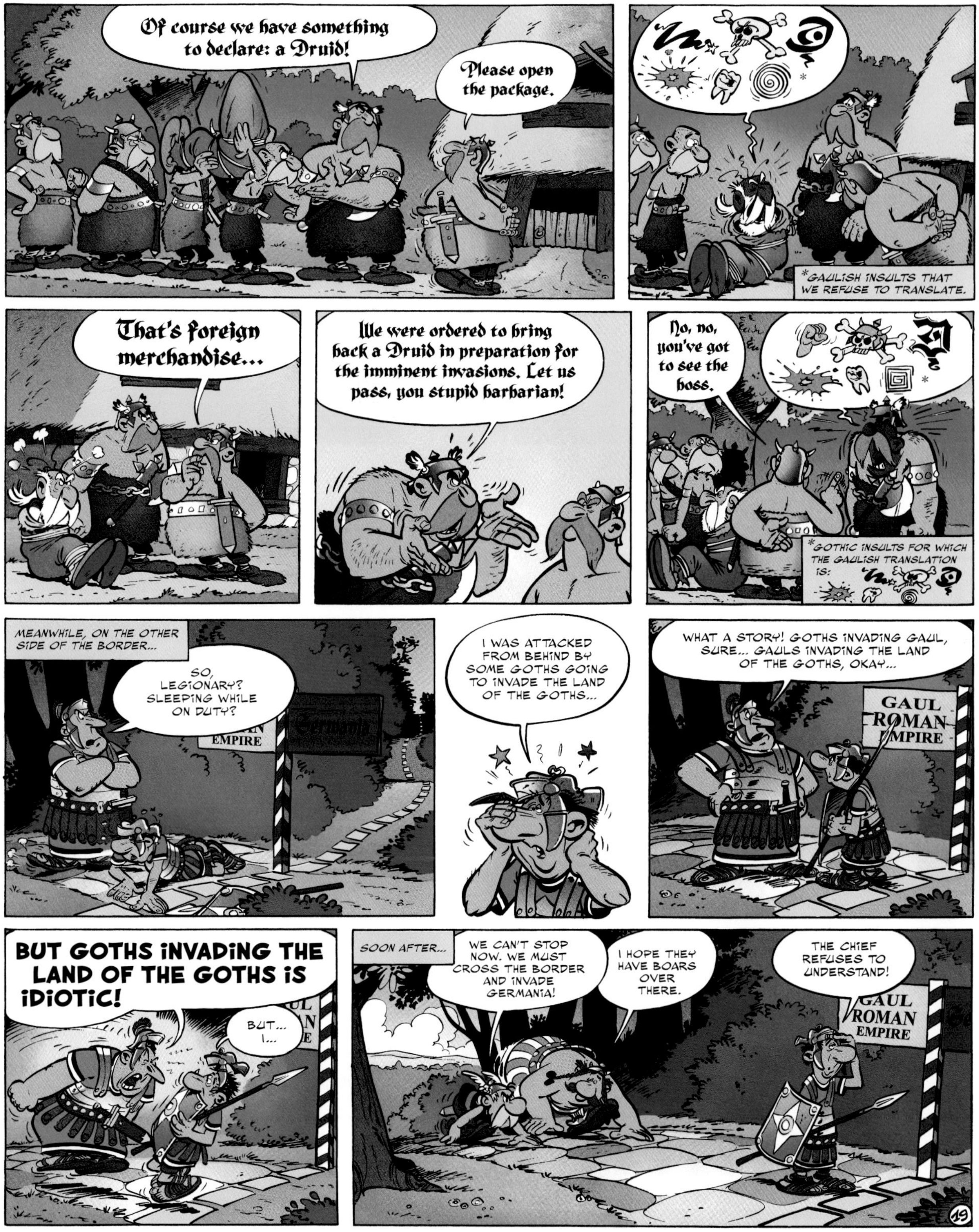

Of course we have something to declare: a Druid!
Please open the package.
*
*GAULISH INSULTS THAT WE REFUSE TO TRANSLATE.
That's foreign merchandise...
We were ordered to bring back a Druid in preparation for the imminent invasions. Let us pass, you stupid barbarian!
No, no, you've got to see the boss.
*
*GOTHIC INSULTS FOR WHICH THE GAULISH TRANSLATION IS:
MEANWHILE, ON THE OTHER SIDE OF THE BORDER...
SO, LEGIONARY? SLEEPING WHILE ON DUTY?
EMPIRE
I WAS ATTACKED FROM BEHIND BY SOME GOTHS GOING TO INVADE THE LAND OF THE GOTHS...
WHAT A STORY! GOTHS INVADING GAUL, SURE... GAULS INVADING THE LAND OF THE GOTHS, OKAY...
GAUL ROMAN EMPIRE
BUT GOTHS INVADING THE LAND OF THE GOTHS IS IDIOTIC!
BUT... I...
SOON AFTER...
WE CAN'T STOP NOW. WE MUST CROSS THE BORDER AND INVADE GERMANIA!
I HOPE THEY HAVE BOARS OVER THERE.
THE CHIEF REFUSES TO UNDERSTAND!
GAUL ROMAN EMPIRE
19

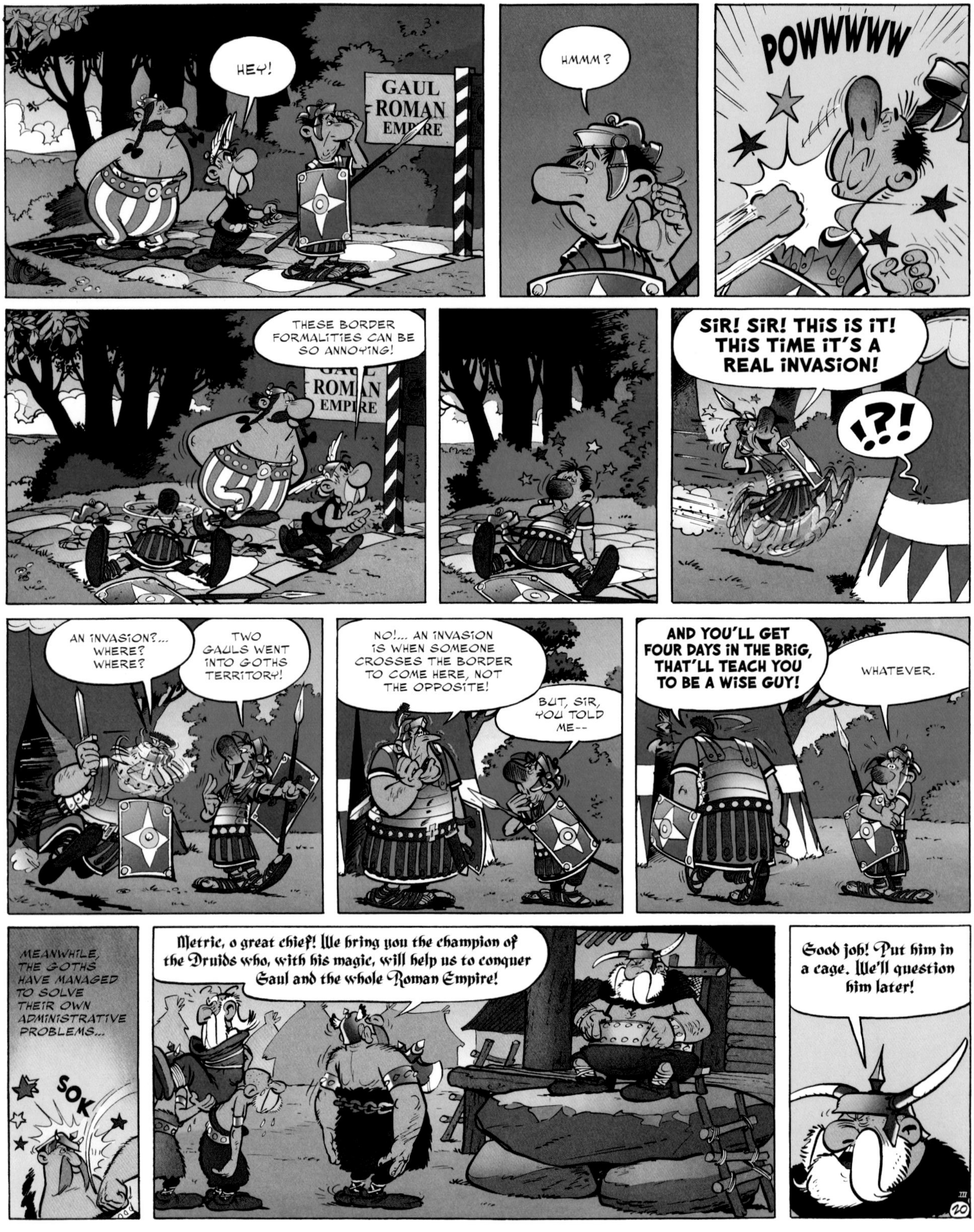

HEY!
GAUL
ROMAN EMPIRE
HMMM?
POWWWWW
THESE BORDER FORMALITIES CAN BE SO ANNOYING!
ROMAN EMPIRE
SIR! SIR! THIS IS IT! THIS TIME IT'S A REAL INVASION!
!?!
AN INVASION?... WHERE? WHERE?
TWO GAULS WENT INTO GOTHS TERRITORY!
NO!... AN INVASION IS WHEN SOMEONE CROSSES THE BORDER TO COME HERE, NOT THE OPPOSITE!
BUT, SIR, YOU TOLD ME--
AND YOU'LL GET FOUR DAYS IN THE BRIG, THAT'LL TEACH YOU TO BE A WISE GUY!
WHATEVER.
MEANWHILE, THE GOTHS HAVE MANAGED TO SOLVE THEIR OWN ADMINISTRATIVE PROBLEMS...
SOK
Metric, o great chief! We bring you the champion of the Druids who, with his magic, will help us to conquer Gaul and the whole Roman Empire!
Good job! Put him in a cage. We'll question him later!

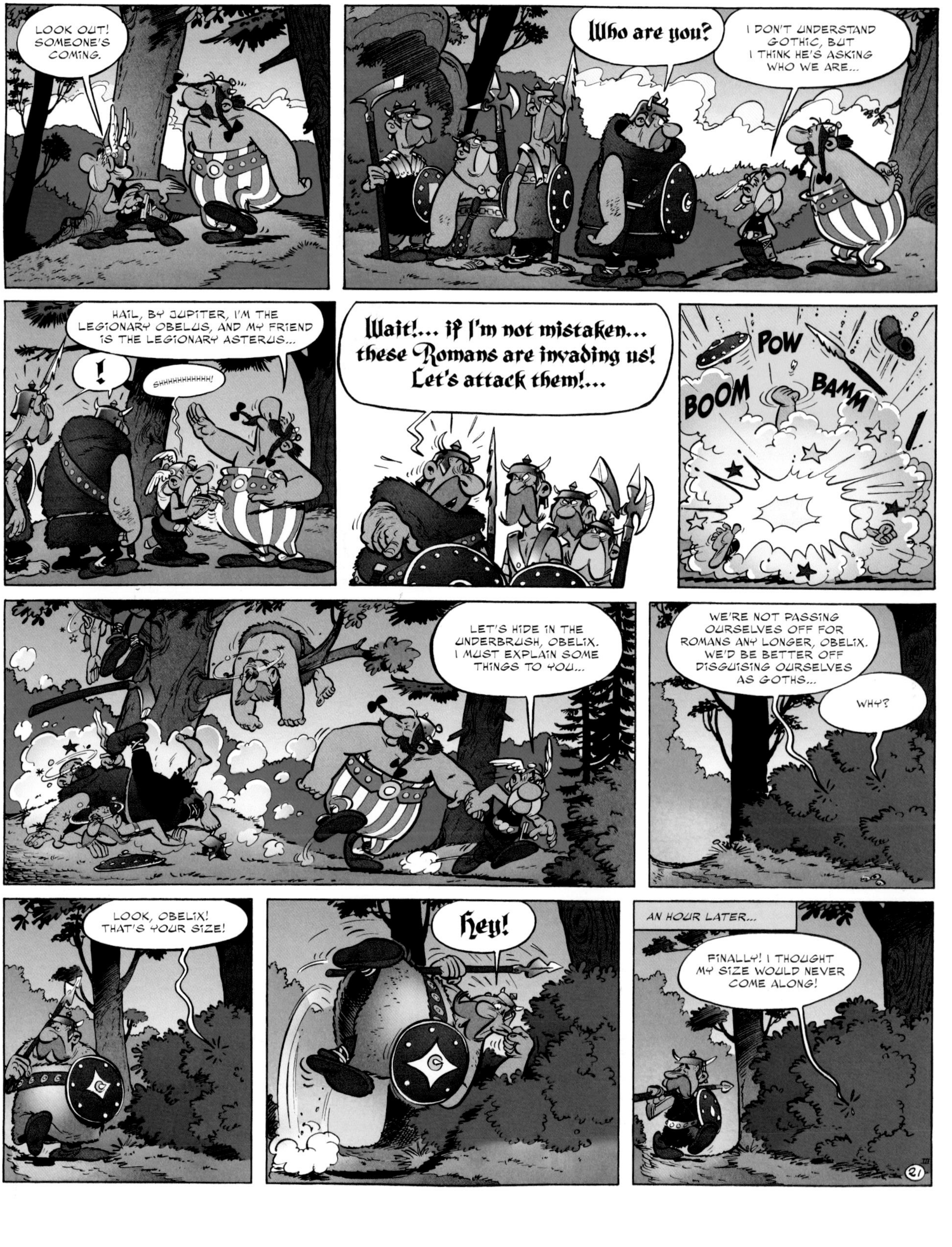
LOOK OUT! SOMEONE'S COMING.
Who are you?
I DON'T UNDERSTAND GOTHIC, BUT I THINK HE'S ASKING WHO WE ARE...
HAIL, BY JUPITER, I'M THE LEGIONARY OBELUS, AND MY FRIEND IS THE LEGIONARY ASTERUS...
!
SHHHHHHHHHHHH!
Wait!... if I'm not mistaken... these Romans are invading us! Let's attack them!...
POW
BOOM
BAMM
LET'S HIDE IN THE UNDERBRUSH, OBELIX. I MUST EXPLAIN SOME THINGS TO YOU...
WE'RE NOT PASSING OURSELVES OFF FOR ROMANS ANY LONGER, OBELIX. WE'D BE BETTER OFF DISGUISING OURSELVES AS GOTHS...
WHY?
LOOK, OBELIX! THAT'S YOUR SIZE!
Hey!
AN HOUR LATER...
FINALLY! I THOUGHT MY SIZE WOULD NEVER COME ALONG!
21

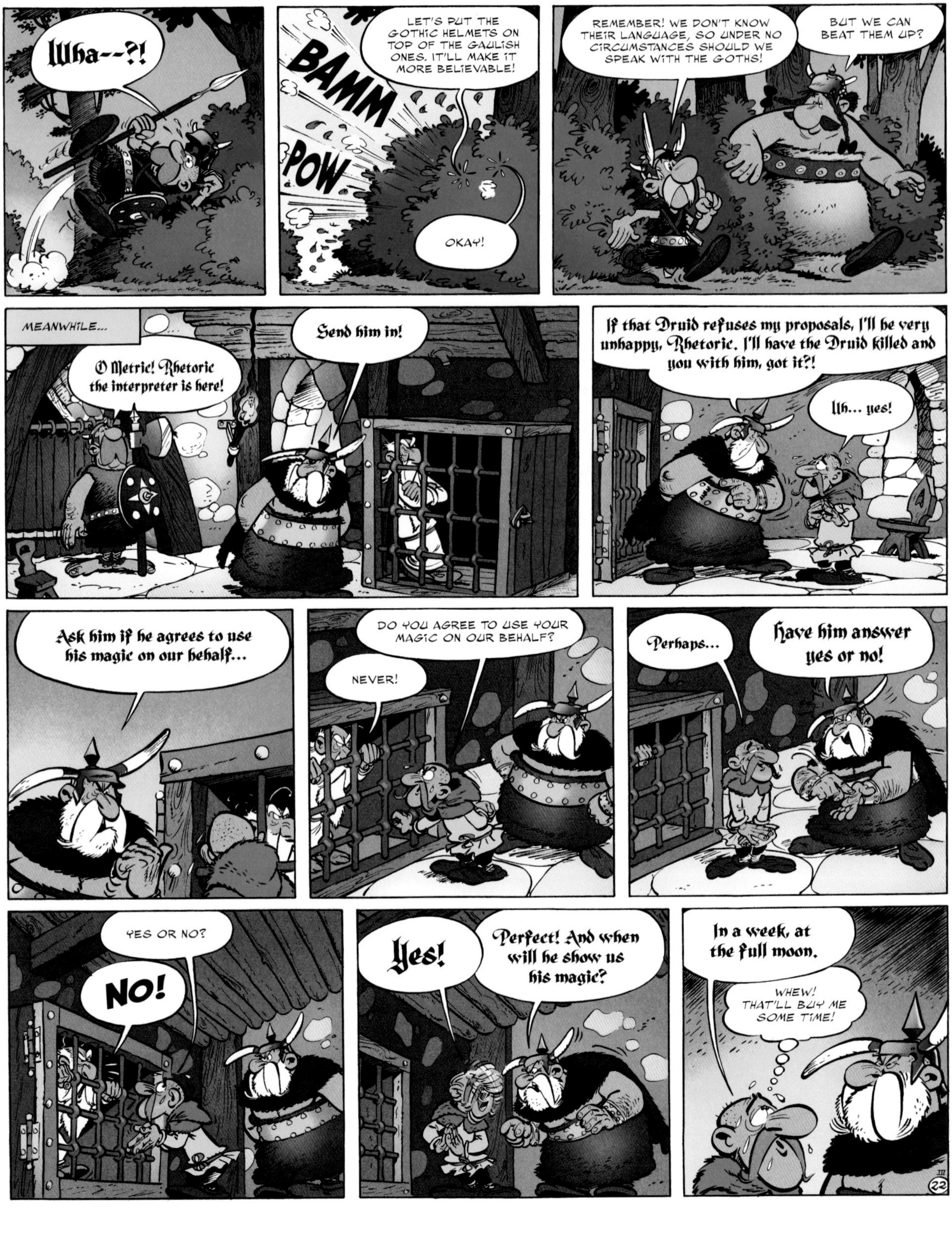
Wha--?!
BAMM
POW
LET'S PUT THE GOTHIC HELMETS ON TOP OF THE GAULISH ONES. IT'LL MAKE IT MORE BELIEVABLE!
OKAY!
REMEMBER! WE DON'T KNOW THEIR LANGUAGE, SO UNDER NO CIRCUMSTANCES SHOULD WE SPEAK WITH THE GOTHS!
BUT WE CAN BEAT THEM UP?
MEANWHILE...
O Metric! Rhetoric the interpreter is here!
Send him in!
If that Druid refuses my proposals, I'll be very unhappy, Rhetoric. I'll have the Druid killed and you with him, got it?!
Uh... yes!
Ask him if he agrees to use his magic on our behalf...
DO YOU AGREE TO USE YOUR MAGIC ON OUR BEHALF?
NEVER!
Perhaps...
Have him answer yes or no!
YES OR NO?
NO!
Yes!
Perfect! And when will he show us his magic?
In a week, at the full moon.
WHEW! THAT'LL BUY ME SOME TIME!
III 22

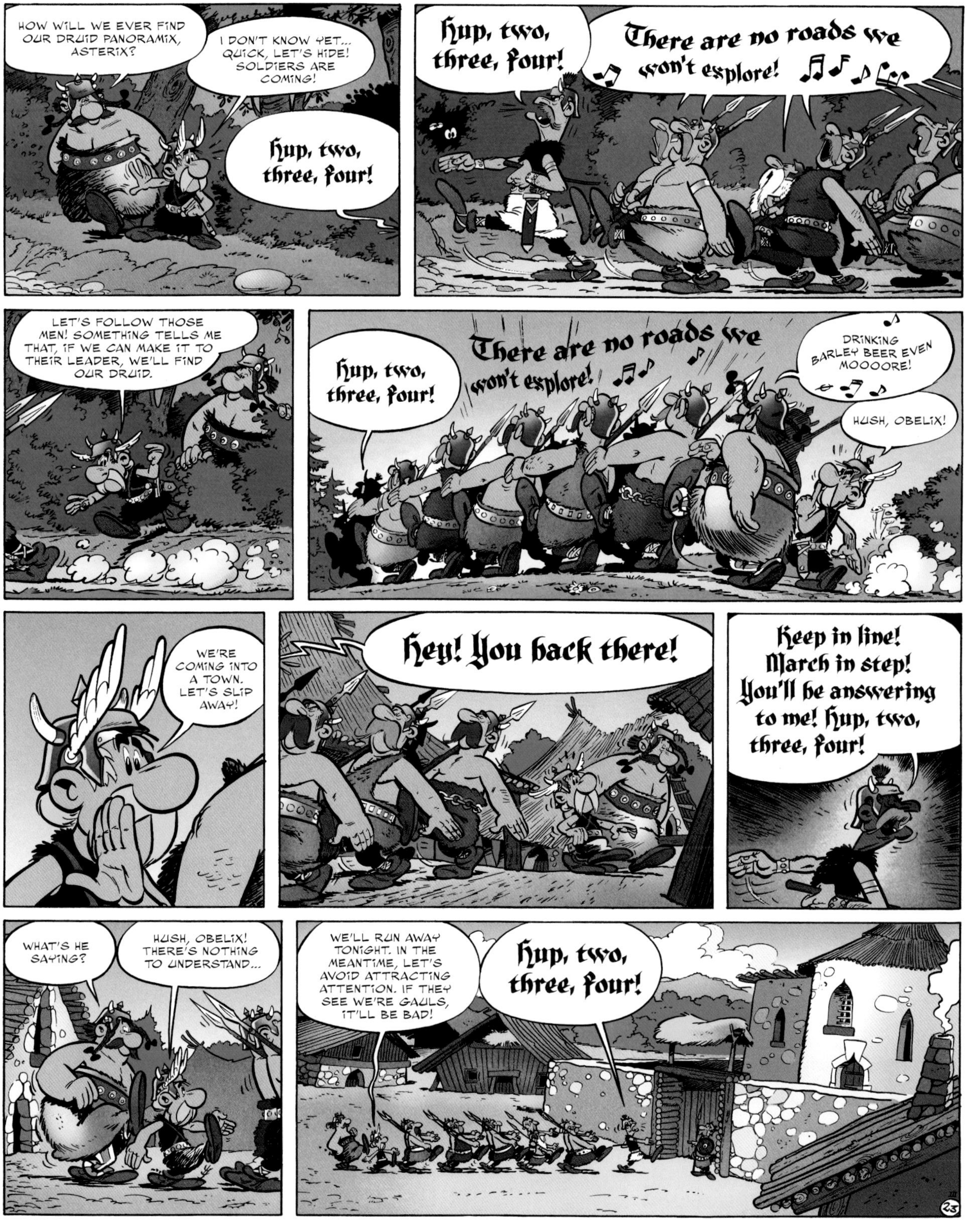
HOW WILL WE EVER FIND OUR DRUID PANORAMIX, ASTERIX?
I DON'T KNOW YET... QUICK, LET'S HIDE! SOLDIERS ARE COMING!
Hup, two, three, four!
Hup, two, three, four!
There are no roads we won't explore!
LET'S FOLLOW THOSE MEN! SOMETHING TELLS ME THAT, IF WE CAN MAKE IT TO THEIR LEADER, WE'LL FIND OUR DRUID.
Hup, two, three, four!
There are no roads we won't explore!
DRINKING BARLEY BEER EVEN MOOOORE!
HUSH, OBELIX!
WE'RE COMING INTO A TOWN. LET'S SLIP AWAY!
Hey! You back there!
Keep in line! March in step! You'll be answering to me! Hup, two, three, four!
WHAT'S HE SAYING?
HUSH, OBELIX! THERE'S NOTHING TO UNDERSTAND...
WE'LL RUN AWAY TONIGHT. IN THE MEANTIME, LET'S AVOID ATTRACTING ATTENTION. IF THEY SEE WE'RE GAULS, IT'LL BE BAD!
Hup, two, three, four!
23

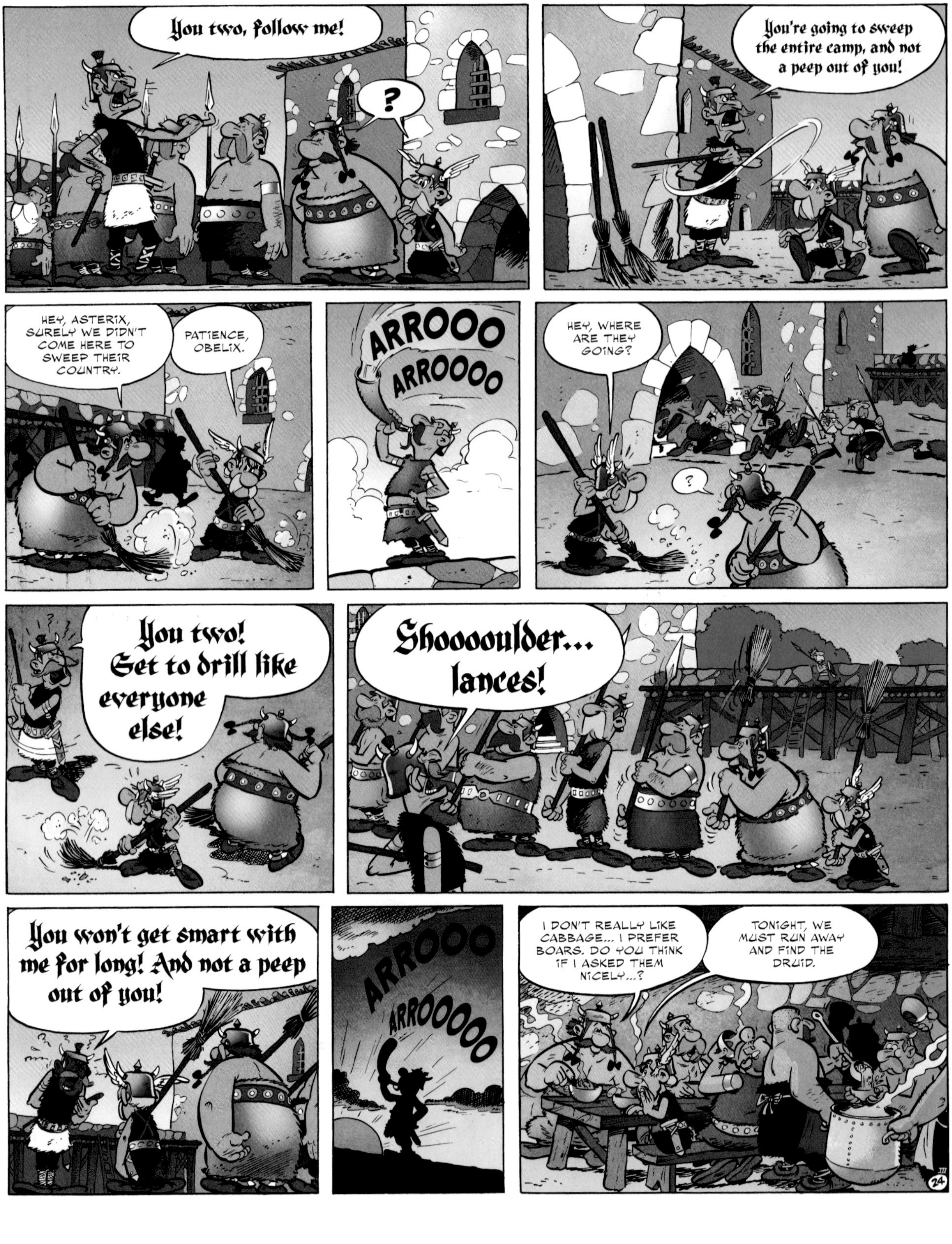
You two, follow me!
?
You're going to sweep the entire camp, and not a peep out of you!
HEY, ASTERIX, SURELY WE DIDN'T COME HERE TO SWEEP THEIR COUNTRY.
PATIENCE, OBELIX.
ARROOO
ARROOOO
HEY, WHERE ARE THEY GOING?
?
You two! Get to drill like everyone else!
Shooooulder... lances!
You won't get smart with me for long! And not a peep out of you!
ARROOO
ARROOOOO
I DON'T REALLY LIKE CABBAGE... I PREFER BOARS. DO YOU THINK IF I ASKED THEM NICELY...?
TONIGHT, WE MUST RUN AWAY AND FIND THE DRUID.
24

ASTERIX AND OBELIX AREN'T THE ONLY ONES PLANNING TO RUN AWAY... FOR, ON THE OTHER SIDE OF TOWN...

I'LL GO TO GAUL. WITH MY LANGUAGE SKILLS, I COULD MAKE A HOME THERE...

HALT!

THE PATROL!

Why, it's Rhetoric the interpreter! Where are you going at this hour?

Vell, I... uh... because... so... or rather...

That's all very shady. Send him to the brig. We'll clear this up tomorrow.

No! No! You're making a mistake! I have connections!

I'M DOOMED! OUR LEADER WILL NEVER FORGIVE ME FOR DECEIVING HIM ABOUT THAT STUBBORN DRUID'S ANSWERS...

MEAN-WHILE...

UNDERSTOOD? NO BRAWLING OR TALKING WITH GOTHS!

OKAY!

!

OH, NO!

Aha, my two rogues! Throw them into prison!

25

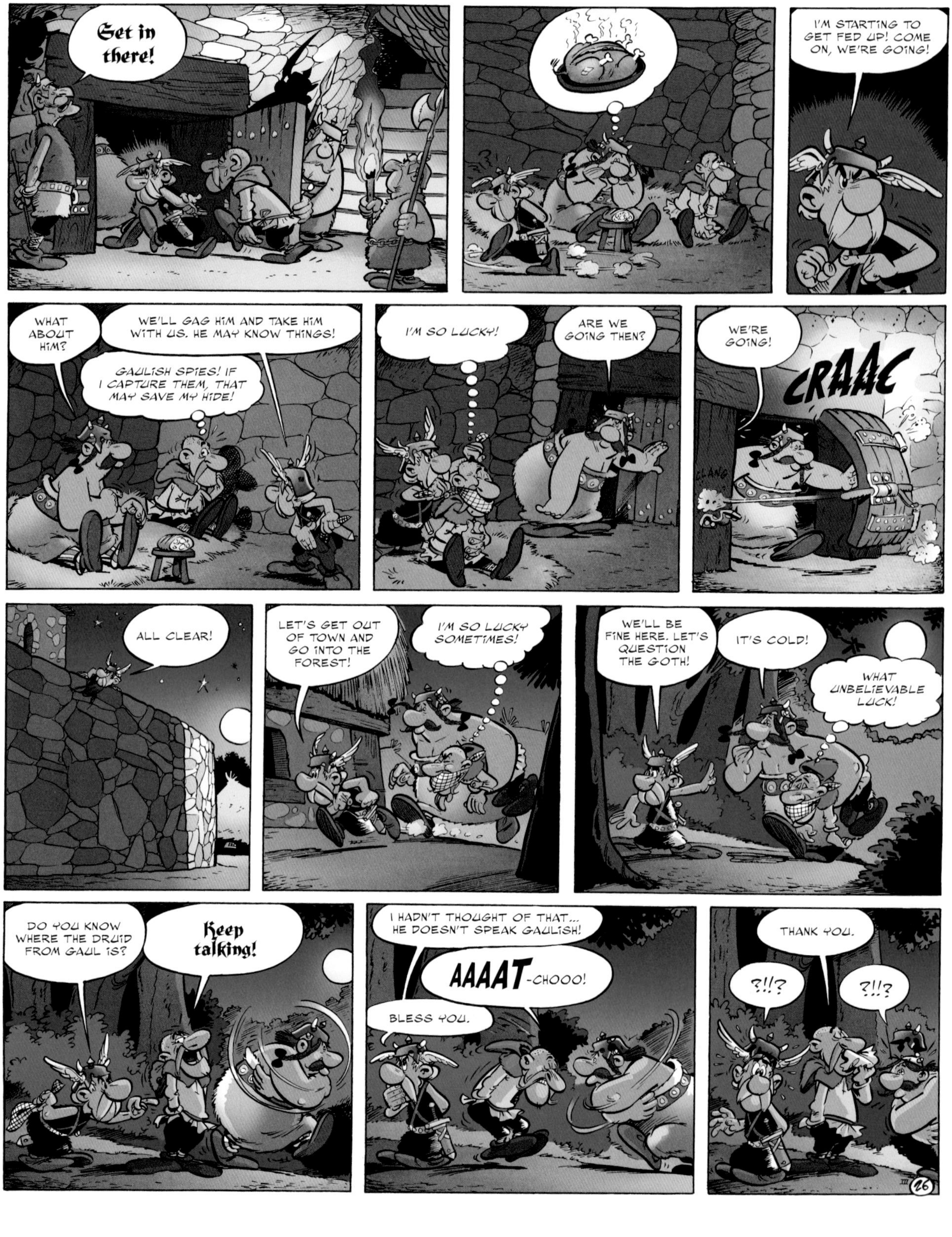
Get in there!
I'M STARTING TO GET FED UP! COME ON, WE'RE GOING!
WHAT ABOUT HIM?
WE'LL GAG HIM AND TAKE HIM WITH US. HE MAY KNOW THINGS!
GAULISH SPIES! IF I CAPTURE THEM, THAT MAY SAVE MY HIDE!
I'M SO LUCKY!
ARE WE GOING THEN?
WE'RE GOING!
CRAAC
CLANG
ALL CLEAR!
LET'S GET OUT OF TOWN AND GO INTO THE FOREST!
I'M SO LUCKY SOMETIMES!
WE'LL BE FINE HERE. LET'S QUESTION THE GOTH!
IT'S COLD!
WHAT UNBELIEVABLE LUCK!
DO YOU KNOW WHERE THE DRUID FROM GAUL IS?
Keep talking!
I HADN'T THOUGHT OF THAT... HE DOESN'T SPEAK GAULISH!
AAAAT-CHOOO!
BLESS YOU.
THANK YOU.
?!!?
?!!?
26

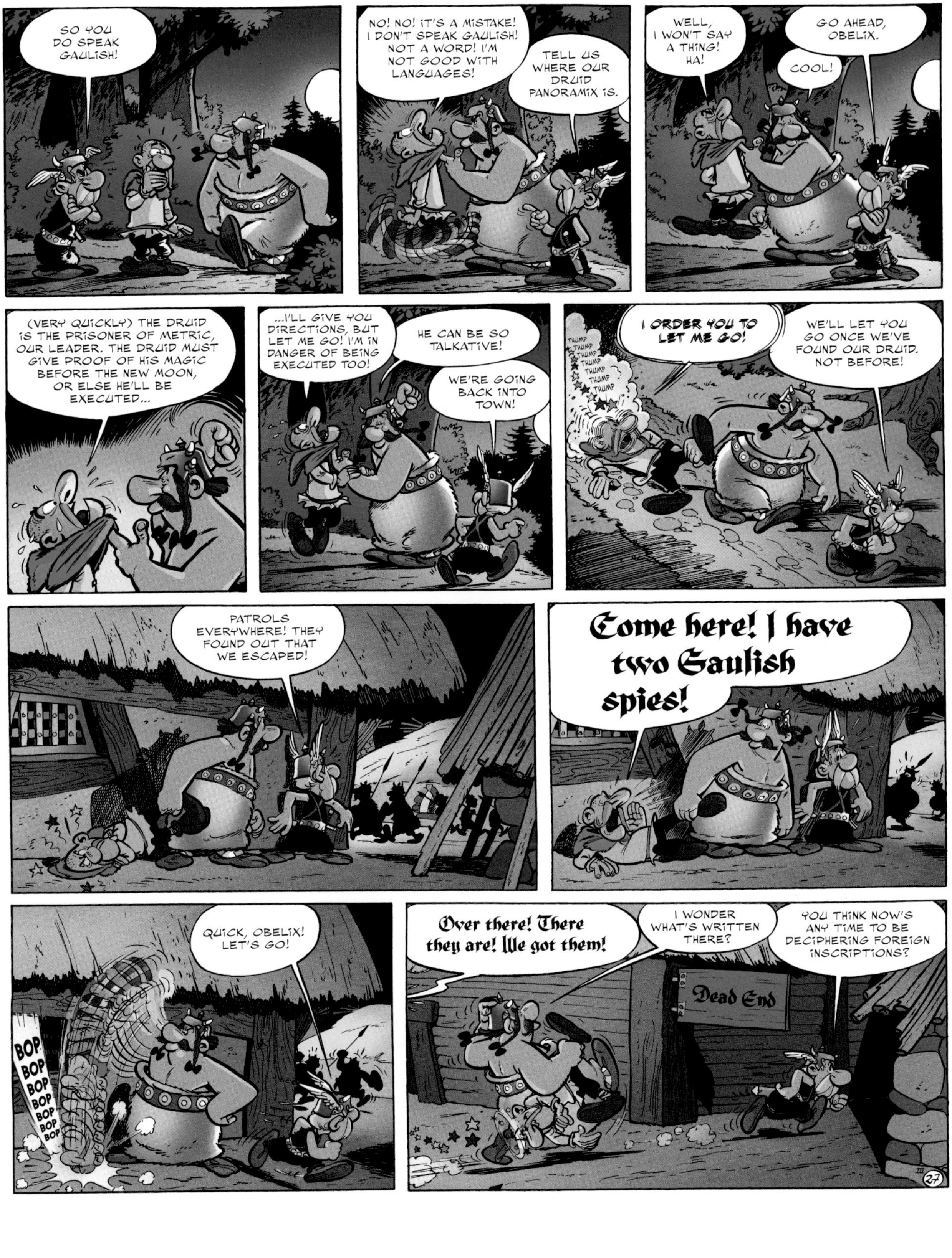
SO YOU DO SPEAK GAULISH!
NO! NO! IT'S A MISTAKE! I DON'T SPEAK GAULISH! NOT A WORD! I'M NOT GOOD WITH LANGUAGES!
TELL US WHERE OUR DRUID PANORAMIX IS.
WELL, I WON'T SAY A THING! HA!
GO AHEAD, OBELIX.
COOL!
(VERY QUICKLY) THE DRUID IS THE PRISONER OF METRIC, OUR LEADER. THE DRUID MUST GIVE PROOF OF HIS MAGIC BEFORE THE NEW MOON, OR ELSE HE'LL BE EXECUTED...
...I'LL GIVE YOU DIRECTIONS, BUT LET ME GO! I'M IN DANGER OF BEING EXECUTED TOO!
HE CAN BE SO TALKATIVE!
WE'RE GOING BACK INTO TOWN!
THUMP THUMP THUMP THUMP THUMP THUMP THUMP
I ORDER YOU TO LET ME GO!
WE'LL LET YOU GO ONCE WE'VE FOUND OUR DRUID. NOT BEFORE!
PATROLS EVERYWHERE! THEY FOUND OUT THAT WE ESCAPED!
Come here! I have two Gaulish spies!
QUICK, OBELIX! LET'S GO!
BOP BOP BOP BOP BOP BOP BOP
Over there! There they are! We got them!
I WONDER WHAT'S WRITTEN THERE?
YOU THINK NOW'S ANY TIME TO BE DECIPHERING FOREIGN INSCRIPTIONS?
Dead End
27

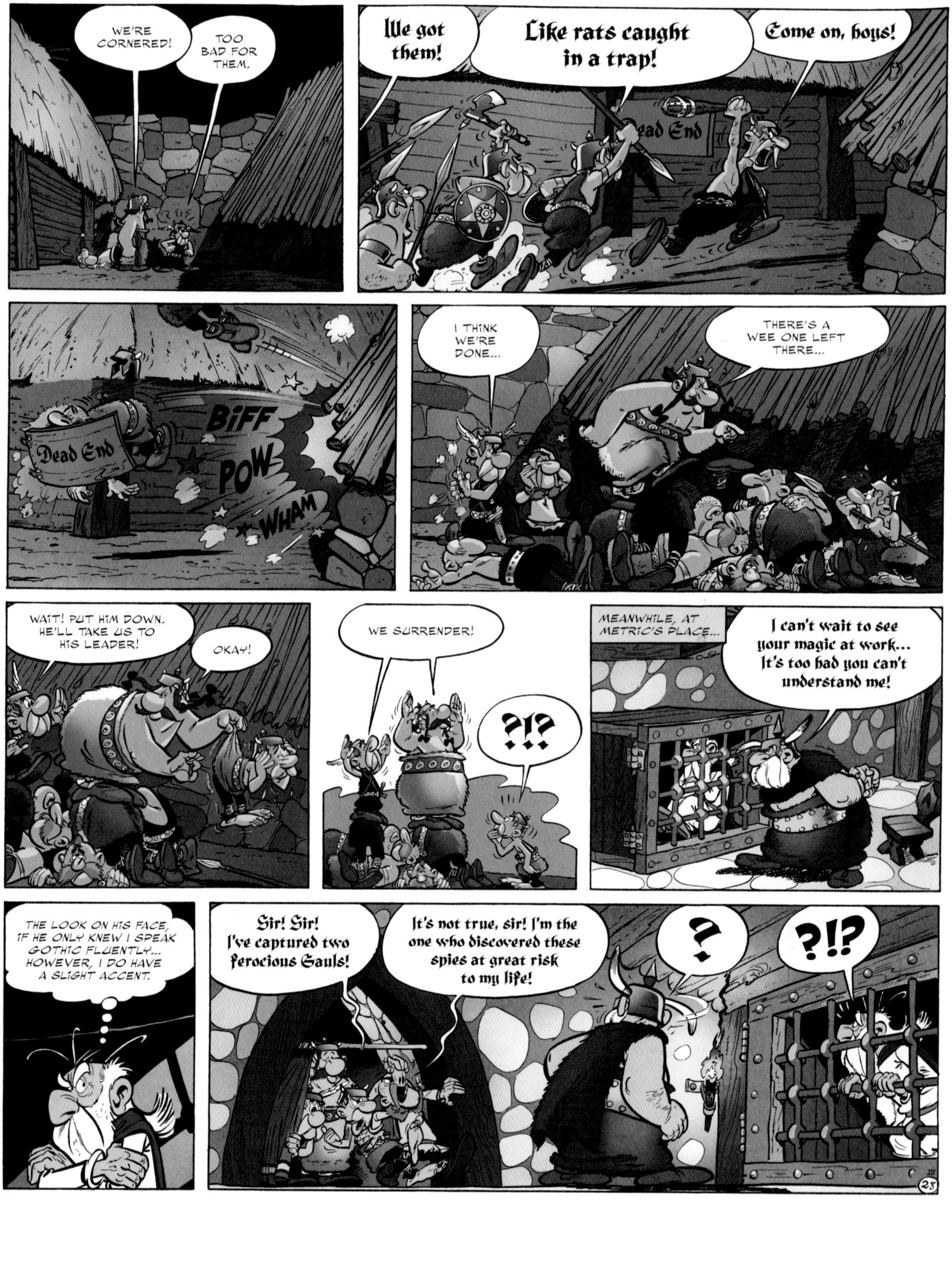
WE'RE CORNERED!
TOO BAD FOR THEM.
We got them!
Like rats caught in a trap!
Come on, boys!
Dead End
Dead End
BIFF
POW
WHAM
I THINK WE'RE DONE...
THERE'S A WEE ONE LEFT THERE...
WAIT! PUT HIM DOWN. HE'LL TAKE US TO HIS LEADER!
OKAY!
WE SURRENDER!
?!?
MEANWHILE, AT METRIC'S PLACE...
I can't wait to see your magic at work... It's too bad you can't understand me!
THE LOOK ON HIS FACE, IF HE ONLY KNEW I SPEAK GOTHIC FLUENTLY... HOWEVER, I DO HAVE A SLIGHT ACCENT.
Sir! Sir! I've captured two ferocious Gauls!
It's not true, sir! I'm the one who discovered these spies at great risk to my life!
?
?!?
28

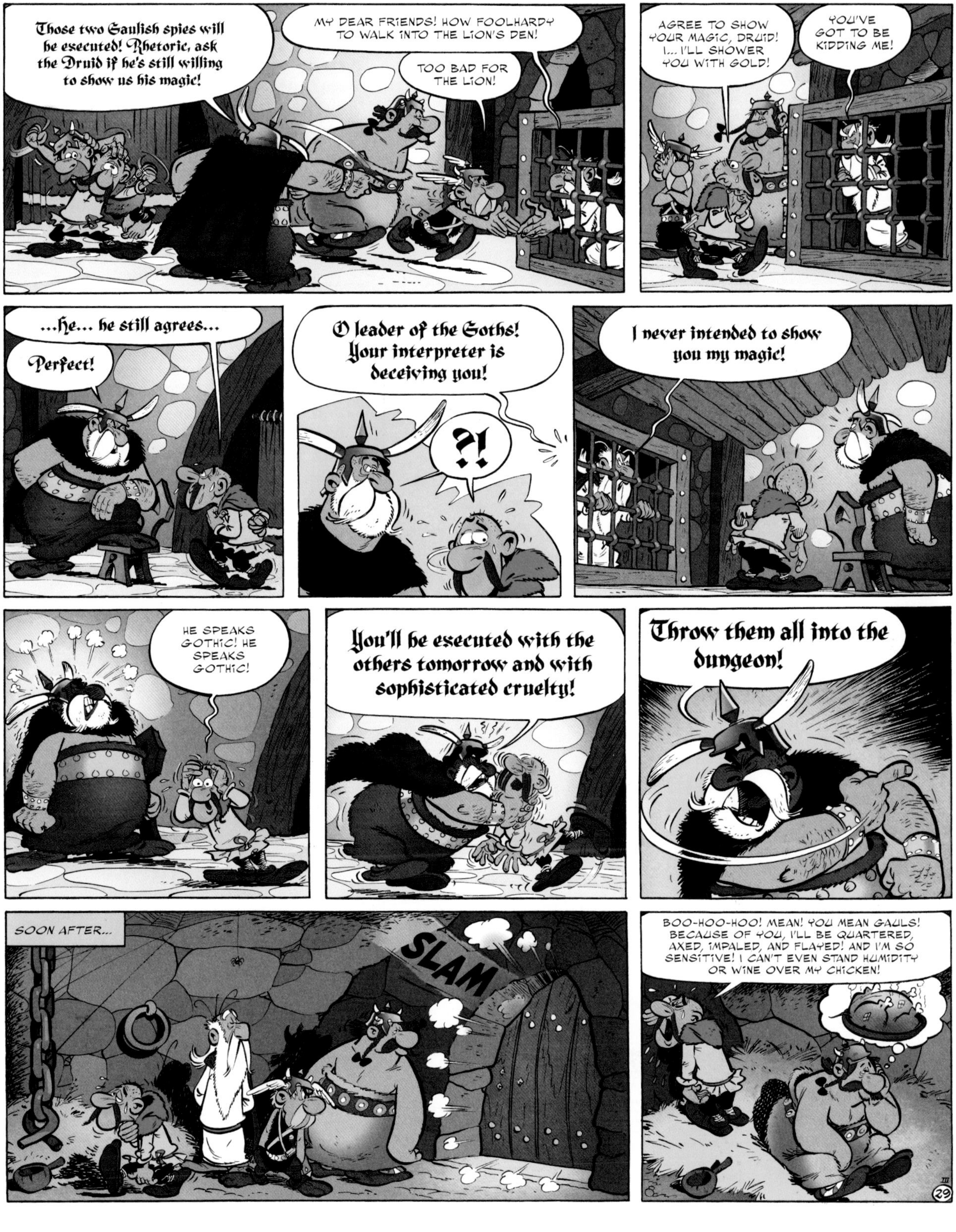
Those two Gaulish spies will be executed! Rhetoric, ask the Druid if he's still willing to show us his magic!
MY DEAR FRIENDS! HOW FOOLHARDY TO WALK INTO THE LION'S DEN!
TOO BAD FOR THE LION!
AGREE TO SHOW YOUR MAGIC, DRUID! I... I'LL SHOWER YOU WITH GOLD!
YOU'VE GOT TO BE KIDDING ME!
...He... he still agrees...
Perfect!
O leader of the Goths! Your interpreter is deceiving you!
?!
I never intended to show you my magic!
HE SPEAKS GOTHIC! HE SPEAKS GOTHIC!
You'll be executed with the others tomorrow and with sophisticated cruelty!
Throw them all into the dungeon!
SOON AFTER...
SLAM
BOO-HOO-HOO! MEAN! YOU MEAN GAULS! BECAUSE OF YOU, I'LL BE QUARTERED, AXED, IMPALED, AND FLAYED! AND I'M SO SENSITIVE! I CAN'T EVEN STAND HUMIDITY OR WINE OVER MY CHICKEN!
III
29

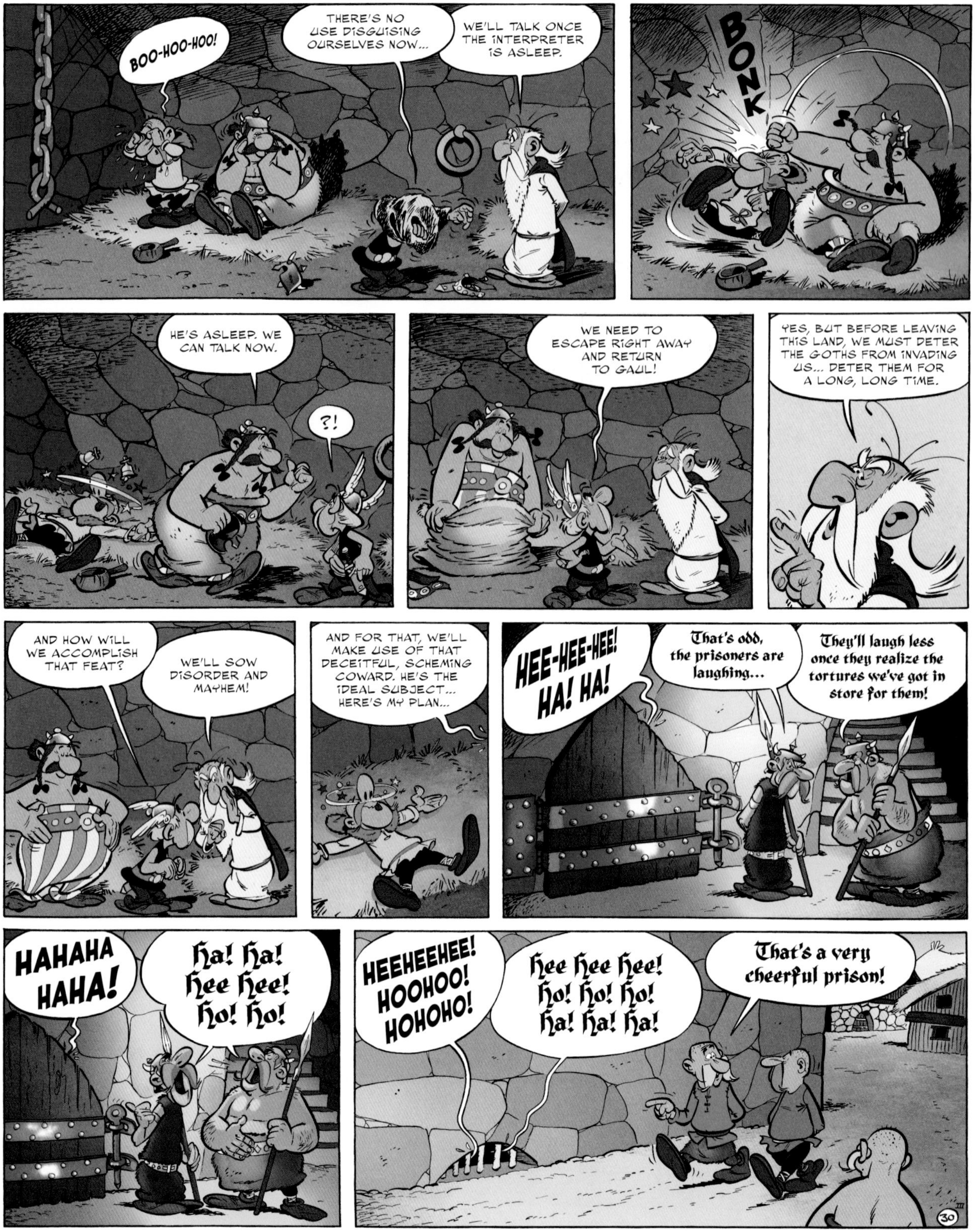
BOO-HOO-HOO!
THERE'S NO USE DISGUISING OURSELVES NOW...
WE'LL TALK ONCE THE INTERPRETER IS ASLEEP.
BONK
HE'S ASLEEP. WE CAN TALK NOW.
?!
WE NEED TO ESCAPE RIGHT AWAY AND RETURN TO GAUL!
YES, BUT BEFORE LEAVING THIS LAND, WE MUST DETER THE GOTHS FROM INVADING US... DETER THEM FOR A LONG, LONG TIME.
AND HOW WILL WE ACCOMPLISH THAT FEAT?
WE'LL SOW DISORDER AND MAYHEM!
AND FOR THAT, WE'LL MAKE USE OF THAT DECEITFUL, SCHEMING COWARD. HE'S THE IDEAL SUBJECT... HERE'S MY PLAN...
HEE-HEE-HEE! HA! HA!
That's odd, the prisoners are laughing...
They'll laugh less once they realize the tortures we've got in store for them!
HAHAHA HAHA!
Ha! Ha! Hee Hee! Ho! Ho!
HEEHEEHEE! HOOHOO! HOHOHO!
Hee Hee Hee! Ho! Ho! Ho! Ha! Ha! Ha!
That's a very cheerful prison!
30

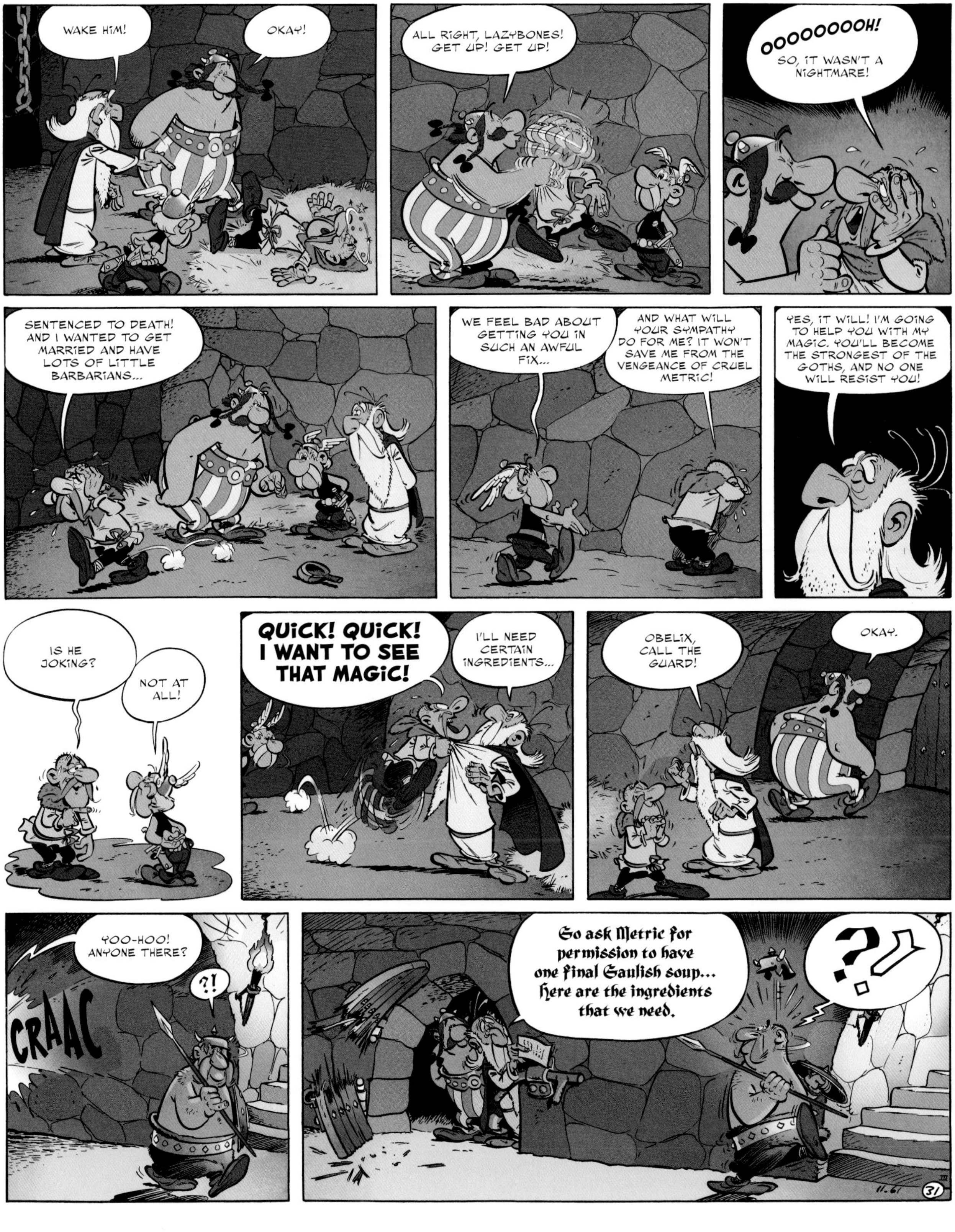
WAKE HIM!
OKAY!
ALL RIGHT, LAZYBONES! GET UP! GET UP!
OOOOOOOOH!
SO, IT WASN'T A NIGHTMARE!
SENTENCED TO DEATH! AND I WANTED TO GET MARRIED AND HAVE LOTS OF LITTLE BARBARIANS...
WE FEEL BAD ABOUT GETTING YOU IN SUCH AN AWFUL FIX...
AND WHAT WILL YOUR SYMPATHY DO FOR ME? IT WON'T SAVE ME FROM THE VENGEANCE OF CRUEL METRIC!
YES, IT WILL! I'M GOING TO HELP YOU WITH MY MAGIC. YOU'LL BECOME THE STRONGEST OF THE GOTHS, AND NO ONE WILL RESIST YOU!
IS HE JOKING?
NOT AT ALL!
QUICK! QUICK! I WANT TO SEE THAT MAGIC!
I'LL NEED CERTAIN INGREDIENTS...
OBELIX, CALL THE GUARD!
OKAY.
YOO-HOO! ANYONE THERE?
CRAAC
?!
So ask Metric for permission to have one final Gaulish soup... Here are the ingredients that we need.
?!
11.61
31

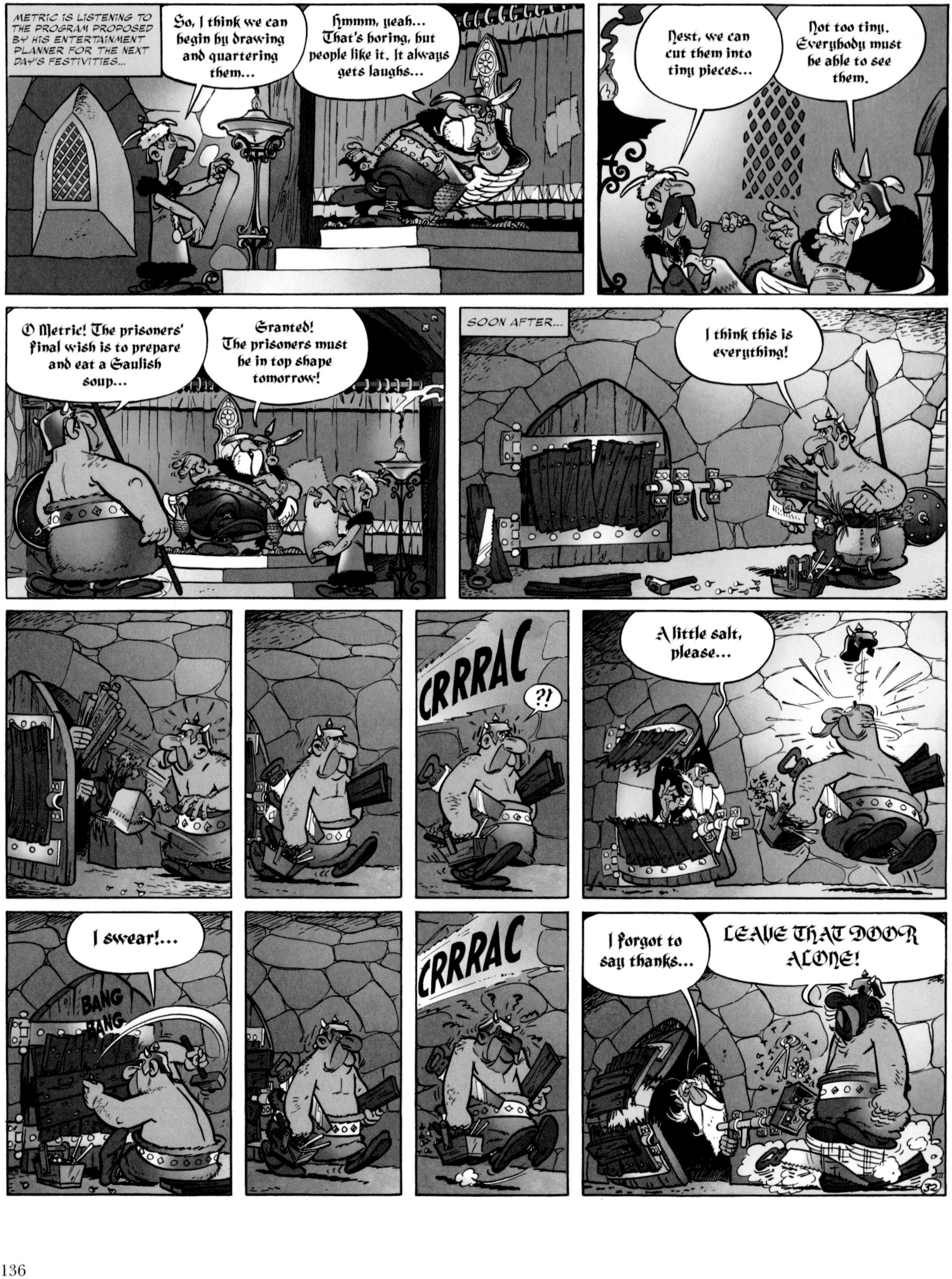

METRIC IS LISTENING TO THE PROGRAM PROPOSED BY HIS ENTERTAINMENT PLANNER FOR THE NEXT DAY'S FESTIVITIES...
So, I think we can begin by drawing and quartering them...
Hmmm, yeah... That's boring, but people like it. It always gets laughs...
Next, we can cut them into tiny pieces...
Not too tiny. Everybody must be able to see them.
O Metric! The prisoners' final wish is to prepare and eat a Gaulish soup...
Granted! The prisoners must be in top shape tomorrow!
SOON AFTER...
I think this is everything!
CRRRAC
?!
A little salt, please...
I swear!...
BANG
BANG
CRRRAC
I forgot to say thanks...
LEAVE THAT DOOR ALONE!

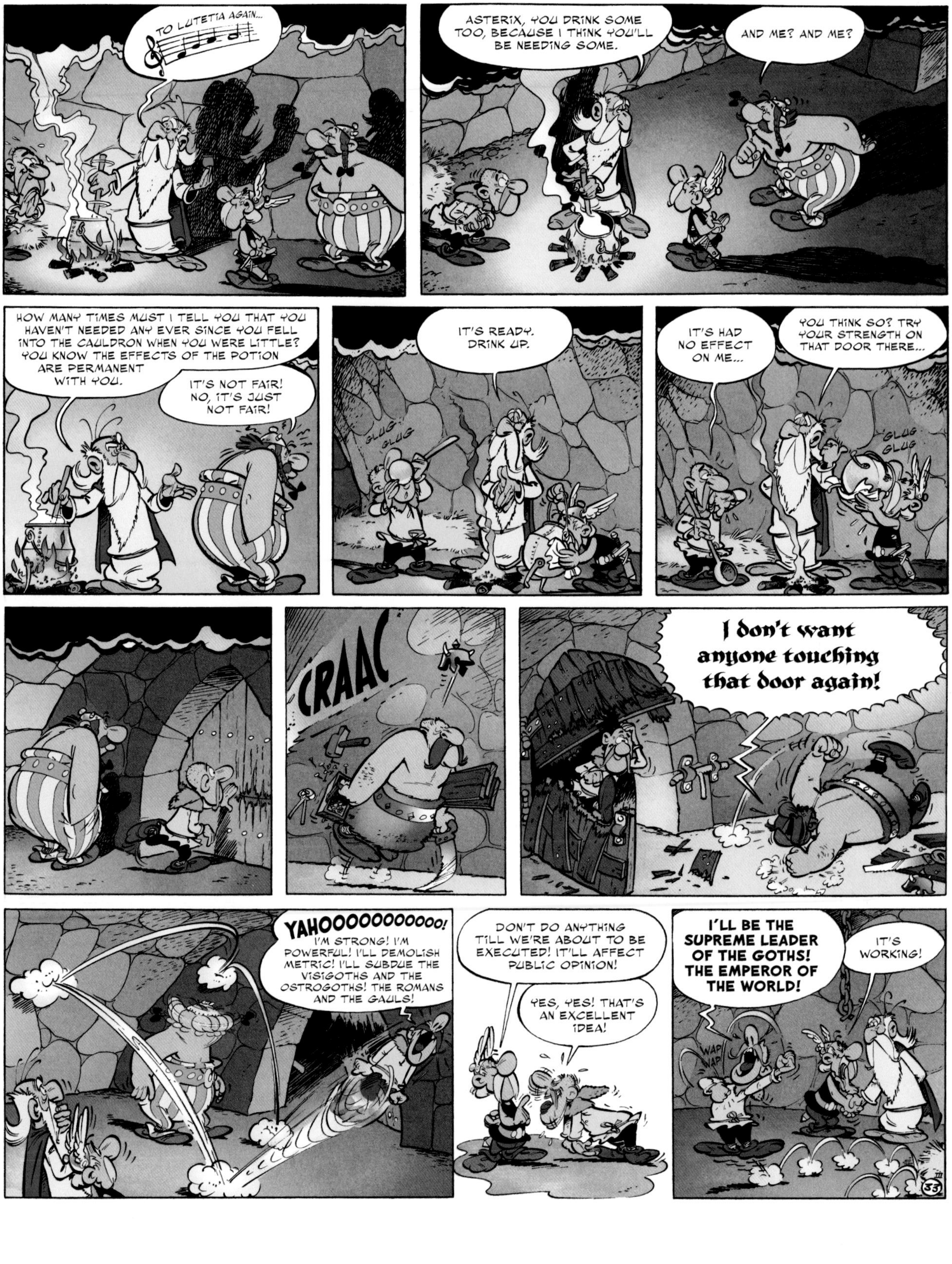

TO LUTETIA AGAIN...
ASTERIX, YOU DRINK SOME TOO, BECAUSE I THINK YOU'LL BE NEEDING SOME.
AND ME? AND ME?
HOW MANY TIMES MUST I TELL YOU THAT YOU HAVEN'T NEEDED ANY EVER SINCE YOU FELL INTO THE CAULDRON WHEN YOU WERE LITTLE? YOU KNOW THE EFFECTS OF THE POTION ARE PERMANENT WITH YOU.
IT'S NOT FAIR! NO, IT'S JUST NOT FAIR!
IT'S READY. DRINK UP.
GLUG GLUG
IT'S HAD NO EFFECT ON ME...
YOU THINK SO? TRY YOUR STRENGTH ON THAT DOOR THERE...
GLUG GLUG
CRAAC
I don't want anyone touching that door again!
YAHOOOOOOOOOOOO! I'M STRONG! I'M POWERFUL! I'LL DEMOLISH METRIC! I'LL SUBDUE THE VISIGOTHS AND THE OSTROGOTHS! THE ROMANS AND THE GAULS!
DON'T DO ANYTHING TILL WE'RE ABOUT TO BE EXECUTED! IT'LL AFFECT PUBLIC OPINION!
YES, YES! THAT'S AN EXCELLENT IDEA!
I'LL BE THE SUPREME LEADER OF THE GOTHS! THE EMPEROR OF THE WORLD!
WAP WAP
IT'S WORKING!
33

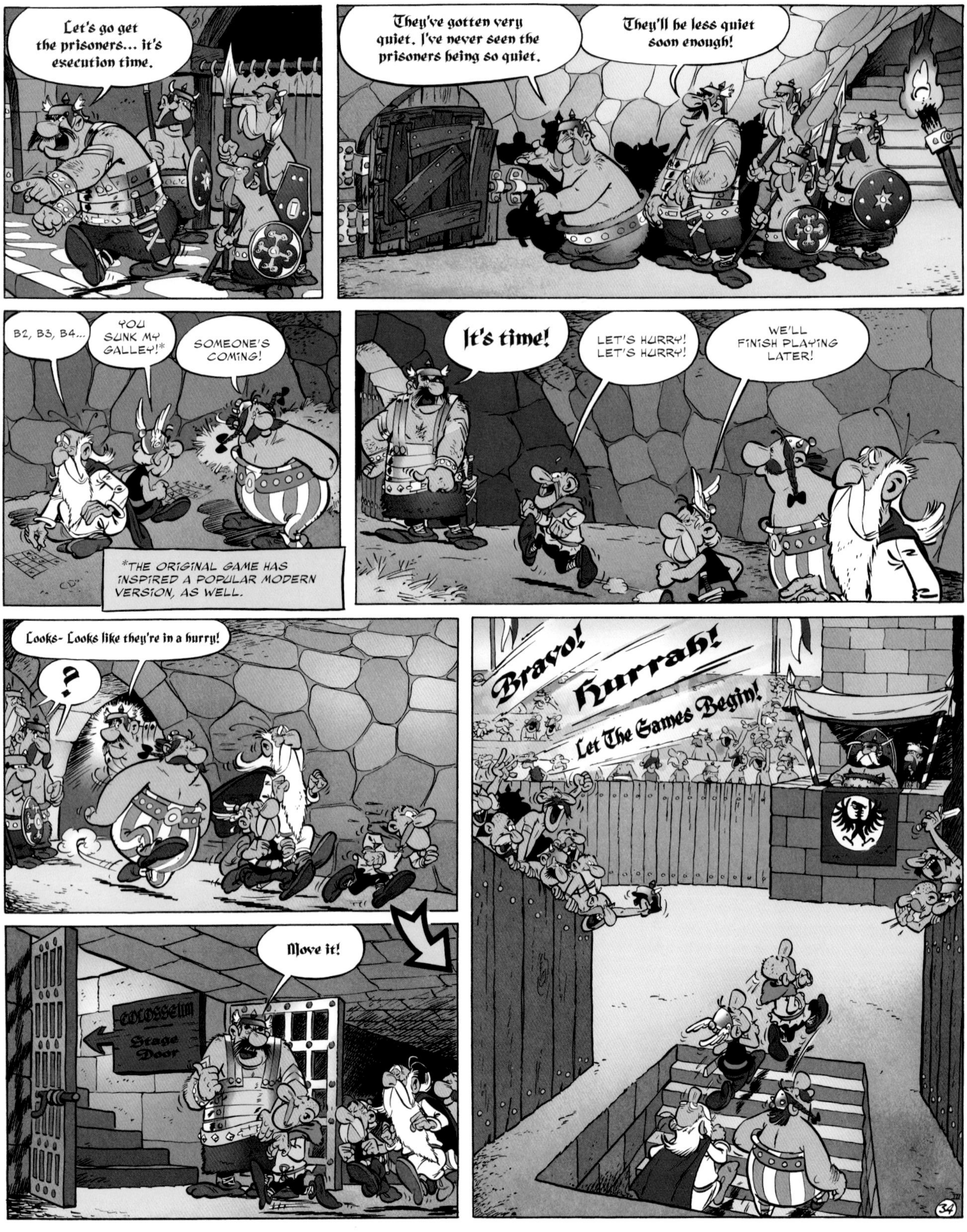
Let's go get the prisoners... it's execution time.
They've gotten very quiet. I've never seen the prisoners being so quiet.
They'll be less quiet soon enough!
B2, B3, B4...
YOU SUNK MY GALLEY!*
SOMEONE'S COMING!
*THE ORIGINAL GAME HAS INSPIRED A POPULAR MODERN VERSION, AS WELL.
It's time!
LET'S HURRY! LET'S HURRY!
WE'LL FINISH PLAYING LATER!
Looks- Looks like they're in a hurry!
?
Bravo!
Hurrah!
Let The Games Begin!
COLOSSEUM
Stage Door
Move it!
34

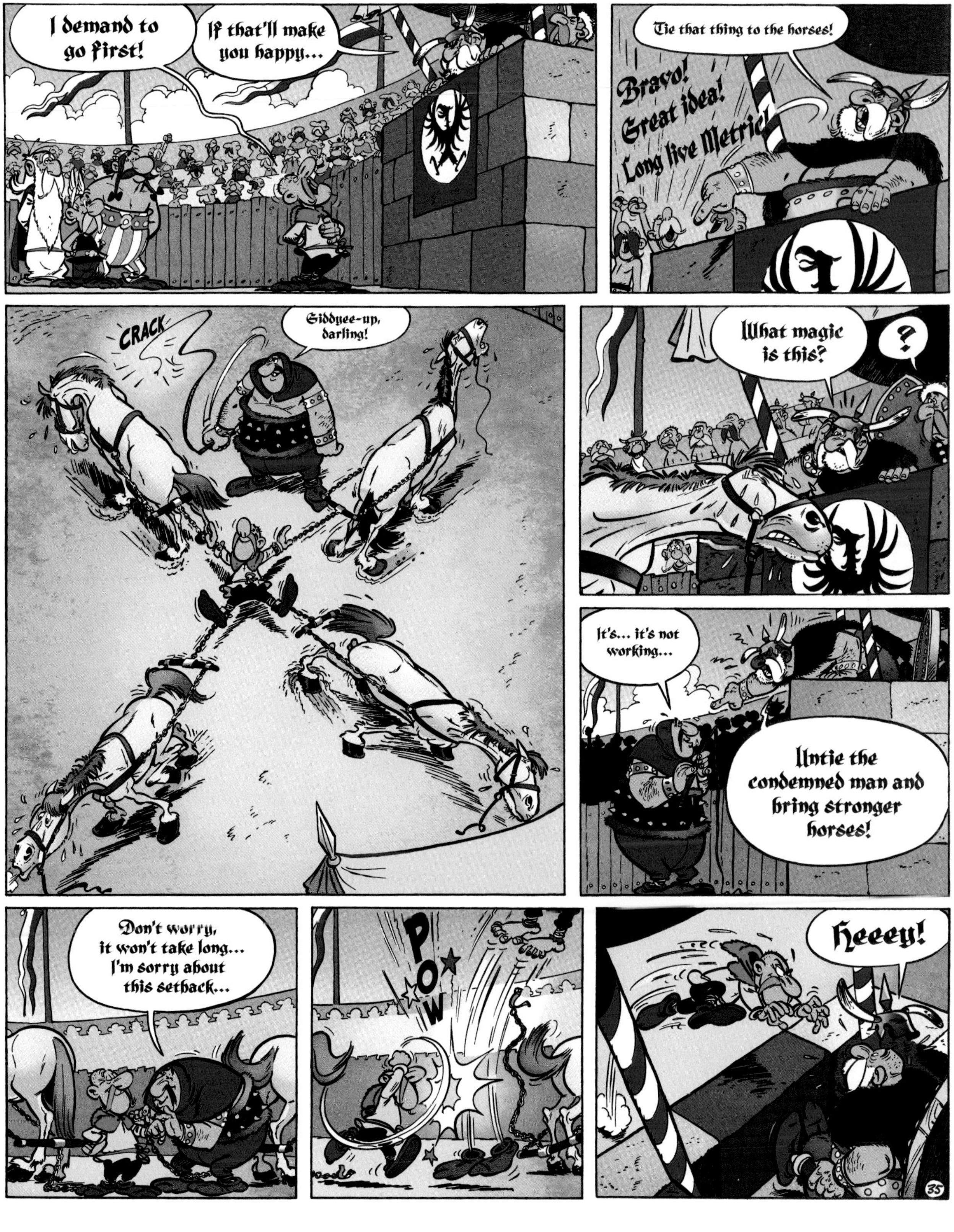

I demand to go first!
If that'll make you happy...
Tie that thing to the horses!
Bravo! Great idea! Long live Metric!
CRACK
Giddyee-up, darling!
What magic is this?
?
It's... it's not working...
Untie the condemned man and bring stronger horses!
Don't worry, it won't take long... I'm sorry about this setback...
POW
Heeey!
35

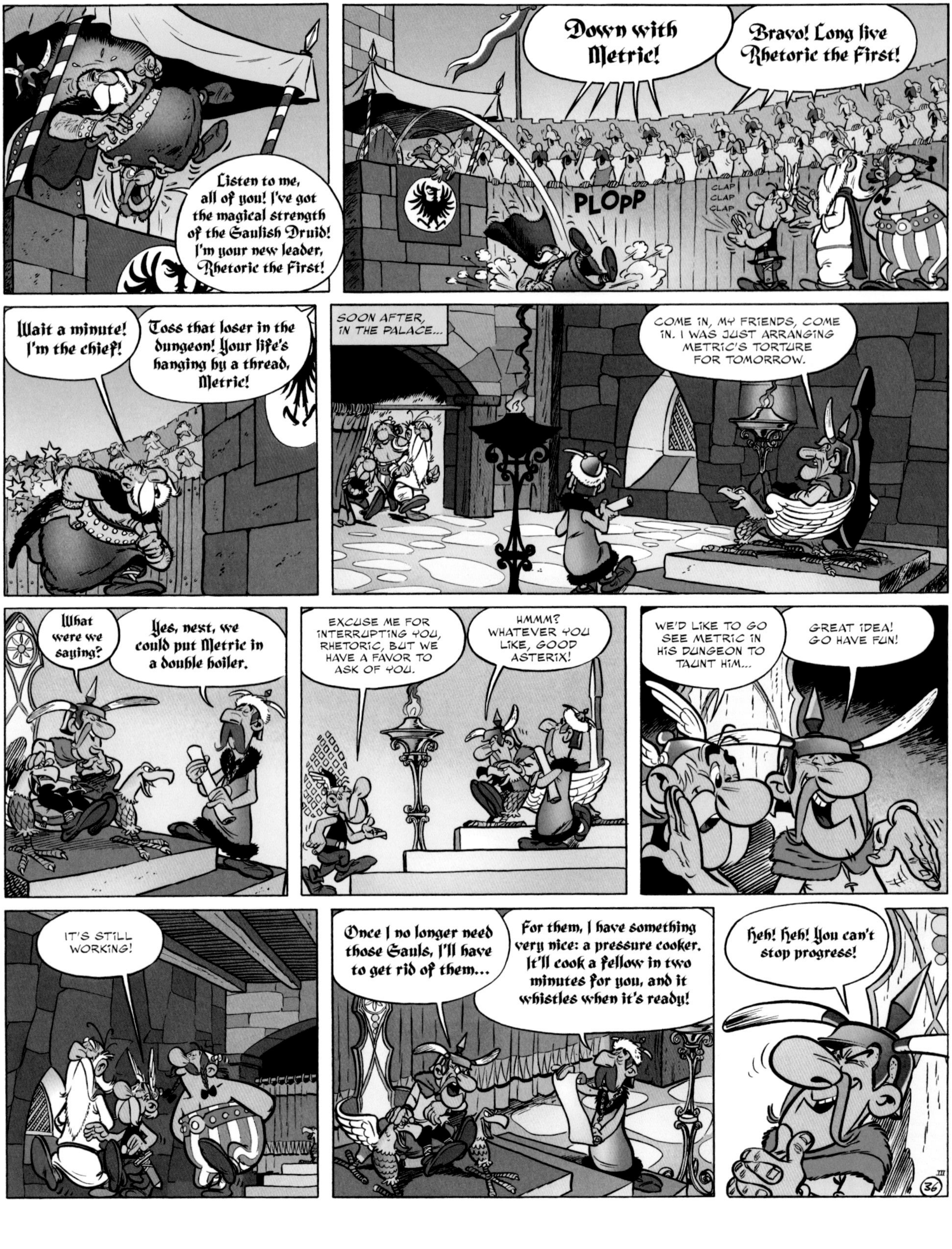
Listen to me, all of you! I've got the magical strength of the Gaulish Druid! I'm your new leader, Rhetoric the First!
Down with Metric!
Bravo! Long live Rhetoric the First!
PLOPP
CLAP CLAP CLAP
Wait a minute! I'm the chief!
Toss that loser in the dungeon! Your life's hanging by a thread, Metric!
SOON AFTER, IN THE PALACE...
COME IN, MY FRIENDS, COME IN. I WAS JUST ARRANGING METRIC'S TORTURE FOR TOMORROW.
What were we saying?
Yes, next, we could put Metric in a double boiler.
EXCUSE ME FOR INTERRUPTING YOU, RHETORIC, BUT WE HAVE A FAVOR TO ASK OF YOU.
HMMM? WHATEVER YOU LIKE, GOOD ASTERIX!
WE'D LIKE TO GO SEE METRIC IN HIS DUNGEON TO TAUNT HIM...
GREAT IDEA! GO HAVE FUN!
IT'S STILL WORKING!
Once I no longer need those Gauls, I'll have to get rid of them...
For them, I have something very nice: a pressure cooker. It'll cook a fellow in two minutes for you, and it whistles when it's ready!
Heh! Heh! You can't stop progress!
III 36

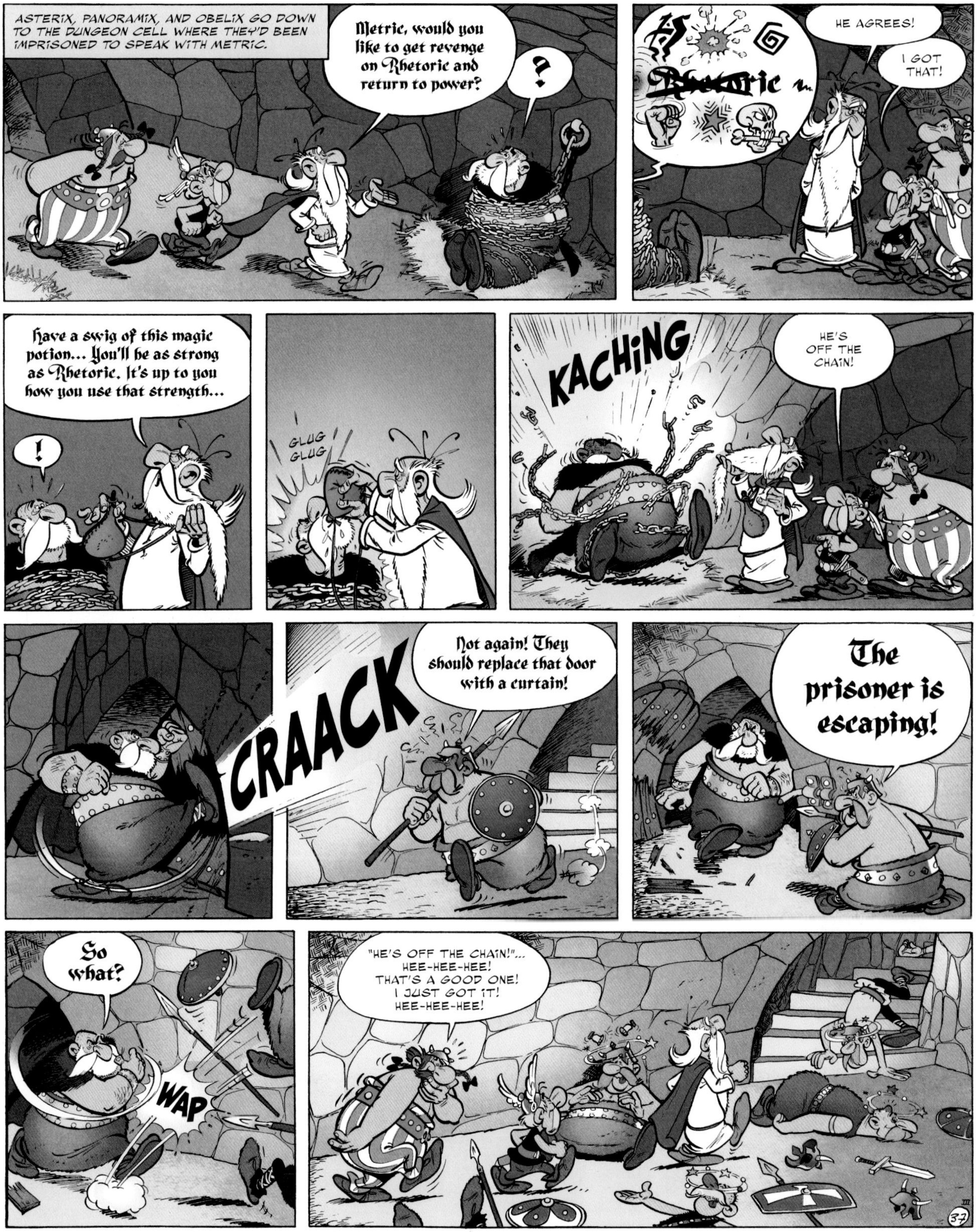

ASTERIX, PANORAMIX, AND OBELIX GO DOWN TO THE DUNGEON CELL WHERE THEY'D BEEN IMPRISONED TO SPEAK WITH METRIC.
Metric, would you like to get revenge on Rhetoric and return to power?
?
Rhetoric
HE AGREES!
I GOT THAT!
Have a swig of this magic potion... You'll be as strong as Rhetoric. It's up to you how you use that strength...
!
GLUG GLUG
KACHING
HE'S OFF THE CHAIN!
CRAACK
Not again! They should replace that door with a curtain!
The prisoner is escaping!
So what?
WAP
"HE'S OFF THE CHAIN!"... HEE-HEE-HEE! THAT'S A GOOD ONE! I JUST GOT IT! HEE-HEE-HEE!

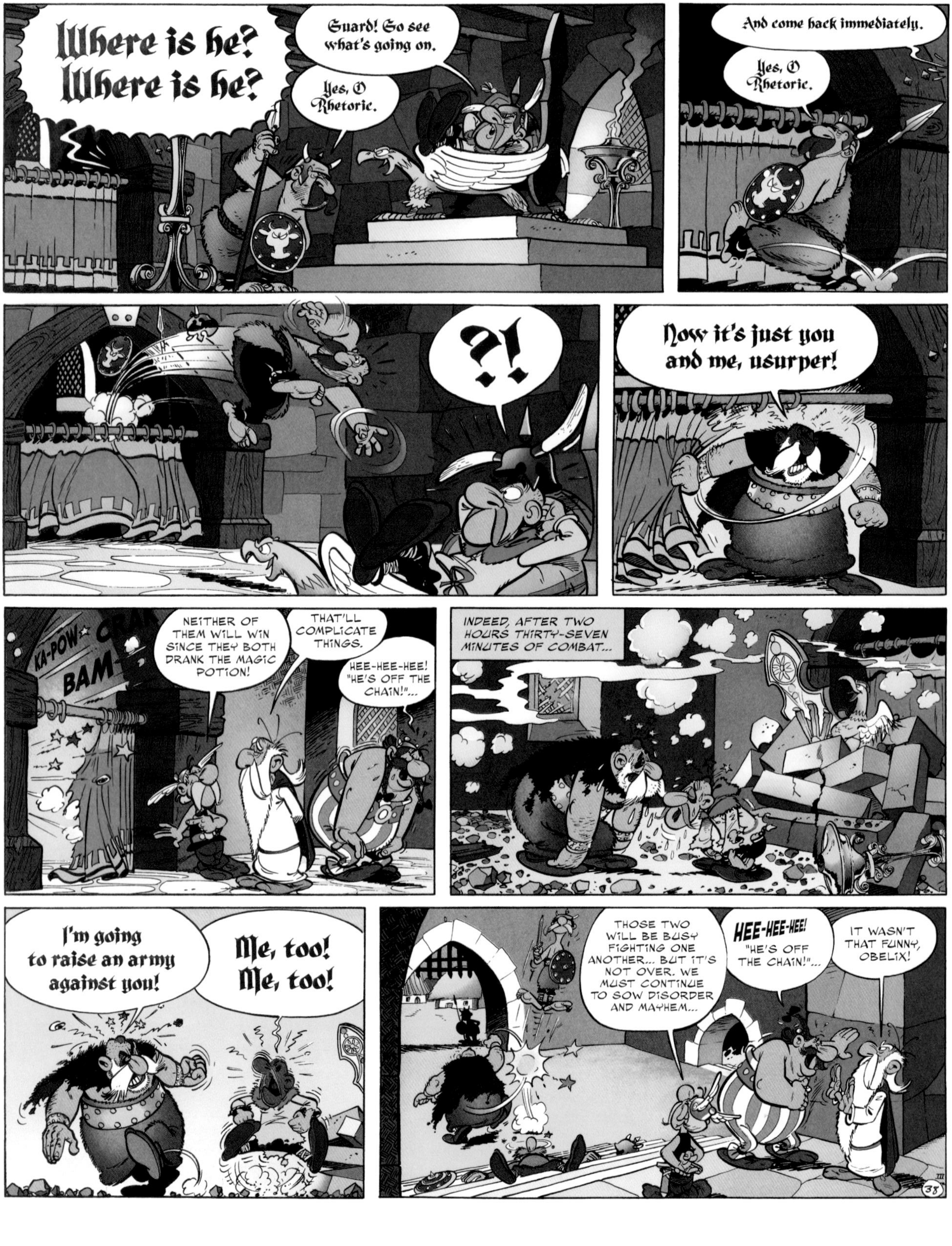

Where is he? Where is he?
Guard! Go see what's going on.
Yes, O Rhetoric.
And come back immediately.
Yes, O Rhetoric.
?!
Now it's just you and me, usurper!
KA-POW
CRAK
BAM
NEITHER OF THEM WILL WIN SINCE THEY BOTH DRANK THE MAGIC POTION!
THAT'LL COMPLICATE THINGS.
HEE-HEE-HEE! "HE'S OFF THE CHAIN!"...
INDEED, AFTER TWO HOURS THIRTY-SEVEN MINUTES OF COMBAT...
I'm going to raise an army against you!
Me, too! Me, too!
THOSE TWO WILL BE BUSY FIGHTING ONE ANOTHER... BUT IT'S NOT OVER. WE MUST CONTINUE TO SOW DISORDER AND MAYHEM...
HEE-HEE-HEE! "HE'S OFF THE CHAIN!"...
IT WASN'T THAT FUNNY, OBELIX!
III
38

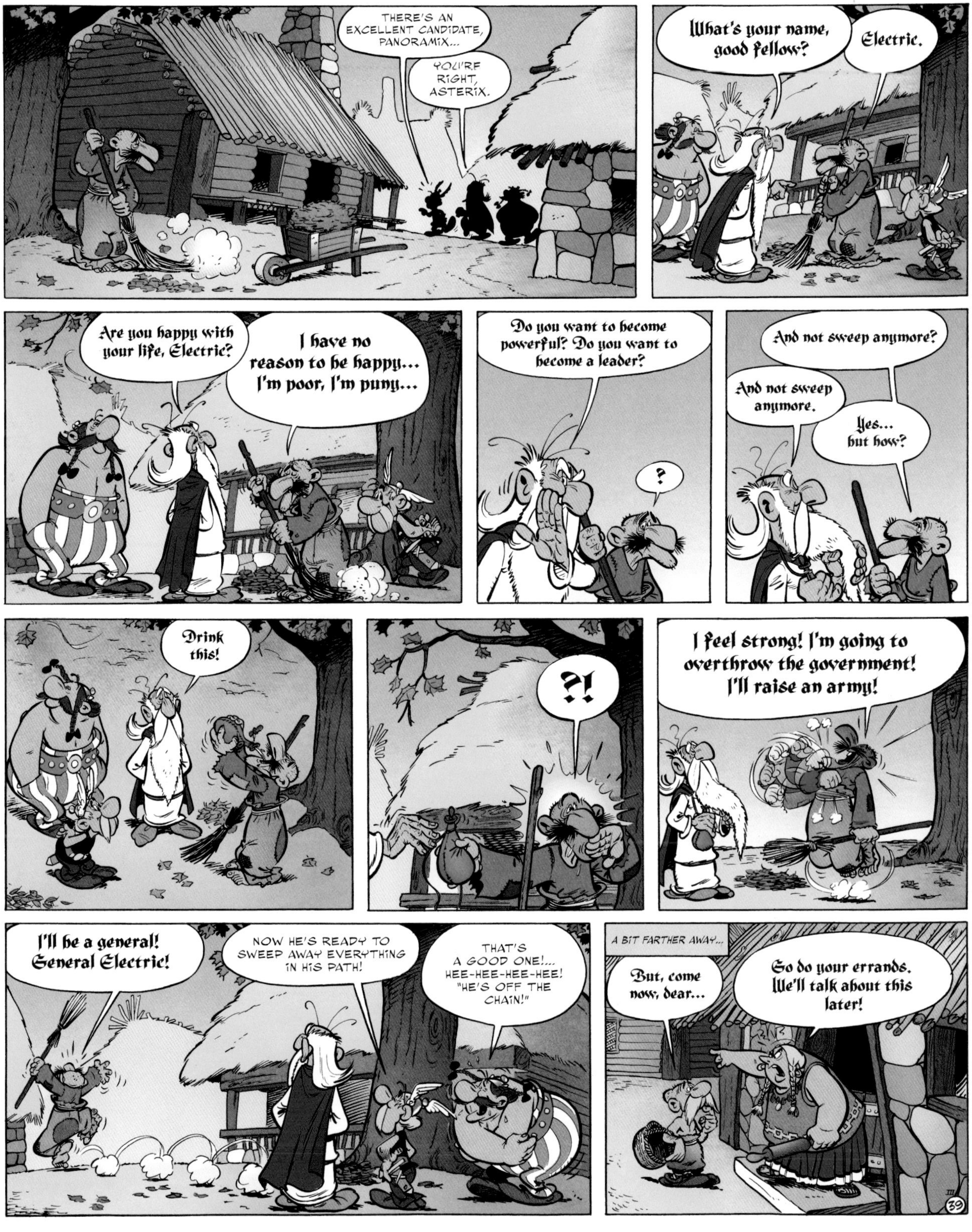
THERE'S AN EXCELLENT CANDIDATE, PANORAMIX...
YOU'RE RIGHT, ASTERIX.
What's your name, good fellow?
Electric.
Are you happy with your life, Electric?
I have no reason to be happy... I'm poor, I'm puny...
Do you want to become powerful? Do you want to become a leader?
?
And not sweep anymore?
And not sweep anymore.
Yes... but how?
Drink this!
?!
I feel strong! I'm going to overthrow the government! I'll raise an army!
I'll be a general! General Electric!
NOW HE'S READY TO SWEEP AWAY EVERYTHING IN HIS PATH!
THAT'S A GOOD ONE!... HEE-HEE-HEE-HEE! "HE'S OFF THE CHAIN!"
A BIT FARTHER AWAY...
But, come now, dear...
So do your errands. We'll talk about this later!
III 39

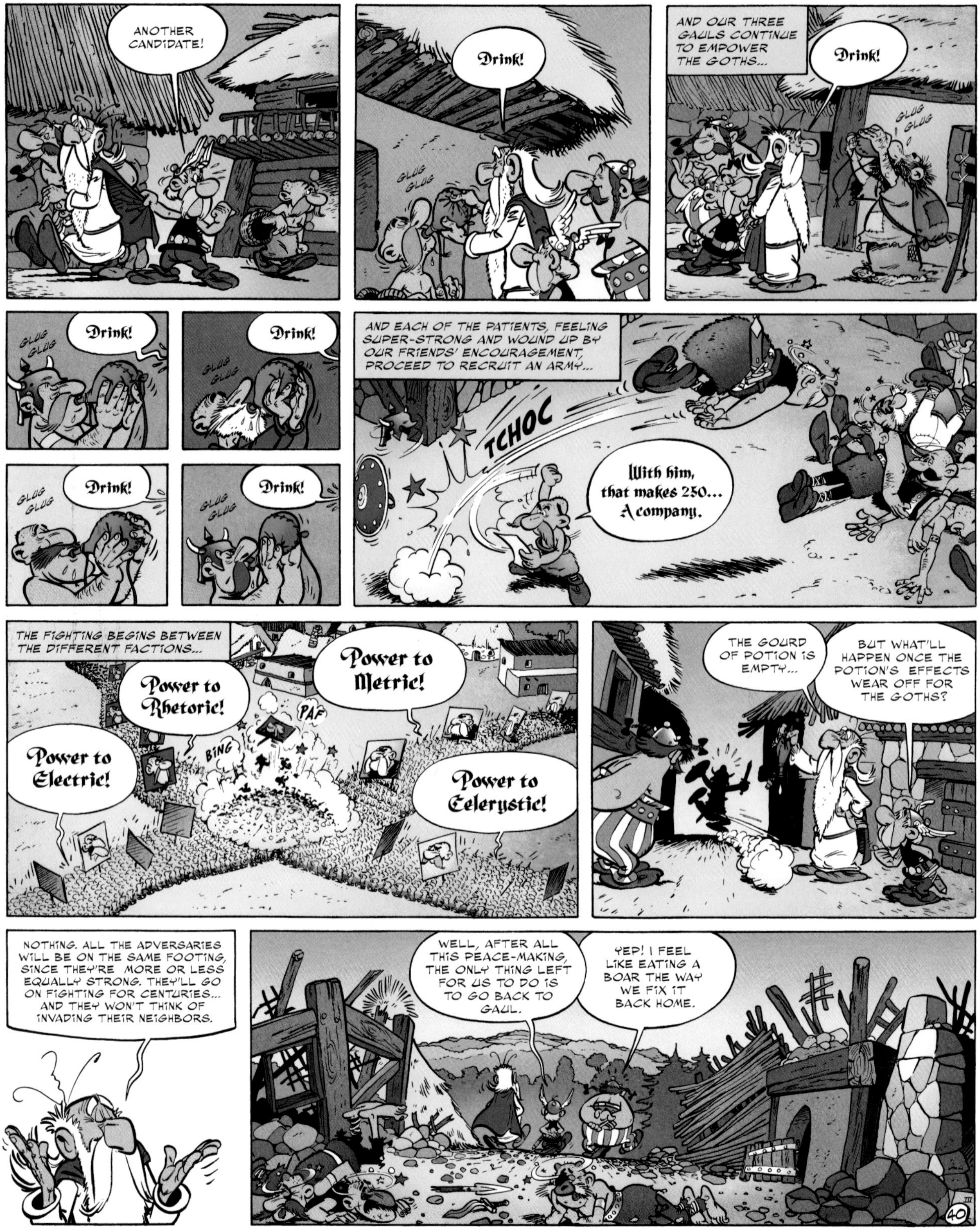
ANOTHER CANDIDATE!
Drink!
AND OUR THREE GAULS CONTINUE TO EMPOWER THE GOTHS...
Drink!
GLUG GLUG
GLUG GLUG
Drink!
GLUG GLUG
Drink!
GLUG GLUG
Drink!
GLUG GLUG
Drink!
AND EACH OF THE PATIENTS, FEELING SUPER-STRONG AND WOUND UP BY OUR FRIENDS' ENCOURAGEMENT, PROCEED TO RECRUIT AN ARMY...
TCHOC
With him, that makes 250... A company.
THE FIGHTING BEGINS BETWEEN THE DIFFERENT FACTIONS...
Power to Electric!
Power to Rhetoric!
BING
PAF
Power to Metric!
Power to Eclerystic!
THE GOURD OF POTION IS EMPTY...
BUT WHAT'LL HAPPEN ONCE THE POTION'S EFFECTS WEAR OFF FOR THE GOTHS?
NOTHING. ALL THE ADVERSARIES WILL BE ON THE SAME FOOTING, SINCE THEY'RE MORE OR LESS EQUALLY STRONG. THEY'LL GO ON FIGHTING FOR CENTURIES... AND THEY WON'T THINK OF INVADING THEIR NEIGHBORS.
WELL, AFTER ALL THIS PEACE-MAKING, THE ONLY THING LEFT FOR US TO DO IS TO GO BACK TO GAUL.
YEP! I FEEL LIKE EATING A BOAR THE WAY WE FIX IT BACK HOME.
III 40

A FEW LEADERS

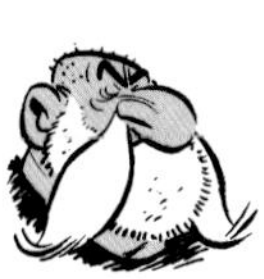

Metric

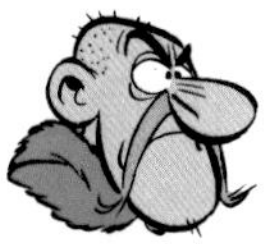

Rhetoric

Total mayhem… THE ASTERIXIAN WARS

Asterix, Panoramix, and Obelix's ruse succeeded beyond their wildest dreams. After drinking the Druid's magic potion, the Goths fought one another relentlessly. We want to tell you the story of those wars, so you'll really understand.

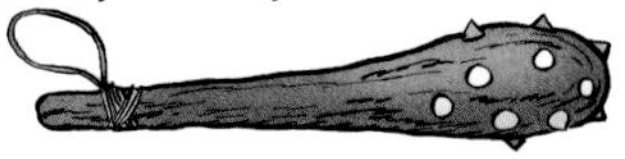

The preferred weapon of the combatants. It wreaks havoc.

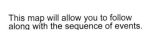

This map will allow you to follow along with the sequence of events.

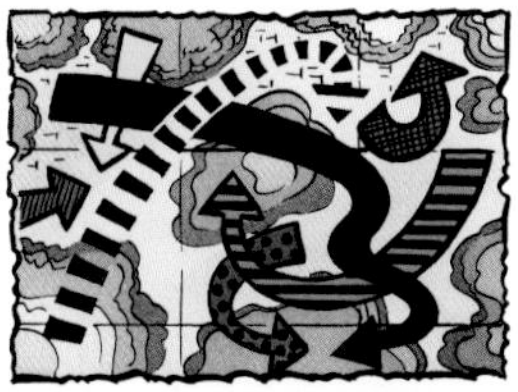

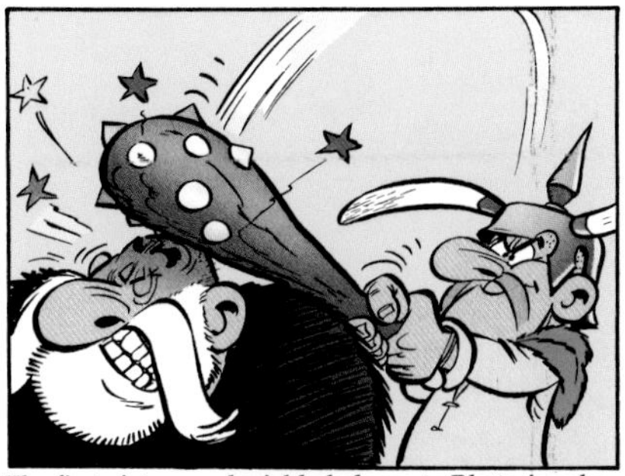

The first victory undeniably belongs to Rhetoric, who, surprised Metric with a switchback move, doesn't hold back and lets him have it – BONK! A temporary defeat, however…

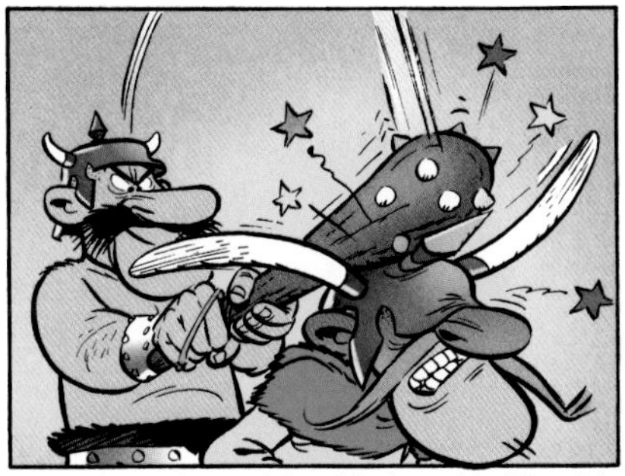

Rhetoric has no time to celebrate his victory. After his switch-back move, however, he's attacked from behind by Lyric, who was his ally. Lyric immediately proclaims himself the supreme leader of the Goths, but the other leaders laugh at him…

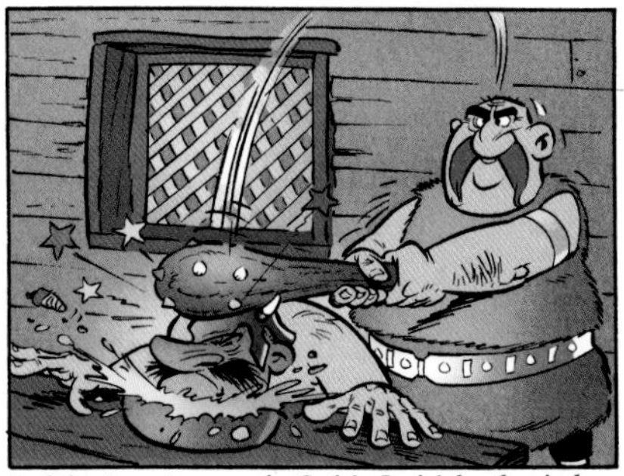

And they're not wrong, for Satiric, Lyric's brother-in-law, pretends to invite Lyric to a family meal and lays an ambush for him. The expression "Keeping it in the family…" was coined during the course of that battle.

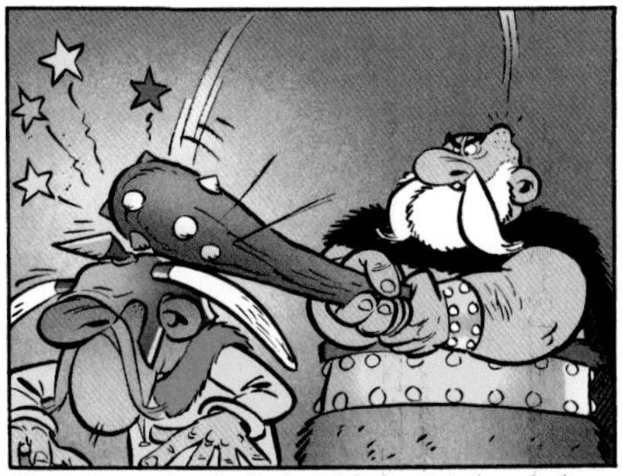

Rhetoric searches for Lyric, with the stated goal of "giving him a couple of smacks" (a historical event), but his rearguard gets surprised by Metric's vanguard, and SMACK! Rhetoric gets run over by Metric.

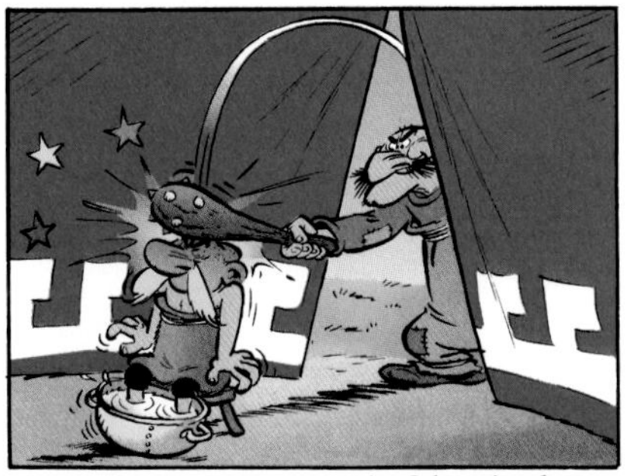

General Electric manages to surprise Celerystic, who was pondering his next campaigns. Euphoric's morale is crushed, but he vows: "I'll end up short-circuiting him!"

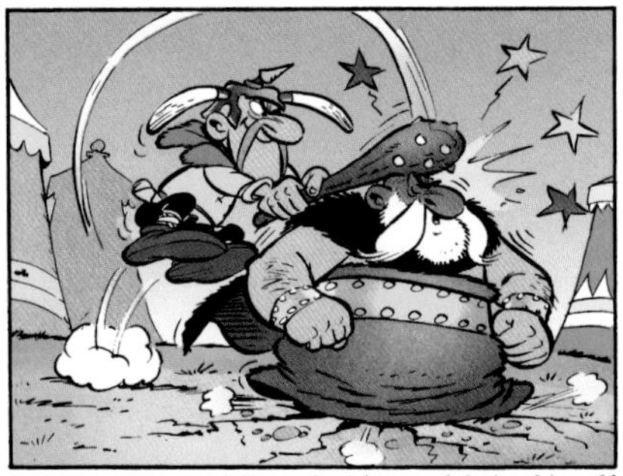

While Electric is widely mocked for proclaiming himself the supreme leader of the Goths, it's Metric's rearguard's turn to be surprised by Rhetoric's vanguard, and BONK! … A very irritated Metric then says, "He's annoying."

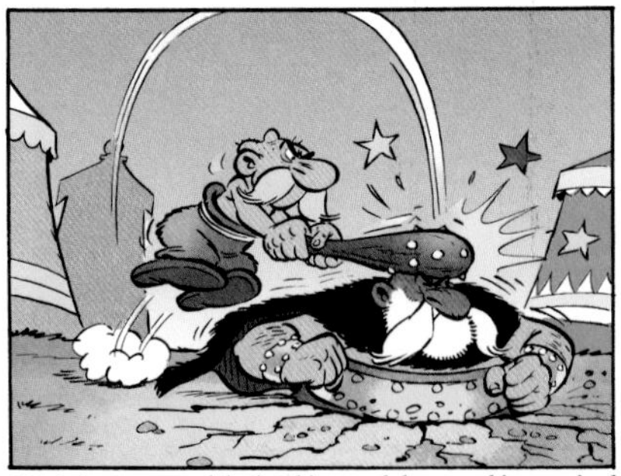

Metric is so annoyed, he lets his guard down and is surprised by Celerystic. The combat doesn't last long. Celerystic, an able politician, then proclaims himself the supreme leader of the Goths. The other supreme leaders laugh at him…

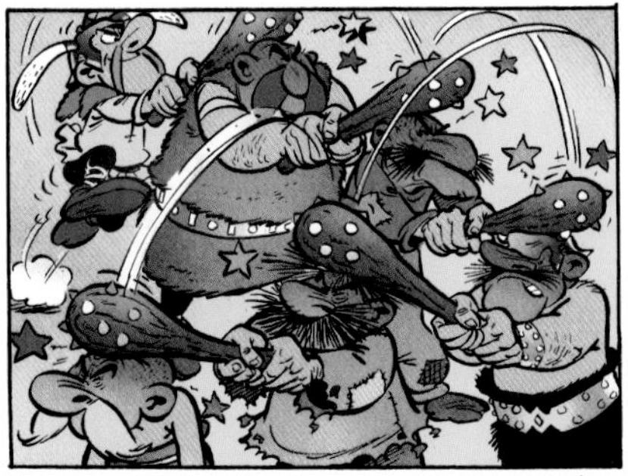

An annoyed Celerystic sets up an encampment and decides to sulk. He's surprised by Karatekic, who will himself be attacked by Lyric, who is defeated in turn by Electric. Electric will be betrayed by Satiric, who'll be beaten by Rhetoric.

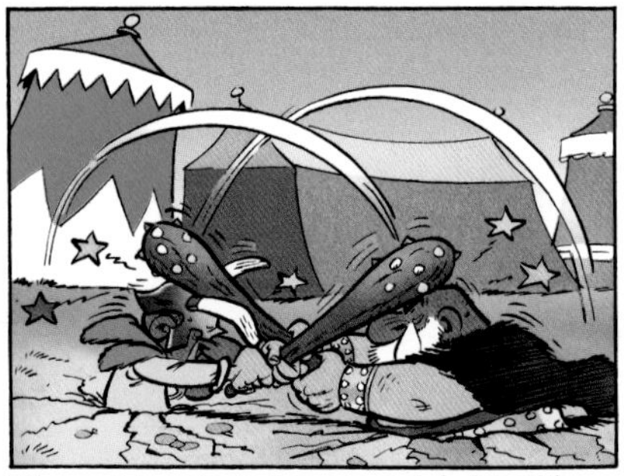

Taking a detour, Rhetoric's vanguard clashes with Metric's vanguard. BONK! BONK! That famous battle in the Asterixian Wars, will go down in history as the "Battle of the Two Losers." And the war goes on…

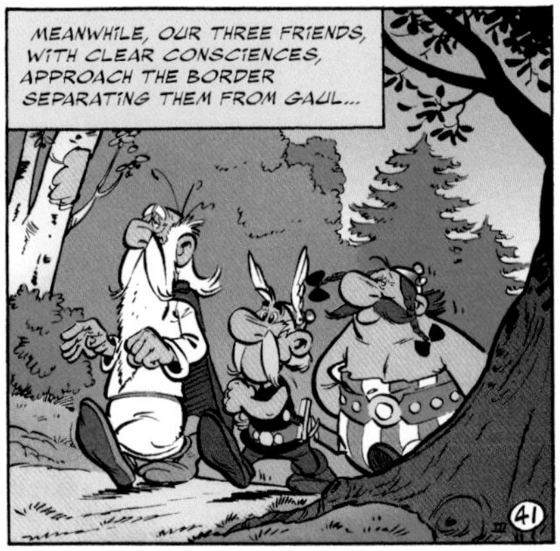
MEANWHILE, OUR THREE FRIENDS, WITH CLEAR CONSCIENCES, APPROACH THE BORDER SEPARATING THEM FROM GAUL...
41

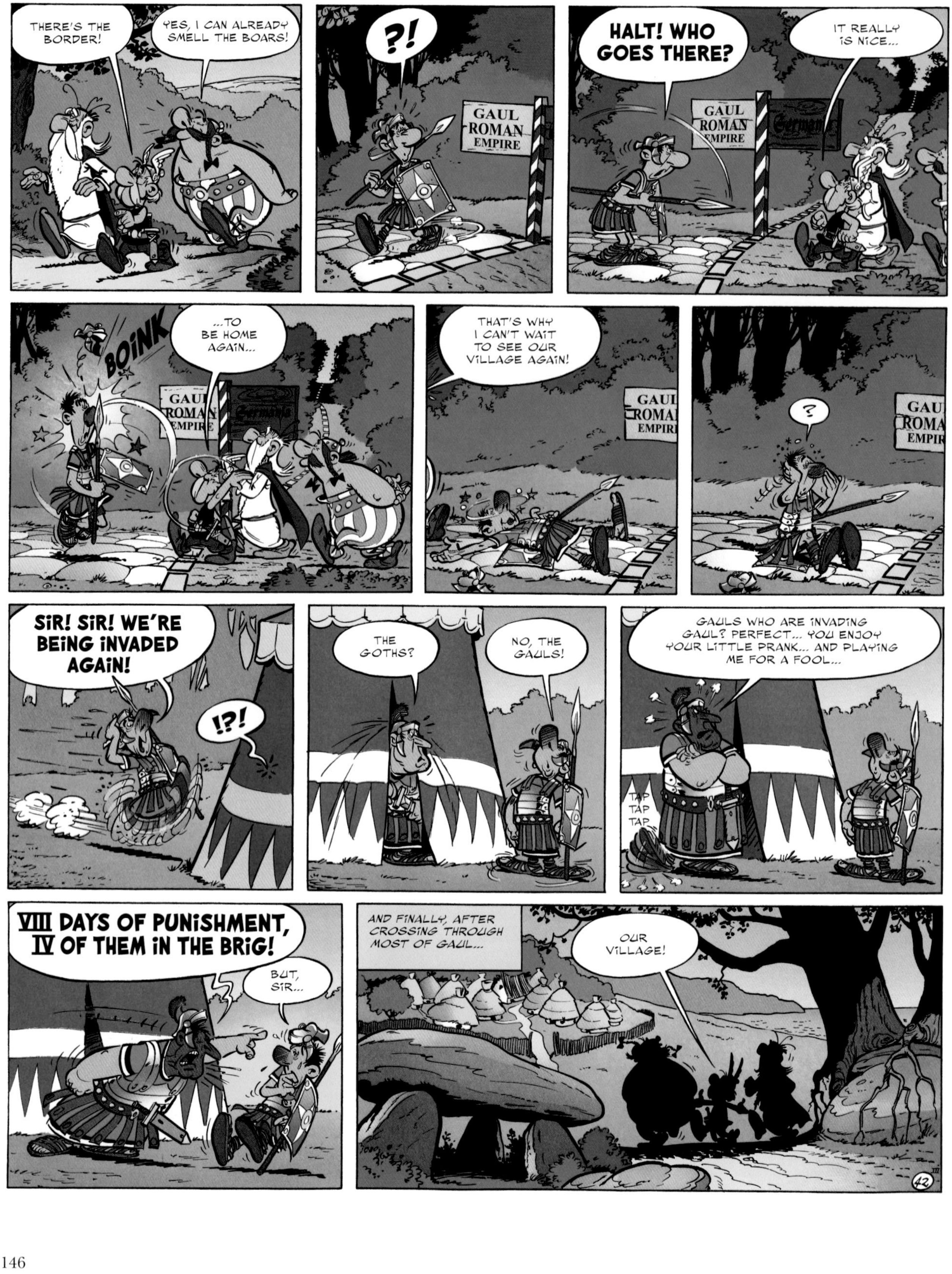

THERE'S THE BORDER!
YES, I CAN ALREADY SMELL THE BOARS!
?!
GAUL ROMAN EMPIRE
HALT! WHO GOES THERE?
IT REALLY IS NICE...
GAUL ROMAN EMPIRE
BOINK
...TO BE HOME AGAIN...
THAT'S WHY I CAN'T WAIT TO SEE OUR VILLAGE AGAIN!
?
SIR! SIR! WE'RE BEING INVADED AGAIN!
!?!
THE GOTHS?
NO, THE GAULS!
GAULS WHO ARE INVADING GAUL? PERFECT... YOU ENJOY YOUR LITTLE PRANK... AND PLAYING ME FOR A FOOL...
TAP TAP TAP
VIII DAYS OF PUNISHMENT, IV OF THEM IN THE BRIG!
BUT, SIR...
AND FINALLY, AFTER CROSSING THROUGH MOST OF GAUL...
OUR VILLAGE!
42

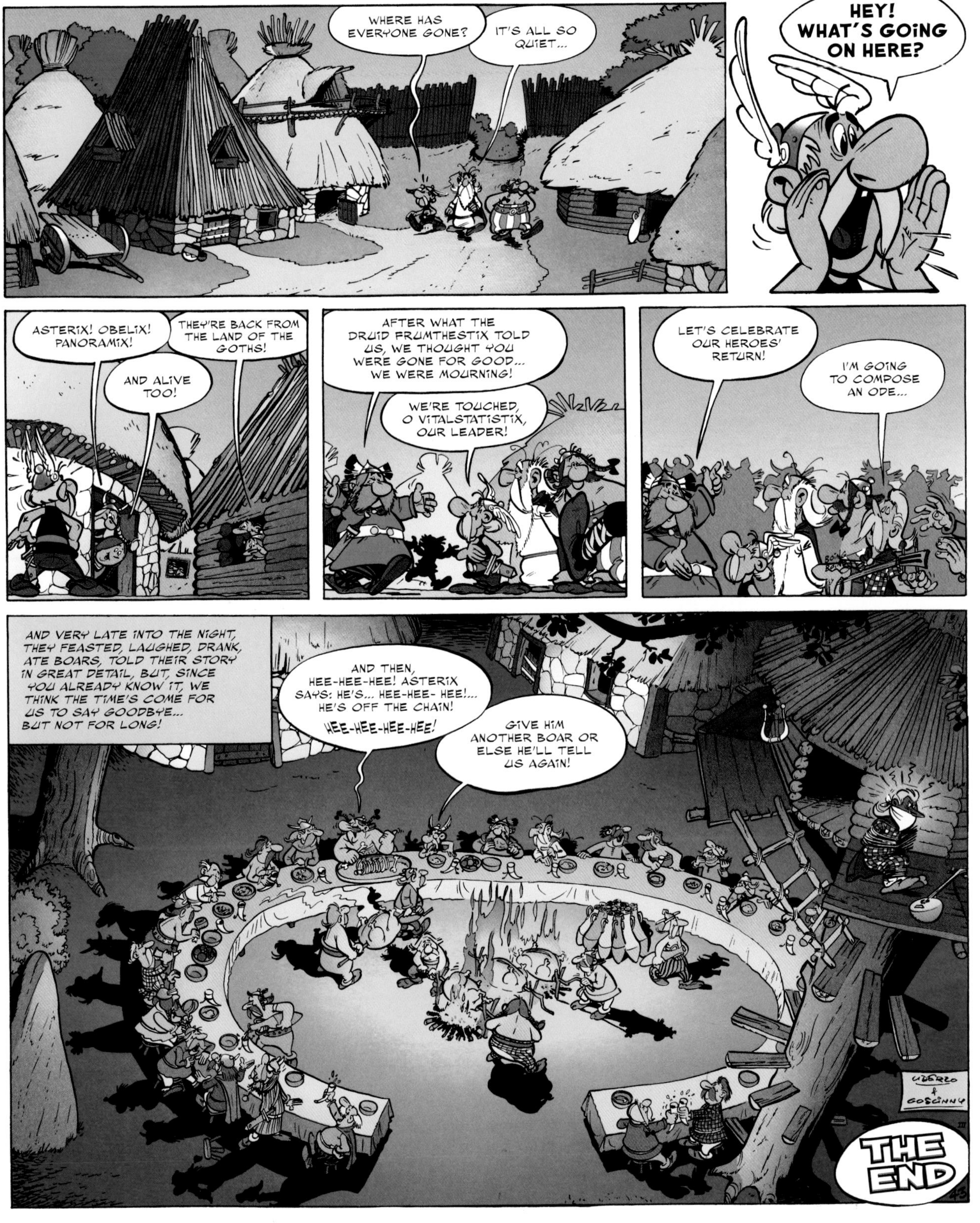

WHERE HAS EVERYONE GONE?
IT'S ALL SO QUIET...
HEY! WHAT'S GOING ON HERE?
ASTERIX! OBELIX! PANORAMIX!
THEY'RE BACK FROM THE LAND OF THE GOTHS!
AND ALIVE TOO!
AFTER WHAT THE DRUID FRUMTHESTIX TOLD US, WE THOUGHT YOU WERE GONE FOR GOOD... WE WERE MOURNING!
WE'RE TOUCHED, O VITALSTATISTIX, OUR LEADER!
LET'S CELEBRATE OUR HEROES' RETURN!
I'M GOING TO COMPOSE AN ODE...
AND VERY LATE INTO THE NIGHT, THEY FEASTED, LAUGHED, DRANK, ATE BOARS, TOLD THEIR STORY IN GREAT DETAIL, BUT, SINCE YOU ALREADY KNOW IT, WE THINK THE TIME'S COME FOR US TO SAY GOODBYE... BUT NOT FOR LONG!
AND THEN, HEE-HEE-HEE! ASTERIX SAYS: HE'S... HEE-HEE- HEE!... HE'S OFF THE CHAIN!
HEE-HEE-HEE-HEE!
GIVE HIM ANOTHER BOAR OR ELSE HE'LL TELL US AGAIN!
UDERZO & GOSCINNY
THE END

WATCH OUT FOR PAPERCUTZ

Welcome to ASTERIX Volume One, collecting the first three ASTERIX graphic novels, "Asterix the Gaul," "Asterix and the Golden Sickle," and "Asterix and the Goths," by René Goscinny and Albert Uderzo. Papercutz is incredibly proud and honored to be the new North American publisher of this classic comics series. As we always say, Papercutz is dedicated to publishing great graphic novels for all ages—and we can't think of a better example of a comics series that can be enjoyed by young and old alike than ASTERIX. That's why we'll be re-presenting ASTERIX in omnibus editions, featuring three stories at a time.

I'm Jim Salicrup, Editor-in-Chief of Papercutz (an honorary citizen of a certain Gaulish village), and unlike Papercutz publisher, Terry Nantier, and millions of others, I didn't grow up reading Asterix, and wish I did. Well, it's never too late! I'm now thrilled to not only get to read ASTERIX from the very beginning, but to also participate in editing the new Americanized translations. The previous excellent English translations by Anthea Bell and Derek Hockridge were wonderful, but our goal is to help make ASTERIX as accessible as possible to new generations here in the USA, while maintaining everything that made ASTERIX great in the first place.

The stories in this volume were created by these two incredibly talented men...

René Goscinny
Writer

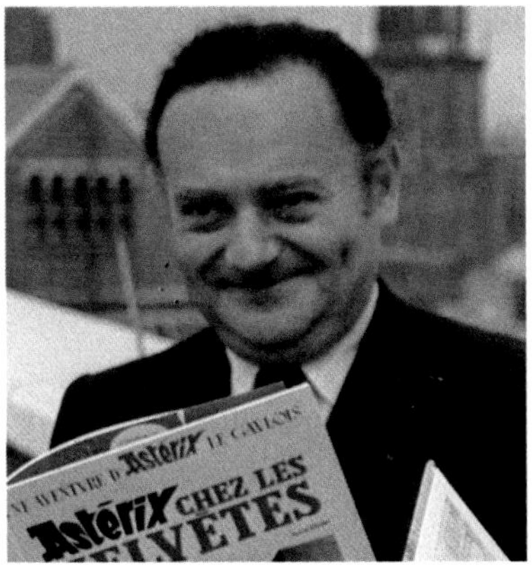

CHEZ LES

René Goscinny was born in Paris in 1926. After growing up in Argentina, he came to the United States where he shared a studio with future MAD magazine creator Harvey Kurtzman and collaborators Will Elder and Jack Davis. In 1959, Goscinny co-founded the magazine *Pilote* which premiered what was to become the most successful comics series in the world: ASTERIX. Unfortunately, René Goscinny died suddenly of a cardiac arrest in 1977 at the age of 51.

Albert Uderzo
Artist

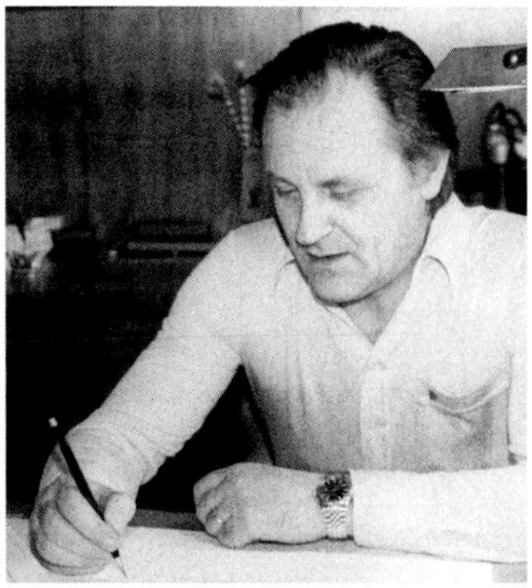

Albert Uderzo was born in France in 1927 to Italian immigrants. In 1959, Goscinny and Uderzo became co-founders of *Pilote* magazine. Their creation, ASTERIX, became a runaway success. At the time of Goscinny's death in 1977, 24 volumes of ASTERIX were completed. Uderzo continued to write and illustrate the ASTERIX graphic novels on his own, publishing 10 volumes. The cover credits still read "Goscinny and Uderzo." After seventy years of drawing, Albert Uderzo decided to put down his pencils and pens. But while he lived a long life, and continued to follow the adventures of his characters under new authors, Uderzo passed away in 2020.

Speaking of the new authors, Jean-Yves Ferri and Didier Conrad, the 38th volume was published in 2019 to celebrate the 60th anniversary of ASTERIX. In the spirit of that celebration, Papercutz published ASTERIX #38 to have it be available to all North American fans. In fact, you can even get a little preview of "The Chieftain's Daughter" on the following pages. So, in this one volume, Papercutz is bringing you the very first ASTERIX stories, and a little bit of the latest adventure as well. Also available now is ASTERIX Volume Two, featuring "Asterix the Gladiator," "Asterix and the Banquet," and "Asterix and Cleopatra" (We hear she has a pretty nose!). As well as volumes 3, 4, and 5 with more to come. Whether you're a longtime ASTERIX fan or an ASTERIX newbie, we sincerely hope you enjoy these Papercutz editions of Goscinny and Uderzo's masterpiece—ASTERIX.

Thanks,
Jim

STAY IN TOUCH!

EMAIL:	salicrup@papercutz.com
WEB:	papercutz.com
TWITTER:	@papercutzgn
INSTAGRAM:	@papercutzgn
FACEBOOK:	PAPERCUTZGRAPHICNOVELS
REGULAR MAIL:	Papercutz, 160 Broadway, Suite 700, East Wing, New York, NY 10038

Go to papercutz.com and sign up for the free Papercutz e-newsletter!

Special preview of ASTERIX #38 "The Chieftain's Daughter"...

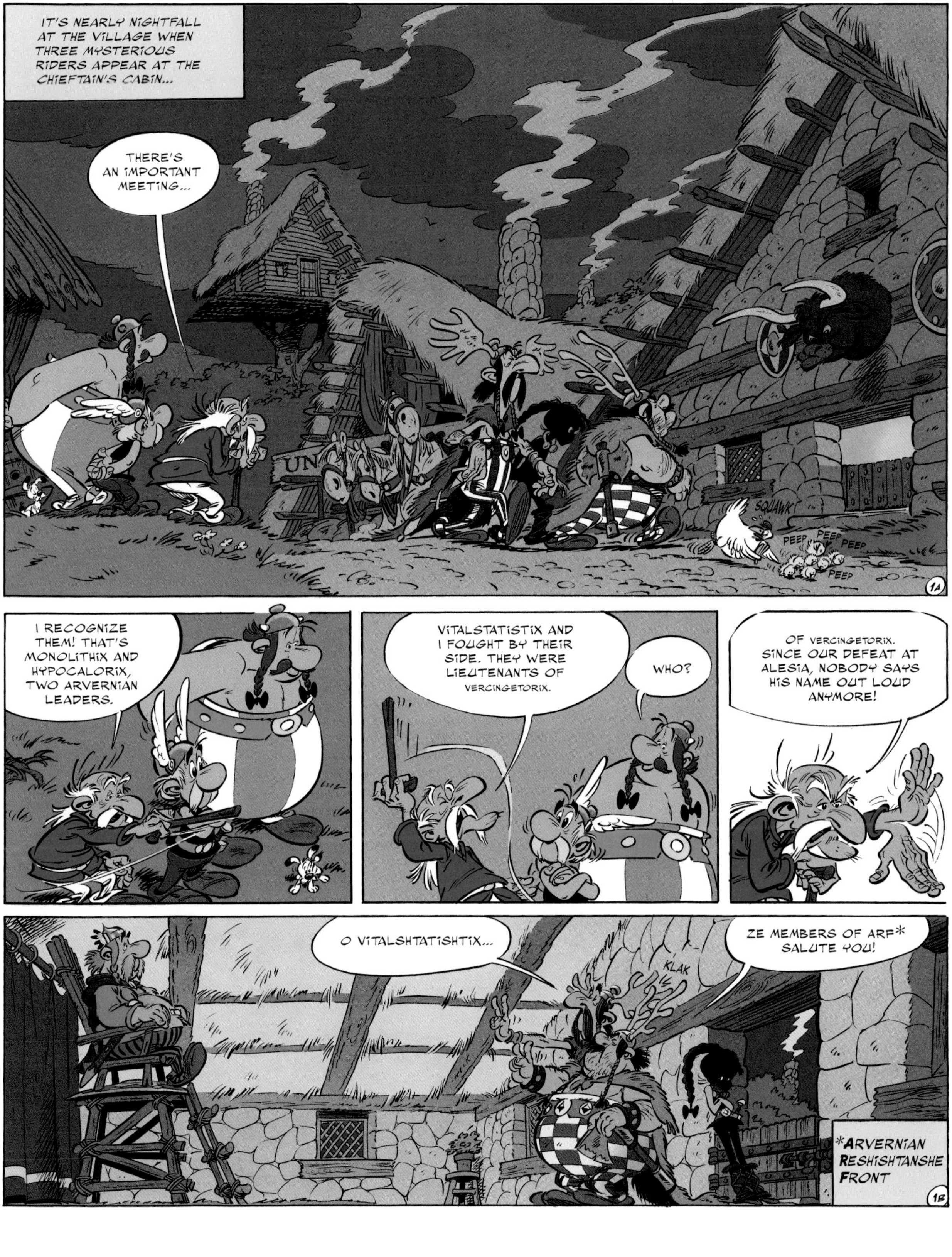

IT'S NEARLY NIGHTFALL AT THE VILLAGE WHEN THREE MYSTERIOUS RIDERS APPEAR AT THE CHIEFTAIN'S CABIN...
THERE'S AN IMPORTANT MEETING...
UN
SQUAWK
PEEP PEEP PEEP
PEEP
1A
I RECOGNIZE THEM! THAT'S MONOLITHIX AND HYPOCALORIX, TWO ARVERNIAN LEADERS.
VITALSTATISTIX AND I FOUGHT BY THEIR SIDE. THEY WERE LIEUTENANTS OF VERCINGETORIX.
WHO?
OF VERCINGETORIX. SINCE OUR DEFEAT AT ALESIA, NOBODY SAYS HIS NAME OUT LOUD ANYMORE!
O VITALSHTATISHTIX...
KLAK
ZE MEMBERS OF ARF* SALUTE YOU!
*ARVERNIAN RESHISHTANSHE FRONT
1B

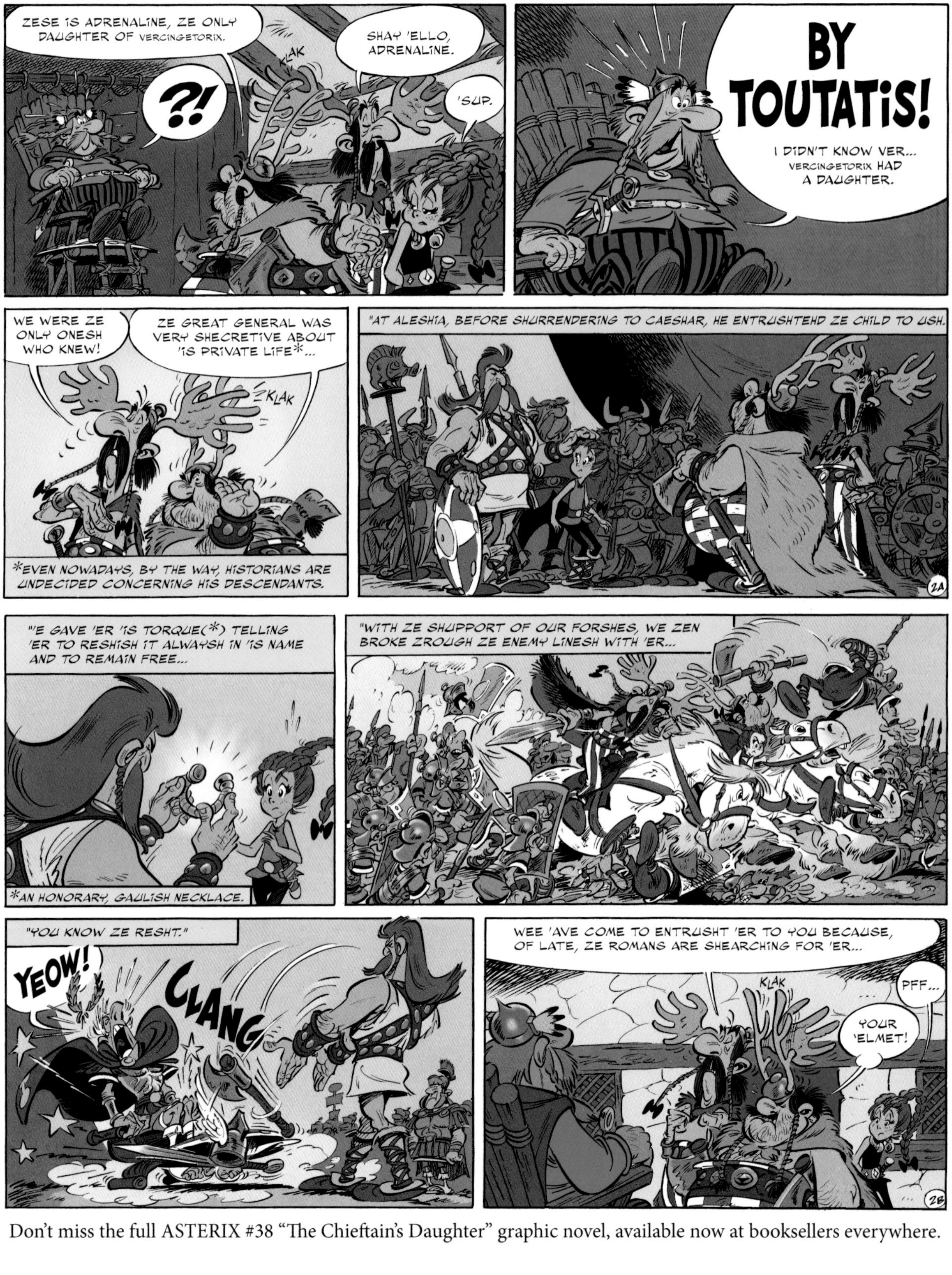
ZESE IS ADRENALINE, ZE ONLY DAUGHTER OF VERCINGETORIX.
SHAY 'ELLO, ADRENALINE.
KLAK
?!
'SUP.
BY TOUTATIS!
I DIDN'T KNOW VER... VERCINGETORIX HAD A DAUGHTER.
WE WERE ZE ONLY ONESH WHO KNEW!
ZE GREAT GENERAL WAS VERY SHECRETIVE ABOUT 'IS PRIVATE LIFE*...
KLAK
*EVEN NOWADAYS, BY THE WAY, HISTORIANS ARE UNDECIDED CONCERNING HIS DESCENDANTS.
"AT ALESHIA, BEFORE SHURRENDERING TO CAESHAR, HE ENTRUSHTEHD ZE CHILD TO USH.
"'E GAVE 'ER 'IS TORQUE(*) TELLING 'ER TO RESHISH IT ALWAYSH IN 'IS NAME AND TO REMAIN FREE...
*AN HONORARY, GAULISH NECKLACE.
"WITH ZE SHUPPORT OF OUR FORSHES, WE ZEN BROKE ZROUGH ZE ENEMY LINESH WITH 'ER...
"YOU KNOW ZE RESHT."
YEOW!
CLANG
WEE 'AVE COME TO ENTRUSHT 'ER TO YOU BECAUSE, OF LATE, ZE ROMANS ARE SHEARCHING FOR 'ER...
KLAK
PFF...
YOUR 'ELMET!

Don't miss the full ASTERIX #38 "The Chieftain's Daughter" graphic novel, available now at booksellers everywhere.